Tarzan and the Jewels of Opar

A Tale of Tarzan

Tarzan and the Jewels of Opar

A Tale of Tarzan

Edgar Rice Burroughs

WILDSIDE PRESS
Doylestown, Pennsylvania

Based on the A.C. McClurg edition of 1918.

Tarzan and the Jewels of Opar
A publication of
WILDSIDE PRESS
P.O. Box 301
Holicong, PA 18928-0301

www.wildsidepress.com

Introduction:

Master of Our Imagination

*I*f there is such a thing as a "collective subconscious" as proposed by Jung, then Edgar Rice Burroughs leapt into it and never left in 1917 when *Tarzan of the Apes* was published in England, and Burroughs's first Mars book found readers. That was the year before the end of the "Great War," a year of great trouble, and the aftermath of the terrible Influenza epidemic. Millions died in Europe and around the world, soldiers within the trenches, and civilians due to disease, starvation, and economic upheaval.

Imagine the Lord of Greystoke, raised in the Jungle. A man of honor, courage, and uncompromising principles, who knew nothing of Continental politics, Bolshevism, or anarchists with knives, guns and bombs. Imagine, too, a Mars of wonder, with great lords, Princesses, barbarians, and wondrous new inventions. And imagine them coming into a world of trouble and strife. Dreams do serve a purpose; and Edgar Rice Burroughs was nothing if not a great and powerful dreamer.

Burroughs's aficionados note that during his life-time, his work "failed to gather critical acclaim, yet influenced a generation." Like so many beloved writ-ers, Burroughs followed the well-known path to story-telling success. Burroughs got a start in writing after some failed attempts at being a salesman, railroad policeman, and other professions; according to official biographies, he even had to pawn his wife's jewelry to make ends meet. He daydreamed and read pulp maga-zines, and one day decided that he could write a better pulp story than the ones he knew, and submitted his first tale to the *All-Story Magazine* at age 35, using the pseudonym "Normal Bean," believing that the story was so far-out and fantastic that no one would be interested. He shouldn't have worried. From that time forward, readers were hooked.

What can you say about a writer who created Tarzan of the Apes, John Carter of Mars, and David Innes of Pellucidar? A writer who took readers — for the first time, and for many, the times that they imagine and dream and remember always — to the African jungles, to the plains and canals of Mars, and to the magical world of Pellucidar? Worlds within our own, far more wondrous than any ever imagined before — Barsoom! Ray Bradbury fully acknowledges his debt to Edgar Rice Burroughs, and in this beautiful, childlike, dream-ing bard's words can we see the reflection of Bur-roughs's dreams today. In truth, nearly every fantasy or science fiction writer, and certainly filmmakers, have drunk from the well of Edgar Rice Burroughs, and drunk deeply.

Ray Bradbury never spoke more movingly than at the Nebula Awards in 2001 in Beverly Hills, California. There is something of magic in him, just as there is something of complete wonder and magic in Edgar Rice Burroughs. Ray Bradbury spoke, as he often does, of the importance of remaining a child, and this is true: there is something of the child in almost every great writer. Do you remember when you were young? How it seemed that if you only wished hard enough and thought hard enough and dreamed long enough, the magic might become real? Toys were not merely playthings, they were real, real friends, real companions, real comrades. And that boy in the jungle that every child knows, swinging from the trees, he can really talk to the lions and the elephants and the crocodiles and to "Cheetah." Tarzan can even talk to Jane. Now, if that's not magic, what is?

No one much compliments Burroughs on his prose, but here is how he introduces John Carter in *A Princess of Mars*: "I am a very old man; how old I do not know. Possibly I am a hundred, possibly more; but I cannot tell because I have never aged as other men, nor do I remember any childhood. So far as I can recollect I have always been a man, a man of about thirty. I appear today as I did forty years and more ago, and yet I feel that I cannot go on living forever; that some day I shall die the real death from which there is no resurrection." Perhaps the suggestion of Carter's agelessness is what offends "critics," but — John Carter may have feared that he would die the "real death," but the truth is — he'll live forever.

Chieftains, Princesses, Adventurers, Barbarians. Lush jungles, garden worlds, and a world within the Earth itself. This is the imagination of a profound dreamer, full of rich images that have fueled more than fifty Tarzan movies and famous Tarzans from Johnny Weismuller and Buster Crabbe to Ron Ely and Christopher Lambert. Fritz Leiber and Philip Jose Farmer have written Tarzan-inspired novels. It doesn't matter how many NASA probes return from Mars empty-handed: dreamers everywhere know that somewhere, sometime, somehow, Barsoom is real.

At the very Nebula Award ceremony where Ray

Bradbury spoke, Philip Jose Farmer was named one of science fiction's "Grand Masters." Farmer came up with the idea that there is some kind of vast genetic "family" of heroes and adventurers, all related, and among these are Tarzan, John Carter, and other beloved Burroughs characters. This all sounds quite insane, but how else to explain this extraordinary combination of heroism, strength, and character?

Just like 1917, we are in a world whose moorings have come loose, a world filled with change, fear, and horrific, cataclysmic events. Perhaps these stories of Edgar Rice Burroughs, filled with wonder, adventure, miracles, heroes and villains as they are, fit the same need today as they did during that long-ago time. A distant jungle, to ponder about and imagine, a hero swinging to the rescue, calling nature itself to his aid. A man of adventure, beyond age and limitations, traversing the magical, mystical land of Mars. Pellucidar, whose very name conjures up images of beauty, mystery and wonder.

We are told that to grow up, we must put aside childish things; but what child ever went to war? What child ever flew a plane into a building which was itself a miracle, killing thousands, like the World Trade Towers? And who was ever too old to breathe in wonder at untold vistas beneath the earth, to think that a Princess of Mars was beautiful, to imagine the gardens of Mars and the deep, green jungles of Africa where a man grew to be a hero untouched by human hand?

Edgar Rice Burroughs himself told everyone that his only aim in writing was to "entertain." He wanted to take people's minds off their troubles for a few moments, give them laughter, pleasure and enjoyment. Few, if any, have ever so entertained. Not just one, but many of his characters are as real to us as if they truly lived, breathed and walked. They are truly immortal: Tarzan will never die; John Carter still lives.

There is too much pain in this world, and too little wonder. Every so often, we receive gifts. And these, like Edgar Rice Burroughs, we ought not question, but rather, treasure.

Edgar Rice Burroughs created a full, rich panoply of characters and worlds of wonder. His work is timeless, like one of his invented worlds: *The Land That Time Forgot.* Edgar Rice Burroughs made pure, unadulterated magic.

— Amy Sterling Casil
February, 2002
Redlands, California

Chapter I

BELGIAN AND ARAB

*L*IEUTENANT ALBERT WERPER had only the prestige of the name he had dishonored to thank for his narrow escape from being cashiered. At first he had been humbly thankful, too, that they had sent him to this Godforsaken Congo post instead of court-martialing him, as he had so justly deserved; but now six months of the monotony, the frightful isolation and the loneliness had wrought a change. The young man brooded continually over his fate. His days were filled with morbid self-pity, which eventually engendered in his weak and vacillating mind a hatred for those who had sent him here — for the very men he had at first inwardly thanked for saving him from the ignominy of degradation.

He regretted the gay life of Brussels as he never had regretted the sins which had snatched him from that gayest of capitals, and as the days passed he came to center his resentment upon the representative in Congo land of the authority which had exiled him —

his captain and immediate superior.

This officer was a cold, taciturn man, inspiring little love in those directly beneath him, yet respected and feared by the black soldiers of his little command.

Werper was accustomed to sit for hours glaring at his superior as the two sat upon the veranda of their common quarters, smoking their evening cigarettes in a silence which neither seemed desirous of breaking. The senseless hatred of the lieutenant grew at last into a form of mania. The captain's natural taciturnity he distorted into a studied attempt to insult him because of his past shortcomings. He imagined that his superior held him in contempt, and so he chafed and fumed inwardly until one evening his madness became suddenly homicidal. He fingered the butt of the revolver at his hip, his eyes narrowed and his brows contracted. At last he spoke.

"You have insulted me for the last time!" he cried, springing to his feet. "I am an officer and a gentleman, and I shall put up with it no longer without an accounting from you, you pig."

The captain, an expression of surprise upon his features, turned toward his junior. He had seen men before with the jungle madness upon them — the madness of solitude and unrestrained brooding, and perhaps a touch of fever.

He rose and extended his hand to lay it upon the other's shoulder. Quiet words of counsel were upon his lips; but they were never spoken. Werper construed his superior's action into an attempt to close with him. His revolver was on a level with the captain's heart, and the latter had taken but a step when Werper pulled the trigger. Without a moan the man sank to the rough planking of the veranda, and as he fell the mists that had clouded Werper's brain lifted, so that he saw himself and the deed that he had done in the same light that those who must judge him would see them.

He heard excited exclamations from the quarters of the soldiers and he heard men running in his direction. They would seize him, and if they didn't kill him they would take him down the Congo to a point where a properly ordered military tribunal would do so just as effectively, though in a more regular manner.

Werper had no desire to die. Never before had he so yearned for life as in this moment that he had so effectively forfeited his right to live. The men were nearing him. What was he to do? He glanced about as though searching for the tangible form of a legitimate excuse for his crime; but he could find only the body of the man he had so causelessly shot down.

In despair, he turned and fled from the oncoming soldiery. Across the compound he ran, his revolver still clutched tightly in his hand. At the gates a sentry halted him. Werper did not pause to parley or to exert the influence of his commission – he merely raised his weapon and shot down the innocent black. A moment later the fugitive had torn open the gates and vanished into the blackness of the jungle, but not before he had transferred the rifle and ammunition belts of the dead sentry to his own person.

All that night Werper fled farther and farther into the heart of the wilderness. Now and again the voice of a lion brought him to a listening halt; but with cocked and ready rifle he pushed ahead again, more fearful of the human huntsmen in his rear than of the wild carnivora ahead.

Dawn came at last, but still the man plodded on. All sense of hunger and fatigue were lost in the terrors of contemplated capture. He could think only of escape. He dared not pause to rest or eat until there was no further danger from pursuit, and so he staggered on until at last he fell and could rise no more. How long he had fled he did not know, or try to know. When he could flee no longer the knowledge that he had reached his limit was hidden from him in the unconsciousness of utter exhaustion.

And thus it was that Achmet Zek, the Arab, found him. Achmet's followers were for running a spear through the body of their hereditary enemy; but Achmet would have it otherwise. First he would question the Belgian. It were easier to question a man first and kill him afterward, than kill him first and then question him.

So he had Lieutenant Albert Werper carried to his own tent, and there slaves administered wine and food in small quantities until at last the prisoner regained consciousness. As he opened his eyes he saw the faces of strange black men about him, and just outside the tent the figure of an Arab. Nowhere was the uniform of his soldiers to be seen.

The Arab turned and seeing the open eyes of the prisoner upon him, entered the tent.

"I am Achmet Zek," he announced. "Who are you, and what were you doing in my country? Where are your soldiers?"

Achmet Zek! Werper's eyes went wide, and his heart sank. He was in the clutches of the most notorious of cut-throats — a hater of all Europeans, especially those who wore the uniform of Belgium. For years the military forces of Belgian Congo had waged a fruitless war upon this man and his followers — a war in which quarter had never been asked nor expected by either side.

But presently in the very hatred of the man for Belgians, Werper saw a faint ray of hope for himself. He, too, was an outcast and an outlaw. So far, at least, they possessed a common interest, and Werper decided to play upon it for all that it might yield.

"I have heard of you," he replied, "and was searching for you. My people have turned against me. I hate them. Even now their soldiers are searching for me, to kill me. I knew that you would protect me from them, for you, too, hate them. In return I will take service with you. I am a trained soldier. I can fight, and your enemies are my enemies."

Achmet Zek eyed the European in silence. In his mind he revolved many thoughts, chief among which was that the unbeliever lied. Of course there was the chance that he did not lie, and if he told the truth then his proposition was one well worthy of consideration, since fighting men were never over plentiful – especially white men with the training and knowledge of military matters that a European officer must possess.

Achmet Zek scowled and Werper's heart sank; but Werper did not know Achmet Zek, who was quite apt to scowl where another would smile, and smile where another would scowl.

"And if you have lied to me," said Achmet Zek, "I will kill you at any time. What return, other than your life, do you expect for your services?"

"My keep only, at first," replied Werper. "Later, if I am worth more, we can easily reach an understanding." Werper's only desire at the moment was to preserve his life. And so the agreement was reached and Lieutenant Albert Werper became a member of the ivory and slave raiding band of the notorious Achmet Zek.

For months the renegade Belgian rode with the savage raider. He fought with a savage abandon, and a vicious cruelty fully equal to that of his fellow desperadoes. Achmet Zek watched his recruit with eagle eye, and with a growing satisfaction which finally found expression in a greater confidence in the man, and resulted in an increased independence of action for Werper.

Achmet Zek took the Belgian into his confidence to a great extent, and at last unfolded to him a pet scheme which the Arab had long fostered, but which he never had found an opportunity to effect. With the aid of a

European, however, the thing might be easily accomplished. He sounded Werper.

"You have heard of the man men call Tarzan?" he asked.

Werper nodded. "I have heard of him; but I do not know him."

"But for him we might carry on our 'trading' in safety and with great profit," continued the Arab. "For years he has fought us, driving us from the richest part of the country, harassing us, and arming the natives that they may repel us when we come to 'trade.' He is very rich. If we could find some way to make him pay us many pieces of gold we should not only be avenged upon him; but repaid for much that he has prevented us from winning from the natives under his protection."

Werper withdrew a cigarette from a jeweled case and lighted it.

"And you have a plan to make him pay?" he asked.

"He has a wife," replied Achmet Zek, "whom men say is very beautiful. She would bring a great price farther north, if we found it too difficult to collect ransom money from this Tarzan."

Werper bent his head in thought. Achmet Zek stood awaiting his reply. What good remained in Albert Werper revolted at the thought of selling a white woman into the slavery and degradation of a Moslem harem. He looked up at Achmet Zek. He saw the Arab's eyes narrow, and he guessed that the other had sensed his antagonism to the plan. What would it mean to Werper to refuse? His life lay in the hands of this semi-barbarian, who esteemed the life of an unbeliever less highly than that of a dog. Werper loved life. What was this woman to him, anyway? She was a European, doubtless, a member of organized society. He was an outcast. The hand of every white man was against him. She was his natural enemy, and if he refused to lend himself to her undoing, Achmet Zek would have him killed.

"You hesitate," murmured the Arab.

"I was but weighing the chances of success," lied Werper, "and my reward. As a European I can gain admittance to their home and table. You have no other with you who could do so much. The risk will be great. I should be well paid, Achmet Zek."

A smile of relief passed over the raider's face.

"Well said, Werper," and Achmet Zek slapped his lieutenant upon the shoulder. "You should be well paid and you shall. Now let us sit together and plan how best the thing may be done," and the two men squatted upon a soft rug beneath the faded silks of Achmet's once gorgeous tent, and talked together in low voices well into the night. Both were tall and bearded, and the exposure to sun and wind had given an almost Arab hue to the European's complexion. In every detail of dress, too, he copied the fashions of his chief, so that outwardly he was as much an Arab as the other. It was late when he arose and retired to his own tent.

The following day Werper spent in overhauling his Belgian uniform, removing from it every vestige of evidence that might indicate its military purposes. From a heterogeneous collection of loot, Achmet Zek procured a pith helmet and a European saddle, and from his black slaves and followers a party of porters, askaris and tent boys to make up a modest safari for a big game hunter. At the head of this party Werper set out from camp.

Chapter II

ON THE ROAD TO OPAR

*I*T WAS TWO weeks later that John Clayton, Lord Greystoke, riding in from a tour of inspection of his vast African estate, glimpsed the head of a column of men crossing the plain that lay between his bungalow and the forest to the north and west.

He reined in his horse and watched the little party as it emerged from a concealing swale. His keen eyes caught the reflection of the sun upon the white helmet of a mounted man, and with the conviction that a wandering European hunter was seeking his hospitality, he wheeled his mount and rode slowly forward to meet the newcomer.

A half hour later he was mounting the steps leading to the veranda of his bungalow, and introducing M. Jules Frecoult to Lady Greystoke.

"I was completely lost," M. Frecoult was explaining. "My head man had never before been in this part of the country and the guides who were to have accompanied me from the last village we passed knew even less of the country than we. They finally deserted us two days since. I am very fortunate indeed to have stumbled so providentially upon succor. I do not know what I should have done, had I not found you."

It was decided that Frecoult and his party should remain several days, or until they were thoroughly rested, when Lord Greystoke would furnish guides to lead them safely back into country with which Frecoult's head man was supposedly familiar.

In his guise of a French gentleman of leisure, Werper found little difficulty in deceiving his host and in ingratiating himself with both Tarzan and Jane Clayton; but the longer he remained the less hopeful he became of an easy accomplishment of his designs.

Lady Greystoke never rode alone at any great distance from the bungalow, and the savage loyalty of the ferocious Waziri warriors who formed a great part of Tarzan's followers seemed to preclude the possibility of a successful attempt at forcible abduction, or of the bribery of the Waziri themselves.

A week passed, and Werper was no nearer the fulfillment of his plan, in so far as he could judge, than upon the day of his arrival, but at that very moment something occurred which gave him renewed hope and set his mind upon an even greater reward than a woman's ransom.

A runner had arrived at the bungalow with the weekly mail, and Lord Greystoke had spent the afternoon in his study reading and answering letters. At dinner he seemed distraught, and early in the evening he excused himself and retired, Lady Greystoke following him very soon after. Werper, sitting upon the veranda, could hear their voices in earnest discussion, and having realized that something of unusual moment was afoot, he quietly rose from his chair, and keeping well in the shadow of the shrubbery growing profusely about the bungalow, made his silent way to a point beneath the window of the room in which his host and hostess slept.

Here he listened, and not without result, for almost the first words he overheard filled him with excitement. Lady Greystoke was speaking as Werper came within hearing.

"I always feared for the stability of the company," she was saying; "but it seems incredible that they should have failed for so enormous a sum — unless there has been some dishonest manipulation."

"That is what I suspect," replied Tarzan; "but whatever the cause, the fact remains that I have lost everything, and there is nothing for it but to return to Opar and get more."

"Oh, John," cried Lady Greystoke, and Werper could feel the shudder through her voice, "is there no other way? I cannot bear to think of you returning to that frightful city. I would rather live in poverty always than to have you risk the hideous dangers of Opar."

"You need have no fear," replied Tarzan, laughing. "I am pretty well able to take care of myself, and were I not, the Waziri who will accompany me will see that no harm befalls me."

"They ran away from Opar once, and left you to your fate," she reminded him.

"They will not do it again," he answered. "They were very much ashamed of themselves, and were coming back when I met them."

"But there must be some other way," insisted the woman.

"There is no other way half so easy to obtain another fortune, as to go to the treasure vaults of Opar and bring it away," he replied. "I shall be very careful, Jane, and the chances are that the inhabitants of Opar will never know that I have been there again and despoiled them of another portion of the treasure, the very existence of which they are as ignorant of as they would be of its value."

The finality in his tone seemed to assure Lady Greystoke that further argument was futile, and so she abandoned the subject.

Werper remained, listening, for a short time, and then, confident that he had overheard all that was necessary and fearing discovery, returned to the veranda, where he smoked numerous cigarettes in rapid succession before retiring.

The following morning at breakfast, Werper announced his intention of making an early departure, and asked Tarzan's permission to hunt big game in the Waziri country on his way out — permission which Lord Greystoke readily granted.

The Belgian consumed two days in completing his preparations, but finally got away with his safari, accompanied by a single Waziri guide whom Lord Greystoke had loaned him. The party made but a single short march when Werper simulated illness, and announced his intention of remaining where he was until he had fully recovered. As they had gone but a short distance from the Greystoke bungalow, Werper dismissed the Waziri guide, telling the warrior that he would send for him when he was able to proceed. The Waziri gone, the Belgian summoned one of Achmet Zek's trusted blacks to his tent, and dispatched him to watch for the departure of Tarzan, returning immediately to advise Werper of the event and the direction taken by the Englishman.

The Belgian did not have long to wait, for the following day his emissary returned with word that Tarzan and a party of fifty Waziri warriors had set out toward the southeast early in the morning.

Werper called his head man to him, after writing a long letter to Achmet Zek. This letter he handed to the head man.

"Send a runner at once to Achmet Zek with this,"

he instructed the head man. "Remain here in camp awaiting further instructions from him or from me. If any come from the bungalow of the Englishman, tell them that I am very ill within my tent and can see no one. Now, give me six porters and six askaris — the strongest and bravest of the safari — and I will march after the Englishman and discover where his gold is hidden."

And so it was that as Tarzan, stripped to the loin cloth and armed after the primitive fashion he best loved, led his loyal Waziri toward the dead city of Opar, Werper, the renegade, haunted his trail through the long, hot days, and camped close behind him by night.

And as they marched, Achmet Zek rode with his entire following southward toward the Greystoke farm.

To Tarzan of the Apes the expedition was in the nature of a holiday outing. His civilization was at best but an outward veneer which he gladly peeled off with his uncomfortable European clothes whenever any reasonable pretext presented itself. It was a woman's love which kept Tarzan even to the semblance of civilization — a condition for which familiarity had bred contempt. He hated the shams and the hypocrisies of it and with the clear vision of an unspoiled mind he had penetrated to the rotten core of the heart of the thing — the cowardly greed for peace and ease and the safe-guarding of property rights. That the fine things of life — art, music and literature — had thriven upon such enervating ideals he strenuously denied, insisting, rather, that they had endured in spite of civilization.

"Show me the fat, opulent coward," he was wont to say, "who ever originated a beautiful ideal. In the clash of arms, in the battle for survival, amid hunger and death and danger, in the face of God as manifested in the display of Nature's most terrific forces, is born all that is finest and best in the human heart and mind."

And so Tarzan always came back to Nature in the

spirit of a lover keeping a long deferred tryst after a period behind prison walls. His Waziri, at marrow, were more civilized than he. They cooked their meat before they ate it and they shunned many articles of food as unclean that Tarzan had eaten with gusto all his life and so insidious is the virus of hypocrisy that even the stalwart ape-man hesitated to give rein to his natural longings before them. He ate burnt flesh when he would have preferred it raw and unspoiled, and he brought down game with arrow or spear when he would far rather have leaped upon it from ambush and sunk his strong teeth in its jugular; but at last the call of the milk of the savage mother that had suckled him in infancy rose to an insistent demand — he craved the hot blood of a fresh kill and his muscles yearned to pit themselves against the savage jungle in the battle for existence that had been his sole birthright for the first twenty years of his life.

Chapter III

THE CALL OF THE JUNGLE

MOVED BY THESE vague yet all-powerful urgings
the ape-man lay awake one night in the little thorn
boma that protected, in a way, his party from the
depredations of the great carnivora of the jungle. A
single warrior stood sleepy guard beside the fire that
yellow eyes out of the darkness beyond the camp made
imperative. The moans and the coughing of the big
cats mingled with the myriad noises of the lesser deni-
zens of the jungle to fan the savage flame in the breast
of this savage English lord. He tossed upon his bed of
grasses, sleepless, for an hour and then he rose, noise-
less as a wraith, and while the Waziri's back was turned,
vaulted the boma wall in the face of the flaming eyes,
swung silently into a great tree and was gone.

For a time in sheer exuberance of animal spirit he
raced swiftly through the middle terrace, swinging
perilously across wide spans from one jungle giant to
the next, and then he clambered upward to the swaying,
lesser boughs of the upper terrace where the moon

shone full upon him and the air was stirred by little
breezes and death lurked ready in each frail branch.
Here he paused and raised his face to Goro, the moon.
With uplifted arm he stood, the cry of the bull ape
quivering upon his lips, yet he remained silent lest he
arouse his faithful Waziri who were all too familiar
with the hideous challenge of their master.

And then he went on more slowly and with greater
stealth and caution, for now Tarzan of the Apes was
seeking a kill. Down to the ground he came in the utter
blackness of the close-set boles and the overhanging
verdure of the jungle.

He stooped from time to time and put his nose close
to earth. He sought and found a wide game trail and
at last his nostrils were rewarded with the scent of the
fresh spoor of Bara, the deer. Tarzan's mouth watered
and a low growl escaped his patrician lips. Sloughed
from him was the last vestige of artificial caste — once
again he was the primeval hunter — -the first man-the
highest caste type of the human race. Up wind he
followed the elusive spoor with a sense of perception
so transcending that of ordinary man as to be incon-
ceivable to us. Through counter currents of the heavy
stench of meat eaters he traced the trail of Bara; the
sweet and cloying stink of Horta, the boar, could not
drown his quarry's scent — the permeating, mellow
musk of the deer's foot.

Presently the body scent of the deer told Tarzan that
his prey was close at hand. It sent him into the trees
again — into the lower terrace where he could watch
the ground below and catch with ears and nose the first
intimation of actual contact with his quarry. Nor was
it long before the ape-man came upon Bara standing
alert at the edge of a moon-bathed clearing. Noiselessly
Tarzan crept through the trees until he was directly over
the deer. In the ape-man's right hand was the long
hunting knife of his father and in his heart the blood

lust of the carnivore. Just for an instant he poised above the unsuspecting Bara and then he launched himself downward upon the sleek back. The impact of his weight carried the deer to its knees and before the animal could regain its feet the knife had found its heart. As Tarzan rose upon the body of his kill to scream forth his hideous victory cry into the face of the moon the wind carried to his nostrils something which froze him to statuesque immobility and silence. His savage eyes blazed into the direction from which the wind had borne down the warning to him and a moment later the grasses at one side of the clearing parted and Numa, the lion, strode majestically into view. His yellow-green eyes were fastened upon Tarzan as he halted just within the clearing and glared enviously at the successful hunter, for Numa had had no luck this night.

From the lips of the ape-man broke a rumbling growl of warning. Numa answered but he did not advance. Instead he stood waving his tail gently to and fro, and presently Tarzan squatted upon his kill and cut a generous portion from a hind quarter. Numa eyed him with growing resentment and rage as, between mouthfuls, the ape-man growled out his savage warnings. Now this particular lion had never before come in contact with Tarzan of the Apes and he was much mystified. Here was the appearance and the scent of a man-thing and Numa had tasted of human flesh and learned that though not the most palatable it was certainly by far the easiest to secure, yet there was that in the bestial growls of the strange creature which reminded him of formidable antagonists and gave him pause, while his hunger and the odor of the hot flesh of Bara goaded him almost to madness. Always Tarzan watched him, guessing what was passing in the little brain of the carnivore and well it was that he did watch him, for at last Numa could stand it no longer. His tail shot suddenly erect and at the same instant the wary ape-man, knowing all too well what the signal portended, grasped the remainder of the deer's hind quarter between his teeth and leaped into a nearby tree as Numa charged him with all the speed and a sufficient semblance of the weight of an express train.

Tarzan's retreat was no indication that he felt fear. Jungle life is ordered along different lines than ours and different standards prevail. Had Tarzan been famished he would, doubtless, have stood his ground and met the lion's charge. He had done the thing before upon more than one occasion, just as in the past he had charged lions himself; but tonight he was far from famished and in the hind quarter he had carried off with him was more raw flesh than he could eat; yet it was with no equanimity that he looked down upon Numa rending the flesh of Tarzan's kill. The presumption of this strange Numa must be punished! And forthwith Tarzan set out to make life miserable for the big cat. Close by were many trees bearing large, hard fruits and to one of these the ape-man swung with the agility of a squirrel. Then commenced a bombardment which brought forth earth-shaking roars from Numa. One after another as rapidly as he could gather and hurl them, Tarzan pelted the hard fruit down upon the lion. It was impossible for the tawny cat to eat under that hail of missiles — he could but roar and growl and dodge and eventually he was driven away entirely from the carcass of Bara, the deer. He went roaring and resentful; but in the very center of the clearing his voice was suddenly hushed and Tarzan saw the great head lower and flatten out, the body crouch and the long tail quiver, as the beast slunk cautiously toward the trees upon the opposite side.

Immediately Tarzan was alert. He lifted his head and sniffed the slow, jungle breeze. What was it that had attracted Numa's attention and taken him soft-footed and silent away from the scene of his discomfiture? Just as the lion disappeared among the trees beyond the clearing Tarzan caught upon the down-coming wind the explanation of his new interest — the scent spoor of man was wafted strongly to the sensitive nostrils. Caching the remainder of the deer's hind quarter in the crotch of a tree the ape-man wiped his greasy palms upon his naked thighs and swung off in pursuit of Numa. A broad, well-beaten elephant path led into the forest from the clearing. Parallel to this slunk Numa, while above him Tarzan moved through the trees, the shadow of a wraith. The savage cat and the savage man saw Numa's quarry almost simultaneously, though both had known before it came within the vision of their eyes that it was a black man. Their sensitive nostrils had told them this much and Tarzan's had told him that the scent spoor was that of a stranger — old and a male, for race and sex and age each has its own distinctive scent. It was an old man that made his way alone through the gloomy jungle, a wrinkled, dried up, little old man hideously scarred and tattooed and strangely garbed, with the skin of a hyena about his shoulders and the dried head mounted upon his grey pate. Tarzan recognized the ear-marks of the witch-doctor and awaited Numa's charge with a feeling of pleasurable anticipation, for the ape-man had no love for witch-doctors; but in the instant that Numa did charge, the white man suddenly recalled that the lion had stolen his kill a few minutes before and that revenge is sweet.

The first intimation the black man had that he was in danger was the crash of twigs as Numa charged through the bushes into the game trail not twenty yards behind him. Then he turned to see a huge, black-maned lion racing toward him and even as he turned, Numa seized him. At the same instant the ape-man dropped from an overhanging limb full upon the lion's back and as he alighted he plunged his knife into the tawny side behind the left shoulder, tangled the fingers of his right hand in the long mane, buried his teeth in Numa's neck and wound his powerful legs about the beast's torso. With a roar of pain and rage, Numa reared up and fell backward upon the ape-man; but still the mighty man-thing clung to his hold and repeatedly the long knife plunged rapidly into his side. Over and over rolled Numa, the lion, clawing and biting at the air, roaring and growling horribly in savage attempt to reach the thing upon its back. More than once was Tarzan almost brushed from his hold. He was battered and bruised and covered with blood from Numa and dirt from the trail, yet not for an instant did he lessen the ferocity of his mad attack nor his grim hold upon the back of his antagonist. To have loosened for an instant his grip there, would have been to bring him within reach of those tearing talons or rending fangs, and have ended forever the grim career of this jungle-bred English lord. Where he had fallen beneath the spring of the lion the witch-doctor lay, torn and bleeding, unable to drag himself away and watched the terrific battle between these two lords of the jungle. His sunken eyes glittered and his wrinkled lips moved over toothless gums as he mumbled weird incantations to the demons of his cult.

For a time he felt no doubt as to the outcome — the strange white man must certainly succumb to terrible Simba — whoever heard of a lone man armed only with a knife slaying so mighty a beast! Yet presently the old black man's eyes went wider and he commenced to have his doubts and misgivings. What wonderful sort of creature was this that battled with Simba and held his own despite the mighty muscles of the king of beasts and slowly there dawned in those sunken eyes, gleaming so brightly from the scarred and wrinkled face, the light of a dawning recollection. Gropingly backward into the past reached the fingers of memory, until at last they seized upon a faint picture, faded and yellow with the passing years. It was the picture of a lithe, white-skinned youth swinging through the trees in company with a band of huge apes, and the old eyes blinked and a great fear came into them — the superstitious fear of one who believes in ghosts and spirits and demons.

And came the time once more when the witch-doctor no longer doubted the outcome of the duel, yet his first judgment was reversed, for now he knew that the jungle god would slay Simba and the old black was even more terrified of his own impending fate at the hands of the victor than he had been by the sure and sudden death which the triumphant lion would have meted out to him. He saw the lion weaken from loss of blood. He saw the mighty limbs tremble and stagger and at last he saw the beast sink down to rise no more. He saw the forest god or demon rise from the vanquished foe, and placing a foot upon the still quivering carcass, raise his face to the moon and bay out a hideous cry that froze the ebbing blood in the veins of the witch-doctor.

Chapter IV

PROPHECY AND FULFILLMENT

THEN TARZAN TURNED his attention to the man. He had not slain Numa to save the Negro — he had merely done it in revenge upon the lion; but now that he saw the old man lying helpless and dying before him something akin to pity touched his savage heart. In his youth he would have slain the witch-doctor without the slightest compunction; but civilization had had its softening effect upon him even as it does upon the nations and races which it touches, though it had not yet gone far enough with Tarzan to render him either cowardly or effeminate. He saw an old man suffering and dying, and he stooped and felt of his wounds and stanched the flow of blood.

"Who are you?" asked the old man in a trembling voice.

"I am Tarzan — Tarzan of the Apes," replied the ape-man and not without a greater touch of pride than he would have said, "I am John Clayton, Lord Greystoke."

The witch-doctor shook convulsively and closed his eyes. When he opened them again there was in them a resignation to whatever horrible fate awaited him at the hands of this feared demon of the woods. "Why do you not kill me?" he asked.

"Why should I kill you?" inquired Tarzan. "You have not harmed me, and anyway you are already dying. Numa, the lion, has killed you."

"You would not kill me?" Surprise and incredulity were in the tones of the quavering old voice.

"I would save you if I could," replied Tarzan, "but that cannot be done. Why did you think I would kill you?"

For a moment the old man was silent. When he spoke it was evidently after some little effort to muster his courage. "I knew you of old," he said, "when you ranged the jungle in the country of Mbonga, the chief. I was already a witch-doctor when you slew Kulonga and the others, and when you robbed our huts and our poison pot. At first I did not remember you; but at last I did — the white-skinned ape that lived with the hairy apes and made life miserable in the village of Mbonga, the chief — the forest god — the Munango-Keewati for whom we set food outside our gates and who came and ate it. Tell me before I die — are you man or devil?"

Tarzan laughed. "I am a man," he said.

The old fellow sighed and shook his head. "You have tried to save me from Simba," he said. "For that I shall reward you. I am a great witch-doctor. Listen to me, white man! I see bad days ahead of you. It is writ in my own blood which I have smeared upon my palm. A god greater even than you will rise up and strike you down. Turn back, Munango-Keewati! Turn back before it is too late. Danger lies ahead of you and danger lurks behind; but greater is the danger before. I see —" He paused and drew a long, gasping breath. Then he crumpled into a little, wrinkled heap and died. Tarzan wondered what else he had seen.

It was very late when the ape-man re-entered the boma and lay down among his black warriors. None had seen him go and none saw him return. He thought about the warning of the old witch-doctor before he fell asleep and he thought of it again after he awoke; but he did not turn back for he was unafraid, though had he known what lay in store for one he loved most in all the world he would have flown through the trees to her side and allowed the gold of Opar to remain forever hidden in its forgotten storehouse.

Behind him that morning another white man pondered something he had heard during the night and very nearly did he give up his project and turn back upon his trail. It was Werper, the murderer, who in the still of the night had heard far away upon the trail ahead of him a sound that had filled his cowardly soul with terror — a sound such as he never before had heard in all his life, nor dreamed that such a frightful thing could emanate from the lungs of a God-created creature. He had heard the victory cry of the bull ape as Tarzan had screamed it forth into the face of Goro, the moon, and he had trembled then and hidden his face; and now in the broad light of a new day he trembled again as he recalled it, and would have turned back from the nameless danger the echo of that frightful sound seemed to portend, had he not stood in even greater fear of Achmet Zek, his master.

And so Tarzan of the Apes forged steadily ahead toward Opar's ruined ramparts and behind him slunk Werper, jackal-like, and only God knew what lay in store for each.

At the edge of the desolate valley, overlooking the golden domes and minarets of Opar, Tarzan halted. By night he would go alone to the treasure vault, reconnoitering, for he had determined that caution should mark his every move upon this expedition.

With the coming of night he set forth, and Werper, who had scaled the cliffs alone behind the ape-man's party, and hidden through the day among the rough boulders of the mountain top, slunk stealthily after him. The boulder-strewn plain between the valley's edge and the mighty granite kopje, outside the city's walls, where lay the entrance to the passage-way leading to the treasure vault, gave the Belgian ample cover as he followed Tarzan toward Opar.

He saw the giant ape-man swing himself nimbly up the face of the great rock. Werper, clawing fearfully during the perilous ascent, sweating in terror, almost palsied by fear, but spurred on by avarice, following upward, until at last he stood upon the summit of the rocky hill.

Tarzan was nowhere in sight. For a time Werper hid behind one of the lesser boulders that were scattered over the top of the hill, but, seeing or hearing nothing of the Englishman, he crept from his place of conceal-ment to undertake a systematic search of his surround-ings, in the hope that he might discover the location of the treasure in ample time to make his escape before Tarzan returned, for it was the Belgian's desire merely to locate the gold, that, after Tarzan had departed, he might come in safety with his followers and carry away as much as he could transport.

He found the narrow cleft leading downward into the heart of the kopje along well-worn, granite steps. He advanced quite to the dark mouth of the tunnel into which the runway disappeared; but here he halted, fearing to enter, lest he meet Tarzan returning.

The ape-man, far ahead of him, groped his way along the rocky passage, until he came to the ancient wooden door. A moment later he stood within the treasure chamber, where, ages since, long-dead hands had ranged the lofty rows of precious ingots for the rulers

of that great continent which now lies submerged
beneath the waters of the Atlantic.

No sound broke the stillness of the subterranean
vault. There was no evidence that another had discovered the forgotten wealth since last the ape-man had
visited its hiding place.

Satisfied, Tarzan turned and retraced his steps toward
the summit of the kopje. Werper, from the concealment of a jutting, granite shoulder, watched him pass
up from the shadows of the stairway and advance
toward the edge of the hill which faced the rim of the
valley where the Waziri awaited the signal of their
master. Then Werper, slipping stealthily from his hiding place, dropped into the somber darkness of the
entrance and disappeared.

Tarzan, halting upon the kopje's edge, raised his
voice in the thunderous roar of a lion. Twice, at regular
intervals, he repeated the call, standing in attentive
silence for several minutes after the echoes of the third
call had died away. And then, from far across the valley,
faintly, came an answering roar — once, twice, thrice.
Basuli, the Waziri chieftain, had heard and replied.

Tarzan again made his way toward the treasure vault,
knowing that in a few hours his blacks would be with
him, ready to bear away another fortune in the
strangely shaped, golden ingots of Opar. In the meantime he would carry as much of the precious metal to
the summit of the kopje as he could.

Six trips he made in the five hours before Basuli
reached the kopje, and at the end of that time he had
transported forty-eight ingots to the edge of the great
boulder, carrying upon each trip a load which might
well have staggered two ordinary men, yet his giant
frame showed no evidence of fatigue, as he helped to
raise his ebon warriors to the hill top with the rope
that had been brought for the purpose.

Six times he had returned to the treasure chamber,

and six times Werper, the Belgian, had cowered in the black shadows at the far end of the long vault. Once again came the ape-man, and this time there came with him fifty fighting men, turning porters for love of the only creature in the world who might command of their fierce and haughty natures such menial service. Fifty-two more ingots passed out of the vaults, making the total of one hundred which Tarzan intended taking away with him.

As the last of the Waziri filed from the chamber, Tarzan turned back for a last glimpse of the fabulous wealth upon which his two inroads had made no appreciable impression. Before he extinguished the single candle he had brought with him for the purpose, and the flickering light of which had cast the first alleviating rays into the impenetrable darkness of the buried chamber, that it had known for the countless ages since it had lain forgotten of man, Tarzan's mind reverted to that first occasion upon which he had entered the treasure vault, coming upon it by chance as he fled from the pits beneath the temple, where he had been hidden by La, the High Priestess of the Sun Worshipers.

He recalled the scene within the temple when he had lain stretched upon the sacrificial altar, while La, with high-raised dagger, stood above him, and the rows of priests and priestesses awaited, in the ecstatic hysteria of fanaticism, the first gush of their victim's warm blood, that they might fill their golden goblets and drink to the glory of their Flaming God.

The brutal and bloody interruption by Tha, the mad priest, passed vividly before the ape-man's recollective eyes, the flight of the votaries before the insane blood lust of the hideous creature, the brutal attack upon La, and his own part of the grim tragedy when he had battled with the infuriated Oparian and left him dead at the feet of the priestess he would have profaned.

This and much more passed through Tarzan's memory as he stood gazing at the long tiers of dull-yellow metal. He wondered if La still ruled the temples of the ruined city whose crumbling walls rose upon the very foundations about him. Had she finally been forced into a union with one of her grotesque priests? It seemed a hideous fate, indeed, for one so beautiful. With a shake of his head, Tarzan stepped to the flickering candle, extinguished its feeble rays and turned toward the exit.

Behind him the spy waited for him to be gone. He had learned the secret for which he had come, and now he could return at his leisure to his waiting followers, bring them to the treasure vault and carry away all the gold that they could stagger under.

The Waziri had reached the outer end of the tunnel, and were winding upward toward the fresh air and the welcome starlight of the kopje's summit, before Tarzan shook off the detaining hand of reverie and started slowly after them.

Once again, and, he thought, for the last time, he closed the massive door of the treasure room. In the darkness behind him Werper rose and stretched his cramped muscles. He stretched forth a hand and lovingly caressed a golden ingot on the nearest tier. He raised it from its immemorial resting place and weighed it in his hands. He clutched it to his bosom in an ecstasy of avarice.

Tarzan dreamed of the happy homecoming which lay before him, of dear arms about his neck, and a soft cheek pressed to his; but there rose to dispel that dream the memory of the old witch-doctor and his warning.

And then, in the span of a few brief seconds, the hopes of both these men were shattered. The one forgot even his greed in the panic of terror — the other was plunged into total forgetfulness of the past by a jagged fragment of rock which gashed a deep cut upon his head.

Chapter V

THE ALTAR
OF THE FLAMING GOD

*I*T WAS AT the moment that Tarzan turned from the closed door to pursue his way to the outer world. The thing came without warning. One instant all was quiet and stability — the next, and the world rocked, the tortured sides of the narrow passageway split and crumbled, great blocks of granite, dislodged from the ceiling, tumbled into the narrow way, choking it, and the walls bent inward upon the wreckage. Beneath the blow of a fragment of the roof, Tarzan staggered back against the door to the treasure room, his weight pushed it open and his body rolled inward upon the floor.

In the great apartment where the treasure lay less damage was wrought by the earthquake. A few ingots toppled from the higher tiers, a single piece of the rocky ceiling splintered off and crashed downward to the floor, and the walls cracked, though they did not collapse.

There was but the single shock, no other followed to

complete the damage undertaken by the first. Werper, thrown to his length by the suddenness and violence of the disturbance, staggered to his feet when he found himself unhurt. Groping his way toward the far end of the chamber, he sought the candle which Tarzan had left stuck in its own wax upon the protruding end of an ingot.

By striking numerous matches the Belgian at last found what he sought, and when, a moment later, the sickly rays relieved the Stygian darkness about him, he breathed a nervous sigh of relief, for the impenetrable gloom had accentuated the terrors of his situation.

As they became accustomed to the light the man turned his eyes toward the door — his one thought now was of escape from this frightful tomb — and as he did so he saw the body of the naked giant lying stretched upon the floor just within the doorway. Werper drew back in sudden fear of detection; but a second glance convinced him that the Englishman was dead. From a great gash in the man's head a pool of blood had collected upon the concrete floor.

Quickly, the Belgian leaped over the prostrate form of his erstwhile host, and without a thought of succor for the man in whom, for aught he knew, life still remained, he bolted for the passageway and safety.

But his renewed hopes were soon dashed. Just beyond the doorway he found the passage completely clogged and choked by impenetrable masses of shattered rock. Once more he turned and re-entered the treasure vault. Taking the candle from its place he commenced a systematic search of the apartment, nor had he gone far before he discovered another door in the opposite end of the room, a door which gave upon creaking hinges to the weight of his body. Beyond the door lay another narrow passageway. Along this Werper made his way, ascending a flight of stone steps to another corridor twenty feet above the level of the first.

The flickering candle lighted the way before him, and a moment later he was thankful for the possession of this crude and antiquated luminant, which, a few hours before he might have looked upon with contempt, for it showed him, just in time, a yawning pit, apparently terminating the tunnel he was traversing.

Before him was a circular shaft. He held the candle above it and peered downward. Below him, at a great distance, he saw the light reflected back from the surface of a pool of water. He had come upon a well. He raised the candle above his head and peered across the black void, and there upon the opposite side he saw the continuation of the tunnel; but how was he to span the gulf?

As he stood there measuring the distance to the opposite side and wondering if he dared venture so great a leap, there broke suddenly upon his startled ears a piercing scream which diminished gradually until it ended in a series of dismal moans. The voice seemed partly human, yet so hideous that it might well have emanated from the tortured throat of a lost soul, writhing in the fires of hell.

The Belgian shuddered and looked fearfully upward, for the scream had seemed to come from above him. As he looked he saw an opening far overhead, and a patch of sky pinked with brilliant stars.

His half-formed intention to call for help was expunged by the terrifying cry — where such a voice lived, no human creatures could dwell. He dared not reveal himself to whatever inhabitants dwelt in the place above him. He cursed himself for a fool that he had ever embarked upon such a mission. He wished himself safely back in the camp of Achmet Zek, and would almost have embraced an opportunity to give himself up to the military authorities of the Congo if by so doing he might be rescued from the frightful predicament in which he now was.

He listened fearfully, but the cry was not repeated, and at last spurred to desperate means, he gathered himself for the leap across the chasm. Going back twenty paces, he took a running start, and at the edge of the well, leaped upward and outward in an attempt to gain the opposite side.

In his hand he clutched the sputtering candle, and as he took the leap the rush of air extinguished it. In utter darkness he flew through space, clutching outward for a hold should his feet miss the invisible ledge.

He struck the edge of the door of the opposite terminus of the rocky tunnel with his knees, slipped backward, clutched desperately for a moment, and at last hung half within and half without the opening; but he was safe. For several minutes he dared not move; but clung, weak and sweating, where he lay. At last, cautiously, he drew himself well within the tunnel, and again he lay at full length upon the floor, fighting to regain control of his shattered nerves.

When his knees struck the edge of the tunnel he had dropped the candle. Presently, hoping against hope that it had fallen upon the floor of the passageway, rather than back into the depths of the well, he rose upon all fours and commenced a diligent search for the little tallow cylinder, which now seemed infinitely more precious to him than all the fabulous wealth of the hoarded ingots of Opar.

And when, at last, he found it, he clasped it to him and sank back sobbing and exhausted. For many minutes he lay trembling and broken; but finally he drew himself to a sitting posture, and taking a match from his pocket, lighted the stump of the candle which remained to him. With the light he found it easier to regain control of his nerves, and presently he was again making his way along the tunnel in search of an avenue of escape. The horrid cry that had come down to him from above through the ancient well-shaft still haunted him, so that he trembled in terror at even the sounds of his own cautious advance.

He had gone forward but a short distance, when, to his chagrin, a wall of masonry barred his farther progress, closing the tunnel completely from top to bottom and from side to side. What could it mean? Werper was an educated and intelligent man. His military training had taught him to use his mind for the purpose for which it was intended. A blind tunnel such as this was senseless. It must continue beyond the wall. Someone, at some time in the past, had had it blocked for an unknown purpose of his own. The man fell to examining the masonry by the light of his candle. To his delight he discovered that the thin blocks of hewn stone of which it was constructed were fitted in loosely without mortar or cement. He tugged upon one of them, and to his joy found that it was easily removable. One after another he pulled out the blocks until he had opened an aperture large enough to admit his body, then he crawled through into a large, low chamber. Across this another door barred his way; but this, too, gave before his efforts, for it was not barred. A long, dark corridor showed before him, but before he had followed it far, his candle burned down until it scorched his fingers. With an oath he dropped it to the floor, where it sputtered for a moment and went out.

Now he was in total darkness, and again terror rode heavily astride his neck. What further pitfalls and dangers lay ahead he could not guess; but that he was as far as ever from liberty he was quite willing to believe, so depressing is utter absence of light to one in unfamiliar surroundings.

Slowly he groped his way along, feeling with his hands upon the tunnel's walls, and cautiously with his feet ahead of him upon the floor before he could take a single forward step. How long he crept on thus he could not guess; but at last, feeling that the tunnel's length was interminable, and exhausted by his efforts, by terror, and loss of sleep, he determined to lie down and rest before proceeding farther.

When he awoke there was no change in the surrounding blackness. He might have slept a second or a day — he could not know; but that he had slept for some time was attested by the fact that he felt refreshed and hungry.

Again he commenced his groping advance; but this time he had gone but a short distance when he emerged into a room, which was lighted through an opening in the ceiling, from which a flight of concrete steps led downward to the floor of the chamber.

Above him, through the aperture, Werper could see sunlight glancing from massive columns, which were twined about by clinging vines. He listened; but he heard no sound other than the soughing of the wind through leafy branches, the hoarse cries of birds, and the chattering of monkeys.

Boldly he ascended the stairway, to find himself in a circular court. Just before him stood a stone altar, stained with rusty-brown discolorations. At the time Werper gave no thought to an explanation of these stains — later their origin became all too hideously apparent to him.

Beside the opening in the floor, just behind the altar, through which he had entered the court from the subterranean chamber below, the Belgian discovered several doors leading from the enclosure upon the level of the floor. Above, and circling the courtyard, was a series of open balconies. Monkeys scampered about the deserted ruins, and gaily plumaged birds flitted in and out among the columns and the galleries far above; but no sign of human presence was discernible. Werper felt relieved. He sighed, as though a great weight had been lifted from his shoulders. He took a step toward one of the exits, and then he halted, wide-eyed in astonishment and terror, for almost at the same instant a dozen doors opened in the courtyard wall and a horde of frightful men rushed in upon him.

They were the priests of the Flaming God of Opar — the same, shaggy, knotted, hideous little men who had dragged Jane Clayton to the sacrificial altar at this very spot years before. Their long arms, their short and crooked legs, their close-set, evil eyes, and their low, receding foreheads gave them a bestial appearance that sent a qualm of paralyzing fright through the shaken nerves of the Belgian.

With a scream he turned to flee back into the lesser terrors of the gloomy corridors and apartments from which he had just emerged, but the frightful men anticipated his intentions. They blocked the way; they seized him, and though he fell, groveling upon his knees before them, begging for his life, they bound him and hurled him to the floor of the inner temple.

The rest was but a repetition of what Tarzan and Jane Clayton had passed through. The priestesses came, and with them La, the High Priestess. Werper was raised and laid across the altar. Cold sweat exuded from his every pore as La raised the cruel, sacrificial knife above him. The death chant fell upon his tortured ears. His staring eyes wandered to the golden goblets from which the hideous votaries would soon quench their inhuman thirst in his own, warm life-blood.

He wished that he might be granted the brief respite of unconsciousness before the final plunge of the keen blade — and then there was a frightful roar that sounded almost in his ears. The High Priestess lowered her dagger. Her eyes went wide in horror. The priestesses, her votaresses, screamed and fled madly toward the exits. The priests roared out their rage and terror according to the temper of their courage. Werper strained his neck about to catch a sight of the cause of their panic, and when, at last he saw it, he too went

cold in dread, for what his eyes beheld was the figure
of a huge lion standing in the center of the temple,
and already a single victim lay mangled beneath his
cruel paws.

Again the lord of the wilderness roared, turning his
baleful gaze upon the altar. La staggered forward,
reeled, and fell across Werper in a swoon.

Chapter VI

THE ARAB RAID

*A*FTER THEIR FIRST terror had subsided subsequent to the shock of the earthquake, Basuli and his warriors hastened back into the passageway in search of Tarzan and two of their own number who were also missing.

They found the way blocked by jammed and distorted rock. For two days they labored to tear a way through to their imprisoned friends; but when, after Herculean efforts, they had unearthed but a few yards of the choked passage, and discovered the mangled remains of one of their fellows they were forced to the conclusion that Tarzan and the second Waziri also lay dead beneath the rock mass farther in, beyond human aid, and no longer susceptible of it.

Again and again as they labored they called aloud the names of their master and their comrade; but no answering call rewarded their listening ears. At last they gave up the search. Tearfully they cast a last look at the shattered tomb of their master, shouldered the heavy

burden of gold that would at least furnish comfort, if
not happiness, to their bereaved and beloved mistress,
and made their mournful way back across the desolate
valley of Opar, and downward through the forests
beyond toward the distant bungalow.

And as they marched what sorry fate was already
drawing down upon that peaceful, happy home!

From the north came Achmet Zek, riding to the
summons of his lieutenant's letter. With him came his
horde of renegade Arabs, outlawed marauders, these,
and equally degraded blacks, garnered from the more
debased and ignorant tribes of savage cannibals
through whose countries the raider passed to and fro
with perfect impunity.

Mugambi, the ebon Hercules, who had shared the
dangers and vicissitudes of his beloved Bwana, from
Jungle Island, almost to the headwaters of the Ugambi,
was the first to note the bold approach of the sinister
caravan.

He it was whom Tarzan had left in charge of the
warriors who remained to guard Lady Greystoke, nor
could a braver or more loyal guardian have been found
in any clime or upon any soil. A giant in stature, a
savage, fearless warrior, the huge black possessed also
soul and judgment in proportion to his bulk and his
ferocity.

Not once since his master had departed had he been
beyond sight or sound of the bungalow, except when
Lady Greystoke chose to canter across the broad plain,
or relieve the monotony of her loneliness by a brief
hunting excursion. On such occasions Mugambi,
mounted upon a wiry Arab, had ridden close at her
horse's heels.

The raiders were still a long way off when the warrior's keen eyes discovered them. For a time he stood
scrutinizing the advancing party in silence, then he
turned and ran rapidly in the direction of the native

huts which lay a few hundred yards below the bungalow.

Here he called out to the lolling warriors. He issued
orders rapidly. In compliance with them the men
seized upon their weapons and their shields. Some ran
to call in the workers from the fields and to warn the
tenders of the flocks and herds. The majority followed
Mugambi back toward the bungalow.

The dust of the raiders was still a long distance away.
Mugambi could not know positively that it hid an
enemy; but he had spent a lifetime of savage life in
savage Africa, and he had seen parties before come thus
unheralded. Sometimes they had come in peace and
sometimes they had come in war — one could never
tell. It was well to be prepared. Mugambi did not like
the haste with which the strangers advanced.

The Greystoke bungalow was not well adapted for
defense. No palisade surrounded it, for, situated as it
was, in the heart of loyal Waziri, its master had anticipated no possibility of an attack in force by any enemy.
Heavy, wooden shutters there were to close the window
apertures against hostile arrows, and these Mugambi
was engaged in lowering when Lady Greystoke appeared upon the veranda.

"Why, Mugambi!" she exclaimed. "What has happened? Why are you lowering the shutters?"

Mugambi pointed out across the plain to where a
white-robed force of mounted men was now distinctly
visible.

"Arabs," he explained. "They come for no good
purpose in the absence of the Great Bwana."

Beyond the neat lawn and the flowering shrubs, Jane
Clayton saw the glistening bodies of her Waziri. The
sun glanced from the tips of their metal-shod spears,
picked out the gorgeous colors in the feathers of their
war bonnets, and reflected the high-lights from the
glossy skins of their broad shoulders and high cheek

bones.

Jane Clayton surveyed them with unmixed feelings of pride and affection. What harm could befall her with such as these to protect her?

The raiders had halted now, a hundred yards out upon the plain. Mugambi had hastened down to join his warriors. He advanced a few yards before them and raising his voice hailed the strangers. Achmet Zek sat straight in his saddle before his henchmen.

"Arab!" cried Mugambi. "What do you here?"

"We come in peace," Achmet Zek called back.

"Then turn and go in peace," replied Mugambi. "We do not want you here. There can be no peace between Arab and Waziri."

Mugambi, although not born in Waziri, had been adopted into the tribe, which now contained no member more jealous of its traditions and its prowess than he.

Achmet Zek drew to one side of his horde, speaking to his men in a low voice. A moment later, without warning, a ragged volley was poured into the ranks of the Waziri. A couple of warriors fell, the others were for charging the attackers; but Mugambi was a cautious as well as a brave leader. He knew the futility of charging mounted men armed with muskets. He withdrew his force behind the shrubbery of the garden. Some he dispatched to various other parts of the grounds surrounding the bungalow. Half a dozen he sent to the bungalow itself with instructions to keep their mistress within doors, and to protect her with their lives.

Adopting the tactics of the desert fighters from which he had sprung, Achmet Zek led his followers at a gallop in a long, thin line, describing a great circle which drew closer and closer in toward the defenders.

At that part of the circle closest to the Waziri, a constant fusillade of shots was poured into the bushes behind which the black warriors had concealed themselves. The latter, on their part, loosed their slim shafts at the nearest of the enemy.

The Waziri, justly famed for their archery, found no cause to blush for their performance that day. Time and again some swarthy horseman threw hands above his head and toppled from his saddle, pierced by a deadly arrow; but the contest was uneven. The Arabs outnumbered the Waziri; their bullets penetrated the shrubbery and found marks that the Arab riflemen had not even seen; and then Achmet Zek circled inward a half mile above the bungalow, tore down a section of the fence, and led his marauders within the grounds.

Across the fields they charged at a mad run. Not again did they pause to lower fences, instead, they drove their wild mounts straight for them, clearing the obstacles as lightly as winged gulls.

Mugambi saw them coming, and, calling those of his warriors who remained, ran for the bungalow and the last stand. Upon the veranda Lady Greystoke stood, rifle in hand. More than a single raider had accounted to her steady nerves and cool aim for his outlawry; more than a single pony raced, riderless, in the wake of the charging horde.

Mugambi pushed his mistress back into the greater security of the interior, and with his depleted force prepared to make a last stand against the foe.

On came the Arabs, shouting and waving their long guns above their heads. Past the veranda they raced, pouring a deadly fire into the kneeling Waziri who discharged their volley of arrows from behind their long, oval shields — shields well adapted, perhaps, to stop a hostile arrow, or deflect a spear; but futile, quite, before the leaden missiles of the riflemen.

From beneath the half-raised shutters of the bungalow other bowmen did effective service in greater security, and after the first assault, Mugambi withdrew his entire force within the building.

Again and again the Arabs charged, at last forming a stationary circle about the little fortress, and outside the effective range of the defenders' arrows. From their new position they fired at will at the windows. One by one the Waziri fell. Fewer and fewer were the arrows that replied to the guns of the raiders, and at last Achmet Zek felt safe in ordering an assault.

Firing as they ran, the bloodthirsty horde raced for the veranda. A dozen of them fell to the arrows of the defenders; but the majority reached the door. Heavy gun butts fell upon it. The crash of splintered wood mingled with the report of a rifle as Jane Clayton fired through the panels upon the relentless foe.

Upon both sides of the door men fell; but at last the frail barrier gave to the vicious assaults of the maddened attackers; it crumpled inward and a dozen swarthy murderers leaped into the living-room. At the far end stood Jane Clayton surrounded by the remnant of her devoted guardians. The floor was covered by the bodies of those who already had given up their lives in her defense. In the forefront of her protectors stood the giant Mugambi. The Arabs raised their rifles to pour in the last volley that would effectually end all resistance; but Achmet Zek roared out a warning order that stayed their trigger fingers.

"Fire not upon the woman!" he cried. "Who harms her, dies. Take the woman alive!"

The Arabs rushed across the room; the Waziri met them with their heavy spears. Swords flashed, long-barreled pistols roared out their sullen death dooms. Mugambi launched his spear at the nearest of the enemy with a force that drove the heavy shaft completely through the Arab's body, then he seized a pistol from another, and grasping it by the barrel brained all who forced their way too near his mistress.

Emulating his example the few warriors who remained to him fought like demons; but one by one they fell, until only Mugambi remained to defend the life and honor of the ape-man's mate.

From across the room Achmet Zek watched the unequal struggle and urged on his minions. In his hands was a jeweled musket. Slowly he raised it to his shoulder, waiting until another move should place Mugambi at his mercy without endangering the lives of the woman or any of his own followers.

At last the moment came, and Achmet Zek pulled the trigger. Without a sound the brave Mugambi sank to the floor at the feet of Jane Clayton.

An instant later she was surrounded and disarmed. Without a word they dragged her from the bungalow. A giant Negro lifted her to the pommel of his saddle, and while the raiders searched the bungalow and out-houses for plunder he rode with her beyond the gates and waited the coming of his master.

Jane Clayton saw the raiders lead the horses from the corral, and drive the herds in from the fields. She saw her home plundered of all that represented intrinsic worth in the eyes of the Arabs, and then she saw the torch applied, and the flames lick up what remained.

And at last, when the raiders assembled after glutting their fury and their avarice, and rode away with her toward the north, she saw the smoke and the flames rising far into the heavens until the winding of the trail into the thick forests hid the sad view from her eyes.

As the flames ate their way into the living-room, reaching out forked tongues to lick up the bodies of the dead, one of that gruesome company whose bloody welterings had long since been stilled, moved again. It was a huge black who rolled over upon his side and opened blood-shot, suffering eyes. Mugambi, whom the Arabs had left for dead, still lived. The hot flames were almost upon him as he raised himself painfully upon his hands and knees and crawled slowly toward the doorway.

Again and again he sank weakly to the floor; but each time he rose again and continued his pitiful way toward safety. After what seemed to him an interminable time, during which the flames had become a veritable fiery furnace at the far side of the room, the great black managed to reach the veranda, roll down the steps, and crawl off into the cool safety of some nearby shrubbery.

All night he lay there, alternately unconscious and painfully sentient; and in the latter state watching with savage hatred the lurid flames which still rose from burning crib and hay cock. A prowling lion roared close at hand; but the giant black was unafraid. There was place for but a single thought in his savage mind — revenge! revenge! revenge!

Chapter VII

THE JEWEL-ROOM OF OPAR

*F*OR SOME TIME Tarzan lay where he had fallen upon the floor of the treasure chamber beneath the ruined walls of Opar. He lay as one dead; but he was not dead. At length he stirred. His eyes opened upon the utter darkness of the room. He raised his hand to his head and brought it away sticky with clotted blood. He sniffed at his fingers, as a wild beast might sniff at the life-blood upon a wounded paw.

Slowly he rose to a sitting posture — listening. No sound reached to the buried depths of his sepulcher. He staggered to his feet, and groped his way about among the tiers of ingots. What was he? Where was he? His head ached; but otherwise he felt no ill effects from the blow that had felled him. The accident he did not recall, nor did he recall aught of what had led up to it.

He let his hands grope unfamiliarly over his limbs, his torso, and his head. He felt of the quiver at his back, the knife in his loin cloth. Something struggled for recognition within his brain. Ah! he had it. There

was something missing. He crawled about upon the
floor, feeling with his hands for the thing that instinct
warned him was gone. At last he found it — the heavy
war spear that in past years had formed so important
a feature of his daily life, almost of his very existence,
so inseparably had it been connected with his every
action since the long-gone day that he had wrested his
first spear from the body of a black victim of his savage
training.

Tarzan was sure that there was another and more
lovely world than that which was confined to the
darkness of the four stone walls surrounding him. He
continued his search and at last found the doorway
leading inward beneath the city and the temple. This
he followed, most incautiously. He came to the stone
steps leading upward to the higher level. He ascended
them and continued onward toward the well.

Nothing spurred his hurt memory to a recollection
of past familiarity with his surroundings. He blundered on through the darkness as though he were
traversing an open plain under the brilliance of a
noonday sun, and suddenly there happened that which
had to happen under the circumstances of his rash
advance.

He reached the brink of the well, stepped outward
into space, lunged forward, and shot downward into
the inky depths below. Still clutching his spear, he
struck the water, and sank beneath its surface, plumb-
ing the depths.

The fall had not injured him, and when he rose to
the surface, he shook the water from his eyes, and
found that he could see. Daylight was filtering into the
well from the orifice far above his head. It illumined
the inner walls faintly. Tarzan gazed about him. On
the level with the surface of the water he saw a large
opening in the dark and slimy wall. He swam to it, and
drew himself out upon the wet floor of a tunnel.

Along this he passed; but now he went warily, for Tarzan of the Apes was learning. The unexpected pit had taught him care in the traversing of dark passage-ways — he needed no second lesson.

For a long distance the passage went straight as an arrow. The floor was slippery, as though at times the rising waters of the well overflowed and flooded it. This, in itself, retarded Tarzan's pace, for it was with difficulty that he kept his footing.

The foot of a stairway ended the passage. Up this he made his way. It turned back and forth many times, leading, at last, into a small, circular chamber, the gloom of which was relieved by a faint light which found ingress through a tubular shaft several feet in diameter which rose from the center of the room's ceiling, upward to a distance of a hundred feet or more, where it terminated in a stone grating through which Tarzan could see a blue and sun-lit sky.

Curiosity prompted the ape-man to investigate his surroundings. Several metal-bound, copper-studded chests constituted the sole furniture of the round room. Tarzan let his hands run over these. He felt of the copper studs, he pulled upon the hinges, and at last, by chance, he raised the cover of one.

An exclamation of delight broke from his lips at sight of the pretty contents. Gleaming and glistening in the subdued light of the chamber, lay a great tray full of brilliant stones. Tarzan, reverted to the primitive by his accident, had no conception of the fabulous value of his find. To him they were but pretty pebbles. He plunged his hands into them and let the priceless gems filter through his fingers. He went to others of the chests, only to find still further stores of precious stones. Nearly all were cut, and from these he gathered a handful and filled the pouch which dangled at his side — the uncut stones he tossed back into the chests.

Unwittingly, the ape-man had stumbled upon the

forgotten jewel-room of Opar. For ages it had lain buried beneath the temple of the Flaming God, midway of one of the many inky passages which the superstitious descendants of the ancient Sun Worshipers had either dared not or cared not to explore.

Tiring at last of this diversion, Tarzan took up his way along the corridor which led upward from the jewel-room by a steep incline. Winding and twisting, but always tending upward, the tunnel led him nearer and nearer to the surface, ending finally in a low-ceiled room, lighter than any that he had as yet discovered.

Above him an opening in the ceiling at the upper end of a flight of concrete steps revealed a brilliant sunlit scene. Tarzan viewed the vine-covered columns in mild wonderment. He puckered his brows in an attempt to recall some recollection of similar things. He was not sure of himself. There was a tantalizing suggestion always present in his mind that something was eluding him — that he should know many things which he did not know.

His earnest cogitation was rudely interrupted by a thunderous roar from the opening above him. Following the roar came the cries and screams of men and women. Tarzan grasped his spear more firmly and ascended the steps. A strange sight met his eyes as he emerged from the semi-darkness of the cellar to the brilliant light of the temple.

The creatures he saw before him he recognized for what they were — men and women, and a huge lion. The men and women were scuttling for the safety of the exits. The lion stood upon the body of one who had been less fortunate than the others. He was in the center of the temple. Directly before Tarzan, a woman stood beside a block of stone. Upon the top of the stone lay stretched a man, and as the ape-man watched the scene, he saw the lion glare terribly at the two who remained within the temple. Another thunderous roar broke from the savage throat, the woman screamed and swooned across the body of the man stretched prostrate upon the stone altar before her.

The lion advanced a few steps and crouched. The tip of his sinuous tail twitched nervously. He was upon the point of charging when his eyes were attracted toward the ape-man.

Werper, helpless upon the altar, saw the great carnivore preparing to leap upon him. He saw the sudden change in the beast's expression as his eyes wandered to something beyond the altar and out of the Belgian's view. He saw the formidable creature rise to a standing position. A figure darted past Werper. He saw a mighty arm upraised, and a stout spear shoot forward toward the lion, to bury itself in the broad chest.

He saw the lion snapping and tearing at the weapon's shaft, and he saw, wonder of wonders, the naked giant who had hurled the missile charging upon the great beast, only a long knife ready to meet those ferocious fangs and talons.

The lion reared up to meet this new enemy. The beast was growling frightfully, and then upon the startled ears of the Belgian, broke a similar savage growl from the lips of the man rushing upon the beast.

By a quick side step, Tarzan eluded the first swinging clutch of the lion's paws. Darting to the beast's side, he leaped upon the tawny back. His arms encircled the maned neck, his teeth sank deep into the brute's flesh. Roaring, leaping, rolling and struggling, the giant cat attempted to dislodge this savage enemy, and all the while one great, brown fist was driving a long keen blade repeatedly into the beast's side.

During the battle, La regained consciousness. Spellbound, she stood above her victim watching the spectacle. It seemed incredible that a human being could best the king of beasts in personal encounter and yet before her very eyes there was taking place just such an improbability.

At last Tarzan's knife found the great heart, and with a final, spasmodic struggle the lion rolled over upon the marble floor, dead. Leaping to his feet the conqueror placed a foot upon the carcass of his kill, raised his face toward the heavens, and gave voice to so hideous a cry that both La and Werper trembled as it reverberated through the temple.

Then the ape-man turned, and Werper recognized him as the man he had left for dead in the treasure room.

Chapter VIII

THE ESCAPE FROM OPAR

WERPER WAS ASTOUNDED. Could this creature be the same dignified Englishman who had entertained him so graciously in his luxurious African home? Could this wild beast, with blazing eyes, and bloody countenance, be at the same time a man? Could the horrid, victory cry he had but just heard have been formed in human throat?

Tarzan was eyeing the man and the woman, a puzzled expression in his eyes, but there was no faintest tinge of recognition. It was as though he had discovered some new species of living creature and was marveling at his find.

La was studying the ape-man's features. Slowly her large eyes opened very wide.

"Tarzan!" she exclaimed, and then, in the vernacular of the great apes which constant association with the anthropoids had rendered the common language of the Oparians: "You have come back to me! La has ignored the mandates of her religion, waiting, always waiting for Tarzan — for her Tarzan. She has taken no mate, for in all the world there was but one with whom La would mate. And now you have come back! Tell me, O Tarzan, that it is for me you have returned."

Werper listened to the unintelligible jargon. He looked from La to Tarzan. Would the latter understand this strange tongue? To the Belgian's surprise, the Englishman answered in a language evidently identical to hers.

"Tarzan," he repeated, musingly. "Tarzan. The name sounds familiar."

"It is your name — you are Tarzan," cried La.

"I am Tarzan?" The ape-man shrugged. "Well, it is a good name — I know no other, so I will keep it; but I do not know you. I did not come hither for you. Why I came, I do not know at all; neither do I know from whence I came. Can you tell me?"

La shook her head. "I never knew," she replied.

Tarzan turned toward Werper and put the same question to him; but in the language of the great apes. The Belgian shook his head.

"I do not understand that language," he said in French.

Without effort, and apparently without realizing that he made the change, Tarzan repeated his question in French. Werper suddenly came to a full realization of the magnitude of the injury of which Tarzan was a victim. The man had lost his memory — no longer could he recollect past events. The Belgian was upon the point of enlightening him, when it suddenly occurred to him that by keeping Tarzan in ignorance, for a time at least, of his true identity, it might be possible to turn the ape-man's misfortune to his own advantage.

"I cannot tell you from whence you came," he said; "but this I can tell you — if we do not get out of this horrible place we shall both be slain upon this bloody altar. The woman was about to plunge her knife into my heart when the lion interrupted the fiendish ritual. Come! Before they recover from their fright and reassemble, let us find a way out of their damnable temple."

Tarzan turned again toward La.

"Why," he asked, "would you have killed this man? Are you hungry?"

The High Priestess cried out in disgust.

"Did he attempt to kill you?" continued Tarzan.

The woman shook her head.

"Then why should you have wished to kill him?" Tarzan was determined to get to the bottom of the thing.

La raised her slender arm and pointed toward the sun.

"We were offering up his soul as a gift to the Flaming God," she said.

Tarzan looked puzzled. He was again an ape, and apes do not understand such matters as souls and Flaming Gods.

"Do you wish to die?" he asked Werper.

The Belgian assured him, with tears in his eyes, that he did not wish to die.

"Very well then, you shall not," said Tarzan. "Come! We will go. This *she* would kill you and keep me for herself. It is no place anyway for a Mangani. I should soon die, shut up behind these stone walls."

He turned toward La. "We are going now," he said.

The woman rushed forward and seized the ape-man's hands in hers.

"Do not leave me!" she cried. "Stay, and you shall be High Priest. La loves you. All Opar shall be yours. Slaves shall wait upon you. Stay, Tarzan of the Apes, and let love reward you."

The ape-man pushed the kneeling woman aside. "Tarzan does not desire you," he said, simply, and stepping to Werper's side he cut the Belgian's bonds and motioned him to follow.

Panting — her face convulsed with rage, La sprang to her feet.

"Stay, you shall!" she screamed. "La will have you — if she cannot have you alive, she will have you dead," and raising her face to the sun she gave voice to the same hideous shriek that Werper had heard once before and Tarzan many times.

In answer to her cry a Babel of voices broke from the surrounding chambers and corridors.

"Come, Guardian Priests!" she cried. "The infidels have profaned the holiest of the holies. Come! Strike terror to their hearts; defend La and her altar; wash clean the temple with the blood of the polluters."

Tarzan understood, though Werper did not. The former glanced at the Belgian and saw that he was unarmed. Stepping quickly to La's side the ape-man seized her in his strong arms and though she fought with all the mad savagery of a demon, he soon disarmed her, handing her long, sacrificial knife to Werper.

"You will need this," he said, and then from each doorway a horde of the monstrous, little men of Opar streamed into the temple.

They were armed with bludgeons and knives, and fortified in their courage by fanatical hate and frenzy. Werper was terrified. Tarzan stood eyeing the foe in proud disdain. Slowly he advanced toward the exit he had chosen to utilize in making his way from the temple. A burly priest barred his way. Behind the first was a score of others. Tarzan swung his heavy spear, clublike, down upon the skull of the priest. The fellow collapsed, his head crushed.

Again and again the weapon fell as Tarzan made his way slowly toward the doorway. Werper pressed close behind, casting backward glances toward the shrieking, dancing mob menacing their rear. He held the sacrificial knife ready to strike whoever might come within its reach; but none came. For a time he wondered that they should so bravely battle with the giant ape-man, yet hesitate to rush upon him, who was relatively so weak. Had they done so he knew that he must have fallen at the first charge. Tarzan had reached the doorway over the corpses of all that had stood to dispute his way, before Werper guessed at the reason for his immunity. The priests feared the sacrificial knife! Willingly would they face death and welcome it if it came while they defended their High Priestess and her altar; but evidently there were deaths, and deaths. Some strange superstition must surround that polished blade, that no Oparian cared to chance a death thrust from it, yet gladly rushed to the slaughter of the ape-man's flaying spear.

Once outside the temple court, Werper communicated his discovery to Tarzan. The ape-man grinned, and let Werper go before him, brandishing the jeweled and holy weapon. Like leaves before a gale, the Oparians scattered in all directions and Tarzan and the Belgian found a clear passage through the corridors and chambers of the ancient temple.

The Belgian's eyes went wide as they passed through the room of the seven pillars of solid gold. With ill-concealed avarice he looked upon the age-old, golden tablets set in the walls of nearly every room and down the sides of many of the corridors. To the ape-man all this wealth appeared to mean nothing.

On the two went, chance leading them toward the broad avenue which lay between the stately piles of the half-ruined edifices and the inner wall of the city. Great apes jabbered at them and menaced them; but Tarzan answered them after their own kind, giving back taunt for taunt, insult for insult, challenge for challenge.

Werper saw a hairy bull swing down from a broken column and advance, stiff-legged and bristling, toward the naked giant. The yellow fangs were bared, angry snarls and barkings rumbled threateningly through the thick and hanging lips.

The Belgian watched his companion. To his horror, he saw the man stoop until his closed knuckles rested upon the ground as did those of the anthropoid. He saw him circle, stiff-legged about the circling ape. He heard the same bestial barkings and growlings issue from the human throat that were coming from the mouth of the brute. Had his eyes been closed he could not have known but that two giant apes were bridling for combat.

But there was no battle. It ended as the majority of such jungle encounters end — one of the boasters loses his nerve, and becomes suddenly interested in a blowing leaf, a beetle, or the lice upon his hairy stomach.

In this instance it was the anthropoid that retired in stiff dignity to inspect an unhappy caterpillar, which he presently devoured. For a moment Tarzan seemed inclined to pursue the argument. He swaggered truculently, stuck out his chest, roared and advanced closer to the bull. It was with difficulty that Werper finally persuaded him to leave well enough alone and continue his way from the ancient city of the Sun Worshipers.

The two searched for nearly an hour before they found the narrow exit through the inner wall. From there the well-worn trail led them beyond the outer fortification to the desolate valley of Opar.

Tarzan had no idea, in so far as Werper could discover, as to where he was or whence he came. He wandered aimlessly about, searching for food, which he discovered beneath small rocks, or hiding in the shade of the scant brush which dotted the ground.

The Belgian was horrified by the hideous menu of his companion. Beetles, rodents and caterpillars were devoured with seeming relish. Tarzan was indeed an ape again.

At last Werper succeeded in leading his companion toward the distant hills which mark the northwestern boundary of the valley, and together the two set out in the direction of the Greystoke bungalow.

What purpose prompted the Belgian in leading the victim of his treachery and greed back toward his former home it is difficult to guess, unless it was that without Tarzan there could be no ransom for Tarzan's wife.

That night they camped in the valley beyond the hills, and as they sat before a little fire where cooked a wild pig that had fallen to one of Tarzan's arrows, the latter sat lost in speculation. He seemed continually to be trying to grasp some mental image which as constantly eluded him.

At last he opened the leathern pouch which hung at his side. From it he poured into the palm of his hand a quantity of glittering gems. The firelight playing upon them conjured a multitude of scintillating rays, and as the wide eyes of the Belgian looked on in rapt fascination, the man's expression at last acknowledged a tangible purpose in courting the society of the ape-man.

Chapter IX

THE THEFT OF THE JEWELS

*F*OR TWO DAYS Werper sought for the party that had accompanied him from the camp to the barrier cliffs; but not until late in the afternoon of the second day did he find clew to its whereabouts, and then in such gruesome form that he was totally unnerved by the sight.

In an open glade he came upon the bodies of three of the blacks, terribly mutilated, nor did it require considerable deductive power to explain their murder. Of the little party only these three had not been slaves. The others, evidently tempted to hope for freedom from their cruel Arab master, had taken advantage of their separation from the main camp, to slay the three representatives of the hated power which held them in slavery, and vanish into the jungle.

Cold sweat exuded from Werper's forehead as he contemplated the fate which chance had permitted him to escape, for had he been present when the conspiracy bore fruit, he, too, must have been of the garnered.

Tarzan showed not the slightest surprise or interest in the discovery. Inherent in him was a calloused familiarity with violent death. The refinements of his recent civilization expunged by the force of the sad calamity which had befallen him, left only the primitive sensibilities which his childhood's training had imprinted indelibly upon the fabric of his mind.

The training of Kala, the examples and precepts of Kerchak, of Tublat, and of Terkoz now formed the basis of his every thought and action. He retained a mechanical knowledge of French and English speech. Werper had spoken to him in French, and Tarzan had replied in the same tongue without conscious realization that he had departed from the anthropoidal speech in which he had addressed La. Had Werper used English, the result would have been the same.

Again, that night, as the two sat before their camp fire, Tarzan played with his shining baubles. Werper asked him what they were and where he had found them. The ape-man replied that they were gay-colored stones, with which he purposed fashioning a necklace, and that he had found them far beneath the sacrificial court of the temple of the Flaming God.

Werper was relieved to find that Tarzan had no conception of the value of the gems. This would make it easier for the Belgian to obtain possession of them. Possibly the man would give them to him for the asking. Werper reached out his hand toward the little pile that Tarzan had arranged upon a piece of flat wood before him.

"Let me see them," said the Belgian.

Tarzan placed a large palm over his treasure. He bared his fighting fangs, and growled. Werper withdrew his hand more quickly than he had advanced it. Tarzan resumed his playing with the gems, and his conversation with Werper as though nothing unusual had occurred. He had but exhibited the beast's jealous protective instinct for a possession. When he killed he shared the meat with Werper; but had Werper ever, by accident, laid a hand upon Tarzan's share, he would have aroused the same savage, and resentful warning.

From that occurrence dated the beginning of a great fear in the breast of the Belgian for his savage companion. He had never understood the transformation that had been wrought in Tarzan by the blow upon his head, other than to attribute it to a form of amnesia. That Tarzan had once been, in truth, a savage, jungle beast, Werper had not known, and so, of course, he could not guess that the man had reverted to the state in which his childhood and young manhood had been spent.

Now Werper saw in the Englishman a dangerous maniac, whom the slightest untoward accident might turn upon him with rending fangs. Not for a moment did Werper attempt to delude himself into the belief that he could defend himself successfully against an attack by the ape-man. His one hope lay in eluding him, and making for the far distant camp of Achmet Zek as rapidly as he could; but armed only with the sacrificial knife, Werper shrank from attempting the journey through the jungle. Tarzan constituted a protection that was by no means despicable, even in the face of the larger carnivora, as Werper had reason to acknowledge from the evidence he had witnessed in the Oparian temple.

Too, Werper had his covetous soul set upon the pouch of gems, and so he was torn between the various emotions of avarice and fear. But avarice it was that burned most strongly in his breast, to the end that he dared the dangers and suffered the terrors of constant association with him he thought a mad man, rather than give up the hope of obtaining possession of the fortune which the contents of the little pouch represented.

Achmet Zek should know nothing of these — these would be for Werper alone, and so soon as he could encompass his design he would reach the coast and take passage for America, where he could conceal himself beneath the veil of a new identity and enjoy to some measure the fruits of his theft. He had it all planned out, did Lieutenant Albert Werper, living in anticipation the luxurious life of the idle rich. He even found himself regretting that America was so provincial, and that nowhere in the new world was a city that might compare with his beloved Brussels.

It was upon the third day of their progress from Opar that the keen ears of Tarzan caught the sound of men behind them. Werper heard nothing above the humming of the jungle insects, and the chattering life of the lesser monkeys and the birds.

For a time Tarzan stood in statuesque silence, listening, his sensitive nostrils dilating as he assayed each passing breeze. Then he withdrew Werper into the concealment of thick brush, and waited. Presently, along the game trail that Werper and Tarzan had been following, there came in sight a sleek, black warrior, alert and watchful.

In single file behind him, there followed, one after another, near fifty others, each burdened with two dull-yellow ingots lashed upon his back. Werper recognized the party immediately as that which had accompanied Tarzan on his journey to Opar. He glanced at the ape-man; but in the savage, watchful eyes he saw no recognition of Basuli and those other loyal Waziri.

When all had passed, Tarzan rose and emerged from concealment. He looked down the trail in the direction the party had gone. Then he turned to Werper.

"We will follow and slay them," he said.

"Why?" asked the Belgian.

"They are black," explained Tarzan. "It was a black

who killed Kala. They are the enemies of the Man-ganis."

Werper did not relish the idea of engaging in a battle with Basuli and his fierce fighting men. And, again, he had welcomed the sight of them returning toward the Greystoke bungalow, for he had begun to have doubts as to his ability to retrace his steps to the Waziri country. Tarzan, he knew, had not the remotest idea of whither they were going. By keeping at a safe dis-tance behind the laden warriors, they would have no difficulty in following them home. Once at the bun-galow, Werper knew the way to the camp of Achmet Zek. There was still another reason why he did not wish to interfere with the Waziri — they were bearing the great bur den of treasure in the direction he wished it borne. The farther they took it, the less the distance that he and Achmet Zek would have to transport it.

He argued with the ape-man therefore, against the latter's desire to exterminate the blacks, and at last he prevailed upon Tarzan to follow them in peace, saying that he was sure they would lead them out of the forest into a rich country, teeming with game.

It was many marches from Opar to the Waziri coun-try; but at last came the hour when Tarzan and the Belgian, following the trail of the warriors, topped the last rise, and saw before them the broad Waziri plain, the winding river, and the distant forests to the north and west.

A mile or more ahead of them, the line of warriors was creeping like a giant caterpillar through the tall grasses of the plain. Beyond, grazing herds of zebra, hartebeest, and topi dotted the level landscape, while closer to the river a bull buffalo, his head and shoulders protruding from the reeds watched the advancing blacks for a moment, only to turn at last and disappear into the safety of his dank and gloomy retreat.

Tarzan looked out across the familiar vista with no

faintest gleam of recognition in his eyes. He saw the
game animals, and his mouth watered; but he did not
look in the direction of his bungalow. Werper, however, did. A puzzled expression entered the Belgian's
eyes. He shaded them with his palms and gazed long
and earnestly toward the spot where the bungalow had
stood. He could not credit the testimony of his eyes —
there was no bungalow — no barns — no outhouses.
The corrals, the hay stacks — all were gone. What could
it mean?

And then, slowly there filtered into Werper's consciousness an explanation of the havoc that had been
wrought in that peaceful valley since last his eyes had
rested upon it — Achmet Zek had been there!

Basuli and his warriors had noted the devastation
the moment they had come in sight of the farm. Now
they hastened on toward it talking excitedly among
themselves in animated speculation upon the cause
and meaning of the catastrophe.

When, at last they crossed the trampled garden and
stood before the charred ruins of their master's bungalow, their greatest fears became convictions in the
light of the evidence about them.

Remnants of human dead, half devoured by prowling hyenas and others of the carnivora which infested
the region, lay rotting upon the ground, and among
the corpses remained sufficient remnants of their
clothing and ornaments to make clear to Basuli the
frightful story of the disaster that had befallen his
master's house.

"The Arabs," he said, as his men clustered about him.

The Waziri gazed about in mute rage for several
minutes. Everywhere they encountered only further
evidence of the ruthlessness of the cruel enemy that
had come during the Great Bwana's absence and laid
waste his property.

"What did they with 'Lady'?" asked one of the blacks.

They had always called Lady Greystoke thus.

"The women they would have taken with them," said Basuli. "Our women and his."

A giant black raised his spear above his head, and gave voice to a savage cry of rage and hate. The others followed his example. Basuli silenced them with a gesture.

"This is no time for useless noises of the mouth," he said. "The Great Bwana has taught us that it is acts by which things are done, not words. Let us save our breath — we shall need it all to follow up the Arabs and slay them. If 'Lady' and our women live the greater the need of haste, and warriors cannot travel fast upon empty lungs."

From the shelter of the reeds along the river, Werper and Tarzan watched the blacks. They saw them dig a trench with their knives and fingers. They saw them lay their yellow burdens in it and scoop the overturned earth back over the tops of the ingots.

Tarzan seemed little interested, after Werper had assured him that that which they buried was not good to eat; but Werper was intensely interested. He would have given much had he had his own followers with him, that he might take away the treasure as soon as the blacks left, for he was sure that they would leave this scene of desolation and death as soon as possible.

The treasure buried, the blacks removed themselves a short distance up wind from the fetid corpses, where they made camp, that they might rest before setting out in pursuit of the Arabs. It was already dusk. Werper and Tarzan sat devouring some pieces of meat they had brought from their last camp. The Belgian was occupied with his plans for the immediate future. He was positive that the Waziri would pursue Achmet Zek, for he knew enough of savage warfare, and of the characteristics of the Arabs and their degraded followers to guess that they had carried the Waziri women off into slavery. This alone would assure immediate pursuit by so warlike a people as the Waziri.

Werper felt that he should find the means and the opportunity to push on ahead, that he might warn Achmet Zek of the coming of Basuli, and also of the location of the buried treasure. What the Arab would now do with Lady Greystoke, in view of the mental affliction of her husband, Werper neither knew nor cared. It was enough that the golden treasure buried upon the site of the burned bungalow was infinitely more valuable than any ransom that would have occurred even to the avaricious mind of the Arab, and if Werper could persuade the raider to share even a portion of it with him he would be well satisfied.

But by far the most important consideration, to Werper, at least, was the incalculably valuable treasure in the little leathern pouch at Tarzan's side. If he could but obtain possession of this! He must! He would!

His eyes wandered to the object of his greed. They measured Tarzan's giant frame, and rested upon the rounded muscles of his arms. It was hopeless. What could he, Werper, hope to accomplish, other than his own death, by an attempt to wrest the gems from their savage owner?

Disconsolate, Werper threw himself upon his side. His head was pillowed on one arm, the other rested across his face in such a way that his eyes were hidden from the ape-man, though one of them was fastened upon him from beneath the shadow of the Belgian's forearm. For a time he lay thus, glowering at Tarzan, and originating schemes for plundering him of his treasure — schemes that were discarded as futile as rapidly as they were born.

Tarzan presently let his own eyes rest upon Werper. The Belgian saw that he was being watched, and lay very still. After a few moments he simulated the regular breathing of deep slumber.

Tarzan had been thinking. He had seen the Waziri bury their belongings. Werper had told him that they were hiding them lest some one find them and take them away. This seemed to Tarzan a splendid plan for safeguarding valuables. Since Werper had evinced a desire to possess his glittering pebbles, Tarzan, with the suspicions of a savage, had guarded the baubles, of whose worth he was entirely ignorant, as zealously as though they spelled life or death to him.

For a long time the ape-man sat watching his companion. At last, convinced that he slept, Tarzan withdrew his hunting knife and commenced to dig a hole in the ground before him. With the blade he loosened up the earth, and with his hands he scooped it out until he had excavated a little cavity a few inches in diameter, and five or six inches in depth. Into this he placed the pouch of jewels. Werper almost forgot to breathe after the fashion of a sleeper as he saw what the ape-man was doing — he scarce repressed an ejaculation of satisfaction.

Tarzan become suddenly rigid as his keen ears noted the cessation of the regular inspirations and expirations of his companion. His narrowed eyes bored straight down upon the Belgian. Werper felt that he was lost — he must risk all on his ability to carry on the deception. He sighed, threw both arms outward, and turned over on his back mumbling as though in the throes of a bad dream. A moment later he resumed the regular breathing.

Now he could not watch Tarzan, but he was sure that the man sat for a long time looking at him. Then, faintly, Werper heard the other's hands scraping dirt, and later patting it down. He knew then that the jewels were buried.

It was an hour before Werper moved again, then he rolled over facing Tarzan and opened his eyes. The ape-man slept. By reaching out his hand Werper could touch the spot where the pouch was buried.

For a long time he lay watching and listening. He moved about, making more noise than necessary, yet Tarzan did not awaken. He drew the sacrificial knife from his belt, and plunged it into the ground. Tarzan did not move. Cautiously the Belgian pushed the blade downward through the loose earth above the pouch. He felt the point touch the soft, tough fabric of the leather. Then he pried down upon the handle. Slowly the little mound of loose earth rose and parted. An instant later a corner of the pouch came into view. Werper pulled it from its hiding place, and tucked it in his shirt. Then he refilled the hole and pressed the dirt carefully down as it had been before.

Greed had prompted him to an act, the discovery of which by his companion could lead only to the most frightful consequences for Werper. Already he could almost feel those strong, white fangs burying themselves in his neck. He shuddered. Far out across the plain a leopard screamed, and in the dense reeds behind him some great beast moved on padded feet.

Werper feared these prowlers of the night; but infinitely more he feared the just wrath of the human beast sleeping at his side. With utmost caution the Belgian arose. Tarzan did not move. Werper took a few steps toward the plain and the distant forest to the northwest, then he paused and fingered the hilt of the long knife in his belt. He turned and looked down upon the sleeper.

"Why not?" he mused. "Then I should be safe."

He returned and bent above the ape-man. Clutched tightly in his hand was the sacrificial knife of the High Priestess of the Flaming God!

Chapter X

ACHMET ZEK
SEES THE JEWELS

MUGAMBI, WEAK AND suffering, had dragged his painful way along the trail of the retreating raiders. He could move but slowly, resting often; but savage hatred and an equally savage desire for vengeance kept him to his task. As the days passed his wounds healed and his strength returned, until at last his giant frame had regained all of its former mighty powers. Now he went more rapidly; but the mounted Arabs had covered a great distance while the wounded black had been painfully crawling after them.

They had reached their fortified camp, and there Achmet Zek awaited the return of his lieutenant, Albert Werper. During the long, rough journey, Jane Clayton had suffered more in anticipation of her impending fate than from the hardships of the road.

Achmet Zek had not deigned to acquaint her with his intentions regarding her future. She prayed that she had been captured in the hope of ransom, for if such should prove the case, no great harm would befall her at the hands of the Arabs; but there was the chance, the horrid chance, that another fate awaited her. She had heard of many women, among whom were white women, who had been sold by outlaws such as Achmet Zek into the slavery of black harems, or taken farther north into the almost equally hideous existence of some Turkish seraglio.

Jane Clayton was of sterner stuff than that which bends in spineless terror before danger. Until hope proved futile she would not give it up; nor did she entertain thoughts of self-destruction only as a final escape from dishonor. So long as Tarzan lived there was every reason to expect succor. No man nor beast who roamed the savage continent could boast the cunning and the powers of her lord and master. To her, he was little short of omnipotent in his native world — this world of savage beasts and savage men. Tarzan would come, and she would be rescued and avenged, of that she was certain. She counted the days that must elapse before he would return from Opar and discover what had transpired during his absence. After that it would be but a short time before he had surrounded the Arab stronghold and punished the motley crew of wrongdoers who inhabited it.

That he could find her she had no slightest doubt. No spoor, however faint, could elude the keen vigilance of his senses. To him, the trail of the raiders would be as plain as the printed page of an open book to her.

And while she hoped, there came through the dark jungle another. Terrified by night and by day, came Albert Werper. A dozen times he had escaped the claws and fangs of the giant carnivora only by what seemed a miracle to him. Armed with nothing more than the knife he had brought with him from Opar, he had made his way through as savage a country as yet exists upon the face of the globe.

By night he had slept in trees. By day he had stumbled fearfully on, often taking refuge among the branches when sight or sound of some great cat warned him from danger. But at last he had come within sight of the palisade behind which were his fierce companions.

At almost the same time Mugambi came out of the jungle before the walled village. As he stood in the shadow of a great tree, reconnoitering, he saw a man, ragged and disheveled, emerge from the jungle almost at his elbow. Instantly he recognized the newcomer as he who had been a guest of his master before the latter had departed for Opar.

The black was upon the point of hailing the Belgian when something stayed him. He saw the white man walking confidently across the clearing toward the village gate. No sane man thus approached a village in this part of Africa unless he was sure of a friendly welcome. Mugambi waited. His suspicions were aroused.

He heard Werper halloo; he saw the gates swing open, and he witnessed the surprised and friendly welcome that was accorded the erstwhile guest of Lord and Lady Greystoke. A light broke upon the understanding of Mugambi. This white man had been a traitor and a spy. It was to him they owed the raid during the absence of the Great Bwana. To his hate for the Arabs, Mugambi added a still greater hate for the white spy.

Within the village Werper passed hurriedly toward the silken tent of Achmet Zek. The Arab arose as his lieutenant entered. His face showed surprise as he viewed the tattered apparel of the Belgian.

"What has happened?" he asked.

Werper narrated all, save the little matter of the pouch of gems which were now tightly strapped about his waist, beneath his clothing. The Arab's eyes narrowed greedily as his henchman described the treasure that the Waziri had buried beside the ruins of the Greystoke bungalow.

"It will be a simple matter now to return and get it," said Achmet Zek. "First we will await the coming of the rash Waziri, and after we have slain them we may take our time to the treasure — none will disturb it where it lies, for we shall leave none alive who knows of its existence.

"And the woman?" asked Werper.

"I shall sell her in the north," replied the raider. "It is the only way, now. She should bring a good price."

The Belgian nodded. He was thinking rapidly. If he could persuade Achmet Zek to send him in command of the party which took Lady Greystoke north it would give him the opportunity he craved to make his escape from his chief. He would forego a share of the gold, if he could but get away unscathed with the jewels.

He knew Achmet Zek well enough by this time to know that no member of his band ever was voluntarily released from the service of Achmet Zek. Most of the few who deserted were recaptured. More than once had Werper listened to their agonized screams as they were tortured before being put to death. The Belgian had no wish to take the slightest chance of recapture.

"Who will go north with the woman," he asked, "while we are returning for the gold that the Waziri buried by the bungalow of the Englishman?"

Achmet Zek thought for a moment. The buried gold was of much greater value than the price the woman would bring. It was necessary to rid himself of her as quickly as possible and it was also well to obtain the gold with the least possible delay. Of all his followers, the Belgian was the most logical lieutenant to entrust with the command of one of the parties. An Arab, as familiar with the trails and tribes as Achmet Zek himself, might collect the woman's price and make good his escape into the far north. Werper, on the other hand, could scarce make his escape alone through a country hostile to Europeans while the men he would send with the Belgian could be carefully selected with a view to preventing Werper from persuading any considerable portion of his command to accompany him should he contemplate desertion of his chief.

At last the Arab spoke: "It is not necessary that we both return for the gold. You shall go north with the woman, carrying a letter to a friend of mine who is always in touch with the best markets for such merchandise, while I return for the gold. We can meet again here when our business is concluded."

Werper could scarce disguise the joy with which he received this welcome decision. And that he did entirely disguise it from the keen and suspicious eyes of Achmet Zek is open to question. However, the decision reached, the Arab and his lieutenant discussed the details of their forthcoming ventures for a short time further, when Werper made his excuses and returned to his own tent for the comforts and luxury of a long-desired bath and shave.

Having bathed, the Belgian tied a small hand mirror to a cord sewn to the rear wall of his tent, placed a rude chair beside an equally rude table that stood beside the glass, and proceeded to remove the rough stubble from his face.

In the catalog of masculine pleasures there is scarce one which imparts a feeling of greater comfort and refreshment than follows a clean shave, and now, with weariness temporarily banished, Albert Werper sprawled in his rickety chair to enjoy a final cigarette before retiring. His thumbs, tucked in his belt in lazy support of the weight of his arms, touched the belt which held the jewel pouch about his waist. He tingled with excitement as he let his mind dwell upon the value of the treasure, which, unknown to all save himself, lay hidden beneath his clothing.

What would Achmet Zek say, if he knew? Werper grinned. How the old rascal's eyes would pop could he but have a glimpse of those scintillating beauties! Werper had never yet had an opportunity to feast his eyes for any great length of time upon them. He had not even counted them — only roughly had he guessed at their value.

He unfastened the belt and drew the pouch from its hiding place. He was alone. The balance of the camp, save the sentries, had retired — none would enter the Belgian's tent. He fingered the pouch, feeling out the shapes and sizes of the precious, little nodules within. He hefted the bag, first in one palm, then in the other, and at last he wheeled his chair slowly around before the table, and in the rays of his small lamp let the glittering gems roll out upon the rough wood.

The refulgent rays transformed the interior of the soiled and squalid canvas to the splendor of a palace in the eyes of the dreaming man. He saw the gilded halls of pleasure that would open their portals to the possessor of the wealth which lay scattered upon this stained and dented table top. He dreamed of joys and luxuries and power which always had been beyond his grasp, and as he dreamed his gaze lifted from the table, as the gaze of a dreamer will, to a far distant goal above the mean horizon of terrestrial commonplaceness.

Unseeing, his eyes rested upon the shaving mirror which still hung upon the tent wall above the table; but his sight was focused far beyond. And then a reflection moved within the polished surface of the tiny glass, the man's eyes shot back out of space to the mirror's face, and in it he saw reflected the grim visage of Achmet Zek, framed in the flaps of the tent doorway behind him.

Werper stifled a gasp of dismay. With rare self-possession he let his gaze drop, without appearing to have halted upon the mirror until it rested again upon the gems. Without haste, he replaced them in the pouch, tucked the latter into his shirt, selected a cigarette from his case, lighted it and rose. Yawning, and stretching his arms above his head, he turned slowly toward the opposite end of the tent. The face of Achmet Zek had disappeared from the opening.

To say that Albert Werper was terrified would be putting it mildly. He realized that he not only had sacrificed his treasure; but his life as well. Achmet Zek would never permit the wealth that he had discovered to slip through his fingers, nor would he forgive the duplicity of a lieutenant who had gained possession of such a treasure without offering to share it with his chief.

Slowly the Belgian prepared for bed. If he were being watched, he could not know; but if so the watcher saw no indication of the nervous excitement which the European strove to conceal. When ready for his blankets, the man crossed to the little table and extinguished the light.

It was two hours later that the flaps at the front of the tent separated silently and gave entrance to a dark-robed figure, which passed noiselessly from the darkness without to the darkness within. Cautiously the prowler crossed the interior. In one hand was a long knife. He came at last to the pile of blankets spread upon several rugs close to one of the tent walls.

Lightly, his fingers sought and found the bulk beneath the blankets — the bulk that should be Albert Werper. They traced out the figure of a man, and then an arm shot upward, poised for an instant and descended. Again and again it rose and fell, and each time the long blade of the knife buried itself in the thing beneath the blankets. But there was an initial lifelessness in the silent bulk that gave the assassin momentary wonder. Feverishly he threw back the coverlets, and searched with nervous hands for the pouch of jewels which he expected to find concealed upon his victim's body.

An instant later he rose with a curse upon his lips. It was Achmet Zek, and he cursed because he had discovered beneath the blankets of his lieutenant only a pile of discarded clothing arranged in the form and semblance of a sleeping man — Albert Werper had fled.

Out into the village ran the chief, calling in angry tones to the sleepy Arabs, who tumbled from their tents in answer to his voice. But though they searched the village again and again they found no trace of the Belgian. Foaming with anger, Achmet Zek called his followers to horse, and though the night was pitchy black they set out to scour the adjoining forest for their quarry.

As they galloped from the open gates, Mugambi, hiding in a nearby bush, slipped, unseen, within the palisade. A score of blacks crowded about the entrance to watch the searchers depart, and as the last of them passed out of the village the blacks seized the portals and drew them to, and Mugambi lent a hand in the work as though the best of his life had been spent among the raiders.

In the darkness he passed, unchallenged, as one of their number, and as they returned from the gates to their respective tents and huts, Mugambi melted into the shadows and disappeared.

For an hour he crept about in the rear of the various huts and tents in an effort to locate that in which his master's mate was imprisoned. One there was which he was reasonably assured contained her, for it was the only hut before the door of which a sentry had been posted. Mugambi was crouching in the shadow of this structure, just around the corner from the unsuspecting guard, when another approached to relieve his comrade.

"The prisoner is safe within?" asked the newcomer.

"She is," replied the other, "for none has passed this doorway since I came."

The new sentry squatted beside the door, while he whom he had relieved made his way to his own hut. Mugambi slunk closer to the corner of the building. In one powerful hand he gripped a heavy knob-stick. No sign of elation disturbed his phlegmatic calm, yet inwardly he was aroused to joy by the proof he had just heard that "Lady" really was within.

The sentry's back was toward the corner of the hut which hid the giant black. The fellow did not see the huge form which silently loomed behind him. The knob-stick swung upward in a curve, and downward again. There was the sound of a dull thud, the crushing of heavy bone, and the sentry slumped into a silent, inanimate lump of clay.

A moment later Mugambi was searching the interior of the hut. At first slowly, calling, "Lady!" in a low whisper, and finally with almost frantic haste, until the truth presently dawned upon him — the hut was empty!

Chapter XI

TARZAN
BECOMES A BEAST AGAIN

*F*OR A MOMENT Werper had stood above the sleeping ape-man, his murderous knife poised for the fatal thrust; but fear stayed his hand. What if the first blow should fail to drive the point to his victim's heart? Werper shuddered in contemplation of the disastrous consequences to himself. Awakened, and even with a few moments of life remaining, the giant could literally tear his assailant to pieces should he choose, and the Belgian had no doubt but that Tarzan would so choose.

Again came the soft sound of padded footsteps in the reeds — closer this time. Werper abandoned his design. Before him stretched the wide plain and escape. The jewels were in his possession. To remain longer was to risk death at the hands of Tarzan, or the jaws of the hunter creeping ever nearer. Turning, he slunk away through the night, toward the distant forest.

Tarzan slept on. Where were those uncanny, guardian powers that had formerly rendered him immune from the dangers of surprise? Could this dull sleeper be the alert, sensitive Tarzan of old?

Perhaps the blow upon his head had numbed his senses, temporarily — who may say? Closer crept the stealthy creature through the reeds. The rustling curtain of vegetation parted a few paces from where the sleeper lay, and the massive head of a lion appeared. The beast surveyed the ape-man intently for a moment, then he crouched, his hind feet drawn well beneath him, his tail lashing from side to side.

It was the beating of the beast's tail against the reeds which awakened Tarzan. Jungle folk do not awaken slowly — instantly, full consciousness and full command of their every faculty returns to them from the depth of profound slumber.

Even as Tarzan opened his eyes he was upon his feet, his spear grasped firmly in his hand and ready for attack. Again was he Tarzan of the Apes, sentient, vigilant, ready.

No two lions have identical characteristics, nor does the same lion invariably act similarly under like circumstances. Whether it was surprise, fear or caution which prompted the lion crouching ready to spring upon the man, is immaterial — the fact remains that he did not carry out his original design, he did not spring at the man at all, but, instead, wheeled and sprang back into the reeds as Tarzan arose and confronted him.

The ape-man shrugged his broad shoulders and looked about for his companion. Werper was nowhere to be seen. At first Tarzan suspected that the man had been seized and dragged off by another lion, but upon examination of the ground he soon discovered that the Belgian had gone away alone out into the plain.

For a moment he was puzzled; but presently came to the conclusion that Werper had been frightened by the approach of the lion, and had sneaked off in terror.

A sneer touched Tarzan's lips as he pondered the man's act — the desertion of a comrade in time of danger, and without warning. Well, if that was the sort of creature Werper was, Tarzan wished nothing more of him. He had gone, and for all the ape-man cared, he might remain away — Tarzan would not search for him.

A hundred yards from where he stood grew a large tree, alone upon the edge of the reedy jungle. Tarzan made his way to it, clambered into it, and finding a comfortable crotch among its branches, reposed himself for uninterrupted sleep until morning.

And when morning came Tarzan slept on long after the sun had risen. His mind, reverted to the primitive, was untroubled by any more serious obligations than those of providing sustenance, and safeguarding his life. Therefore, there was nothing to awaken for until danger threatened, or the pangs of hunger assailed. It was the latter which eventually aroused him.

Opening his eyes, he stretched his giant thews, yawned, rose and gazed about him through the leafy foliage of his retreat. Across the wasted meadowlands and fields of John Clayton, Lord Greystoke, Tarzan of the Apes looked, as a stranger, upon the moving figures of Basuli and his braves as they prepared their morning meal and made ready to set out upon the expedition which Basuli had planned after discovering the havoc and disaster which had befallen the estate of his dead master.

The ape-man eyed the blacks with curiosity. In the back of his brain loitered a fleeting sense of familiarity with all that he saw, yet he could not connect any of the various forms of life, animate and inanimate, which had fallen within the range of his vision since he had emerged from the darkness of the pits of Opar, with any particular event of the past.

Hazily he recalled a grim and hideous form, hairy, ferocious. A vague tenderness dominated his savage sentiments as this phantom memory struggled for recognition. His mind had reverted to his childhood days — it was the figure of the giant she-ape, Kala, that he saw; but only half recognized. He saw, too, other grotesque, manlike forms. They were of Terkoz, Tublat, Kerchak, and a smaller, less ferocious figure, that was Neeta, the little playmate of his boyhood.

Slowly, very slowly, as these visions of the past animated his lethargic memory, he came to recognize them. They took definite shape and form, adjusting themselves nicely to the various incidents of his life with which they had been intimately connected. His boyhood among the apes spread itself in a slow panorama before him, and as it unfolded it induced within him a mighty longing for the companionship of the shaggy, low-browed brutes of his past.

He watched the blacks scatter their cook fire and depart; but though the face of each of them had but recently been as familiar to him as his own, they awakened within him no recollections whatsoever.

When they had gone, he descended from the tree and sought food. Out upon the plain grazed numerous herds of wild ruminants. Toward a sleek, fat bunch of zebra he wormed his stealthy way. No intricate process of reasoning caused him to circle widely until he was down wind from his prey — he acted instinctively. He took advantage of every form of cover as he crawled upon all fours and often flat upon his stomach toward them.

A plump young mare and a fat stallion grazed nearest to him as he neared the herd. Again it was instinct which selected the former for his meat. A low bush grew but a few yards from the unsuspecting two. The ape-man reached its shelter. He gathered his spear firmly in his grasp. Cautiously he drew his feet beneath him. In a single swift move he rose and cast his heavy weapon at the mare's side. Nor did he wait to note the effect of his assault, but leaped cat-like after his spear, his hunting knife in his hand.

For an instant the two animals stood motionless. The tearing of the cruel barb into her side brought a sudden scream of pain and fright from the mare, and then they both wheeled and broke for safety; but Tarzan of the Apes, for a distance of a few yards, could equal the speed of even these, and the first stride of the mare found her overhauled, with a savage beast at her shoulder. She turned, biting and kicking at her foe. Her mate hesitated for an instant, as though about to rush to her assistance; but a backward glance revealed to him the flying heels of the balance of the herd, and with a snort and a shake of his head he wheeled and dashed away.

Clinging with one hand to the short mane of his quarry, Tarzan struck again and again with his knife at the unprotected heart. The result had, from the first, been inevitable. The mare fought bravely, but hopelessly, and presently sank to the earth, her heart pierced. The ape-man placed a foot upon her carcass and raised his voice in the victory call of the Mangani. In the distance, Basuli halted as the faint notes of the hideous scream broke upon his ears.

"The great apes," he said to his companion. "It has been long since I have heard them in the country of the Waziri. What could have brought them back?"

Tarzan grasped his kill and dragged it to the partial seclusion of the bush which had hidden his own near approach, and there he squatted upon it, cut a huge hunk of flesh from the loin and proceeded to satisfy his hunger with the warm and dripping meat.

Attracted by the shrill screams of the mare, a pair of hyenas slunk presently into view. They trotted to a point a few yards from the gorging ape-man, and halted. Tarzan looked up, bared his fighting fangs and growled. The hyenas returned the compliment, and withdrew a couple of paces. They made no move to attack; but continued to sit at a respectful distance until Tarzan had concluded his meal. After the ape-man had cut a few strips from the carcass to carry with him, he walked slowly off in the direction of the river to quench his thirst. His way lay directly toward the hyenas, nor did he alter his course because of them.

With all the lordly majesty of Numa, the lion, he strode straight toward the growling beasts. For a moment they held their ground, bristling and defiant; but only for a moment, and then slunk away to one side while the indifferent ape-man passed them on his lordly way. A moment later they were tearing at the remains of the zebra.

Back to the reeds went Tarzan, and through them toward the river. A herd of buffalo, startled by his approach, rose ready to charge or to fly. A great bull pawed the ground and bellowed as his bloodshot eyes discovered the intruder; but the ape-man passed across their front as though ignorant of their existence. The bull's bellowing lessened to a low rumbling, he turned and scraped a horde of flies from his side with his muzzle, cast a final glance at the ape-man and resumed his feeding. His numerous family either followed his example or stood gazing after Tarzan in mild-eyed curiosity, until the opposite reeds swallowed him from view.

At the river, Tarzan drank his fill and bathed. During the heat of the day he lay up under the shade of a tree near the ruins of his burned barns. His eyes wandered out across the plain toward the forest, and a longing for the pleasures of its mysterious depths possessed his thoughts for a considerable time. With the next sun he would cross the open and enter the forest! There was no hurry — there lay before him an endless vista of tomorrows with naught to fill them but the satisfying of the appetites and caprices of the moment.

The ape-man's mind was untroubled by regret for the past, or aspiration for the future. He could lie at full length along a swaying branch, stretching his giant limbs, and luxuriating in the blessed peace of utter thoughtlessness, without an apprehension or a worry to sap his nervous energy and rob him of his peace of mind. Recalling only dimly any other existence, the ape-man was happy. Lord Greystoke had ceased to exist.

For several hours Tarzan lolled upon his swaying, leafy couch until once again hunger and thirst suggested an excursion. Stretching lazily he dropped to the ground and moved slowly toward the river. The game trail down which he walked had become by ages of use a deep, narrow trench, its walls topped on either side by impenetrable thicket and dense-growing trees closely interwoven with thick-stemmed creepers and lesser vines inextricably matted into two solid ramparts of vegetation. Tarzan had almost reached the point where the trail debouched upon the open river bottom when he saw a family of lions approaching along the path from the direction of the river. The ape-man counted seven — a male and two lionesses, full grown, and four young lions as large and quite as formidable as their parents. Tarzan halted, growling, and the lions paused, the great male in the lead baring his fangs and rumbling forth a warning roar. In his hand the ape-man held his heavy spear; but he had no intention of pitting his puny weapon against seven lions; yet he stood there growling and roaring and the lions did likewise. It was purely an exhibition of jungle bluff. Each was trying to frighten off the other. Neither wished to turn back and give way, nor did either at first desire to precipitate an encounter. The lions were fed sufficiently so as not to be goaded by pangs of hunger and as for Tarzan he seldom ate the meat of the carnivores; but a point of ethics was at stake and neither side wished to back down. So they stood there facing one another, making all sorts of hideous noises the while they hurled jungle invective back and forth. How long this bloodless duel would have persisted it is difficult to say, though eventually Tarzan would have been forced to yield to superior numbers.

There came, however, an interruption which put an end to the deadlock and it came from Tarzan's rear. He and the lions had been making so much noise that neither could hear anything above their concerted bedlam, and so it was that Tarzan did not hear the great bulk bearing down upon him from behind until an instant before it was upon him, and then he turned to see Buto, the rhinoceros, his little, pig eyes blazing, charging madly toward him and already so close that escape seemed impossible; yet so perfectly were mind and muscles coordinated in this unspoiled, primitive man that almost simultaneously with the sense perception of the threatened danger he wheeled and hurled his spear at Buto's chest. It was a heavy spear shod with iron, and behind it were the giant muscles of the ape-man, while coming to meet it was the enormous weight of Buto and the momentum of his rapid rush. All that happened in the instant that Tarzan turned to meet the charge of the irascible rhinoceros might take long to tell, and yet would have taxed the swiftest lens to record. As his spear left his hand the ape-man was looking down upon the mighty horn lowered to toss him, so close was Buto to him. The spear entered the rhinoceros' neck at its junction with the left shoulder and passed almost entirely through the beast's body, and at the instant that he launched it, Tarzan leaped straight into the air alighting upon Buto's back but escaping the mighty horn.

Then Buto espied the lions and bore madly down upon them while Tarzan of the Apes leaped nimbly into the tangled creepers at one side of the trail. The first lion met Buto's charge and was tossed high over the back of the maddened brute, torn and dying, and then the six remaining lions were upon the rhinoceros, rending and tearing the while they were being gored or trampled. From the safety of his perch Tarzan watched the royal battle with the keenest interest, for the more intelligent of the jungle folk are interested in such encounters. They are to them what the race-track and the prize ring, the theater and the movies are to us. They see them often; but always they enjoy them for no two are precisely alike.

For a time it seemed to Tarzan that Buto, the rhinoceros, would prove victor in the gory battle. Already had he accounted for four of the seven lions and badly wounded the three remaining when in a momentary lull in the encounter he sank limply to his knees and rolled over upon his side. Tarzan's spear had done its work. It was the man-made weapon which killed the great beast that might easily have survived the assault of seven mighty lions, for Tarzan's spear had pierced the great lungs, and Buto, with victory almost in sight, succumbed to internal hemorrhage.

Then Tarzan came down from his sanctuary and as the wounded lions, growling, dragged themselves away, the ape-man cut his spear from the body of Buto, hacked off a steak and vanished into the jungle. The episode was over. It had been all in the day's work — something which you and I might talk about for a lifetime Tarzan dismissed from his mind the moment that the scene passed from his sight.

Chapter XII

LA SEEKS VENGEANCE

SWINGING BACK THROUGH the jungle in a wide circle the ape-man came to the river at another point, drank and took to the trees again and while he hunted, all oblivious of his past and careless of his future, there came through the dark jungles and the open, parklike places and across the wide meadows, where grazed the countless herbivora of the mysterious continent, a weird and terrible caravan in search of him. There were fifty frightful men with hairy bodies and gnarled and crooked legs. They were armed with knives and great bludgeons and at their head marched an almost naked woman, beautiful beyond compare. It was La of Opar, High Priestess of the Flaming God, and fifty of her horrid priests searching for the purloiner of the sacred sacrificial knife.

Never before had La passed beyond the crumbling outer walls of Opar; but never before had need been so insistent. The sacred knife was gone! Handed down through countless ages it had come to her as a heritage

and an insignia of her religious office and regal authority from some long-dead progenitor of lost and forgotten Atlantis. The loss of the crown jewels or the Great
Seal of England could have brought no greater consternation to a British king than did the pilfering of the
sacred knife bring to La, the Oparian, Queen and High
Priestess of the degraded remnants of the oldest civilization upon earth. When Atlantis, with all her mighty
cities and her cultivated fields and her great commerce
and culture and riches sank into the sea long ages since,
she took with her all but a handful of her colonists
working the vast gold mines of Central Africa. From
these and their degraded slaves and a later intermixture
of the blood of the anthropoids sprung the gnarled
men of Opar; but by some queer freak of fate, aided
by natural selection, the old Atlantean strain had remained pure and undegraded in the females descended
from a single princess of the royal house of Atlantis
who had been in Opar at the time of the great catastrophe. Such was La.

Burning with white-hot anger was the High Priestess,
her heart a seething, molten mass of hatred for Tarzan
of the Apes. The zeal of the religious fanatic whose
altar has been desecrated was triply enhanced by the
rage of a woman scorned. Twice had she thrown her
heart at the feet of the godlike ape-man and twice had
she been repulsed. La knew that she was beautiful —
and she was beautiful, not by the standards of prehis-
toric Atlantis alone, but by those of modern times was
La physically a creature of perfection. Before Tarzan
came that first time to Opar, La had never seen a
human male other than the grotesque and knotted
men of her clan. With one of these she must mate
sooner or later that the direct line of high priestesses
might not be broken, unless Fate should bring other
men to Opar. Before Tarzan came upon his first visit,
La had had no thought that such men as he existed,

for she knew only her hideous little priests and the bulls of the tribe of great anthropoids that had dwelt from time immemorial in and about Opar, until they had come to be looked upon almost as equals by the Oparians. Among the legends of Opar were tales of godlike men of the olden time and of black men who had come more recently; but these latter had been enemies who killed and robbed. And, too, these legends always held forth the hope that some day that nameless continent from which their race had sprung, would rise once more out of the sea and with slaves at the long sweeps would send her carven, gold-picked galleys forth to succor the long-exiled colonists.

The coming of Tarzan had aroused within La's breast the wild hope that at last the fulfillment of this ancient prophecy was at hand; but more strongly still had it aroused the hot fires of love in a heart that never otherwise would have known the meaning of that all-consuming passion, for such a wondrous creature as La could never have felt love for any of the repulsive priests of Opar. Custom, duty and religious zeal might have commanded the union; but there could have been no love on La's part. She had grown to young woman-hood a cold and heartless creature, daughter of a thousand other cold, heartless, beautiful women who had never known love. And so when love came to her it liberated all the pent passions of a thousand genera-tions, transforming La into a pulsing, throbbing vol-cano of desire, and with desire thwarted this great force of love and gentleness and sacrifice was transmuted by its own fires into one of hatred and revenge.

It was in a state of mind superinduced by these conditions that La led forth her jabbering company to retrieve the sacred emblem of her high office and wreak vengeance upon the author of her wrongs. To Werper she gave little thought. The fact that the knife had been in his hand when it departed from Opar brought down no thoughts of vengeance upon his head. Of course, he should be slain when captured; but his death would give La no pleasure — she looked for that in the contemplated death agonies of Tarzan. He should be tortured. His should be a slow and frightful death. His punishment should be adequate to the immensity of his crime. He had wrested the sacred knife from La; he had lain sacrilegious hands upon the High Priestess of the Flaming God; he had desecrated the altar and the temple. For these things he should die; but he had scorned the love of La, the woman, and for this he should die horribly with great anguish.

The march of La and her priests was not without its adventures. Unused were these to the ways of the jungle, since seldom did any venture forth from behind Opar's crumbling walls, yet their very numbers protected them and so they came without fatalities far along the trail of Tarzan and Werper. Three great apes accompanied them and to these was delegated the business of tracking the quarry, a feat beyond the senses of the Oparians. La commanded. She arranged the order of march, she selected the camps, she set the hour for halting and the hour for resuming and though she was inexperienced in such matters, her native intelligence was so far above that of the men or the apes that she did better than they could have done. She was a hard taskmaster, too, for she looked down with loathing and contempt upon the misshapen creatures amongst which cruel Fate had thrown her and to some extent vented upon them her dissatisfaction and her thwarted love. She made them build her a strong protection and shelter each night and keep a great fire burning before it from dusk to dawn. When she tired of walking they were forced to carry her upon an improvised litter, nor did one dare to question her authority or her right to such services. In fact they did not question either. To them she was a goddess and each loved her and each hoped that he would be chosen as her mate, so they slaved for her and bore the stinging lash of her displeasure and the habitually haughty disdain of her manner without a murmur.

For many days they marched, the apes following the trail easily and going a little distance ahead of the body of the caravan that they might warn the others of impending danger. It was during a noonday halt while all were lying resting after a tiresome march that one of the apes rose suddenly and sniffed the breeze. In a low guttural he cautioned the others to silence and a moment later was swinging quietly up wind into the jungle. La and the priests gathered silently together, the hideous little men fingering their knives and bludgeons, and awaited the return of the shaggy anthropoid.

Nor had they long to wait before they saw him emerge from a leafy thicket and approach them. Straight to La he came and in the language of the great apes which was also the language of decadent Opar he addressed her.

"The great Tarmangani lies asleep there," he said, pointing in the direction from which he had just come. "Come and we can kill him."

"Do not kill him," commanded La in cold tones. "Bring the great Tarmangani to me alive and unhurt. The vengeance is La's. Go; but make no sound!" and she waved her hands to include all her followers.

Cautiously the weird party crept through the jungle in the wake of the great ape until at last he halted them with a raised hand and pointed upward and a little ahead. There they saw the giant form of the ape-man stretched along a low bough and even in sleep one hand grasped a stout limb and one strong, brown leg reached out and overlapped another. At ease lay Tarzan of the Apes, sleeping heavily upon a full stomach and dreaming of Numa, the lion, and Horta, the boar, and other creatures of the jungle. No intimation of danger assailed the dormant faculties of the ape-man — he saw no crouching hairy figures upon the ground beneath him nor the three apes that swung quietly into the tree beside him.

The first intimation of danger that came to Tarzan was the impact of three bodies as the three apes leaped upon him and hurled him to the ground, where he alighted half stunned beneath their combined weight and was immediately set upon by the fifty hairy men or as many of them as could swarm upon his person. Instantly the ape-man became the center of a whirling, striking, biting maelstrom of horror. He fought nobly but the odds against him were too great. Slowly they overcame him though there was scarce one of them that did not feel the weight of his mighty fist or the rending of his fangs.

Chapter XIII

CONDEMNED TO TORTURE
AND DEATH

*L*A HAD FOLLOWED her company and when she saw them clawing and biting at Tarzan, she raised her voice and cautioned them not to kill him. She saw that he was weakening and that soon the greater numbers would prevail over him, nor had she long to wait before the mighty jungle creature lay helpless and bound at her feet.

"Bring him to the place at which we stopped," she commanded and they carried Tarzan back to the little clearing and threw him down beneath a tree.

"Build me a shelter!" ordered La. "We shall stop here tonight and tomorrow in the face of the Flaming God, La will offer up the heart of this defiler of the temple. Where is the sacred knife? Who took it from him?"

But no one had seen it and each was positive in his assurance that the sacrificial weapon had not been upon Tarzan's person when they captured him. The ape-man looked upon the menacing creatures which surrounded him and snarled his defiance. He looked upon La and smiled. In the face of death he was unafraid.

"Where is the knife?" La asked him.

"I do not know," replied Tarzan. "The man took it with him when he slipped away during the night. Since you are so desirous for its return I would look for him and get it back for you, did you not hold me prisoner; but now that I am to die I cannot get it back. Of what good was your knife, anyway? You can make another. Did you follow us all this way for nothing more than a knife? Let me go and find him and I will bring it back to you."

La laughed a bitter laugh, for in her heart she knew that Tarzan's sin was greater than the purloining of the sacrificial knife of Opar; yet as she looked at him lying bound and helpless before her, tears rose to her eyes so that she had to turn away to hide them; but she remained inflexible in her determination to make him pay in frightful suffering and in eventual death for daring to spurn the love of La.

When the shelter was completed La had Tarzan transferred to it. "All night I shall torture him," she muttered to her priests, "and at the first streak of dawn you may prepare the flaming altar upon which his heart shall be offered up to the Flaming God. Gather wood well filled with pitch, lay it in the form and size of the altar at Opar in the center of the clearing that the Flaming God may look down upon our handiwork and be pleased."

During the balance of the day the priests of Opar were busy erecting an altar in the center of the clearing, and while they worked they chanted weird hymns in the ancient tongue of that lost continent that lies at the bottom of the Atlantic. They knew not the meanings of the words they mouthed; they but repeated the ritual that had been handed down from preceptor to neophyte since that long-gone day when the ancestors of the Piltdown man still swung by their tails in the humid jungles that are England now.

And in the shelter of the hut, La paced to and fro beside the stoic ape-man. Resigned to his fate was Tarzan. No hope of succor gleamed through the dead black of the death sentence hanging over him. He knew that his giant muscles could not part the many strands that bound his wrists and ankles, for he had strained often, but ineffectually for release. He had no hope of outside help and only enemies surrounded him within the camp, and yet he smiled at La as she paced nervously back and forth the length of the shelter.

And La? She fingered her knife and looked down upon her captive. She glared and muttered but she did not strike. "Tonight!" she thought. "Tonight, when it is dark I will torture him." She looked upon his perfect, godlike figure and upon his handsome, smiling face and then she steeled her heart again by thoughts of her love spurned; by religious thoughts that damned the infidel who had desecrated the holy of holies; who had taken from the blood-stained altar of Opar the offering to the Flaming God — and not once but thrice. Three times had Tarzan cheated the god of her fathers. At the thought La paused and knelt at his side. In her hand was a sharp knife. She placed its point against the ape-man's side and pressed upon the hilt; but Tarzan only smiled and shrugged his shoulders.

How beautiful he was! La bent low over him, looking into his eyes. How perfect was his figure. She compared it with those of the knurled and knotted men from whom she must choose a mate, and La shuddered at the thought. Dusk came and after dusk came night. A great fire blazed within the little thorn boma about the camp. The flames played upon the new altar erected in the center of the clearing, arousing in the mind of the High Priestess of the Flaming God a picture of the event of the coming dawn. She saw this giant and perfect form writhing amid the flames of the burning pyre. She saw those smiling lips, burned and blackened, falling away from the strong, white teeth. She saw the shock of black hair tousled upon Tarzan's well-shaped head disappear in a spurt of flame. She saw these and many other frightful pictures as she stood with closed eyes and clenched fists above the object of her hate — ah! was it hate that La of Opar felt?

The darkness of the jungle night had settled down upon the camp, relieved only by the fitful flarings of the fire that was kept up to warn off the man-eaters. Tarzan lay quietly in his bonds. He suffered from thirst and from the cutting of the tight strands about his wrists and ankles; but he made no complaint. A jungle beast was Tarzan with the stoicism of the beast and the intelligence of man. He knew that his doom was sealed — that no supplications would avail to temper the severity of his end and so he wasted no breath in pleadings; but waited patiently in the firm conviction that his sufferings could not endure forever.

In the darkness La stooped above him. In her hand was a sharp knife and in her mind the determination to initiate his torture without further delay. The knife was pressed against his side and La's face was close to his when a sudden burst of flame from new branches thrown upon the fire without, lighted up the interior of the shelter. Close beneath her lips La saw the perfect features of the forest god and into her woman's heart welled all the great love she had felt for Tarzan since first she had seen him, and all the accumulated passion of the years that she had dreamed of him.

Dagger in hand, La, the High Priestess, towered above the helpless creature that had dared to violate the sanctuary of her deity. There should be no torture — there should be instant death. No longer should the defiler of the temple pollute the sight of the lord god almighty. A single stroke of the heavy blade and then the corpse to the flaming pyre without. The knife arm stiffened ready for the downward plunge, and then La, the woman, collapsed weakly upon the body of the man she loved.

She ran her hands in mute caress over his naked flesh; she covered his forehead, his eyes, his lips with hot kisses; she covered him with her body as though to protect him from the hideous fate she had ordained for him, and in trembling, piteous tones she begged him for his love. For hours the frenzy of her passion possessed the burning hand-maiden of the Flaming God, until at last sleep overpowered her and she lapsed into unconsciousness beside the man she had sworn to torture and to slay. And Tarzan, untroubled by thoughts of the future, slept peacefully in La's embrace.

At the first hint of dawn the chanting of the priests of Opar brought Tarzan to wakefulness. Initiated in low and subdued tones, the sound soon rose in volume to the open diapason of barbaric blood lust. La stirred. Her perfect arm pressed Tarzan closer to her — a smile parted her lips and then she awoke, and slowly the smile faded and her eyes went wide in horror as the significance of the death chant impinged upon her understanding.

"Love me, Tarzan!" she cried. "Love me, and you shall be saved."

Tarzan's bonds hurt him. He was suffering the tortures of long-restricted circulation. With an angry growl he rolled over with his back toward La. That was her answer! The High Priestess leaped to her feet. A hot flush of shame mantled her cheek and then she went dead white and stepped to the shelter's entrance.

"Come, Priests of the Flaming God!" she cried, "and make ready the sacrifice."

The warped things advanced and entered the shelter. They laid hands upon Tarzan and bore him forth, and as they chanted they kept time with their crooked bodies, swaying to and fro to the rhythm of their song of blood and death. Behind them came La, swaying too; but not in unison with the chanted cadence. White and drawn was the face of the High Priestess — white and drawn with unrequited love and hideous terror of the moments to come. Yet stern in her resolve was La. The infidel should die! The scorner of her love should pay the price upon the fiery altar. She saw them lay the perfect body there upon the rough branches. She saw the High Priest, he to whom custom would unite her — bent, crooked, gnarled, stunted, hideous — advance with the flaming torch and stand awaiting her command to apply it to the faggots surrounding the sacrificial pyre. His hairy, bestial face was distorted in a yellow-fanged grin of anticipatory enjoyment. His hands were cupped to receive the life blood of the victim — the red nectar that at Opar would have filled the golden sacrificial goblets.

La approached with upraised knife, her face turned toward the rising sun and upon her lips a prayer to the burning deity of her people. The High Priest looked questioningly toward her — the brand was burning close to his hand and the faggots lay temptingly near. Tarzan closed his eyes and awaited the end. He knew that he would suffer, for he recalled the faint memories of past burns. He knew that he would suffer and die; but he did not flinch. Death is no great adventure to the jungle bred who walk hand-in-hand with the grim specter by day and lie down at his side by night through all the years of their lives. It is doubtful that the ape-man even speculated upon what came after death. As a matter of fact as his end approached, his mind was occupied by thoughts of the pretty pebbles he had lost, yet his every faculty still was open to what passed around him.

He felt La lean over him and he opened his eyes. He

saw her white, drawn face and he saw tears blinding her eyes. "Tarzan, my Tarzan!" she moaned, "tell me that you love me — that you will return to Opar with me — and you shall live. Even in the face of the anger of my people I will save you. This last chance I give you. What is your answer?"

At the last moment the woman in La had triumphed over the High Priestess of a cruel cult. She saw upon the altar the only creature that ever had aroused the fires of love within her virgin breast; she saw the beast-faced fanatic who would one day be her mate, unless she found another less repulsive, standing with the burning torch ready to ignite the pyre; yet with all her mad passion for the ape-man she would give the word to apply the flame if Tarzan's final answer was unsatisfactory. With heaving bosom she leaned close above him. "Yes or no?" she whispered.

Through the jungle, out of the distance, came faintly a sound that brought a sudden light of hope to Tarzan's eyes. He raised his voice in a weird scream that sent La back from him a step or two. The impatient priest grumbled and switched the torch from one hand to the other at the same time holding it closer to the tinder at the base of the pyre.

"Your answer!" insisted La. "What is your answer to the love of La of Opar?"

Closer came the sound that had attracted Tarzan's attention and now the others heard it — the shrill trumpeting of an elephant. As La looked wide-eyed into Tarzan's face, there to read her fate for happiness or heartbreak, she saw an expression of concern shadow his features. Now, for the first time, she guessed the meaning of Tarzan's shrill scream — he had summoned Tantor, the elephant, to his rescue! La's brows contracted in a savage scowl. "You refuse La!" she cried. "Then die! The torch!" she commanded, turning toward the priest.

Tarzan looked up into her face. "Tantor is coming," he said. "I thought that he would rescue me; but I know now from his voice that he will slay me and you and all that fall in his path, searching out with the cunning of Sheeta, the panther, those who would hide from him, for Tantor is mad with the madness of love."

La knew only too well the insane ferocity of a bull elephant in *must*. She knew that Tarzan had not exaggerated. She knew that the devil in the cunning, cruel brain of the great beast might send it hither and thither hunting through the forest for those who escaped its first charge, or the beast might pass on without returning — no one might guess which.

"I cannot love you, La," said Tarzan in a low voice. "I do not know why, for you are very beautiful. I could not go back and live in Opar — I who have the whole broad jungle for my range. No, I cannot love you but I cannot see you die beneath the goring tusks of mad Tantor. Cut my bonds before it is too late. Already he is almost upon us. Cut them and I may yet save you."

A little spiral of curling smoke rose from one corner of the pyre — the flames licked upward, crackling. La stood there like a beautiful statue of despair gazing at Tarzan and at the spreading flames. In a moment they would reach out and grasp him. From the tangled forest came the sound of cracking limbs and crashing trunks — Tantor was coming down upon them, a huge Juggernaut of the jungle. The priests were becoming uneasy. They cast apprehensive glances in the direction of the approaching elephant and then back at La.

"Fly!" she commanded them and then she stooped and cut the bonds securing her prisoner's feet and hands. In an instant Tarzan was upon the ground. The priests screamed out their rage and disappointment. He with the torch took a menacing step toward La and the ape-man. "Traitor!" He shrieked at the woman. "For this you too shall die!" Raising his bludgeon he rushed upon the High Priestess; but Tarzan was there before her. Leaping in to close quarters the ape-man seized the upraised weapon and wrenched it from the hands of the frenzied fanatic and then the priest closed upon him with tooth and nail. Seizing the stocky, stunted body in his mighty hands Tarzan raised the creature high above his head, hurling him at his fellows who were now gathered ready to bear down upon their erstwhile captive. La stood proudly with ready knife behind the ape-man. No faint sign of fear marked her perfect brow — only haughty disdain for her priests and admiration for the man she loved so hopelessly filled her thoughts.

Suddenly upon this scene burst the mad bull — a huge tusker, his little eyes inflamed with insane rage. The priests stood for an instant paralyzed with terror; but Tarzan turned and gathering La in his arms raced for the nearest tree. Tantor bore down upon him trumpeting shrilly. La clung with both white arms about the ape-man's neck. She felt him leap into the air and marveled at his strength and his ability as, burdened with her weight, he swung nimbly into the lower branches of a large tree and quickly bore her upward beyond reach of the sinuous trunk of the pachyderm.

Momentarily baffled here, the huge elephant wheeled and bore down upon the hapless priests who had now scattered, terror-stricken, in every direction. The nearest he gored and threw high among the branches of a tree. One he seized in the coils of his trunk and broke upon a huge bole, dropping the mangled pulp to charge, trumpeting, after another. Two he trampled beneath his huge feet and by then the others had disappeared into the jungle. Now Tantor turned his attention once more to Tarzan for one of the symptoms of madness is a revulsion of affection — objects of sane love become the objects of insane hatred. Peculiar in the unwritten annals of the jungle was the proverbial love that had existed between the ape-man and the tribe of Tantor. No elephant in all the jungle would harm the Tarmangani — the white-ape; but with the madness of *must* upon him the great bull sought to destroy his long-time play-fellow.

Back to the tree where La and Tarzan perched came Tantor, the elephant. He reared up with his forefeet against the bole and reached high toward them with his long trunk; but Tarzan had foreseen this and clambered beyond the bull's longest reach. Failure but tended to further enrage the mad creature. He bellowed and trumpeted and screamed until the earth shook to the mighty volume of his noise. He put his head against the tree and pushed and the tree bent before his mighty strength; yet still it held.

The actions of Tarzan were peculiar in the extreme. Had Numa, or Sabor, or Sheeta, or any other beast of the jungle been seeking to destroy him, the ape-man would have danced about hurling missiles and invectives at his assailant. He would have insulted and taunted them, reviling in the jungle Billingsgate he knew so well; but now he sat silent out of Tantor's reach and upon his handsome face was an expression of deep sorrow and pity, for of all the jungle folk Tarzan loved Tantor the best. Could he have slain him he would not have thought of doing so. His one idea was to escape, for he knew that with the passing of the *must* Tantor would be sane again and that once more he might stretch at full length upon that mighty back and make foolish speech into those great, flapping ears.

Finding that the tree would not fall to his pushing, Tantor was but enraged the more. He looked up at the two perched high above him, his red-rimmed eyes blazing with insane hatred, and then he wound his trunk about the bole of the tree, spread his giant feet wide apart and tugged to uproot the jungle giant. A huge creature was Tantor, an enormous bull in the full prime of all his stupendous strength. Mightily he strove until presently, to Tarzan's consternation, the great tree gave slowly at the roots. The ground rose in little mounds and ridges about the base of the bole, the tree tilted — in another moment it would be uprooted and fall.

The ape-man whirled La to his back and just as the tree inclined slowly in its first movement out of the perpendicular, before the sudden rush of its final collapse, he swung to the branches of a lesser neighbor. It was a long and perilous leap. La closed her eyes and shuddered; but when she opened them again she found herself safe and Tarzan whirling onward through the forest. Behind them the uprooted tree crashed heavily to the ground, carrying with it the lesser trees in its path and then Tantor, realizing that his prey had escaped him, set up once more his hideous trumpeting and followed at a rapid charge upon their trail.

Chapter XIV

A PRIESTESS
BUT YET A WOMAN

AT FIRST LA closed her eyes and clung to Tarzan in terror, though she made no outcry; but presently she gained sufficient courage to look about her, to look down at the ground beneath and even to keep her eyes open during the wide, perilous swings from tree to tree, and then there came over her a sense of safety because of her confidence in the perfect physical creature in whose strength and nerve and agility her fate lay. Once she raised her eyes to the burning sun and murmured a prayer of thanks to her pagan god that she had not been permitted to destroy this godlike man, and her long lashes were wet with tears. A strange anomaly was La of Opar — a creature of circumstance torn by conflicting emotions. Now the cruel and bloodthirsty creature of a heartless god and again a melting woman filled with compassion and tenderness. Sometimes the incarnation of jealousy and revenge and sometimes a sobbing maiden, generous and forgiving; at once a virgin and a wanton; but always — a woman. Such was La.

She pressed her cheek close to Tarzan's shoulder. Slowly she turned her head until her hot lips were pressed against his flesh. She loved him and would gladly have died for him; yet within an hour she had been ready to plunge a knife into his heart and might again within the coming hour.

A hapless priest seeking shelter in the jungle chanced to show himself to enraged Tantor. The great beast turned to one side, bore down upon the crooked, little man, snuffed him out and then, diverted from his course, blundered away toward the south. In a few minutes even the noise of his trumpeting was lost in the distance.

Tarzan dropped to the ground and La slipped to her feet from his back. "Call your people together," said Tarzan.

"They will kill me," replied La.

"They will not kill you," contradicted the ape-man. "No one will kill you while Tarzan of the Apes is here. Call them and we will talk with them."

La raised her voice in a weird, flutelike call that carried far into the jungle on every side. From near and far came answering shouts in the barking tones of the Oparian priests: "We come! We come!" Again and again, La repeated her summons until singly and in pairs the greater portion of her following approached and halted a short distance away from the High Priestess and her savior. They came with scowling brows and threatening mien. When all had come Tarzan addressed them.

"Your La is safe," said the ape-man. "Had she slain me she would now herself be dead and many more of you; but she spared me that I might save her. Go your way with her back to Opar, and Tarzan will go his way into the jungle. Let there be peace always between

Tarzan and La. What is your answer?"

The priests grumbled and shook their heads. They spoke together and La and Tarzan could see that they were not favorably inclined toward the proposition. They did not wish to take La back and they did wish to complete the sacrifice of Tarzan to the Flaming God. At last the ape-man became impatient.

"You will obey the commands of your queen," he said, "and go back to Opar with her or Tarzan of the Apes will call together the other creatures of the jungle and slay you all. La saved me that I might save you and her. I have served you better alive than I could have dead. If you are not all fools you will let me go my way in peace and you will return to Opar with La. I know not where the sacred knife is; but you can fashion another. Had I not taken it from La you would have slain me and now your god must be glad that I took it since I have saved his priestess from love-mad Tantor. Will you go back to Opar with La, promising that no harm shall befall her?"

The priests gathered together in a little knot arguing and discussing. They pounded upon their breasts with their fists; they raised their hands and eyes to their fiery god; they growled and barked among themselves until it became evident to Tarzan that one of their number was preventing the acceptance of his proposal. This was the High Priest whose heart was filled with jealous rage because La openly acknowledged her love for the stranger, when by the worldly customs of their cult she should have belonged to him. Seemingly there was to be no solution of the problem until another priest stepped forth and, raising his hand, addressed La.

"Cadj, the High Priest," he announced, "would sacrifice you both to the Flaming God; but all of us except Cadj would gladly return to Opar with our queen."

"You are many against one," spoke up Tarzan. "Why should you not have your will? Go your way with La to Opar and if Cadj interferes slay him."

The priests of Opar welcomed this suggestion with loud cries of approval. To them it appeared nothing short of divine inspiration. The influence of ages of unquestioning obedience to high priests had made it seem impossible to them to question his authority; but when they realized that they could force him to their will they were as happy as children with new toys.

They rushed forward and seized Cadj. They talked in loud menacing tones into his ear. They threatened him with bludgeon and knife until at last he acquiesced in their demands, though sullenly, and then Tarzan stepped close before Cadj.

"Priest," he said, "La goes back to her temple under the protection of her priests and the threat of Tarzan of the Apes that whoever harms her shall die. Tarzan will go again to Opar before the next rains and if harm has befallen La, woe betide Cadj, the High Priest."

Sullenly Cadj promised not to harm his queen.

"Protect her," cried Tarzan to the other Oparians. "Protect her so that when Tarzan comes again he will find La there to greet him."

"La will be there to greet thee," exclaimed the High Priestess, "and La will wait, longing, always longing, until you come again. Oh, tell me that you will come!"

"Who knows?" asked the ape-man as he swung quickly into the trees and raced off toward the east.

For a moment La stood looking after him, then her head drooped, a sigh escaped her lips and like an old woman she took up the march toward distant Opar.

Through the trees raced Tarzan of the Apes until the darkness of night had settled upon the jungle, then he lay down and slept, with no thought beyond the morrow and with even La but the shadow of a memory within his consciousness.

But a few marches to the north Lady Greystoke looked forward to the day when her mighty lord and master should discover the crime of Achmet Zek, and be speeding to rescue and avenge, and even as she pictured the coming of John Clayton, the object of her thoughts squatted almost naked, beside a fallen log, beneath which he was searching with grimy fingers for a chance beetle or a luscious grub.

Two days elapsed following the theft of the jewels before Tarzan gave them a thought. Then, as they chanced to enter his mind, he conceived a desire to play with them again, and, having nothing better to do than satisfy the first whim which possessed him, he rose and started across the plain from the forest in which he had spent the preceding day.

Though no mark showed where the gems had been buried, and though the spot resembled the balance of an unbroken stretch several miles in length, where the reeds terminated at the edge of the meadowland, yet the ape-man moved with unerring precision directly to the place where he had hid his treasure.

With his hunting knife he upturned the loose earth, beneath which the pouch should be; but, though he excavated to a greater distance than the depth of the original hole there was no sign of pouch or jewels. Tarzan's brow clouded as he discovered that he had been despoiled. Little or no reasoning was required to convince him of the identity of the guilty party, and with the same celerity that had marked his decision to unearth the jewels, he set out upon the trail of the thief.

Though the spoor was two days old, and practically obliterated in many places, Tarzan followed it with comparative ease. A white man could not have followed it twenty paces twelve hours after it had been made, a black man would have lost it within the first mile; but Tarzan of the Apes had been forced in childhood to develop senses that an ordinary mortal scarce ever uses.

We may note the garlic and whisky on the breath of

a fellow strap hanger, or the cheap perfume emanating from the person of the wondrous lady sitting in front of us, and deplore the fact of our sensitive noses; but, as a matter of fact, we cannot smell at all, our olfactory organs are practically atrophied, by comparison with the development of the sense among the beasts of the wild.

Where a foot is placed an effluvium remains for a considerable time. It is beyond the range of our sensibilities; but to a creature of the lower orders, especially to the hunters and the hunted, as interesting and ofttimes more lucid than is the printed page to us.

Nor was Tarzan dependent alone upon his sense of smell. Vision and hearing had been brought to a marvelous state of development by the necessities of his early life, where survival itself depended almost daily upon the exercise of the keenest vigilance and the constant use of all his faculties.

And so he followed the old trail of the Belgian through the forest and toward the north; but because of the age of the trail he was constrained to a far from rapid progress. The man he followed was two days ahead of him when Tarzan took up the pursuit, and each day he gained upon the ape-man. The latter, however, felt not the slightest doubt as to the outcome. Some day he would overhaul his quarry — he could bide his time in peace until that day dawned. Doggedly he followed the faint spoor, pausing by day only to kill and eat, and at night only to sleep and refresh himself.

Occasionally he passed parties of savage warriors; but these he gave a wide berth, for he was hunting with a purpose that was not to be distracted by the minor accidents of the trail.

These parties were of the collecting hordes of the Waziri and their allies which Basuli had scattered his messengers broadcast to summon. They were marching to a common rendezvous in preparation for an assault upon the stronghold of Achmet Zek; but to Tarzan they were enemies — he retained no conscious memory of any friendship for the black men.

It was night when he halted outside the palisaded village of the Arab raider. Perched in the branches of a great tree he gazed down upon the life within the enclosure. To this place had the spoor led him. His quarry must be within; but how was he to find him among so many huts? Tarzan, although cognizant of his mighty powers, realized also his limitations. He knew that he could not successfully cope with great numbers in open battle. He must resort to the stealth and trickery of the wild beast, if he were to succeed.

Sitting in the safety of his tree, munching upon the leg bone of Horta, the boar, Tarzan waited a favorable opportunity to enter the village. For awhile he gnawed at the bulging, round ends of the large bone, splintering off small pieces between his strong jaws, and sucking at the delicious marrow within; but all the time he cast repeated glances into the village. He saw white-robed figures, and half-naked blacks; but not once did he see one who resembled the stealer of the gems.

Patiently he waited until the streets were deserted by all save the sentries at the gates, then he dropped lightly to the ground, circled to the opposite side of the village and approached the palisade.

At his side hung a long, rawhide rope — a natural and more dependable evolution from the grass rope of his childhood. Loosening this, he spread the noose upon the ground behind him, and with a quick movement of his wrist tossed the coils over one of the sharpened projections of the summit of the palisade.

Drawing the noose taut, he tested the solidity of its hold. Satisfied, the ape-man ran nimbly up the vertical wall, aided by the rope which he clutched in both hands. Once at the top it required but a moment to gather the dangling rope once more into its coils, make it fast again at his waist, take a quick glance downward within the palisade, and, assured that no one lurked directly beneath him, drop softly to the ground.

Now he was within the village. Before him stretched a series of tents and native huts. The business of exploring each of them would be fraught with danger; but danger was only a natural factor of each day's life — it never appalled Tarzan. The chances appealed to him — the chances of life and death, with his prowess and his faculties pitted against those of a worthy antagonist.

It was not necessary that he enter each habitation — through a door, a window or an open chink, his nose told him whether or not his prey lay within. For some time he found one disappointment following upon the heels of another in quick succession. No spoor of the Belgian was discernible. But at last he came to a tent where the smell of the thief was strong. Tarzan listened, his ear close to the canvas at the rear, but no sound came from within.

At last he cut one of the pin ropes, raised the bottom of the canvas, and intruded his head within the interior. All was quiet and dark. Tarzan crawled cautiously within — the scent of the Belgian was strong; but it was not live scent. Even before he had examined the interior minutely, Tarzan knew that no one was within it.

In one corner he found a pile of blankets and clothing scattered about; but no pouch of pretty pebbles. A careful examination of the balance of the tent revealed nothing more, at least nothing to indicate the presence of the jewels; but at the side where the blankets and clothing lay, the ape-man discovered that the tent wall had been loosened at the bottom, and presently he sensed that the Belgian had recently passed out of the tent by this avenue.

Tarzan was not long in following the way that his prey had fled. The spoor led always in the shadow and at the rear of the huts and tents of the village — it was quite evident to Tarzan that the Belgian had gone alone and secretly upon his mission. Evidently he feared the inhabitants of the village, or at least his work had been of such a nature that he dared not risk detection.

At the back of a native hut the spoor led through a small hole recently cut in the brush wall and into the dark interior beyond. Fearlessly, Tarzan followed the trail. On hands and knees, he crawled through the small aperture. Within the hut his nostrils were assailed by many odors; but clear and distinct among them was one that half aroused a latent memory of the past — it was the faint and delicate odor of a woman. With the cognizance of it there rose in the breast of the ape-man a strange uneasiness — the result of an irresistible force which he was destined to become acquainted with anew — the instinct which draws the male to his mate.

In the same hut was the scent spoor of the Belgian, too, and as both these assailed the nostrils of the ape-man, mingling one with the other, a jealous rage leaped and burned within him, though his memory held before the mirror of recollection no image of the she to which he had attached his desire.

Like the tent he had investigated, the hut, too, was empty, and after satisfying himself that his stolen pouch was secreted nowhere within, he left, as he had entered, by the hole in the rear wall.

Here he took up the spoor of the Belgian, followed it across the clearing, over the palisade, and out into the dark jungle beyond.

Chapter XV

THE FLIGHT OF WERPER

AFTER WERPER HAD arranged the dummy in his bed, and sneaked out into the darkness of the village beneath the rear wall of his tent, he had gone directly to the hut in which Jane Clayton was held captive.

Before the doorway squatted a black sentry. Werper approached him boldly, spoke a few words in his ear, handed him a package of tobacco, and passed into the hut. The black grinned and winked as the European disappeared within the darkness of the interior.

The Belgian, being one of Achmet Zek's principal lieutenants, might naturally go where he wished within or without the village, and so the sentry had not questioned his right to enter the hut with the white, woman prisoner.

Within, Werper called in French and in a low whisper: "Lady Greystoke! It is I, M. Frecoult. Where are you?" But there was no response. Hastily the man felt around the interior, groping blindly through the darkness with outstretched hands. There was no one within!

Werper's astonishment surpassed words. He was on the point of stepping without to question the sentry, when his eyes, becoming accustomed to the dark, discovered a blotch of lesser blackness near the base of the rear wall of the hut. Examination revealed the fact that the blotch was an opening cut in the wall. It was large enough to permit the passage of his body, and assured as he was that Lady Greystoke had passed out through the aperture in an attempt to escape the village, he lost no time in availing himself of the same avenue; but neither did he lose time in a fruitless search for Jane Clayton.

His own life depended upon the chance of his eluding, or outdistancing Achmet Zek, when that worthy should have discovered that he had escaped. His original plan had contemplated connivance in the escape of Lady Greystoke for two very good and sufficient reasons. The first was that by saving her he would win the gratitude of the English, and thus lessen the chance of his extradition should his identity and his crime against his superior officer be charged against him.

The second reason was based upon the fact that only one direction of escape was safely open to him. He could not travel to the west because of the Belgian possessions which lay between him and the Atlantic. The south was closed to him by the feared presence of the savage ape-man he had robbed. To the north lay the friends and allies of Achmet Zek. Only toward the east, through British East Africa, lay reasonable assurance of freedom.

Accompanied by a titled Englishwoman whom he had rescued from a frightful fate, and his identity vouched for by her as that of a Frenchman by the name of Frecoult, he had looked forward, and not without reason, to the active assistance of the British from the moment that he came in contact with their first outpost.

But now that Lady Greystoke had disappeared, though he still looked toward the east for hope, his chances were lessened, and another, subsidiary design completely dashed. From the moment that he had first laid eyes upon Jane Clayton he had nursed within his breast a secret passion for the beautiful American wife of the English lord, and when Achmet Zek's discovery of the jewels had necessitated flight, the Belgian had dreamed, in his planning, of a future in which he might convince Lady Greystoke that her husband was dead, and by playing upon her gratitude win her for himself.

At that part of the village farthest from the gates, Werper discovered that two or three long poles, taken from a nearby pile which had been collected for the construction of huts, had been leaned against the top of the palisade, forming a precarious, though not impossible avenue of escape.

Rightly, he inferred that thus had Lady Greystoke found the means to scale the wall, nor did he lose even a moment in following her lead. Once in the jungle he struck out directly eastward.

A few miles south of him, Jane Clayton lay panting among the branches of a tree in which she had taken refuge from a prowling and hungry lioness.

Her escape from the village had been much easier than she had anticipated. The knife which she had used to cut her way through the brush wall of the hut to freedom she had found sticking in the wall of her prison, doubtless left there by accident when a former tenant had vacated the premises.

To cross the rear of the village, keeping always in the densest shadows, had required but a few moments, and the fortunate circumstance of the discovery of the hut poles lying so near the palisade had solved for her the problem of the passage of the high wall.

For an hour she had followed the old game trail toward the south, until there fell upon her trained hearing the stealthy padding of a stalking beast behind her. The nearest tree gave her instant sanctuary, for she was too wise in the ways of the jungle to chance her safety for a moment after discovering that she was being hunted.

Werper, with better success, traveled slowly onward until dawn, when, to his chagrin, he discovered a mounted Arab upon his trail. It was one of Achmet Zek's minions, many of whom were scattered in all directions through the forest, searching for the fugitive Belgian.

Jane Clayton's escape had not yet been discovered when Achmet Zek and his searchers set forth to overhaul Werper. The only man who had seen the Belgian after his departure from his tent was the black sentry before the doorway of Lady Greystoke's prison hut, and he had been silenced by the discovery of the dead body of the man who had relieved him, the sentry that Mugambi had dispatched.

The bribe taker naturally inferred that Werper had slain his fellow and dared not admit that he had permitted him to enter the hut, fearing as he did, the anger of Achmet Zek. So, as chance directed that he should be the one to discover the body of the sentry when the first alarm had been given following Achmet Zek's discovery that Werper had outwitted him, the crafty black had dragged the dead body to the interior of a nearby tent, and himself resumed his station before the doorway of the hut in which he still believed the woman to be.

With the discovery of the Arab close behind him, the Belgian hid in the foliage of a leafy bush. Here the trail ran straight for a considerable distance, and down the shady forest aisle, beneath the overarching branches of the trees, rode the white-robed figure of the pursuer.

Nearer and nearer he came. Werper crouched closer

to the ground behind the leaves of his hiding place. Across the trail a vine moved. Werper's eyes instantly centered upon the spot. There was no wind to stir the foliage in the depths of the jungle. Again the vine moved. In the mind of the Belgian only the presence of a sinister and malevolent force could account for the phenomenon.

The man's eyes bored steadily into the screen of leaves upon the opposite side of the trail. Gradually a form took shape beyond them — a tawny form, grim and terrible, with yellow-green eyes glaring fearsomely across the narrow trail straight into his.

Werper could have screamed in fright, but up the trail was coming the messenger of another death, equally sure and no less terrible. He remained silent, almost paralyzed by fear. The Arab approached. Across the trail from Werper the lion crouched for the spring, when suddenly his attention was attracted toward the horseman.

The Belgian saw the massive head turn in the direction of the raider and his heart all but ceased its beating as he awaited the result of this interruption. At a walk the horseman approached. Would the nervous animal he rode take fright at the odor of the carnivore, and, bolting, leave Werper still to the mercies of the king of beasts?

But he seemed unmindful of the near presence of the great cat. On he came, his neck arched, champing at the bit between his teeth. The Belgian turned his eyes again toward the lion. The beast's whole attention now seemed riveted upon the horseman. They were abreast the lion now, and still the brute did not spring. Could he be but waiting for them to pass before returning his attention to the original prey? Werper shuddered and half rose. At the same instant the lion sprang from his place of concealment, full upon the mounted man. The horse, with a shrill neigh of terror, shrank sideways almost upon the Belgian, the lion dragged the helpless Arab from his saddle, and the horse leaped back into the trail and fled away toward the west.

But he did not flee alone. As the frightened beast had pressed in upon him, Werper had not been slow to note the quickly emptied saddle and the opportunity it presented. Scarcely had the lion dragged the Arab down from one side, than the Belgian, seizing the pommel of the saddle and the horse's mane, leaped upon the horse's back from the other.

A half hour later a naked giant, swinging easily through the lower branches of the trees, paused, and with raised head, and dilating nostrils sniffed the morning air. The smell of blood fell strong upon his senses, and mingled with it was the scent of Numa, the lion. The giant cocked his head upon one side and listened.

From a short distance up the trail came the unmistakable noises of the greedy feeding of a lion. The crunching of bones, the gulping of great pieces, the contented growling, all attested the nearness of the king at table.

Tarzan approached the spot, still keeping to the branches of the trees. He made no effort to conceal his approach, and presently he had evidence that Numa had heard him, from the ominous, rumbling warning that broke from a thicket beside the trail.

Halting upon a low branch just above the lion Tarzan looked down upon the grisly scene. Could this unrecognizable thing be the man he had been trailing? The ape-man wondered. From time to time he had descended to the trail and verified his judgment by the evidence of his scent that the Belgian had followed this game trail toward the east.

Now he proceeded beyond the lion and his feast, again descended and examined the ground with his nose. There was no scent spoor here of the man he had been trailing. Tarzan returned to the tree. With keen eyes he searched the ground about the mutilated corpse for a sign of the missing pouch of pretty pebbles; but naught could he see of it.

He scolded Numa and tried to drive the great beast away; but only angry growls rewarded his efforts. He tore small branches from a nearby limb and hurled them at his ancient enemy. Numa looked up with bared fangs, grinning hideously, but he did not rise from his kill.

Then Tarzan fitted an arrow to his bow, and drawing the slim shaft far back let drive with all the force of the tough wood that only he could bend. As the arrow sank deeply into his side, Numa leaped to his feet with a roar of mingled rage and pain. He leaped futilely at the grinning ape-man, tore at the protruding end of the shaft, and then, springing into the trail, paced back and forth beneath his tormentor. Again Tarzan loosed a swift bolt. This time the missile, aimed with care, lodged in the lion's spine. The great creature halted in its tracks, and lurched awkwardly forward upon its face, paralyzed.

Tarzan dropped to the trail, ran quickly to the beast's side, and drove his spear deep into the fierce heart, then after recovering his arrows turned his attention to the mutilated remains of the animal's prey in the nearby thicket.

The face was gone. The Arab garments aroused no doubt as to the man's identity, since he had trailed him into the Arab camp and out again, where he might easily have acquired the apparel. So sure was Tarzan that the body was that of he who had robbed him that he made no effort to verify his deductions by scent among the conglomerate odors of the great carnivore and the fresh blood of the victim.

He confined his attentions to a careful search for the pouch, but nowhere upon or about the corpse was any sign of the missing article or its contents. The ape-man was disappointed — possibly not so much because of the loss of the colored pebbles as with Numa for robbing him of the pleasures of revenge.

Wondering what could have become of his possessions, the ape-man turned slowly back along the trail in the direction from which he had come. In his mind he revolved a plan to enter and search the Arab camp, after darkness had again fallen. Taking to the trees, he moved directly south in search of prey, that he might satisfy his hunger before midday, and then lie up for the afternoon in some spot far from the camp, where he might sleep without fear of discovery until it came time to prosecute his design.

Scarcely had he quitted the trail when a tall, black warrior, moving at a dogged trot, passed toward the east. It was Mugambi, searching for his mistress. He continued along the trail, halting to examine the body of the dead lion. An expression of puzzlement crossed his features as he bent to search for the wounds which had caused the death of the jungle lord. Tarzan had removed his arrows, but to Mugambi the proof of death was as strong as though both the lighter missiles and the spear still protruded from the carcass.

The black looked furtively about him. The body was still warm, and from this fact he reasoned that the killer was close at hand, yet no sign of living man appeared. Mugambi shook his head, and continued along the trail, but with redoubled caution.

All day he traveled, stopping occasionally to call aloud the single word, "Lady," in the hope that at last she might hear and respond; but in the end his loyal devotion brought him to disaster.

From the northeast, for several months, Abdul Mourak, in command of a detachment of Abyssinian soldiers, had been assiduously searching for the Arab raider, Achmet Zek, who, six months previously, had affronted the majesty of Abdul Mourak's emperor by conducting a slave raid within the boundaries of Menelek's domain.

And now it happened that Abdul Mourak had halted for a short rest at noon upon this very day and along the same trail that Werper and Mugambi were following toward the east.

It was shortly after the soldiers had dismounted that the Belgian, unaware of their presence, rode his tired mount almost into their midst, before he had discovered them. Instantly he was surrounded, and a volley of questions hurled at him, as he was pulled from his horse and led toward the presence of the commander.

Falling back upon his European nationality, Werper assured Abdul Mourak that he was a Frenchman, hunting in Africa, and that he had been attacked by strangers, his safari killed or scattered, and himself escaping only by a miracle.

From a chance remark of the Abyssinian, Werper discovered the purpose of the expedition, and when he realized that these men were the enemies of Achmet Zek, he took heart, and immediately blamed his predicament upon the Arab.

Lest, however, he might again fall into the hands of the raider, he discouraged Abdul Mourak in the further prosecution of his pursuit, assuring the Abyssinian that Achmet Zek commanded a large and dangerous force, and also that he was marching rapidly toward the south.

Convinced that it would take a long time to overhaul the raider, and that the chances of engagement made the outcome extremely questionable, Mourak, none too unwillingly, abandoned his plan and gave the necessary orders for his command to pitch camp where they were, preparatory to taking up the return march toward Abyssinia the following morning.

It was late in the afternoon that the attention of the

camp was attracted toward the west by the sound of a powerful voice calling a single word, repeated several times: "Lady! Lady! Lady!"

True to their instincts of precaution, a number of Abyssinians, acting under orders from Abdul Mourak, advanced stealthily through the jungle toward the author of the call.

A half hour later they returned, dragging Mugambi among them. The first person the big black's eyes fell upon as he was hustled into the presence of the Abyssinian officer, was M. Jules Frecoult, the Frenchman who had been the guest of his master and whom he last had seen entering the village of Achmet Zek under circumstances which pointed to his familiarity and friendship for the raiders.

Between the disasters that had befallen his master and his master's house, and the Frenchman, Mugambi saw a sinister relationship, which kept him from recalling to Werper's attention the identity which the latter evidently failed to recognize.

Pleading that he was but a harmless hunter from a tribe farther south, Mugambi begged to be allowed to go upon his way; but Abdul Mourak, admiring the warrior's splendid physique, decided to take him back to Adis Abeba and present him to Menelek. A few moments later Mugambi and Werper were marched away under guard, and the Belgian learned for the first time, that he too was a prisoner rather than a guest. In vain he protested against such treatment, until a strapping soldier struck him across the mouth and threatened to shoot him if he did not desist.

Mugambi took the matter less to heart, for he had not the slightest doubt but that during the course of the journey he would find ample opportunity to elude the vigilance of his guards and make good his escape. With this idea always uppermost in his mind, he courted the good opinion of the Abyssinians, asked them many questions about their emperor and their country, and evinced a growing desire to reach their destination, that he might enjoy all the good things which they assured him the city of Adis Abeba contained. Thus he disarmed their suspicions, and each day found a slight relaxation of their watchfulness over him.

By taking advantage of the fact that he and Werper always were kept together, Mugambi sought to learn what the other knew of the whereabouts of Tarzan, or the authorship of the raid upon the bungalow, as well as the fate of Lady Greystoke; but as he was confined to the accidents of conversation for this information, not daring to acquaint Werper with his true identity, and as Werper was equally anxious to conceal from the world his part in the destruction of his host's home and happiness, Mugambi learned nothing – at least in this way.

But there came a time when he learned a very surprising thing, by accident.

The party had camped early in the afternoon of a sultry day, upon the banks of a clear and beautiful stream. The bottom of the river was gravelly, there was no indication of crocodiles, those menaces to promiscuous bathing in the rivers of certain portions of the dark continent, and so the Abyssinians took advantage of the opportunity to perform long-deferred, and much needed, ablutions.

As Werper, who, with Mugambi, had been given permission to enter the water, removed his clothing, the black noted the care with which he unfastened something which circled his waist, and which he took off with his shirt, keeping the latter always around and concealing the object of his suspicious solicitude.

It was this very carefulness which attracted the black's attention to the thing, arousing a natural curiosity in the warrior's mind, and so it chanced that when the Belgian, in the nervousness of overcaution, fumbled the hidden article and dropped it, Mugambi saw it as it fell upon the ground, spilling a portion of its contents on the sward.

Now Mugambi had been to London with his master. He was not the unsophisticated savage that his apparel proclaimed him. He had mingled with the cosmopolitan hordes of the greatest city in the world; he had visited museums and inspected shop windows; and, besides, he was a shrewd and intelligent man.

The instant that the jewels of Opar rolled, scintillating, before his astonished eyes, he recognized them for what they were; but he recognized something else, too, that interested him far more deeply than the value of the stones. A thousand times he had seen the leathern pouch which dangled at his master's side, when Tarzan of the Apes had, in a spirit of play and adventure, elected to return for a few hours to the primitive manners and customs of his boyhood, and surrounded by his naked warriors hunt the lion and the leopard, the buffalo and the elephant after the manner he loved best.

Werper saw that Mugambi had seen the pouch and the stones. Hastily he gathered up the precious gems and returned them to their container, while Mugambi, assuming an air of indifference, strolled down to the river for his bath.

The following morning Abdul Mourak was enraged and chagrined to discover that this huge, black prisoner had escaped during the night, while Werper was terrified for the same reason, until his trembling fingers discovered the pouch still in its place beneath his shirt, and within it the hard outlines of its contents.

Chapter XVI

TARZAN AGAIN LEADS
THE MANGANI

ACHMET ZEK WITH two of his followers had circled far to the south to intercept the flight of his deserting lieutenant, Werper. Others had spread out in various directions, so that a vast circle had been formed by them during the night, and now they were beating in toward the center.

Achmet and the two with him halted for a short rest just before noon. They squatted beneath the trees upon the southern edge of a clearing. The chief of the raiders was in ill humor. To have been outwitted by an unbeliever was bad enough; but to have, at the same time, lost the jewels upon which he had set his avaricious heart was altogether too much — Allah must, indeed be angry with his servant.

Well, he still had the woman. She would bring a fair price in the north, and there was, too, the buried treasure beside the ruins of the Englishman's house.

A slight noise in the jungle upon the opposite side

of the clearing brought Achmet Zek to immediate and alert attention. He gathered his rifle in readiness for instant use, at the same time motioning his followers to silence and concealment. Crouching behind the bushes the three waited, their eyes fastened upon the far side of the open space.

Presently the foliage parted and a woman's face appeared, glancing fearfully from side to side. A moment later, evidently satisfied that no immediate danger lurked before her, she stepped out into the clearing in full view of the Arab.

Achmet Zek caught his breath with a muttered exclamation of incredulity and an imprecation. The woman was the prisoner he had thought safely guarded at his camp!

Apparently she was alone, but Achmet Zek waited that he might make sure of it before seizing her. Slowly Jane Clayton started across the clearing. Twice already since she had quitted the village of the raiders had she barely escaped the fangs of carnivora, and once she had almost stumbled into the path of one of the searchers. Though she was almost despairing of ever reaching safety she still was determined to fight on, until death or success terminated her endeavors.

As the Arabs watched her from the safety of their concealment, and Achmet Zek noted with satisfaction that she was walking directly into his clutches, another pair of eyes looked down upon the entire scene from the foliage of an adjacent tree.

Puzzled, troubled eyes they were, for all their gray and savage glint, for their owner was struggling with an intangible suggestion of the familiarity of the face and figure of the woman below him.

A sudden crashing of the bushes at the point from which Jane Clayton had emerged into the clearing brought her to a sudden stop and attracted the attention of the Arabs and the watcher in the tree to the same point.

The woman wheeled about to see what new danger menaced her from behind, and as she did so a great, anthropoid ape waddled into view. Behind him came another and another; but Lady Greystoke did not wait to learn how many more of the hideous creatures were so close upon her trail.

With a smothered scream she rushed toward the opposite jungle, and as she reached the bushes there, Achmet Zek and his two henchmen rose up and seized her. At the same instant a naked, brown giant dropped from the branches of a tree at the right of the clearing.

Turning toward the astonished apes he gave voice to a short volley of low gutturals, and without waiting to note the effect of his words upon them, wheeled and charged for the Arabs.

Achmet Zek was dragging Jane Clayton toward his tethered horse. His two men were hastily unfastening all three mounts. The woman, struggling to escape the Arab, turned and saw the ape-man running toward her. A glad light of hope illuminated her face.

"John!" she cried. "Thank God that you have come in time."

Behind Tarzan came the great apes, wondering, but obedient to his summons. The Arabs saw that they would not have time to mount and make their escape before the beasts and the man were upon them. Achmet Zek recognized the latter as the redoubtable enemy of such as he, and he saw, too, in the circumstance an opportunity to rid himself forever of the menace of the ape-man's presence.

Calling to his men to follow his example he raised his rifle and leveled it upon the charging giant. His followers, acting with no less alacrity than himself, fired almost simultaneously, and with the reports of the rifles, Tarzan of the Apes and two of his hairy henchmen pitched forward among the jungle grasses.

The noise of the rifle shots brought the balance of the apes to a wondering pause, and, taking advantage of their momentary distraction, Achmet Zek and his fellows leaped to their horses' backs and galloped away with the now hopeless and grief-stricken woman.

Back to the village they rode, and once again Lady Greystoke found herself incarcerated in the filthy, little hut from which she had thought to have escaped for good. But this time she was not only guarded by an additional sentry, but bound as well.

Singly and in twos the searchers who had ridden out with Achmet Zek upon the trail of the Belgian, returned empty handed. With the report of each the raider's rage and chagrin increased, until he was in such a transport of ferocious anger that none dared approach him. Threatening and cursing, Achmet Zek paced up and down the floor of his silken tent; but his temper served him naught — Werper was gone and with him the fortune in scintillating gems which had aroused the cupidity of his chief and placed the sentence of death upon the head of the lieutenant.

With the escape of the Arabs the great apes had turned their attention to their fallen comrades. One was dead, but another and the great white ape still breathed. The hairy monsters gathered about these two, grumbling and muttering after the fashion of their kind.

Tarzan was the first to regain consciousness. Sitting up, he looked about him. Blood was flowing from a wound in his shoulder. The shock had thrown him down and dazed him; but he was far from dead. Rising slowly to his feet he let his eyes wander toward the spot where last he had seen the she, who had aroused within his savage breast such strange emotions.

"Where is she?" he asked.

"The Tarmangani took her away," replied one of the apes. "Who are you who speak the language of the

Mangani?"

"I am Tarzan," replied the ape-man; "mighty hunter, greatest of fighters. When I roar, the jungle is silent and trembles with terror. I am Tarzan of the Apes. I have been away; but now I have come back to my people."

"Yes," spoke up an old ape, "he is Tarzan. I know him. It is well that he has come back. Now we shall have good hunting."

The other apes came closer and sniffed at the ape-man. Tarzan stood very still, his fangs half bared, and his muscles tense and ready for action; but there was none there to question his right to be with them, and presently, the inspection satisfactorily concluded, the apes again returned their attention to the other survivor.

He too was but slightly wounded, a bullet, grazing his skull, having stunned him, so that when he regained consciousness he was apparently as fit as ever.

The apes told Tarzan that they had been traveling toward the east when the scent spoor of the she had attracted them and they had stalked her. Now they wished to continue upon their interrupted march; but Tarzan preferred to follow the Arabs and take the woman from them. After a considerable argument it was decided that they should first hunt toward the east for a few days and then return and search for the Arabs, and as time is of little moment to the ape folk, Tarzan acceded to their demands, he, himself, having reverted to a mental state but little superior to their own.

Another circumstance which decided him to postpone pursuit of the Arabs was the painfulness of his wound. It would be better to wait until that had healed before he pitted himself again against the guns of the Tarmangani.

And so, as Jane Clayton was pushed into her prison hut and her hands and feet securely bound, her natural

protector roamed off toward the east in company with
a score of hairy monsters, with whom he rubbed shoulders as familiarly as a few months before he had mingled with his immaculate fellow-members of one of
London's most select and exclusive clubs.

But all the time there lurked in the back of his
injured brain a troublesome conviction that he had no
business where he was — that he should be, for some
unaccountable reason, elsewhere and among another
sort of creature. Also, there was the compelling urge to
be upon the scent of the Arabs, undertaking the rescue
of the woman who had appealed so strongly to his
savage sentiments; though the thought-word which
naturally occurred to him in the contemplation of the
venture, was "capture," rather than "rescue."

To him she was as any other jungle she, and he had
set his heart upon her as his mate. For an instant, as
he had approached closer to her in the clearing where
the Arabs had seized her, the subtle aroma which had
first aroused his desires in the hut that had imprisoned
her had fallen upon his nostrils, and told him that he
had found the creature for whom he had developed so
sudden and inexplicable a passion.

The matter of the pouch of jewels also occupied his
thoughts to some extent, so that he found a double
urge for his return to the camp of the raiders. He would
obtain possession of both his pretty pebbles and the
she. Then he would return to the great apes with his
new mate and his baubles, and leading his hairy companions into a far wilderness beyond the ken of man,
live out his life, hunting and battling among the lower
orders after the only manner which he now recollected.

He spoke to his fellow-apes upon the matter, in an
attempt to persuade them to accompany him; but all
except Taglat and Chulk refused. The latter was young
and strong, endowed with a greater intelligence than
his fellows, and therefore the possessor of better devel-

oped powers of imagination. To him the expedition savored of adventure, and so appealed, strongly. With Taglat there was another incentive — a secret and sinister incentive, which, had Tarzan of the Apes had knowledge of it, would have sent him at the other's throat in jealous rage.

Taglat was no longer young; but he was still a formidable beast, mightily muscled, cruel, and, because of his greater experience, crafty and cunning. Too, he was of giant proportions, the very weight of his huge bulk serving ofttimes to discount in his favor the superior agility of a younger antagonist.

He was of a morose and sullen disposition that marked him even among his frowning fellows, where such characteristics are the rule rather than the exception, and, though Tarzan did not guess it, he hated the ape-man with a ferocity that he was able to hide only because the dominant spirit of the nobler creature had inspired within him a species of dread which was as powerful as it was inexplicable to him.

These two, then, were to be Tarzan's companions upon his return to the village of Achmet Zek. As they set off, the balance of the tribe vouchsafed them but a parting stare, and then resumed the serious business of feeding.

Tarzan found difficulty in keeping the minds of his fellows set upon the purpose of their adventure, for the mind of an ape lacks the power of long-sustained concentration. To set out upon a long journey, with a definite destination in view, is one thing, to remember that purpose and keep it uppermost in one's mind continually is quite another. There are so many things to distract one's attention along the way.

Chulk was, at first, for rushing rapidly ahead as though the village of the raiders lay but an hour's march before them instead of several days; but within a few minutes a fallen tree attracted his attention with its suggestion of rich and succulent forage beneath, and when Tarzan, missing him, returned in search, he found Chulk squatting beside the rotting bole, from beneath which he was assiduously engaged in digging out the grubs and beetles, whose kind form a considerable proportion of the diet of the apes.

Unless Tarzan desired to fight there was nothing to do but wait until Chulk had exhausted the storehouse, and this he did, only to discover that Taglat was now missing. After a considerable search, he found that worthy gentleman contemplating the sufferings of an injured rodent he had pounced upon. He would sit in apparent indifference, gazing in another direction, while the crippled creature, wriggled slowly and painfully away from him, and then, just as his victim felt assured of escape, he would reach out a giant palm and slam it down upon the fugitive. Again and again he repeated this operation, until, tiring of the sport, he ended the sufferings of his plaything by devouring it.

Such were the exasperating causes of delay which retarded Tarzan's return journey toward the village of Achmet Zek; but the ape-man was patient, for in his mind was a plan which necessitated the presence of Chulk and Taglat when he should have arrived at his destination.

It was not always an easy thing to maintain in the vacillating minds of the anthropoids a sustained interest in their venture. Chulk was wearying of the continued marching and the infrequency and short duration of the rests. He would gladly have abandoned this search for adventure had not Tarzan continually filled his mind with alluring pictures of the great stores of food which were to be found in the village of Tarmangani.

Taglat nursed his secret purpose to better advantage than might have been expected of an ape, yet there were times when he, too, would have abandoned the adventure had not Tarzan cajoled him on.

It was mid-afternoon of a sultry, tropical day when the keen senses of the three warned them of the proximity of the Arab camp. Stealthily they approached, keeping to the dense tangle of growing things which made concealment easy to their uncanny jungle craft.

First came the giant ape-man, his smooth, brown skin glistening with the sweat of exertion in the close, hot confines of the jungle. Behind him crept Chulk and Taglat, grotesque and shaggy caricatures of their godlike leader.

Silently they made their way to the edge of the clearing which surrounded the palisade, and here they clambered into the lower branches of a large tree overlooking the village occupied by the enemy, the better to spy upon his goings and comings.

A horseman, white burnoosed, rode out through the gateway of the village. Tarzan, whispering to Chulk and Taglat to remain where they were, swung, monkey-like, through the trees in the direction of the trail the Arab was riding. From one jungle giant to the next he sped with the rapidity of a squirrel and the silence of a ghost.

The Arab rode slowly onward, unconscious of the danger hovering in the trees behind him. The ape-man made a slight detour and increased his speed until he had reached a point upon the trail in advance of the horseman. Here he halted upon a leafy bough which overhung the narrow, jungle trail. On came the victim, humming a wild air of the great desert land of the north. Above him poised the savage brute that was today bent upon the destruction of a human life — the same creature who a few months before, had occupied his seat in the House of Lords at London, a respected and distinguished member of that august body.

The Arab passed beneath the overhanging bough, there was a slight rustling of the leaves above, the horse snorted and plunged as a brown-skinned creature dropped upon its rump. A pair of mighty arms encircled the Arab and he was dragged from his saddle to the trail.

Ten minutes later the ape-man, carrying the outer garments of an Arab bundled beneath an arm, rejoined his companions. He exhibited his trophies to them, explaining in low gutturals the details of his exploit. Chulk and Taglat fingered the fabrics, smelled of them, and, placing them to their ears, tried to listen to them.

Then Tarzan led them back through the jungle to the trail, where the three hid themselves and waited. Nor had they long to wait before two of Achmet Zek's blacks, clothed in habiliments similar to their master's, came down the trail on foot, returning to the camp.

One moment they were laughing and talking together — the next they lay stretched in death upon the trail, three mighty engines of destruction bending over them. Tarzan removed their outer garments as he had removed those of his first victim, and again retired with Chulk and Taglat to the greater seclusion of the tree they had first selected.

Here the ape-man arranged the garments upon his shaggy fellows and himself, until, at a distance, it might have appeared that three white-robed Arabs squatted silently among the branches of the forest.

Until dark they remained where they were, for from his point of vantage, Tarzan could view the enclosure within the palisade. He marked the position of the hut in which he had first discovered the scent spoor of the she he sought. He saw the two sentries standing before its doorway, and he located the habitation of Achmet Zek, where something told him he would most likely find the missing pouch and pebbles.

Chulk and Taglat were, at first, greatly interested in their wonderful raiment. They fingered the fabric, smelled of it, and regarded each other intently with every mark of satisfaction and pride. Chulk, a humorist in his way, stretched forth a long and hairy arm, and grasping the hood of Taglat's burnoose pulled it down over the latter's eyes, extinguishing him, snuffer-like, as it were.

The older ape, pessimistic by nature, recognized no such thing as humor. Creatures laid their paws upon him for but two things — to search for fleas and to attack. The pulling of the Tarmangani-scented thing about his head and eyes could not be for the performance of the former act; therefore it must be the latter. He was attacked! Chulk had attacked him.

With a snarl he was at the other's throat, not even waiting to lift the woolen veil which obscured his vision. Tarzan leaped upon the two, and swaying and toppling upon their insecure perch the three great beasts tussled and snapped at one another until the ape-man finally succeeded in separating the enraged anthropoids.

An apology is unknown to these savage progenitors of man, and explanation a laborious and usually futile process, Tarzan bridged the dangerous gulf by distracting their attention from their altercation to a consideration of their plans for the immediate future. Accustomed to frequent arguments in which more hair than blood is wasted, the apes speedily forget such trivial encounters, and presently Chulk and Taglat were again squatting in close proximity to each other and peaceful repose, awaiting the moment when the ape-man should lead them into the village of the Tarmangani.

It was long after darkness had fallen, that Tarzan led his companions from their hiding place in the tree to the ground and around the palisade to the far side of the village.

Gathering the skirts of his burnoose, beneath one arm, that his legs might have free action, the ape-man took a short running start, and scrambled to the top of the barrier. Fearing lest the apes should rend their garments to shreds in a similar attempt, he had directed them to wait below for him, and himself securely perched upon the summit of the palisade he unslung his spear and lowered one end of it to Chulk.

The ape seized it, and while Tarzan held tightly to the upper end, the anthropoid climbed quickly up the shaft until with one paw he grasped the top of the wall. To scramble then to Tarzan's side was the work of but an instant. In like manner Taglat was conducted to their sides, and a moment later the three dropped silently within the enclosure.

Tarzan led them first to the rear of the hut in which Jane Clayton was confined, where, through the roughly repaired aperture in the wall, he sought with his sensitive nostrils for proof that the she he had come for was within.

Chulk and Taglat, their hairy faces pressed close to that of the patrician, sniffed with him. Each caught the scent spoor of the woman within, and each reacted according to his temperament and his habits of thought.

It left Chulk indifferent. The she was for Tarzan — all that he desired was to bury his snout in the food-stuffs of the Tarmangani. He had come to eat his fill without labor — Tarzan had told him that that should be his reward, and he was satisfied.

But Taglat's wicked, bloodshot eyes, narrowed to the realization of the nearing fulfillment of his carefully nursed plan. It is true that sometimes during the several days that had elapsed since they had set out upon their expedition it had been difficult for Taglat to hold his idea uppermost in his mind, and on several occasions he had completely forgotten it, until Tarzan, by a chance word, had recalled it to him, but, for an ape, Taglat had done well.

Now, he licked his chops, and he made a sickening, sucking noise with his flabby lips as he drew in his breath.

Satisfied that the she was where he had hoped to find her, Tarzan led his apes toward the tent of Achmet Zek. A passing Arab and two slaves saw them, but the night was dark and the white burnooses hid the hairy limbs of the apes and the giant figure of their leader, so that the three, by squatting down as though in conversation, were passed by, unsuspected. To the rear of the tent they made their way. Within, Achmet Zek conversed with several of his lieutenants. Without, Tarzan listened.

Chapter XVII

THE DEADLY PERIL
OF JANE CLAYTON

*L*IEUTENANT ALBERT WERPER, terrified by contemplation of the fate which might await him at Adis Abeba, cast about for some scheme of escape, but after the black Mugambi had eluded their vigilance the Abyssinians redoubled their precautions to prevent Werper following the lead of the Negro.

For some time Werper entertained the idea of bribing Abdul Mourak with a portion of the contents of the pouch; but fearing that the man would demand all the gems as the price of liberty, the Belgian, influenced by avarice, sought another avenue from his dilemma.

It was then that there dawned upon him the possibility of the success of a different course which would still leave him in possession of the jewels, while at the same time satisfying the greed of the Abyssinian with the conviction that he had obtained all that Werper had to offer.

And so it was that a day or so after Mugambi had

disappeared, Werper asked for an audience with Abdul Mourak. As the Belgian entered the presence of his captor the scowl upon the features of the latter boded ill for any hope which Werper might entertain, still he fortified himself by recalling the common weakness of mankind, which permits the most inflexible of natures to bend to the consuming desire for wealth.

Abdul Mourak eyed him, frowningly. "What do you want now?" he asked.

"My liberty," replied Werper.

The Abyssinian sneered. "And you disturbed me thus to tell me what any fool might know," he said.

"I can pay for it," said Werper.

Abdul Mourak laughed loudly. "Pay for it?" he cried. "What with — the rags that you have upon your back? Or, perhaps you are concealing beneath your coat a thousand pounds of ivory. Get out! You are a fool. Do not bother me again or I shall have you whipped."

But Werper persisted. His liberty and perhaps his life depended upon his success.

"Listen to me," he pleaded. "If I can give you as much gold as ten men may carry will you promise that I shall be conducted in safety to the nearest English commissioner?"

"As much gold as ten men may carry!" repeated Abdul Mourak. "You are crazy. Where have you so much gold as that?"

"I know where it is hid," said Werper. "Promise, and I will lead you to it — if ten loads is enough?"

Abdul Mourak had ceased to laugh. He was eyeing the Belgian intently. The fellow seemed sane enough — yet ten loads of gold! It was preposterous. The Abyssinian thought in silence for a moment.

"Well, and if I promise," he said. "How far is this gold?"

"A long week's march to the south," replied Werper.

"And if we do not find it where you say it is, do you

realize what your punishment will be?"

"If it is not there I will forfeit my life," replied the Belgian. "I know it is there, for I saw it buried with my own eyes. And more — there are not only ten loads, but as many as fifty men may carry. It is all yours if you will promise to see me safely delivered into the protection of the English."

"You will stake your life against the finding of the gold?" asked Abdul.

Werper assented with a nod.

"Very well," said the Abyssinian, "I promise, and even if there be but five loads you shall have your freedom; but until the gold is in my possession you remain a prisoner."

"I am satisfied," said Werper. "Tomorrow we start?"

Abdul Mourak nodded, and the Belgian returned to his guards. The following day the Abyssinian soldiers were surprised to receive an order which turned their faces from the northeast to the south. And so it happened that upon the very night that Tarzan and the two apes entered the village of the raiders, the Abyssinians camped but a few miles to the east of the same spot.

While Werper dreamed of freedom and the unmolested enjoyment of the fortune in his stolen pouch, and Abdul Mourak lay awake in greedy contemplation of the fifty loads of gold which lay but a few days farther to the south of him, Achmet Zek gave orders to his lieutenants that they should prepare a force of fighting men and carriers to proceed to the ruins of the Englishman's *douar* on the morrow and bring back the fabulous fortune which his renegade lieutenant had told him was buried there.

And as he delivered his instructions to those within, a silent listener crouched without his tent, waiting for the time when he might enter in safety and prosecute his search for the missing pouch and the pretty pebbles that had caught his fancy.

At last the swarthy companions of Achmet Zek quitted his tent, and the leader went with them to smoke a pipe with one of their number, leaving his own silken habitation unguarded. Scarcely had they left the interior when a knife blade was thrust through the fabric of the rear wall, some six feet above the ground, and a swift downward stroke opened an entrance to those who waited beyond.

Through the opening stepped the ape-man, and close behind him came the huge Chulk; but Taglat did not follow them. Instead he turned and slunk through the darkness toward the hut where the she who had arrested his brutish interest lay securely bound. Before the doorway the sentries sat upon their haunches, conversing in monotones. Within, the young woman lay upon a filthy sleeping mat, resigned, through utter hopelessness to whatever fate lay in store for her until the opportunity arrived which would permit her to free herself by the only means which now seemed even remotely possible — the hitherto detested act of self-destruction.

Creeping silently toward the sentries, a white-burnoosed figure approached the shadows at one end of the hut. The meager intellect of the creature denied it the advantage it might have taken of its disguise. Where it could have walked boldly to the very sides of the sentries, it chose rather to sneak upon them, unseen, from the rear.

It came to the corner of the hut and peered around. The sentries were but a few paces away; but the ape did not dare expose himself, even for an instant, to those feared and hated thunder-sticks which the Tarmangani knew so well how to use, if there were another and safer method of attack.

Taglat wished that there was a tree nearby from the overhanging branches of which he might spring upon his unsuspecting prey; but, though there was no tree, the idea gave birth to a plan. The eaves of the hut were just above the heads of the sentries — from them he could leap upon the Tarmangani, unseen. A quick snap of those mighty jaws would dispose of one of them before the other realized that they were attacked, and the second would fall an easy prey to the strength, agility and ferocity of a second quick charge.

Taglat withdrew a few paces to the rear of the hut, gathered himself for the effort, ran quickly forward and leaped high into the air. He struck the roof directly above the rear wall of the hut, and the structure, reinforced by the wall beneath, held his enormous weight for an instant, then he moved forward a step, the roof sagged, the thatching parted and the great anthropoid shot through into the interior.

The sentries, hearing the crashing of the roof poles, leaped to their feet and rushed into the hut. Jane Clayton tried to roll aside as the great form lit upon the floor so close to her that one foot pinned her clothing to the ground.

The ape, feeling the movement beside him, reached down and gathered the girl in the hollow of one mighty arm. The burnoose covered the hairy body so that Jane Clayton believed that a human arm supported her, and from the extremity of hopelessness a great hope sprang into her breast that at last she was in the keeping of a rescuer.

The two sentries were now within the hut, but hesitating because of doubt as to the nature of the cause of the disturbance. Their eyes, not yet accustomed to the darkness of the interior, told them nothing, nor did they hear any sound, for the ape stood silently awaiting their attack.

Seeing that they stood without advancing, and realizing that, handicapped as he was by the weight of the she, he could put up but a poor battle, Taglat elected to risk a sudden break for liberty. Lowering his head, he charged straight for the two sentries who blocked the doorway. The impact of his mighty shoulders bowled them over upon their backs, and before they could scramble to their feet, the ape was gone, darting in the shadows of the huts toward the palisade at the far end of the village.

The speed and strength of her rescuer filled Jane Clayton with wonder. Could it be that Tarzan had survived the bullet of the Arab? Who else in all the jungle could bear the weight of a grown woman as lightly as he who held her? She spoke his name; but there was no response. Still she did not give up hope.

At the palisade the beast did not even hesitate. A single mighty leap carried it to the top, where it poised but for an instant before dropping to the ground upon the opposite side. Now the girl was almost positive that she was safe in the arms of her husband, and when the ape took to the trees and bore her swiftly into the jungle, as Tarzan had done at other times in the past, belief became conviction.

In a little moonlit glade, a mile or so from the camp of the raiders, her rescuer halted and dropped her to the ground. His roughness surprised her, but still she had no doubts. Again she called him by name, and at the same instant the ape, fretting under the restraints of the unaccustomed garments of the Tarmangani, tore the burnoose from him, revealing to the eyes of the horror-struck woman the hideous face and hairy form of a giant anthropoid.

With a piteous wail of terror, Jane Clayton swooned, while, from the concealment of a nearby bush, Numa, the lion, eyed the pair hungrily and licked his chops.

Tarzan, entering the tent of Achmet Zek, searched the interior thoroughly. He tore the bed to pieces and scattered the contents of box and bag about the floor. He investigated whatever his eyes discovered, nor did those keen organs overlook a single article within the habitation of the raider chief; but no pouch or pretty pebbles rewarded his thoroughness.

Satisfied at last that his belongings were not in the possession of Achmet Zek, unless they were on the person of the chief himself, Tarzan decided to secure the person of the she before further prosecuting his search for the pouch.

Motioning for Chulk to follow him, he passed out of the tent by the same way that he had entered it, and walking boldly through the village, made directly for the hut where Jane Clayton had been imprisoned.

He noted with surprise the absence of Taglat, whom he had expected to find awaiting him outside the tent of Achmet Zek; but, accustomed as he was to the unreliability of apes, he gave no serious attention to the present defection of his surly companion. So long as Taglat did not cause interference with his plans, Tarzan was indifferent to his absence.

As he approached the hut, the ape-man noticed that a crowd had collected about the entrance. He could see that the men who composed it were much excited, and fearing lest Chulk's disguise should prove inadequate to the concealment of his true identity in the face of so many observers, he commanded the ape to betake himself to the far end of the village, and there await him.

As Chulk waddled off, keeping to the shadows, Tarzan advanced boldly toward the excited group before the doorway of the hut. He mingled with the blacks and the Arabs in an endeavor to learn the cause of the commotion, in his interest forgetting that he alone of the assemblage carried a spear, a bow and arrows, and thus might become an object of suspicious attention.

Shouldering his way through the crowd he approached the doorway, and had almost reached it when one of the Arabs laid a hand upon his shoulder, crying:

"Who is this?" at the same time snatching back the hood from the ape-man's face.

Tarzan of the Apes in all his savage life had never been accustomed to pause in argument with an antagonist. The primitive instinct of self-preservation acknowledges many arts and wiles; but argument is not one of them, nor did he now waste precious time in an attempt to convince the raiders that he was not a wolf in sheep's clothing. Instead he had his unmasker by the throat ere the man's words had scarce quitted his lips, and hurling him from side to side brushed away those who would have swarmed upon him.

Using the Arab as a weapon, Tarzan forced his way quickly to the doorway, and a moment later was within the hut. A hasty examination revealed the fact that it was empty, and his sense of smell discovered, too, the scent spoor of Taglat, the ape. Tarzan uttered a low, ominous growl. Those who were pressing forward at the doorway to seize him, fell back as the savage notes of the bestial challenge smote upon their ears. They looked at one another in surprise and consternation. A man had entered the hut alone, and yet with their own ears they had heard the voice of a wild beast within. What could it mean? Had a lion or a leopard sought sanctuary in the interior, unbeknown to the sentries?

Tarzan's quick eyes discovered the opening in the roof, through which Taglat had fallen. He guessed that the ape had either come or gone by way of the break, and while the Arabs hesitated without, he sprang, catlike, for the opening, grasped the top of the wall and clambered out upon the roof, dropping instantly to the ground at the rear of the hut.

When the Arabs finally mustered courage to enter the hut, after firing several volleys through the walls, they found the interior deserted. At the same time Tarzan, at the far end of the village, sought for Chulk;

but the ape was nowhere to be found.

Robbed of his she, deserted by his companions, and as much in ignorance as ever as to the whereabouts of his pouch and pebbles, it was an angry Tarzan who climbed the palisade and vanished into the darkness of the jungle.

For the present he must give up the search for his pouch, since it would be paramount to self-destruction to enter the Arab camp now while all its inhabitants were aroused and upon the alert.

In his escape from the village, the ape-man had lost the spoor of the fleeing Taglat, and now he circled widely through the forest in an endeavor to again pick it up.

Chulk had remained at his post until the cries and shots of the Arabs had filled his simple soul with terror, for above all things the ape folk fear the thunder-sticks of the Tarmangani; then he had clambered nimbly over the palisade, tearing his burnoose in the effort, and fled into the depths of the jungle, grumbling and scolding as he went.

Tarzan, roaming the jungle in search of the trail of Taglat and the she, traveled swiftly. In a little moonlit glade ahead of him the great ape was bending over the prostrate form of the woman Tarzan sought. The beast was tearing at the bonds that confined her ankles and wrists, pulling and gnawing upon the cords.

The course the ape-man was taking would carry him but a short distance to the right of them, and though he could not have seen them the wind was bearing down from them to him, carrying their scent spoor strongly toward him.

A moment more and Jane Clayton's safety might have been assured, even though Numa, the lion, was already gathering himself in preparation for a charge; but Fate, already all too cruel, now outdid herself — the wind veered suddenly for a few moments, the scent spoor that would have led the ape-man to the girl's side was wafted in the opposite direction; Tarzan passed within fifty yards of the tragedy that was being enacted in the glade, and the opportunity was gone beyond recall.

Chapter XVIII

THE FIGHT
FOR THE TREASURE

*I*T WAS MORNING before Tarzan could bring himself to a realization of the possibility of failure of his
quest, and even then he would only admit that success
was but delayed. He would eat and sleep, and then set
forth again. The jungle was wide; but wide too were the
experience and cunning of Tarzan. Taglat might travel
far; but Tarzan would find him in the end, though he
had to search every tree in the mighty forest.

Soliloquizing thus, the ape-man followed the spoor
of Bara, the deer, the unfortunate upon which he had
decided to satisfy his hunger. For half an hour the trail
led the ape-man toward the east along a well-marked
game path, when suddenly, to the stalker's
astonishment, the quarry broke into sight, racing
madly back along the narrow way straight toward the
hunter.

Tarzan, who had been following along the trail,
leaped so quickly to the concealing verdure at the side

that the deer was still unaware of the presence of an enemy in this direction, and while the animal was still some distance away, the ape-man swung into the lower branches of the tree which overhung the trail. There he crouched, a savage beast of prey, awaiting the coming of its victim.

What had frightened the deer into so frantic a retreat, Tarzan did not know — Numa, the lion, perhaps, or Sheeta, the panther; but whatsoever it was mattered little to Tarzan of the Apes — he was ready and willing to defend his kill against any other denizen of the jungle. If he were unable to do it by means of physical prowess, he had at his command another and a greater power — his shrewd intelligence.

And so, on came the running deer, straight into the jaws of death. The ape-man turned so that his back was toward the approaching animal. He poised with bent knees upon the gently swaying limb above the trail, timing with keen ears the nearing hoof beats of frightened Bara.

In a moment the victim flashed beneath the limb and at the same instant the ape-man above sprang out and down upon its back. The weight of the man's body carried the deer to the ground. It stumbled forward once in a futile effort to rise, and then mighty muscles dragged its head far back, gave the neck a vicious wrench, and Bara was dead.

Quick had been the killing, and equally quick were the ape-man's subsequent actions, for who might know what manner of killer pursued Bara, or how close at hand he might be? Scarce had the neck of the victim snapped than the carcass was hanging over one of Tarzan's broad shoulders, and an instant later the ape-man was perched once more among the lower branches of a tree above the trail, his keen, gray eyes scanning the pathway down which the deer had fled.

Nor was it long before the cause of Bara's fright

became evident to Tarzan, for presently came the unmistakable sounds of approaching horsemen. Dragging his kill after him the ape-man ascended to the middle terrace, and settling himself comfortably in the crotch of a tree where he could still view the trail beneath, cut a juicy steak from the deer's loin, and burying his strong, white teeth in the hot flesh proceeded to enjoy the fruits of his prowess and his cunning.

Nor did he neglect the trail beneath while he satisfied his hunger. His sharp eyes saw the muzzle of the leading horse as it came into view around a bend in the tortuous trail, and one by one they scrutinized the riders as they passed beneath him in single file.

Among them came one whom Tarzan recognized, but so schooled was the ape-man in the control of his emotions that no slightest change of expression, much less any hysterical demonstration that might have revealed his presence, betrayed the fact of his inward excitement.

Beneath him, as unconscious of his presence as were the Abyssinians before and behind him, rode Albert Werper, while the ape-man scrutinized the Belgian for some sign of the pouch which he had stolen.

As the Abyssinians rode toward the south, a giant figure hovered ever upon their trail — a huge, almost naked white man, who carried the bloody carcass of a deer upon his shoulders, for Tarzan knew that he might not have another opportunity to hunt for some time if he were to follow the Belgian.

To endeavor to snatch him from the midst of the armed horsemen, not even Tarzan would attempt other than in the last extremity, for the way of the wild is the way of caution and cunning, unless they be aroused to rashness by pain or anger.

So the Abyssinians and the Belgian marched southward and Tarzan of the Apes swung silently after them through the swaying branches of the middle terrace.

A two days' march brought them to a level plain beyond which lay mountains — a plain which Tarzan remembered and which aroused within him vague half memories and strange longings. Out upon the plain the horsemen rode, and at a safe distance behind them crept the ape-man, taking advantage of such cover as the ground afforded.

Beside a charred pile of timbers the Abyssinians halted, and Tarzan, sneaking close and concealing himself in nearby shrubbery, watched them in wonderment. He saw them digging up the earth, and he wondered if they had hidden meat there in the past and now had come for it. Then he recalled how he had buried his pretty pebbles, and the suggestion that had caused him to do it. They were digging for the things the blacks had buried here!

Presently he saw them uncover a dirty, yellow object, and he witnessed the joy of Werper and of Abdul Mourak as the grimy object was exposed to view. One by one they unearthed many similar pieces, all of the same uniform, dirty yellow, until a pile of them lay upon the ground, a pile which Abdul Mourak fondled and petted in an ecstasy of greed.

Something stirred in the ape-man's mind as he looked long upon the golden ingots. Where had he seen such before? What were they? Why did these Tarmangani covet them so greatly? To whom did they belong?

He recalled the black men who had buried them. The things must be theirs. Werper was stealing them as he had stolen Tarzan's pouch of pebbles. The ape-man's eyes blazed in anger. He would like to find the black men and lead them against these thieves. He wondered where their village might be.

As all these things ran through the active mind, a party of men moved out of the forest at the edge of the plain and advanced toward the ruins of the burned bungalow.

Abdul Mourak, always watchful, was the first to see them, but already they were halfway across the open. He called to his men to mount and hold themselves in readiness, for in the heart of Africa who may know whether a strange host be friend or foe?

Werper, swinging into his saddle, fastened his eyes upon the newcomers, then, white and trembling he turned toward Abdul Mourak.

"It is Achmet Zek and his raiders," he whispered. "They are come for the gold."

It must have been at about the same instant that Achmet Zek discovered the pile of yellow ingots and realized the actuality of what he had already feared since first his eyes had alighted upon the party beside the ruins of the Englishman's bungalow. Someone had forestalled him — another had come for the treasure ahead of him.

The Arab was crazed by rage. Recently everything had gone against him. He had lost the jewels, the Belgian, and for the second time he had lost the Englishwoman. Now some one had come to rob him of this treasure which he had thought as safe from disturbance here as though it never had been mined.

He cared not whom the thieves might be. They would not give up the gold without a battle, of that he was certain, and with a wild whoop and a command to his followers, Achmet Zek put spurs to his horse and dashed down upon the Abyssinians, and after him, waving their long guns above their heads, yelling and cursing, came his motley horde of cut-throat followers.

The men of Abdul Mourak met them with a volley which emptied a few saddles, and then the raiders were among them, and sword, pistol and musket, each was doing its most hideous and bloody work.

Achmet Zek, spying Werper at the first charge, bore

down upon the Belgian, and the latter, terrified by contemplation of the fate he deserved, turned his horse's head and dashed madly away in an effort to escape. Shouting to a lieutenant to take command, and urging him upon pain of death to dispatch the Abyssinians and bring the gold back to his camp, Achmet Zek set off across the plain in pursuit of the Belgian, his wicked nature unable to forego the pleasures of revenge, even at the risk of sacrificing the treasure.

As the pursued and the pursuer raced madly toward the distant forest the battle behind them raged with bloody savageness. No quarter was asked or given by either the ferocious Abyssinians or the murderous cut-throats of Achmet Zek.

From the concealment of the shrubbery Tarzan watched the sanguinary conflict which so effectually surrounded him that he found no loop-hole through which he might escape to follow Werper and the Arab chief.

The Abyssinians were formed in a circle which included Tarzan's position, and around and into them galloped the yelling raiders, now darting away, now charging in to deliver thrusts and cuts with their curved swords.

Numerically the men of Achmet Zek were superior, and slowly but surely the soldiers of Menelek were being exterminated. To Tarzan the result was immaterial. He watched with but a single purpose — to escape the ring of blood-mad fighters and be away after the Belgian and his pouch.

When he had first discovered Werper upon the trail where he had slain Bara, he had thought that his eyes must be playing him false, so certain had he been that the thief had been slain and devoured by Numa; but after following the detachment for two days, with his keen eyes always upon the Belgian, he no longer doubted the identity of the man, though he was put to it to explain the identity of the mutilated corpse he had supposed was the man he sought.

As he crouched in hiding among the unkempt shrubbery which so short a while since had been the delight and pride of the wife he no longer recalled, an Arab and an Abyssinian wheeled their mounts close to his position as they slashed at each other with their swords.

Step by step the Arab beat back his adversary until the latter's horse all but trod upon the ape-man, and then a vicious cut clove the black warrior's skull, and the corpse toppled backward almost upon Tarzan.

As the Abyssinian tumbled from his saddle the possibility of escape which was represented by the riderless horse electrified the ape-man to instant action. Before the frightened beast could gather himself for flight a naked giant was astride his back. A strong hand had grasped his bridle rein, and the surprised Arab discovered a new foe in the saddle of him, whom he had slain.

But this enemy wielded no sword, and his spear and bow remained upon his back. The Arab, recovered from his first surprise, dashed in with raised sword to annihilate this presumptuous stranger. He aimed a mighty blow at the ape-man's head, a blow which swung harmlessly through thin air as Tarzan ducked from its path, and then the Arab felt the other's horse brushing his leg, a great arm shot out and encircled his waist, and before he could recover himself he was dragged from his saddle, and forming a shield for his antagonist was borne at a mad run straight through the encircling ranks of his fellows.

Just beyond them he was tossed aside upon the ground, and the last he saw of his strange foeman the latter was galloping off across the plain in the direction of the forest at its farther edge.

For another hour the battle raged nor did it cease

until the last of the Abyssinians lay dead upon the ground, or had galloped off toward the north in flight. But a handful of men escaped, among them Abdul Mourak.

The victorious raiders collected about the pile of golden ingots which the Abyssinians had uncovered, and there awaited the return of their leader. Their exultation was slightly tempered by the glimpse they had had of the strange apparition of the naked white man galloping away upon the horse of one of their foemen and carrying a companion who was now among them expatiating upon the superhuman strength of the ape-man. None of them there but was familiar with the name and fame of Tarzan of the Apes, and the fact that they had recognized the white giant as the ferocious enemy of the wrongdoers of the jungle, added to their terror, for they had been assured that Tarzan was dead.

Naturally superstitious, they fully believed that they had seen the disembodied spirit of the dead man, and now they cast fearful glances about them in expectation of the ghost's early return to the scene of the ruin they had inflicted upon him during their recent raid upon his home, and discussed in affrighted whispers the probable nature of the vengeance which the spirit would inflict upon them should he return to find them in possession of his gold.

As they conversed their terror grew, while from the concealment of the reeds along the river below them a small party of naked, black warriors watched their every move. From the heights beyond the river these black men had heard the noise of the conflict, and creeping warily down to the stream had forded it and advanced through the reeds until they were in a position to watch every move of the combatants.

For a half hour the raiders awaited Achmet Zek's return, their fear of the earlier return of the ghost of

Tarzan constantly undermining their loyalty to and fear of their chief. Finally one among them voiced the desires of all when he announced that he intended riding forth toward the forest in search of Achmet Zek. Instantly every man of them sprang to his mount.

"The gold will be safe here," cried one. "We have killed the Abyssinians and there are no others to carry it away. Let us ride in search of Achmet Zek!"

And a moment later, amidst a cloud of dust, the raiders were galloping madly across the plain, and out from the concealment of the reeds along the river, crept a party of black warriors toward the spot where the golden ingots of Opar lay piled on the ground.

Werper had still been in advance of Achmet Zek when he reached the forest; but the latter, better mounted, was gaining upon him. Riding with the reckless courage of desperation the Belgian urged his mount to greater speed even within the narrow confines of the winding, game trail that the beast was following.

Behind him he could hear the voice of Achmet Zek crying to him to halt; but Werper only dug the spurs deeper into the bleeding sides of his panting mount. Two hundred yards within the forest a broken branch lay across the trail. It was a small thing that a horse might ordinarily take in his natural stride without noticing its presence; but Werper's horse was jaded, his feet were heavy with weariness, and as the branch caught between his front legs he stumbled, was unable to recover himself, and went down, sprawling in the trail.

Werper, going over his head, rolled a few yards farther on, scrambled to his feet and ran back. Seizing the reins he tugged to drag the beast to his feet; but the animal would not or could not rise, and as the Belgian cursed and struck at him, Achmet Zek appeared in view.

Instantly the Belgian ceased his efforts with the dying animal at his feet, and seizing his rifle, dropped behind the horse and fired at the oncoming Arab.

His bullet, going low, struck Achmet Zek's horse in the breast, bringing him down a hundred yards from where Werper lay preparing to fire a second shot.

The Arab, who had gone down with his mount, was standing astride him, and seeing the Belgian's strategic position behind his fallen horse, lost no time in taking up a similar one behind his own.

And there the two lay, alternately firing at and cursing each other, while from behind the Arab, Tarzan of the Apes approached to the edge of the forest. Here he heard the occasional shots of the duelists, and choosing the safer and swifter avenue of the forest branches to the uncertain transportation afforded by a half-broken Abyssinian pony, took to the trees.

Keeping to one side of the trail, the ape-man came presently to a point where he could look down in comparative safety upon the fighters. First one and then the other would partially raise himself above his breastwork of horseflesh, fire his weapon and immediately drop flat behind his shelter, where he would reload and repeat the act a moment later.

Werper had but little ammunition, having been hastily armed by Abdul Mourak from the body of one of the first of the Abyssinians who had fallen in the fight about the pile of ingots, and now he realized that soon he would have used his last bullet, and be at the mercy of the Arab — a mercy with which he was well acquainted.

Facing both death and despoilment of his treasure, the Belgian cast about for some plan of escape, and the only one that appealed to him as containing even a remote possibility of success hinged upon the chance of bribing Achmet Zek.

Werper had fired all but a single cartridge, when,

during a lull in the fighting, he called aloud to his opponent.

"Achmet Zek," he cried, "Allah alone knows which one of us may leave our bones to rot where he lies upon this trail today if we keep up our foolish battle. You wish the contents of the pouch I wear about my waist, and I wish my life and my liberty even more than I do the jewels. Let us each, then, take that which he most desires and go our separate ways in peace. I will lay the pouch upon the carcass of my horse, where you may see it, and you, in turn, will lay your gun upon your horse, with butt toward me. Then I will go away, leaving the pouch to you, and you will let me go in safety. I want only my life, and my freedom."

The Arab thought in silence for a moment. Then he spoke. His reply was influenced by the fact that he had expended his last shot.

"Go your way, then," he growled, "leaving the pouch in plain sight behind you. See, I lay my gun thus, with the butt toward you. Go."

Werper removed the pouch from about his waist. Sorrowfully and affectionately he let his fingers press the hard outlines of the contents. Ah, if he could extract a little handful of the precious stones! But Achmet Zek was standing now, his eagle eyes commanding a plain view of the Belgian and his every act.

Regretfully Werper laid the pouch, its contents undisturbed, upon the body of his horse, rose, and taking his rifle with him, backed slowly down the trail until a turn hid him from the view of the watchful Arab.

Even then Achmet Zek did not advance, fearful as he was of some such treachery as he himself might have been guilty of under like circumstances; nor were his suspicions groundless, for the Belgian, no sooner had he passed out of the range of the Arab's vision, halted behind the bole of a tree, where he still commanded an unobstructed view of his dead horse and the pouch, and raising his rifle covered the spot where the other's body must appear when he came forward to seize the treasure.

But Achmet Zek was no fool to expose himself to the blackened honor of a thief and a murderer. Taking his long gun with him, he left the trail, entering the rank and tangled vegetation which walled it, and crawling slowly forward on hands and knees he paralleled the trail; but never for an instant was his body exposed to the rifle of the hidden assassin.

Thus Achmet Zek advanced until he had come opposite the dead horse of his enemy. The pouch lay there in full view, while a short distance along the trail, Werper waited in growing impatience and nervousness, wondering why the Arab did not come to claim his reward.

Presently he saw the muzzle of a rifle appear suddenly and mysteriously a few inches above the pouch, and before he could realize the cunning trick that the Arab had played upon him the sight of the weapon was adroitly hooked into the rawhide thong which formed the carrying strap of the pouch, and the latter was drawn quickly from his view into the dense foliage at the trail's side.

Not for an instant had the raider exposed a square inch of his body, and Werper dared not fire his one remaining shot unless every chance of a successful hit was in his favor.

Chuckling to himself, Achmet Zek withdrew a few paces farther into the jungle, for he was as positive that Werper was waiting nearby for a chance to pot him as though his eyes had penetrated the jungle trees to the figure of the hiding Belgian, fingering his rifle behind the bole of the buttressed giant.

Werper did not dare advance — his cupidity would not permit him to depart, and so he stood there, his rifle ready in his hands, his eyes watching the trail before him with cat-like intensity.

But there was another who had seen the pouch and recognized it, who did advance with Achmet Zek, hovering above him, as silent and as sure as death itself, and as the Arab, finding a little spot less overgrown with bushes than he had yet encountered, prepared to gloat his eyes upon the contents of the pouch, Tarzan paused directly above him, intent upon the same object.

Wetting his thin lips with his tongue, Achmet Zek loosened the tie strings which closed the mouth of the pouch, and cupping one claw-like hand poured forth a portion of the contents into his palm.

A single look he took at the stones lying in his hand. His eyes narrowed, a curse broke from his lips, and he hurled the small objects upon the ground, disdainfully. Quickly he emptied the balance of the contents until he had scanned each separate stone, and as he dumped them all upon the ground and stamped upon them his rage grew until the muscles of his face worked in demon-like fury, and his fingers clenched until his nails bit into the flesh.

Above, Tarzan watched in wonderment. He had been curious to discover what all the powwow about his pouch had meant. He wanted to see what the Arab would do after the other had gone away, leaving the pouch behind him, and, having satisfied his curiosity, he would then have pounced upon Achmet Zek and taken the pouch and his pretty pebbles away from him, for did they not belong to Tarzan?

He saw the Arab now throw aside the empty pouch, and grasping his long gun by the barrel, clublike, sneak stealthily through the jungle beside the trail along which Werper had gone.

As the man disappeared from his view, Tarzan dropped to the ground and commenced gathering up the spilled contents of the pouch, and the moment that he obtained his first near view of the scattered pebbles he understood the rage of the Arab, for instead of the glittering and scintillating gems which had first caught and held the attention of the ape-man, the pouch now contained but a collection of ordinary river pebbles.

Chapter XIX

JANE CLAYTON AND THE BEASTS OF THE JUNGLE

MUGAMBI, AFTER HIS successful break for liberty, had fallen upon hard times. His way had led him through a country with which he was unfamiliar, a jungle country in which he could find no water, and but little food, so that after several days of wandering he found himself so reduced in strength that he could barely drag himself along.

It was with growing difficulty that he found the strength necessary to construct a shelter by night wherein he might be reasonably safe from the large carnivora, and by day he still further exhausted his strength in digging for edible roots, and searching for water.

A few stagnant pools at considerable distances apart saved him from death by thirst; but his was a pitiable state when finally he stumbled by accident upon a large river in a country where fruit was abundant, and small game which he might bag by means of a combination of stealth, cunning, and a crude knob-stick which he had fashioned from a fallen limb.

Realizing that he still had a long march ahead of him before he could reach even the outskirts of the Waziri country, Mugambi wisely decided to remain where he was until he had recuperated his strength and health. A few days' rest would accomplish wonders for him, he knew, and he could ill afford to sacrifice his chances for a safe return by setting forth handicapped by weakness.

And so it was that he constructed a substantial thorn boma, and rigged a thatched shelter within it, where he might sleep by night in security, and from which he sallied forth by day to hunt the flesh which alone could return to his giant thews their normal prowess.

One day, as he hunted, a pair of savage eyes discovered him from the concealment of the branches of a great tree beneath which the black warrior passed. Bloodshot, wicked eyes they were, set in a fierce and hairy face.

They watched Mugambi make his little kill of a small rodent, and they followed him as he returned to his hut, their owner moving quietly through the trees upon the trail of the Negro.

The creature was Chulk, and he looked down upon the unconscious man more in curiosity than in hate. The wearing of the Arab burnoose which Tarzan had placed upon his person had aroused in the mind of the anthropoid a desire for similar mimicry of the Tarmangani. The burnoose, though, had obstructed his movements and proven such a nuisance that the ape had long since torn it from him and thrown it away.

Now, however, he saw a Gomangani arrayed in less cumbersome apparel — a loin cloth, a few copper ornaments and a feather headdress. These were more in line with Chulk's desires than a flowing robe which was constantly getting between one's legs, and catching upon every limb and bush along the leafy trail.

Chulk eyed the pouch, which, suspended over Mugambi's shoulder, swung beside his black hip. This took his fancy, for it was ornamented with feathers and a fringe, and so the ape hung about Mugambi's boma, waiting an opportunity to seize either by stealth or might some object of the black's apparel.

Nor was it long before the opportunity came. Feeling safe within his thorny enclosure, Mugambi was wont to stretch himself in the shade of his shelter during the heat of the day, and sleep in peaceful security until the declining sun carried with it the enervating temperature of midday.

Watching from above, Chulk saw the black warrior stretched thus in the unconsciousness of sleep one sultry afternoon. Creeping out upon an overhanging branch the anthropoid dropped to the ground within the boma. He approached the sleeper upon padded feet which gave forth no sound, and with an uncanny woodcraft that rustled not a leaf or a grass blade.

Pausing beside the man, the ape bent over and examined his belongings. Great as was the strength of Chulk there lay in the back of his little brain a something which deterred him from arousing the man to combat — a sense that is inherent in all the lower orders, a strange fear of man, that rules even the most powerful of the jungle creatures at times.

To remove Mugambi's loin cloth without awakening him would be impossible, and the only detachable things were the knob-stick and the pouch, which had fallen from the black's shoulder as he rolled in sleep.

Seizing these two articles, as better than nothing at all, Chulk retreated with haste, and every indication of nervous terror, to the safety of the tree from which he had dropped, and, still haunted by that indefinable terror which the close proximity of man awakened in his breast, fled precipitately through the jungle.

Aroused by attack, or supported by the presence of another of his kind, Chulk could have braved the presence of a score of human beings, but alone — ah, that was a different matter — alone, and unenraged.

It was some time after Mugambi awoke that he missed the pouch. Instantly he was all excitement. What could have become of it? It had been at his side when he lay down to sleep — of that he was certain, for had he not pushed it from beneath him when its bulging bulk, pressing against his ribs, caused him discomfort? Yes, it had been there when he lay down to sleep. How then had it vanished?

Mugambi's savage imagination was filled with visions of the spirits of departed friends and enemies, for only to the machinations of such as these could he attribute the disappearance of his pouch and knobstick in the first excitement of the discovery of their loss; but later and more careful investigation, such as his woodcraft made possible, revealed indisputable evidence of a more material explanation than his excited fancy and superstition had at first led him to accept.

In the trampled turf beside him was the faint impress of huge, manlike feet. Mugambi raised his brows as the truth dawned upon him. Hastily leaving the boma he searched in all directions about the enclosure for some farther sign of the tell-tale spoor. He climbed trees and sought for evidence of the direction of the thief's flight; but the faint signs left by a wary ape who elects to travel through the trees eluded the woodcraft of Mugambi. Tarzan might have followed them; but no ordinary mortal could perceive them, or perceiving, translate.

The black, now strengthened and refreshed by his rest, felt ready to set out again for Waziri, and finding himself another knob-stick, turned his back upon the river and plunged into the mazes of the jungle.

As Taglat struggled with the bonds which secured the

ankles and wrists of his captive, the great lion that eyed
the two from behind a nearby clump of bushes wormed
closer to his intended prey.

The ape's back was toward the lion. He did not see
the broad head, fringed by its rough mane, protruding
through the leafy wall. He could not know that the
powerful hind paws were gathering close beneath the
tawny belly preparatory to a sudden spring, and his
first intimation of impending danger was the thunderous and triumphant roar which the charging lion
could no longer suppress.

Scarce pausing for a backward glance, Taglat abandoned the unconscious woman and fled in the opposite direction from the horrid sound which had broken
in so unexpected and terrifying a manner upon his
startled ears; but the warning had come too late to save
him, and the lion, in his second bound, alighted full
upon the broad shoulders of the anthropoid.

As the great bull went down there was awakened in
him to the full all the cunning, all the ferocity, all the
physical prowess which obey the mightiest of the fundamental laws of nature, the law of self-preservation,
and turning upon his back he closed with the carnivore
in a death struggle so fearless and abandoned, that for
a moment the great Numa himself may have trembled
for the outcome.

Seizing the lion by the mane, Taglat buried his
yellowed fangs deep in the monster's throat, growling
hideously through the muffled gag of blood and hair.
Mixed with the ape's voice the lion's roars of rage and
pain reverberated through the jungle, till the lesser
creatures of the wild, startled from their peaceful pur-
suits, scurried fearfully away.

Rolling over and over upon the turf the two battled
with demoniac fury, until the colossal cat, by doubling
his hind paws far up beneath his belly sank his talons
deep into Taglat's chest, then, ripping downward with

all his strength, Numa accomplished his design, and the disemboweled anthropoid, with a last spasmodic struggle, relaxed in limp and bloody dissolution beneath his titanic adversary.

Scrambling to his feet, Numa looked about quickly in all directions, as though seeking to detect the possible presence of other foes; but only the still and unconscious form of the girl, lying a few paces from him met his gaze, and with an angry growl he placed a forepaw upon the body of his kill and raising his head gave voice to his savage victory cry.

For another moment he stood with fierce eyes roving to and fro about the clearing. At last they halted for a second time upon the girl. A low growl rumbled from the lion's throat. His lower jaw rose and fell, and the slaver drooled and dripped upon the dead face of Taglat.

Like two yellow-green augurs, wide and unblinking, the terrible eyes remained fixed upon Jane Clayton. The erect and majestic pose of the great frame shrank suddenly into a sinister crouch as, slowly and gently as one who treads on eggs, the devil-faced cat crept forward toward the girl.

Beneficent Fate maintained her in happy unconsciousness of the dread presence sneaking stealthily upon her. She did not know when the lion paused at her side. She did not hear the sniffing of his nostrils as he smelled about her. She did not feel the heat of the fetid breath upon her face, nor the dripping of the saliva from the frightful jaws half opened so close above her.

Finally the lion lifted a forepaw and turned the body of the girl half over, then he stood again eyeing her as though still undetermined whether life was extinct or not. Some noise or odor from the nearby jungle attracted his attention for a moment. His eyes did not again return to Jane Clayton, and presently he left her, walked over to the remains of Taglat, and crouching down upon his kill with his back toward the girl, proceeded to devour the ape.

It was upon this scene that Jane Clayton at last opened her eyes. Inured to danger, she maintained her self-possession in the face of the startling surprise which her new-found consciousness revealed to her. She neither cried out nor moved a muscle, until she had taken in every detail of the scene which lay within the range of her vision.

She saw that the lion had killed the ape, and that he was devouring his prey less than fifty feet from where she lay; but what could she do? Her hands and feet were bound. She must wait then, in what patience she could command, until Numa had eaten and digested the ape, when, without doubt, he would return to feast upon her, unless, in the meantime, the dread hyenas should discover her, or some other of the numerous prowling carnivora of the jungle.

As she lay tormented by these frightful thoughts, she suddenly became conscious that the bonds at her wrists and ankles no longer hurt her, and then of the fact that her hands were separated, one lying upon either side of her, instead of both being confined at her back.

Wonderingly she moved a hand. What miracle had been performed? It was not bound! Stealthily and noiselessly she moved her other limbs, only to discover that she was free. She could not know how the thing had happened, that Taglat, gnawing upon them for sinister purposes of his own, had cut them through but an instant before Numa had frightened him from his victim.

For a moment Jane Clayton was overwhelmed with joy and thanksgiving; but only for a moment. What good was her new-found liberty in the face of the frightful beast crouching so close beside her? If she could have had this chance under different conditions, how happily she would have taken advantage of it; but now it was given to her when escape was practically impossible.

The nearest tree was a hundred feet away, the lion less than fifty. To rise and attempt to reach the safety of those tantalizing branches would be but to invite instant destruction, for Numa would doubtless be too jealous of this future meal to permit it to escape with ease. And yet, too, there was another possibility – a chance which hinged entirely upon the unknown temper of the great beast.

His belly already partially filled, he might watch with indifference the departure of the girl; yet could she afford to chance so improbable a contingency? She doubted it. Upon the other hand she was no more minded to allow this frail opportunity for life to entirely elude her without taking or attempting to take some advantage from it.

She watched the lion narrowly. He could not see her without turning his head more than halfway around. She would attempt a ruse. Silently she rolled over in the direction of the nearest tree, and away from the lion, until she lay again in the same position in which Numa had left her, but a few feet farther from him.

Here she lay breathless watching the lion; but the beast gave no indication that he had heard aught to arouse his suspicions. Again she rolled over, gaining a few more feet and again she lay in rigid contemplation of the beast's back.

During what seemed hours to her tense nerves, Jane Clayton continued these tactics, and still the lion fed on in apparent unconsciousness that his second prey was escaping him. Already the girl was but a few paces from the tree – a moment more and she would be close enough to chance springing to her feet, throwing caution aside and making a sudden, bold dash for safety. She was halfway over in her turn, her face away from the lion, when he suddenly turned his great head and fastened his eyes upon her. He saw her roll over upon her side away from him, and then her eyes were turned again toward him, and the cold sweat broke from the girl's every pore as she realized that with life almost within her grasp, death had found her out.

For a long time neither the girl nor the lion moved. The beast lay motionless, his head turned upon his shoulders and his glaring eyes fixed upon the rigid victim, now nearly fifty yards away. The girl stared back straight into those cruel orbs, daring not to move even a muscle.

The strain upon her nerves was becoming so unbearable that she could scarcely restrain a growing desire to scream, when Numa deliberately turned back to the business of feeding; but his back-layed ears attested a sinister regard for the actions of the girl behind him.

Realizing that she could not again turn without attracting his immediate and perhaps fatal attention, Jane Clayton resolved to risk all in one last attempt to reach the tree and clamber to the lower branches.

Gathering herself stealthily for the effort, she leaped suddenly to her feet, but almost simultaneously the lion sprang up, wheeled and with wide-distended jaws and terrific roars, charged swiftly down upon her.

Those who have spent lifetimes hunting the big game of Africa will tell you that scarcely any other creature in the world attains the speed of a charging lion. For the short distance that the great cat can maintain it, it resembles nothing more closely than the onrushing of a giant locomotive under full speed, and so, though the distance that Jane Clayton must cover was relatively small, the terrific speed of the lion rendered her hopes of escape almost negligible.

Yet fear can work wonders, and though the upward spring of the lion as he neared the tree into which she was scrambling brought his talons in contact with her boots she eluded his raking grasp, and as he hurtled against the bole of her sanctuary, the girl drew herself into the safety of the branches above his reach.

For some time the lion paced, growling and moaning, beneath the tree in which Jane Clayton crouched, panting and trembling. The girl was a prey to the nervous reaction from the frightful ordeal through which she had so recently passed, and in her overwrought state it seemed that never again should she dare descend to the ground among the fearsome dangers which infested the broad stretch of jungle that she knew must lie between herself and the nearest village of her faithful Waziri.

It was almost dark before the lion finally quit the clearing, and even had his place beside the remnants of the mangled ape not been immediately usurped by a pack of hyenas, Jane Clayton would scarcely have dared venture from her refuge in the face of impending night, and so she composed herself as best she could for the long and tiresome wait, until daylight might offer some means of escape from the dread vicinity in which she had witnessed such terrifying adventures.

Tired nature at last overcame even her fears, and she dropped into a deep slumber, cradled in a comparatively safe, though rather uncomfortable, position against the bole of the tree, and supported by two large branches which grew outward, almost horizontally, but a few inches apart.

The sun was high in the heavens when she at last awoke, and beneath her was no sign either of Numa or the hyenas. Only the clean-picked bones of the ape, scattered about the ground, attested the fact of what had transpired in this seemingly peaceful spot but a few hours before.

Both hunger and thirst assailed her now, and realizing that she must descend or die of starvation, she at last summoned courage to undertake the ordeal of continuing her journey through the jungle.

Descending from the tree, she set out in a southerly direction, toward the point where she believed the plains of Waziri lay, and though she knew that only ruin and desolation marked the spot where once her happy home had stood, she hoped that by coming to the broad plain she might eventually reach one of the numerous Waziri villages that were scattered over the surrounding country, or chance upon a roving band of these indefatigable huntsmen.

The day was half spent when there broke unexpectedly upon her startled ears the sound of a rifle shot not far ahead of her. As she paused to listen, this first shot was followed by another and another and another. What could it mean? The first explanation which sprung to her mind attributed the firing to an encounter between the Arab raiders and a party of Waziri; but as she did not know upon which side victory might rest, or whether she were behind friend or foe, she dared not advance nearer on the chance of revealing herself to an enemy.

After listening for several minutes she became convinced that no more than two or three rifles were engaged in the fight, since nothing approximating the sound of a volley reached her ears; but still she hesitated to approach, and at last, determining to take no chance, she climbed into the concealing foliage of a tree beside the trail she had been following and there fearfully awaited whatever might reveal itself.

As the firing became less rapid she caught the sound of men's voices, though she could distinguish no words, and at last the reports of the guns ceased, and she heard two men calling to each other in loud tones. Then there was a long silence which was finally broken by the stealthy padding of footfalls on the trail ahead of her, and in another moment a man appeared in view backing toward her, a rifle ready in his hands, and his eyes directed in careful watchfulness along the way that he had come.

Almost instantly Jane Clayton recognized the man as M. Jules Frecoult, who so recently had been a guest in her home. She was upon the point of calling to him in glad relief when she saw him leap quickly to one side and hide himself in the thick verdure at the trail's side. It was evident that he was being followed by an enemy, and so Jane Clayton kept silent, lest she distract Frecoult's attention, or guide his foe to his hiding place.

Scarcely had Frecoult hidden himself than the figure of a white-robed Arab crept silently along the trail in pursuit. From her hiding place, Jane Clayton could see both men plainly. She recognized Achmet Zek as the leader of the band of ruffians who had raided her home and made her a prisoner, and as she saw Frecoult, the supposed friend and ally, raise his gun and take careful aim at the Arab, her heart stood still and every power of her soul was directed upon a fervent prayer for the accuracy of his aim.

Achmet Zek paused in the middle of the trail. His keen eyes scanned every bush and tree within the radius of his vision. His tall figure presented a perfect target to the perfidious assassin. There was a sharp report, and a little puff of smoke arose from the bush that hid the Belgian, as Achmet Zek stumbled forward and pitched, face down, upon the trail.

As Werper stepped back into the trail, he was startled by the sound of a glad cry from above him, and as he wheeled about to discover the author of this unexpected interruption, he saw Jane Clayton drop lightly from a nearby tree and run forward with outstretched hands to congratulate him upon his victory.

Chapter XX

JANE CLAYTON
AGAIN A PRISONER

*T*HOUGH HER CLOTHES were torn and her hair disheveled, Albert Werper realized that he never before had looked upon such a vision of loveliness as that which Lady Greystoke presented in the relief and joy which she felt in coming so unexpectedly upon a friend and rescuer when hope had seemed so far away.

If the Belgian had entertained any doubts as to the woman's knowledge of his part in the perfidious attack upon her home and herself, it was quickly dissipated by the genuine friendliness of her greeting. She told him quickly of all that had befallen her since he had departed from her home, and as she spoke of the death of her husband her eyes were veiled by the tears which she could not repress.

"I am shocked," said Werper, in well-simulated sympathy; "but I am not surprised. That devil there," and he pointed toward the body of Achmet Zek, "has terrorized the entire country. Your Waziri are either exterminated, or have been driven out of their country, far to the south. The men of Achmet Zek occupy the plain about your former home — there is neither sanctuary nor escape in that direction. Our only hope lies in traveling northward as rapidly as we may, of coming to the camp of the raiders before the knowledge of Achmet Zek's death reaches those who were left there, and of obtaining, through some ruse, an escort toward the north.

"I think that the thing can be accomplished, for I was a guest of the raider's before I knew the nature of the man, and those at the camp are not aware that I turned against him when I discovered his villainy.

"Come! We will make all possible haste to reach the camp before those who accompanied Achmet Zek upon his last raid have found his body and carried the news of his death to the cut-throats who remained behind. It is our only hope, Lady Greystoke, and you must place your entire faith in me if I am to succeed. Wait for me here a moment while I take from the Arab's body the wallet that he stole from me," and Werper stepped quickly to the dead man's side, and, kneeling, sought with quick fingers the pouch of jewels. To his consternation, there was no sign of them in the garments of Achmet Zek. Rising, he walked back along the trail, searching for some trace of the missing pouch or its contents; but he found nothing, even though he searched carefully the vicinity of his dead horse, and for a few paces into the jungle on either side. Puzzled, disappointed and angry, he at last returned to the girl. "The wallet is gone," he explained, crisply, "and I dare not delay longer in search of it. We must reach the camp before the returning raiders."

Unsuspicious of the man's true character, Jane Clayton saw nothing peculiar in his plans, or in his specious explanation of his former friendship for the raider, and so she grasped with alacrity the seeming hope for safety which he proffered her, and turning about she set out with Albert Werper toward the hostile camp in which she so lately had been a prisoner.

It was late in the afternoon of the second day before they reached their destination, and as they paused upon the edge of the clearing before the gates of the walled village, Werper cautioned the girl to accede to whatever he might suggest by his conversation with the raiders.

"I shall tell them," he said, "that I apprehended you after you escaped from the camp, that I took you to Achmet Zek, and that as he was engaged in a stubborn battle with the Waziri, he directed me to return to camp with you, to obtain here a sufficient guard, and to ride north with you as rapidly as possible and dispose of you at the most advantageous terms to a certain slave broker whose name he gave me."

Again the girl was deceived by the apparent frankness of the Belgian. She realized that desperate situations required desperate handling, and though she trembled inwardly at the thought of again entering the vile and hideous village of the raiders she saw no better course than that which her companion had suggested.

Calling aloud to those who tended the gates, Werper, grasping Jane Clayton by the arm, walked boldly across the clearing. Those who opened the gates to him permitted their surprise to show clearly in their expressions. That the discredited and hunted lieutenant should be thus returning fearlessly of his own volition, seemed to disarm them quite as effectually as his manner toward Lady Greystoke had deceived her.

The sentries at the gate returned Werper's salutations, and viewed with astonishment the prisoner whom he brought into the village with him.

Immediately the Belgian sought the Arab who had been left in charge of the camp during Achmet Zek's absence, and again his boldness disarmed suspicion and won the acceptance of his false explanation of his return. The fact that he had brought back with him the woman prisoner who had escaped, added strength to his claims, and Mohammed Beyd soon found himself fraternizing good-naturedly with the very man whom he would have slain without compunction had he discovered him alone in the jungle a half hour before.

Jane Clayton was again confined to the prison hut she had formerly occupied, but as she realized that this was but a part of the deception which she and Frecoult were playing upon the credulous raiders, it was with quite a different sensation that she again entered the vile and filthy interior, from that which she had previously experienced, when hope was so far away.

Once more she was bound and sentries placed before the door of her prison; but before Werper left her he whispered words of cheer into her ear. Then he left, and made his way back to the tent of Mohammed Beyd. He had been wondering how long it would be before the raiders who had ridden out with Achmet Zek would return with the murdered body of their chief, and the more he thought upon the matter the greater his fears became, that without accomplices his plan would fail.

What, even, if he got away from the camp in safety before any returned with the true story of his guilt — of what value would this advantage be other than to protract for a few days his mental torture and his life? These hard riders, familiar with every trail and bypath, would get him long before he could hope to reach the coast.

As these thoughts passed through his mind he entered the tent where Mohammed Beyd sat cross-legged upon a rug, smoking. The Arab looked up as the European came into his presence.

"Greetings, O Brother!" he said.

"Greetings!" replied Werper.

For a while neither spoke further. The Arab was the first to break the silence.

"And my master, Achmet Zek, was well when last you saw him?" he asked.

"Never was he safer from the sins and dangers of mortality," replied the Belgian.

"It is well," said Mohammed Beyd, blowing a little puff of blue smoke straight out before him.

Again there was silence for several minutes.

"And if he were dead?" asked the Belgian, determined to lead up to the truth, and attempt to bribe Mohammed Beyd into his service.

The Arab's eyes narrowed and he leaned forward, his gaze boring straight into the eyes of the Belgian.

"I have been thinking much, Werper, since you returned so unexpectedly to the camp of the man whom you had deceived, and who sought you with death in his heart. I have been with Achmet Zek for many years — his own mother never knew him so well as I. He never forgives — much less would he again trust a man who had once betrayed him; that I know.

"I have thought much, as I said, and the result of my thinking has assured me that Achmet Zek is dead — for otherwise you would never have dared return to his camp, unless you be either a braver man or a bigger fool than I have imagined. And, if this evidence of my judgment is not sufficient, I have but just now received from your own lips even more confirmatory witness — for did you not say that Achmet Zek was never more safe from the sins and dangers of mortality?

"Achmet Zek is dead — you need not deny it. I was not his mother, or his mistress, so do not fear that my wailings shall disturb you. Tell me why you have come back here. Tell me what you want, and, Werper, if you still possess the jewels of which Achmet Zek told me, there is no reason why you and I should not ride north together and divide the ransom of the white woman and the contents of the pouch you wear about your person. Eh?"

The evil eyes narrowed, a vicious, thin-lipped smile tortured the villainous face, as Mohammed Beyd grinned knowingly into the face of the Belgian.

Werper was both relieved and disturbed by the Arab's attitude. The complacency with which he accepted the death of his chief lifted a considerable burden of apprehension from the shoulders of Achmet Zek's assassin; but his demand for a share of the jewels boded ill for Werper when Mohammed Beyd should have learned that the precious stones were no longer in the Belgian's possession.

To acknowledge that he had lost the jewels might be to arouse the wrath or suspicion of the Arab to such an extent as would jeopardize his new-found chances of escape. His one hope seemed, then, to lie in fostering Mohammed Beyd's belief that the jewels were still in his possession, and depend upon the accidents of the future to open an avenue of escape.

Could he contrive to tent with the Arab upon the march north, he might find opportunity in plenty to remove this menace to his life and liberty — it was worth trying, and, further, there seemed no other way out of his difficulty.

"Yes," he said, "Achmet Zek is dead. He fell in battle with a company of Abyssinian cavalry that held me captive. During the fighting I escaped; but I doubt if any of Achmet Zek's men live, and the gold they sought is in the possession of the Abyssinians. Even now they are doubtless marching on this camp, for they were sent by Menelek to punish Achmet Zek and his followers for a raid upon an Abyssinian village. There are many of them, and if we do not make haste to escape we shall all suffer the same fate as Achmet Zek."

Mohammed Beyd listened in silence. How much of the unbeliever's story he might safely believe he did not know; but as it afforded him an excuse for deserting the village and making for the north he was not inclined to cross-question the Belgian too minutely.

"And if I ride north with you," he asked, "half the jewels and half the ransom of the woman shall be mine?"

"Yes," replied Werper.

"Good," said Mohammed Beyd. "I go now to give the order for the breaking of camp early on the morrow," and he rose to leave the tent.

Werper laid a detaining hand upon his arm.

"Wait," he said, "let us determine how many shall accompany us. It is not well that we be burdened by the women and children, for then indeed we might be overtaken by the Abyssinians. It would be far better to select a small guard of your bravest men, and leave word behind that we are riding *west*. Then, when the Abyssinians come they will be put upon the wrong trail should they have it in their hearts to pursue us, and if they do not they will at least ride north with less rapidity than as though they thought that we were ahead of them."

"The serpent is less wise than thou, Werper," said Mohammed Beyd with a smile. "It shall be done as you say. Twenty men shall accompany us, and we shall ride *west* — when we leave the village."

"Good," cried the Belgian, and so it was arranged.

Early the next morning Jane Clayton, after an almost sleepless night, was aroused by the sound of voices outside her prison, and a moment later, M. Frecoult, and two Arabs entered. The latter unbound her ankles and lifted her to her feet. Then her wrists were loosed, she was given a handful of dry bread, and led out into the faint light of dawn.

She looked questioningly at Frecoult, and at a moment that the Arab's attention was attracted in another direction the man leaned toward her and whispered that all was working out as he had planned. Thus assured, the young woman felt a renewal of the hope which the long and miserable night of bondage had almost expunged.

Shortly after, she was lifted to the back of a horse, and surrounded by Arabs, was escorted through the gateway of the village and off into the jungle toward the west. Half an hour later the party turned north, and northerly was their direction for the balance of the march.

M. Frecoult spoke with her but seldom, and she understood that in carrying out his deception he must maintain the semblance of her captor, rather than protector, and so she suspected nothing though she saw the friendly relations which seemed to exist between the European and the Arab leader of the band.

If Werper succeeded in keeping himself from conversation with the young woman, he failed signally to expel her from his thoughts. A hundred times a day he found his eyes wandering in her direction and feasting themselves upon her charms of face and figure. Each hour his infatuation for her grew, until his desire to possess her gained almost the proportions of madness.

If either the girl or Mohammed Beyd could have guessed what passed in the mind of the man which each thought a friend and ally, the apparent harmony of the little company would have been rudely disturbed.

Werper had not succeeded in arranging to tent with Mohammed Beyd, and so he revolved many plans for the assassination of the Arab that would have been greatly simplified had he been permitted to share the other's nightly shelter.

Upon the second day out Mohammed Beyd reined his horse to the side of the animal on which the captive was mounted. It was, apparently, the first notice which the Arab had taken of the girl; but many times during these two days had his cunning eyes peered greedily from beneath the hood of his burnoose to gloat upon the beauties of the prisoner.

Nor was this hidden infatuation of any recent origin. He had conceived it when first the wife of the Englishman had fallen into the hands of Achmet Zek; but while that austere chieftain lived, Mohammed Beyd had not even dared hope for a realization of his imaginings.

Now, though, it was different — only a despised dog of a Christian stood between himself and possession of the girl. How easy it would be to slay the unbeliever, and take unto himself both the woman and the jewels! With the latter in his possession, the ransom which might be obtained for the captive would form no great inducement to her relinquishment in the face of the pleasures of sole ownership of her. Yes, he would kill Werper, retain all the jewels and keep the Englishwoman.

He turned his eyes upon her as she rode along at his side. How beautiful she was! His fingers opened and closed — skinny, brown talons itching to feel the soft flesh of the victim in their remorseless clutch.

"Do you know," he asked leaning toward her, "where this man would take you?"

Jane Clayton nodded affirmatively.

"And you are willing to become the plaything of a black sultan?"

The girl drew herself up to her full height, and turned her head away; but she did not reply. She feared lest her knowledge of the ruse that M. Frecoult was playing upon the Arab might cause her to betray herself through an insufficient display of terror and aversion.

"You can escape this fate," continued the Arab; "Mohammed Beyd will save you," and he reached out a

brown hand and seized the fingers of her right hand
in a grasp so sudden and so fierce that this brutal
passion was revealed as clearly in the act as though his
lips had confessed it in words. Jane Clayton wrenched
herself from his grasp.

"You beast!" she cried. "Leave me or I shall call M.
Frecoult."

Mohammed Beyd drew back with a scowl. His thin,
upper lip curled upward, revealing his smooth, white
teeth.

"M. Frecoult?" he jeered. "There is no such person.
The man's name is Werper. He is a liar, a thief, and a
murderer. He killed his captain in the Congo country
and fled to the protection of Achmet Zek. He led
Achmet Zek to the plunder of your home. He followed
your husband, and planned to steal his gold from him.
He has told me that you think him your protector, and
he has played upon this to win your confidence that
it might be easier to carry you north and sell you into
some black sultan's harem. Mohammed Beyd is your
only hope," and with this assertion to provide the
captive with food for thought, the Arab spurred forward toward the head of the column.

Jane Clayton could not know how much of Mohammed Beyd's indictment might be true, or how much
false; but at least it had the effect of dampening her
hopes and causing her to review with suspicion every
past act of the man upon whom she had been looking
as her sole protector in the midst of a world of enemies
and dangers.

On the march a separate tent had been provided for
the captive, and at night it was pitched between those
of Mohammed Beyd and Werper. A sentry was posted
at the front and another at the back, and with these
precautions it had not been thought necessary to con-
fine the prisoner to bonds. The evening following her
interview with Mohammed Beyd, Jane Clayton sat for

some time at the opening of her tent watching the rough activities of the camp. She had eaten the meal that had been brought her by Mohammed Beyd's Negro slave — a meal of cassava cakes and a nondescript stew in which a new-killed monkey, a couple of squirrels and the remains of a zebra, slain the previous day, were impartially and unsavorily combined; but the one-time Baltimore belle had long since submerged in the stern battle for existence, an estheticism which formerly revolted at much slighter provocation.

As the girl's eyes wandered across the trampled jungle clearing, already squalid from the presence of man, she no longer apprehended either the nearer objects of the foreground, the uncouth men laughing or quarreling among themselves, or the jungle beyond, which circumscribed the extreme range of her material vision. Her gaze passed through all these, unseeing, to center itself upon a distant bungalow and scenes of happy security which brought to her eyes tears of mingled joy and sorrow. She saw a tall, broad-shouldered man riding in from distant fields; she saw herself waiting to greet him with an armful of fresh-cut roses from the bushes which flanked the little rustic gate before her. All this was gone, vanished into the past, wiped out by the torches and bullets and hatred of these hideous and degenerate men. With a stifled sob, and a little shudder, Jane Clayton turned back into her tent and sought the pile of unclean blankets which were her bed. Throwing herself face downward upon them she sobbed forth her misery until kindly sleep brought her, at least temporary, relief.

And while she slept a figure stole from the tent that stood to the right of hers. It approached the sentry before the doorway and whispered a few words in the man's ear. The latter nodded, and strode off through the darkness in the direction of his own blankets. The figure passed to the rear of Jane Clayton's tent and spoke again to the sentry there, and this man also left, following in the trail of the first.

Then he who had sent them away stole silently to the tent flap and untying the fastenings entered with the noiselessness of a disembodied spirit.

Chapter XXI

THE FLIGHT TO THE JUNGLE

SLEEPLESS UPON His blankets, Albert Werper let his evil mind dwell upon the charms of the woman in the nearby tent. He had noted Mohammed Beyd's sudden interest in the girl, and judging the man by his own standards, had guessed at the basis of the Arab's sudden change of attitude toward the prisoner.

And as he let his imaginings run riot they aroused within him a bestial jealousy of Mohammed Beyd, and a great fear that the other might encompass his base designs upon the defenseless girl. By a strange process of reasoning, Werper, whose designs were identical with the Arab's, pictured himself as Jane Clayton's protector, and presently convinced himself that the attentions which might seem hideous to her if proffered by Mohammed Beyd, would be welcomed from Albert Werper.

Her husband was dead, and Werper fancied that he could replace in the girl's heart the position which had been vacated by the act of the grim reaper. He could

offer Jane Clayton marriage — a thing which Mohammed Beyd would not offer, and which the girl would
spurn from him with as deep disgust as she would his
unholy lust.

It was not long before the Belgian had succeeded in
convincing himself that the captive not only had every
reason for having conceived sentiments of love for
him; but that she had by various feminine methods
acknowledged her new-born affection.

And then a sudden resolution possessed him. He
threw the blankets from him and rose to his feet.
Pulling on his boots and buckling his cartridge belt
and revolver about his hips he stepped to the flap of
his tent and looked out. There was no sentry before
the entrance to the prisoner's tent! What could it
mean? Fate was indeed playing into his hands.

Stepping outside he passed to the rear of the girl's
tent. There was no sentry there, either! And now,
boldly, he walked to the entrance and stepped within.

Dimly the moonlight illumined the interior. Across
the tent a figure bent above the blankets of a bed. There
was a whispered word, and another figure rose from
the blankets to a sitting position. Slowly Albert Werper's eyes were becoming accustomed to the half darkness of the tent. He saw that the figure leaning over
the bed was that of a man, and he guessed at the truth
of the nocturnal visitor's identity.

A sullen, jealous rage enveloped him. He took a step
in the direction of the two. He heard a frightened cry
break from the girl's lips as she recognized the features
of the man above her, and he saw Mohammed Beyd
seize her by the throat and bear her back upon the
blankets.

Cheated passion cast a red blur before the eyes of
the Belgian. No! The man should not have her. She
was for him and him alone. He would not be robbed
of his rights.

Quickly he ran across the tent and threw himself upon the back of Mohammed Beyd. The latter, though surprised by this sudden and unexpected attack, was not one to give up without a battle. The Belgian's fingers were feeling for his throat, but the Arab tore them away, and rising wheeled upon his adversary. As they faced each other Werper struck the Arab a heavy blow in the face, sending him staggering backward. If he had followed up his advantage he would have had Mohammed Beyd at his mercy in another moment; but instead he tugged at his revolver to draw it from its holster, and Fate ordained that at that particular moment the weapon should stick in its leather scabbard.

Before he could disengage it, Mohammed Beyd had recovered himself and was dashing upon him. Again Werper struck the other in the face, and the Arab returned the blow. Striking at each other and ceaselessly attempting to clinch, the two battled about the small interior of the tent, while the girl, wide-eyed in terror and astonishment, watched the duel in frozen silence.

Again and again Werper struggled to draw his weapon. Mohammed Beyd, anticipating no such opposition to his base desires, had come to the tent unarmed, except for a long knife which he now drew as he stood panting during the first brief rest of the encounter.

"Dog of a Christian," he whispered, "look upon this knife in the hands of Mohammed Beyd! Look well, unbeliever, for it is the last thing in life that you shall see or feel. With it Mohammed Beyd will cut out your black heart. If you have a God pray to him now — in a minute more you shall be dead," and with that he rushed viciously upon the Belgian, his knife raised high above his head.

Werper was still dragging futilely at his weapon. The

Arab was almost upon him. In desperation the European waited until Mohammed Beyd was all but against him, then he threw himself to one side to the floor of the tent, leaving a leg extended in the path of the Arab.

The trick succeeded. Mohammed Beyd, carried on by the momentum of his charge, stumbled over the projecting obstacle and crashed to the ground. Instantly he was up again and wheeling to renew the battle; but Werper was on foot ahead of him, and now his revolver, loosened from its holster, flashed in his hand.

The Arab dove headfirst to grapple with him, there was a sharp report, a lurid gleam of flame in the darkness, and Mohammed Beyd rolled over and over upon the floor to come to a final rest beside the bed of the woman he had sought to dishonor.

Almost immediately following the report came the sound of excited voices in the camp without. Men were calling back and forth to one another asking the meaning of the shot. Werper could hear them running hither and thither, investigating.

Jane Clayton had risen to her feet as the Arab died, and now she came forward with outstretched hands toward Werper.

"How can I ever thank you, my friend?" she asked. "And to think that only today I had almost believed the infamous story which this beast told me of your perfidy and of your past. Forgive me, M. Frecoult. I might have known that a white man and a gentleman could be naught else than the protector of a woman of his own race amid the dangers of this savage land."

Werper's hands dropped limply at his sides. He stood looking at the girl; but he could find no words to reply to her. Her innocent arraignment of his true purposes was unanswerable.

Outside, the Arabs were searching for the author of the disturbing shot. The two sentries who had been relieved and sent to their blankets by Mohammed Beyd were the first to suggest going to the tent of the prisoner. It occurred to them that possibly the woman had successfully defended herself against their leader.

Werper heard the men approaching. To be apprehended as the slayer of Mohammed Beyd would be equivalent to a sentence of immediate death. The fierce and brutal raiders would tear to pieces a Christian who had dared spill the blood of their leader. He must find some excuse to delay the finding of Mohammed Beyd's dead body.

Returning his revolver to its holster, he walked quickly to the entrance of the tent. Parting the flaps he stepped out and confronted the men, who were rapidly approaching. Somehow he found within him the necessary bravado to force a smile to his lips, as he held up his hand to bar their farther progress.

"The woman resisted," he said, "and Mohammed Beyd was forced to shoot her. She is not dead — only slightly wounded. You may go back to your blankets. Mohammed Beyd and I will look after the prisoner;" then he turned and re-entered the tent, and the raiders, satisfied by this explanation, gladly returned to their broken slumbers.

As he again faced Jane Clayton, Werper found himself animated by quite different intentions than those which had lured him from his blankets but a few minutes before. The excitement of his encounter with Mohammed Beyd, as well as the dangers which he now faced at the hands of the raiders when morning must inevitably reveal the truth of what had occurred in the tent of the prisoner that night, had naturally cooled the hot passion which had dominated him when he entered the tent.

But another and stronger force was exerting itself in the girl's favor. However low a man may sink, honor and chivalry, has he ever possessed them, are never entirely eradicated from his character, and though Albert Werper had long since ceased to evidence the slightest claim to either the one or the other, the spontaneous acknowledgment of them which the girl's speech had presumed had reawakened them both within him.

For the first time he realized the almost hopeless and frightful position of the fair captive, and the depths of ignominy to which he had sunk, that had made it possible for him, a well-born, European gentleman, to have entertained even for a moment the part that he had taken in the ruin of her home, happiness, and herself.

Too much of baseness already lay at the threshold of his conscience for him ever to hope entirely to redeem himself; but in the first, sudden burst of contrition the man conceived an honest intention to undo, in so far as lay within his power, the evil that his criminal avarice had brought upon this sweet and unoffending woman.

As he stood apparently listening to the retreating footsteps — Jane Clayton approached him.

"What are we to do now?" she asked. "Morning will bring discovery of this," and she pointed to the still body of Mohammed Beyd. "They will kill you when they find him."

For a time Werper did not reply, then he turned suddenly toward the woman.

"I have a plan," he cried. "It will require nerve and courage on your part; but you have already shown that you possess both. Can you endure still more?"

"I can endure anything," she replied with a brave smile, "that may offer us even a slight chance for escape."

"You must simulate death," he explained, "while I carry you from the camp. I will explain to the sentries that Mohammed Beyd has ordered me to take your body into the jungle. This seemingly unnecessary act I shall explain upon the grounds that Mohammed Beyd had conceived a violent passion for you and that he so regretted the act by which he had become your slayer that he could not endure the silent reproach of your lifeless body."

The girl held up her hand to stop. A smile touched her lips.

"Are you quite mad?" she asked. "Do you imagine that the sentries will credit any such ridiculous tale?"

"You do not know them," he replied. "Beneath their rough exteriors, despite their calloused and criminal natures, there exists in each a well-defined strain of romantic emotionalism — you will find it among such as these throughout the world. It is romance which lures men to lead wild lives of outlawry and crime. The ruse will succeed — never fear."

Jane Clayton shrugged. "We can but try it — and then what?"

"I shall hide you in the jungle," continued the Belgian, "coming for you alone and with two horses in the morning."

"But how will you explain Mohammed Beyd's death?" she asked. "It will be discovered before ever you can escape the camp in the morning."

"I shall not explain it," replied Werper. "Mohammed Beyd shall explain it himself — we must leave that to him. Are you ready for the venture?"

"Yes."

"But wait, I must get you a weapon and ammunition," and Werper walked quickly from the tent.

Very shortly he returned with an extra revolver and ammunition belt strapped about his waist.

"Are you ready?" he asked.

"Quite ready," replied the girl.

"Then come and throw yourself limply across my left shoulder," and Werper knelt to receive her.

"There," he said, as he rose to his feet. "Now, let your arms, your legs and your head hang limply. Remember that you are dead."

A moment later the man walked out into the camp, the body of the woman across his shoulder.

A thorn boma had been thrown up about the camp, to discourage the bolder of the hungry carnivora. A couple of sentries paced to and fro in the light of a fire which they kept burning brightly. The nearer of these looked up in surprise as he saw Werper approaching.

"Who are you?" he cried. "What have you there?"

Werper raised the hood of his burnoose that the fellow might see his face.

"This is the body of the woman," he explained. "Mohammed Beyd has asked me to take it into the jungle, for he cannot bear to look upon the face of her whom he loved, and whom necessity compelled him to slay. He suffers greatly — he is inconsolable. It was with difficulty that I prevented him taking his own life."

Across the speaker's shoulder, limp and frightened, the girl waited for the Arab's reply. He would laugh at this preposterous story; of that she was sure. In an instant he would unmask the deception that M. Frecoult was attempting to practice upon him, and they would both be lost. She tried to plan how best she might aid her would-be rescuer in the fight which must most certainly follow within a moment or two.

Then she heard the voice of the Arab as he replied to M. Frecoult.

"Are you going alone, or do you wish me to awaken someone to accompany you?" he asked, and his tone denoted not the least surprise that Mohammed Beyd had suddenly discovered such remarkably sensitive characteristics.

"I shall go alone," replied Werper, and he passed on and out through the narrow opening in the boma, by which the sentry stood.

A moment later he had entered among the boles of the trees with his burden, and when safely hidden from the sentry's view lowered the girl to her feet, with a low, "sh-sh," when she would have spoken.

Then he led her a little farther into the forest, halted beneath a large tree with spreading branches, buckled a cartridge belt and revolver about her waist, and assisted her to clamber into the lower branches.

"Tomorrow," he whispered, "as soon as I can elude them, I will return for you. Be brave, Lady Greystoke — we may yet escape."

"Thank you," she replied in a low tone. "You have been very kind, and very brave."

Werper did not reply, and the darkness of the night hid the scarlet flush of shame which swept upward across his face. Quickly he turned and made his way back to camp. The sentry, from his post, saw him enter his own tent; but he did not see him crawl under the canvas at the rear and sneak cautiously to the tent which the prisoner had occupied, where now lay the dead body of Mohammed Beyd.

Raising the lower edge of the rear wall, Werper crept within and approached the corpse. Without an instant's hesitation he seized the dead wrists and dragged the body upon its back to the point where he had just entered. On hands and knees he backed out as he had come in, drawing the corpse after him. Once outside the Belgian crept to the side of the tent and surveyed as much of the camp as lay within his vision — no one was watching.

Returning to the body, he lifted it to his shoulder, and risking all on a quick sally, ran swiftly across the narrow opening which separated the prisoner's tent from that of the dead man. Behind the silken wall he halted and lowered his burden to the ground, and there he remained motionless for several minutes, listening.

Satisfied, at last, that no one had seen him, he stooped and raised the bottom of the tent wall, backed in and dragged the thing that had been Mohammed Beyd after him. To the sleeping rugs of the dead raider he drew the corpse, then he fumbled about in the darkness until he had found Mohammed Beyd's revolver. With the weapon in his hand he returned to the side of the dead man, kneeled beside the bedding, and inserted his right hand with the weapon beneath the rugs, piled a number of thicknesses of the closely woven fabric over and about the revolver with his left hand. Then he pulled the trigger, and at the same time he coughed.

The muffled report could not have been heard above the sound of his cough by one directly outside the tent. Werper was satisfied. A grim smile touched his lips as he withdrew the weapon from the rugs and placed it carefully in the right hand of the dead man, fixing three of the fingers around the grip and the index finger inside the trigger guard.

A moment longer he tarried to rearrange the disordered rugs, and then he left as he had entered, fastening down the rear wall of the tent as it had been before he had raised it.

Going to the tent of the prisoner he removed there also the evidence that someone might have come or gone beneath the rear wall. Then he returned to his own tent, entered, fastened down the canvas, and crawled into his blankets.

The following morning he was awakened by the excited voice of Mohammed Beyd's slave calling to him at the entrance of his tent.

"Quick! Quick!" cried the black in a frightened tone. "Come! Mohammed Beyd is dead in his tent — dead by his own hand."

Werper sat up quickly in his blankets at the first alarm, a startled expression upon his countenance; but at the last words of the black a sigh of relief escaped his lips and a slight smile replaced the tense lines upon his face.

"I come," he called to the slave, and drawing on his boots, rose and went out of his tent.

Excited Arabs and blacks were running from all parts of the camp toward the silken tent of Mohammed Beyd, and when Werper entered he found a number of the raiders crowded about the corpse, now cold and stiff.

Shouldering his way among them, the Belgian halted beside the dead body of the raider. He looked down in silence for a moment upon the still face, then he wheeled upon the Arabs.

"Who has done this thing?" he cried. His tone was both menacing and accusing. "Who has murdered Mohammed Beyd?"

A sudden chorus of voices arose in tumultuous protest.

"Mohammed Beyd was not murdered," they cried. "He died by his own hand. This, and Allah, are our witnesses," and they pointed to a revolver in the dead man's hand.

For a time Werper pretended to be skeptical; but at last permitted himself to be convinced that Mohammed Beyd had indeed killed himself in remorse for the death of the white woman he had, all unknown to his followers, loved so devotedly.

Werper himself wrapped the blankets of the dead man about the corpse, taking care to fold inward the scorched and bullet-torn fabric that had muffled the report of the weapon he had fired the night before. Then six husky blacks carried the body out into the clearing where the camp stood, and deposited it in a shallow grave. As the loose earth fell upon the silent form beneath the tell-tale blankets, Albert Werper heaved another sigh of relief — his plan had worked out even better than he had dared hope.

With Achmet Zek and Mohammed Beyd both dead, the raiders were without a leader, and after a brief conference they decided to return into the north on visits to the various tribes to which they belonged, Werper, after learning the direction they intended taking, announced that for his part, he was going east to the coast, and as they knew of nothing he possessed which any of them coveted, they signified their willingness that he should go his way.

As they rode off, he sat his horse in the center of the clearing watching them disappear one by one into the jungle, and thanked his God that he had at last escaped their villainous clutches.

When he could no longer hear any sound of them, he turned to the right and rode into the forest toward the tree where he had hidden Lady Greystoke, and drawing rein beneath it, called up in a gay and hopeful voice a pleasant, "Good morning!"

There was no reply, and though his eyes searched the thick foliage above him, he could see no sign of the girl. Dismounting, he quickly climbed into the tree, where he could obtain a view of all its branches. The tree was empty — Jane Clayton had vanished during the silent watches of the jungle night.

Chapter XXII

TARZAN RECOVERS
HIS REASON

As TARZAN LET the pebbles from the recovered pouch run through his fingers, his thoughts returned to the pile of yellow ingots about which the Arabs and the Abyssinians had waged their relentless battle.

What was there in common between that pile of dirty metal and the beautiful, sparkling pebbles that had formerly been in his pouch? What was the metal? From whence had it come? What was that tantalizing half-conviction which seemed to demand the recognition of his memory that the yellow pile for which these men had fought and died had been intimately connected with his past — that it had been his?

What had been his past? He shook his head. Vaguely the memory of his apish childhood passed slowly in review — then came a strangely tangled mass of faces, figures and events which seemed to have no relation to Tarzan of the Apes, and yet which were, even in their fragmentary form, familiar.

Slowly and painfully, recollection was attempting to reassert itself, the hurt brain was mending, as the cause of its recent failure to function was being slowly absorbed or removed by the healing processes of perfect circulation.

The people who now passed before his mind's eye for the first time in weeks wore familiar faces; but yet he could neither place them in the niches they had once filled in his past life, nor call them by name. One was a fair she, and it was her face which most often moved through the tangled recollections of his convalescing brain. Who was she? What had she been to Tarzan of the Apes? He seemed to see her about the very spot upon which the pile of gold had been unearthed by the Abyssinians; but the surroundings were vastly different from those which now obtained.

There was a building — there were many buildings — and there were hedges, fences, and flowers. Tarzan puckered his brow in puzzled study of the wonderful problem. For an instant he seemed to grasp the whole of a true explanation, and then, just as success was within his grasp, the picture faded into a jungle scene where a naked, white youth danced in company with a band of hairy, primordial ape-things.

Tarzan shook his head and sighed. Why was it that he could not recollect? At least he was sure that in some way the pile of gold, the place where it lay, the subtle aroma of the elusive she he had been pursuing, the memory figure of the white woman, and he himself, were inextricably connected by the ties of a forgotten past.

If the woman belonged there, what better place to search or await her than the very spot which his broken recollections seemed to assign to her? It was worth trying. Tarzan slipped the thong of the empty pouch over his shoulder and started off through the trees in the direction of the plain.

At the outskirts of the forest he met the Arabs returning in search of Achmet Zek. Hiding, he let them pass, and then resumed his way toward the charred ruins of the home he had been almost upon the point of recalling to his memory.

His journey across the plain was interrupted by the discovery of a small herd of antelope in a little swale, where the cover and the wind were well combined to make stalking easy. A fat yearling rewarded a half hour of stealthy creeping and a sudden, savage rush, and it was late in the afternoon when the ape-man settled himself upon his haunches beside his kill to enjoy the fruits of his skill, his cunning, and his prowess.

His hunger satisfied, thirst next claimed his attention. The river lured him by the shortest path toward its refreshing waters, and when he had drunk, night already had fallen and he was some half mile or more down stream from the point where he had seen the pile of yellow ingots, and where he hoped to meet the memory woman, or find some clew to her whereabouts or her identity.

To the jungle bred, time is usually a matter of small moment, and haste, except when engendered by terror, by rage, or by hunger, is distasteful. Today was gone. Therefore tomorrow, of which there was an infinite procession, would answer admirably for Tarzan's further quest. And, besides, the ape-man was tired and would sleep.

A tree afforded him the safety, seclusion and comforts of a well-appointed bedchamber, and to the chorus of the hunters and the hunted of the wild river bank he soon dropped off into deep slumber.

Morning found him both hungry and thirsty again, and dropping from his tree he made his way to the drinking place at the river's edge. There he found Numa, the lion, ahead of him. The big fellow was lapping the water greedily, and at the approach of

Tarzan along the trail in his rear, he raised his head, and turning his gaze backward across his maned shoulders glared at the intruder. A low growl of warning rumbled from his throat; but Tarzan, guessing that the beast had but just quitted his kill and was well filled, merely made a slight detour and continued to the river, where he stopped a few yards above the tawny cat, and dropping upon his hands and knees plunged his face into the cool water. For a moment the lion continued to eye the man; then he resumed his drinking, and man and beast quenched their thirst side by side each apparently oblivious of the other's presence.

Numa was the first to finish. Raising his head, he gazed across the river for a few minutes with that stony fixity of attention which is a characteristic of his kind. But for the ruffling of his black mane to the touch of the passing breeze he might have been wrought from golden bronze, so motionless, so statuesque his pose.

A deep sigh from the cavernous lungs dispelled the illusion. The mighty head swung slowly around until the yellow eyes rested upon the man. The bristled lip curved upward, exposing yellow fangs. Another warning growl vibrated the heavy jowls, and the king of beasts turned majestically about and paced slowly up the trail into the dense reeds.

Tarzan of the Apes drank on, but from the corners of his gray eyes he watched the great brute's every move until he had disappeared from view, and, after, his keen ears marked the movements of the carnivore.

A plunge in the river was followed by a scant breakfast of eggs which chance discovered to him, and then he set off up river toward the ruins of the bungalow where the golden ingots had marked the center of yesterday's battle.

And when he came upon the spot, great was his surprise and consternation, for the yellow metal had disappeared. The earth, trampled by the feet of horses and men, gave no clew. It was as though the ingots had evaporated into thin air.

The ape-man was at a loss to know where to turn or what next to do. There was no sign of any spoor which might denote that the she had been here. The metal was gone, and if there was any connection between the she and the metal it seemed useless to wait for her now that the latter had been removed elsewhere.

Everything seemed to elude him — the pretty pebbles, the yellow metal, the she, his memory. Tarzan was disgusted. He would go back into the jungle and look for Chulk, and so he turned his steps once more toward the forest. He moved rapidly, swinging across the plain in a long, easy trot, and at the edge of the forest, taking to the trees with the agility and speed of a small monkey.

His direction was aimless — he merely raced on and on through the jungle, the joy of unfettered action his principal urge, with the hope of stumbling upon some clew to Chulk or the she, a secondary incentive.

For two days he roamed about, killing, eating, drinking and sleeping wherever inclination and the means to indulge it occurred simultaneously. It was upon the morning of the third day that the scent spoor of horse and man were wafted faintly to his nostrils. Instantly he altered his course to glide silently through the branches in the direction from which the scent came.

It was not long before he came upon a solitary horseman riding toward the east. Instantly his eyes confirmed what his nose had previously suspected — the rider was he who had stolen his pretty pebbles. The light of rage flared suddenly in the gray eyes as the ape-man dropped lower among the branches until he moved almost directly above the unconscious Werper.

There was a quick leap, and the Belgian felt a heavy body hurtle onto the rump of his terror-stricken mount. The horse, snorting, leaped forward. Giant arms encircled the rider, and in the twinkling of an eye he was dragged from his saddle to find himself lying in the narrow trail with a naked, white giant kneeling upon his breast.

Recognition came to Werper with the first glance at his captor's face, and a pallor of fear overspread his features. Strong fingers were at his throat, fingers of steel. He tried to cry out, to plead for his life; but the cruel fingers denied him speech, as they were as surely denying him life.

"The pretty pebbles?" cried the man upon his breast. "What did you with the pretty pebbles — with Tarzan's pretty pebbles?"

The fingers relaxed to permit a reply. For some time Werper could only choke and cough — at last he regained the powers of speech.

"Achmet Zek, the Arab, stole them from me," he cried; "he made me give up the pouch and the pebbles."

"I saw all that," replied Tarzan; "but the pebbles in the pouch were not the pebbles of Tarzan — they were only such pebbles as fill the bottoms of the rivers, and the shelving banks beside them. Even the Arab would not have them, for he threw them away in anger when he had looked upon them. It is my pretty pebbles that I want — where are they?"

"I do not know, I do not know," cried Werper. "I gave them to Achmet Zek or he would have killed me. A few minutes later he followed me along the trail to slay me, although he had promised to molest me no further, and I shot and killed him; but the pouch was not upon his person and though I searched about the jungle for some time I could not find it."

"I found it, I tell you," growled Tarzan, "and I also found the pebbles which Achmet Zek had thrown away in disgust. They were not Tarzan's pebbles. You have hidden them! Tell me where they are or I will kill you," and the brown fingers of the ape-man closed a little tighter upon the throat of his victim.

Werper struggled to free himself. "My God, Lord Greystoke," he managed to scream, "would you commit murder for a handful of stones?"

The fingers at his throat relaxed, a puzzled, far-away expression softened the gray eyes.

"Lord Greystoke!" repeated the ape-man. "Lord Greystoke! Who is Lord Greystoke? Where have I heard that name before?"

"Why man, you are Lord Greystoke," cried the Belgian. "You were injured by a falling rock when the earthquake shattered the passage to the underground chamber to which you and your black Waziri had come to fetch golden ingots back to your bungalow. The blow shattered your memory. You are John Clayton, Lord Greystoke — don't you remember?"

"John Clayton, Lord Greystoke!" repeated Tarzan. Then for a moment he was silent. Presently his hand went falteringly to his forehead, an expression of wonderment filled his eyes — of wonderment and sudden understanding. The forgotten name had reawakened the returning memory that had been struggling to reassert itself. The ape-man relinquished his grasp upon the throat of the Belgian, and leaped to his feet.

"God!" he cried, and then, "Jane!" Suddenly he turned toward Werper. "My wife?" he asked. "What has become of her? The farm is in ruins. You know. You have had something to do with all this. You followed me to Opar, you stole the jewels which I thought but pretty pebbles. You are a crook! Do not try to tell me that you are not."

"He is worse than a crook," said a quiet voice close behind them.

Tarzan turned in astonishment to see a tall man in uniform standing in the trail a few paces from him. Back of the man were a number of black soldiers in the uniform of the Congo Free State.

"He is a murderer, Monsieur," continued the officer. "I have followed him for a long time to take him back to stand trial for the killing of his superior officer."

Werper was upon his feet now, gazing, white and trembling, at the fate which had overtaken him even in the fastness of the labyrinthine jungle. Instinctively he turned to flee; but Tarzan of the Apes reached out a strong hand and grasped him by the shoulder.

"Wait!" said the ape-man to his captive. "This gentleman wishes you, and so do I. When I am through with you, he may have you. Tell me what has become of my wife."

The Belgian officer eyed the almost naked, white giant with curiosity. He noted the strange contrast of primitive weapons and apparel, and the easy, fluent French which the man spoke. The former denoted the lowest, the latter the highest type of culture. He could not quite determine the social status of this strange creature; but he knew that he did not relish the easy assurance with which the fellow presumed to dictate when he might take possession of the prisoner.

"Pardon me," he said, stepping forward and placing his hand on Werper's other shoulder; "but this gentleman is my prisoner. He must come with me."

"When I am through with him," replied Tarzan, quietly.

The officer turned and beckoned to the soldiers standing in the trail behind him. A company of uniformed blacks stepped quickly forward and pushing past the three, surrounded the ape-man and his captive.

"Both the law and the power to enforce it are upon my side," announced the officer. "Let us have no trouble. If you have a grievance against this man you may return with me and enter your charge regularly before an authorized tribunal."

"Your legal rights are not above suspicion, my friend," replied Tarzan, "and your power to enforce your commands are only apparent — not real. You have presumed to enter British territory with an armed force. Where is your authority for this invasion? Where are the extradition papers which warrant the arrest of this man? And what assurance have you that I cannot bring an armed force about you that will prevent your return to the Congo Free State?"

The Belgian lost his temper. "I have no disposition to argue with a naked savage," he cried. "Unless you wish to be hurt you will not interfere with me. Take the prisoner, Sergeant!"

Werper raised his lips close to Tarzan's ear. "Keep me from them, and I can show you the very spot where I saw your wife last night," he whispered. "She cannot be far from here at this very minute."

The soldiers, following the signal from their sergeant, closed in to seize Werper. Tarzan grabbed the Belgian about the waist, and bearing him beneath his arm as he might have borne a sack of flour, leaped forward in an attempt to break through the cordon. His right fist caught the nearest soldier upon the jaw and sent him hurtling backward upon his fellows. Clubbed rifles were torn from the hands of those who barred his way, and right and left the black soldiers stumbled aside in the face of the ape-man's savage break for liberty.

So completely did the blacks surround the two that they dared not fire for fear of hitting one of their own number, and Tarzan was already through them and upon the point of dodging into the concealing mazes of the jungle when one who had sneaked upon him from behind struck him a heavy blow upon the head with a rifle.

In an instant the ape-man was down and a dozen black soldiers were upon his back. When he regained consciousness he found himself securely bound, as was Werper also. The Belgian officer, success having

crowned his efforts, was in good humor, and inclined
to chaff his prisoners about the ease with which they
had been captured; but from Tarzan of the Apes he
elicited no response. Werper, however, was voluble in
his protests. He explained that Tarzan was an English
lord; but the officer only laughed at the assertion, and
advised his prisoner to save his breath for his defense
in court.

As soon as Tarzan regained his senses and it was
found that he was not seriously injured, the prisoners
were hastened into line and the return march toward
the Congo Free State boundary commenced.

Toward evening the column halted beside a stream,
made camp and prepared the evening meal. From the
thick foliage of the nearby jungle a pair of fierce eyes
watched the activities of the uniformed blacks with
silent intensity and curiosity. From beneath beetling
brows the creature saw the boma constructed, the fires
built, and the supper prepared.

Tarzan and Werper had been lying bound behind a
small pile of knapsacks from the time that the company had halted; but with the preparation of the meal
completed, their guard ordered them to rise and come
forward to one of the fires where their hands would be
unfettered that they might eat.

As the giant ape-man rose, a startled expression of
recognition entered the eyes of the watcher in the
jungle, and a low guttural broke from the savage lips.
Instantly Tarzan was alert, but the answering growl
died upon his lips, suppressed by the fear that it might
arouse the suspicions of the soldiers.

Suddenly an inspiration came to him. He turned
toward Werper.

"I am going to speak to you in a loud voice and in
a tongue which you do not understand. Appear to
listen intently to what I say, and occasionally mumble
something as though replying in the same language —

our escape may hinge upon the success of your efforts."

Werper nodded in assent and understanding, and immediately there broke from the lips of his companion a strange jargon which might have been compared with equal propriety to the barking and growling of a dog and the chattering of monkeys.

The nearer soldiers looked in surprise at the apeman. Some of them laughed, while others drew away in evident superstitious fear. The officer approached the prisoners while Tarzan was still jabbering, and halted behind them, listening in perplexed interest. When Werper mumbled some ridiculous jargon in reply his curiosity broke bounds, and he stepped forward, demanding to know what language it was that they spoke.

Tarzan had gauged the measure of the man's culture from the nature and quality of his conversation during the march, and he rested the success of his reply upon the estimate he had made.

"Greek," he explained.

"Oh, I thought it was Greek," replied the officer; "but it has been so many years since I studied it that I was not sure. In future, however, I will thank you to speak in a language which I am more familiar with."

Werper turned his head to hide a grin, whispering to Tarzan: "It was Greek to him all right — and to me, too."

But one of the black soldiers mumbled in a low voice to a companion: "I have heard those sounds before — once at night when I was lost in the jungle, I heard the hairy men of the trees talking among themselves, and their words were like the words of this white man. I wish that we had not found him. He is not a man at all — he is a bad spirit, and we shall have bad luck if we do not let him go," and the fellow rolled his eyes fearfully toward the jungle.

His companion laughed nervously, and moved

away, to repeat the conversation, with variations and exaggerations, to others of the black soldiery, so that it was not long before a frightful tale of black magic and sudden death was woven about the giant prisoner, and had gone the rounds of the camp.

And deep in the gloomy jungle amidst the darkening shadows of the falling night a hairy, manlike creature swung swiftly southward upon some secret mission of his own.

Chapter XXIII

A NIGHT OF TERROR

*T*O JANE CLAYTON, waiting in the tree where Werper had placed her, it seemed that the long night would never end, yet end it did at last, and within an hour of the coming of dawn her spirits leaped with renewed hope at sight of a solitary horseman approaching along the trail.

The flowing burnoose, with its loose hood, hid both the face and the figure of the rider; but that it was M. Frecoult the girl well knew, since he had been garbed as an Arab, and he alone might be expected to seek her hiding place.

That which she saw relieved the strain of the long night vigil; but there was much that she did not see. She did not see the black face beneath the white hood, nor the file of ebon horsemen beyond the trail's bend riding slowly in the wake of their leader. These things she did not see at first, and so she leaned downward toward the approaching rider, a cry of welcome forming in her throat.

At the first word the man looked up, reining in in surprise, and as she saw the black face of Abdul Mourak, the Abyssinian, she shrank back in terror among the branches; but it was too late. The man had seen her, and now he called to her to descend. At first she refused; but when a dozen black cavalrymen drew up behind their leader, and at Abdul Mourak's command one of them started to climb the tree after her she realized that resistance was futile, and came slowly down to stand upon the ground before this new captor and plead her cause in the name of justice and humanity.

Angered by recent defeat, and by the loss of the gold, the jewels, and his prisoners, Abdul Mourak was in no mood to be influenced by any appeal to those softer sentiments to which, as a matter of fact, he was almost a stranger even under the most favorable conditions.

He looked for degradation and possible death in punishment for his failures and his misfortunes when he should have returned to his native land and made his report to Menelek; but an acceptable gift might temper the wrath of the emperor, and surely this fair flower of another race should be gratefully received by the black ruler!

When Jane Clayton had concluded her appeal, Abdul Mourak replied briefly that he would promise her protection; but that he must take her to his emperor. The girl did not need ask him why, and once again hope died within her breast. Resignedly she permitted herself to be lifted to a seat behind one of the troopers, and again, under new masters, her journey was resumed toward what she now began to believe was her inevitable fate.

Abdul Mourak, bereft of his guides by the battle he had waged against the raiders, and himself unfamiliar with the country, had wandered far from the trail he should have followed, and as a result had made but little progress toward the north since the beginning of his flight. Today he was beating toward the west in the hope of coming upon a village where he might obtain guides; but night found him still as far from a realization of his hopes as had the rising sun.

It was a dispirited company which went into camp, waterless and hungry, in the dense jungle. Attracted by the horses, lions roared about the boma, and to their hideous din was added the shrill neighs of the terror-stricken beasts they hunted. There was little sleep for man or beast, and the sentries were doubled that there might be enough on duty both to guard against the sudden charge of an overbold, or overhungry lion, and to keep the fire blazing which was an even more effectual barrier against them than the thorny boma.

It was well past midnight, and as yet Jane Clayton, notwithstanding that she had passed a sleepless night the night before, had scarcely more than dozed. A sense of impending danger seemed to hang like a black pall over the camp. The veteran troopers of the black emperor were nervous and ill at ease. Abdul Mourak left his blankets a dozen times to pace restlessly back and forth between the tethered horses and the crackling fire. The girl could see his great frame silhouetted against the lurid glare of the flames, and she guessed from the quick, nervous movements of the man that he was afraid.

The roaring of the lions rose in sudden fury until the earth trembled to the hideous chorus. The horses shrilled their neighs of terror as they lay back upon their halter ropes in their mad endeavors to break loose. A trooper, braver than his fellows, leaped among the kicking, plunging, fear-maddened beasts in a futile attempt to quiet them. A lion, large, and fierce, and courageous, leaped almost to the boma, full in the bright light from the fire. A sentry raised his piece and fired, and the little leaden pellet unstoppered the vials of hell upon the terror-stricken camp.

The shot ploughed a deep and painful furrow in the lion's side, arousing all the bestial fury of the little brain; but abating not a whit the power and vigor of the great body.

Unwounded, the boma and the flames might have turned him back; but now the pain and the rage wiped caution from his mind, and with a loud, and angry roar he topped the barrier with an easy leap and was among the horses.

What had been pandemonium before became now an indescribable tumult of hideous sound. The stricken horse upon which the lion leaped shrieked out its terror and its agony. Several about it broke their tethers and plunged madly about the camp. Men leaped from their blankets and with guns ready ran toward the picket line, and then from the jungle beyond the boma a dozen lions, emboldened by the example of their fellow charged fearlessly upon the camp.

Singly and in twos and threes they leaped the boma, until the little enclosure was filled with cursing men and screaming horses battling for their lives with the green-eyed devils of the jungle.

With the charge of the first lion, Jane Clayton had scrambled to her feet, and now she stood horror-struck at the scene of savage slaughter that swirled and eddied about her. Once a bolting horse knocked her down, and a moment later a lion, leaping in pursuit of another terror-stricken animal, brushed her so closely that she was again thrown from her feet.

Amidst the cracking of the rifles and the growls of the carnivora rose the death screams of stricken men and horses as they were dragged down by the blood-mad cats. The leaping carnivora and the plunging horses, prevented any concerted action by the Abyssinians — it was every man for himself — and in the melee, the defenseless woman was either forgotten or ignored by her black captors. A score of times was her life menaced by charging lions, by plunging horses, or by the wildly fired bullets of the frightened troopers, yet there was no chance of escape, for now with the fiendish cunning of their kind, the tawny hunters commenced to circle about their prey, hemming them within a ring of mighty, yellow fangs, and sharp, long talons. Again and again an individual lion would dash suddenly among the frightened men and horses, and occasionally a horse, goaded to frenzy by pain or terror, succeeded in racing safely through the circling lions, leaping the boma, and escaping into the jungle; but for the men and the woman no such escape was possible.

A horse, struck by a stray bullet, fell beside Jane Clayton, a lion leaped across the expiring beast full upon the breast of a black trooper just beyond. The man clubbed his rifle and struck futilely at the broad head, and then he was down and the carnivore was standing above him.

Shrieking out his terror, the soldier clawed with puny fingers at the shaggy breast in vain endeavor to push away the grinning jaws. The lion lowered his head, the gaping fangs closed with a single sickening crunch upon the fear-distorted face, and turning strode back across the body of the dead horse dragging his limp and bloody burden with him.

Wide-eyed the girl stood watching. She saw the carnivore step upon the corpse, stumblingly, as the grisly thing swung between its forepaws, and her eyes remained fixed in fascination while the beast passed within a few paces of her.

The interference of the body seemed to enrage the lion. He shook the inanimate clay venomously. He growled and roared hideously at the dead, insensate thing, and then he dropped it and raised his head to look about in search of some living victim upon which to wreak his ill temper. His yellow eyes fastened themselves balefully upon the figure of the girl, the bristling lips raised, disclosing the grinning fangs. A terrific roar broke from the savage throat, and the great beast crouched to spring upon this new and helpless victim.

Quiet had fallen early upon the camp where Tarzan and Werper lay securely bound. Two nervous sentries paced their beats, their eyes rolling often toward the impenetrable shadows of the gloomy jungle. The others slept or tried to sleep — all but the ape-man. Silently and powerfully he strained at the bonds which fettered his wrists.

The muscles knotted beneath the smooth, brown skin of his arms and shoulders, the veins stood out upon his temples from the force of his exertions — a strand parted, another and another, and one hand was free. Then from the jungle came a low guttural, and the ape-man became suddenly a silent, rigid statue, with ears and nostrils straining to span the black void where his eyesight could not reach.

Again came the uncanny sound from the thick verdure beyond the camp. A sentry halted abruptly, straining his eyes into the gloom. The kinky wool upon his head stiffened and raised. He called to his comrade in a hoarse whisper.

"Did you hear it?" he asked.

The other came closer, trembling.

"Hear what?"

Again was the weird sound repeated, followed almost immediately by a similar and answering sound from the camp. The sentries drew close together, watching the black spot from which the voice seemed to come.

Trees overhung the boma at this point which was upon the opposite side of the camp from them. They dared not approach. Their terror even prevented them from arousing their fellows — they could only stand in frozen fear and watch for the fearsome apparition they momentarily expected to see leap from the jungle.

Nor had they long to wait. A dim, bulky form dropped lightly from the branches of a tree into the camp. At sight of it one of the sentries recovered command of his muscles and his voice. Screaming loudly to awaken the sleeping camp, he leaped toward the flickering watch fire and threw a mass of brush upon it.

The white officer and the black soldiers sprang from their blankets. The flames leaped high upon the rejuvenated fire, lighting the entire camp, and the awakened men shrank back in superstitious terror from the sight that met their frightened and astonished vision.

A dozen huge and hairy forms loomed large beneath the trees at the far side of the enclosure. The white giant, one hand freed, had struggled to his knees and was calling to the frightful, nocturnal visitors in a hideous medley of bestial gutturals, barkings and growlings.

Werper had managed to sit up. He, too, saw the savage faces of the approaching anthropoids and scarcely knew whether to be relieved or terror-stricken.

Growling, the great apes leaped forward toward Tarzan and Werper. Chulk led them. The Belgian officer called to his men to fire upon the intruders; but the Negroes held back, filled as they were with superstitious terror of the hairy treemen, and with the conviction that the white giant who could thus summon the beasts of the jungle to his aid was more than human.

Drawing his own weapon, the officer fired, and Tarzan fearing the effect of the noise upon his really timid friends called to them to hasten and fulfill his commands.

A couple of the apes turned and fled at the sound of the firearm; but Chulk and a half dozen others waddled rapidly forward, and, following the ape-man's directions, seized both him and Werper and bore them off toward the jungle.

By dint of threats, reproaches and profanity the Belgian officer succeeded in persuading his trembling command to fire a volley after the retreating apes. A ragged, straggling volley it was, but at least one of its bullets found a mark, for as the jungle closed about the hairy rescuers, Chulk, who bore Werper across one broad shoulder, staggered and fell.

In an instant he was up again; but the Belgian guessed from his unsteady gait that he was hard hit. He lagged far behind the others, and it was several minutes after they had halted at Tarzan's command before he came slowly up to them, reeling from side to side, and at last falling again beneath the weight of his burden and the shock of his wound.

As Chulk went down he dropped Werper, so that the latter fell face downward with the body of the ape lying half across him. In this position the Belgian felt something resting against his hands, which were still bound at his back — something that was not a part of the hairy body of the ape.

Mechanically the man's fingers felt of the object resting almost in their grasp — it was a soft pouch, filled with small, hard particles. Werper gasped in wonderment as recognition filtered through the incredulity of his mind. It was impossible, and yet — it was true!

Feverishly he strove to remove the pouch from the ape and transfer it to his own possession; but the restricted radius to which his bonds held his hands prevented this, though he did succeed in tucking the pouch with its precious contents inside the waist band of his trousers.

Tarzan, sitting at a short distance, was busy with the remaining knots of the cords which bound him. Presently he flung aside the last of them and rose to his feet. Approaching Werper he knelt beside him. For a moment he examined the ape.

"Quite dead," he announced. "It is too bad — he was a splendid creature," and then he turned to the work of liberating the Belgian.

He freed his hands first, and then commenced upon the knots at his ankles.

"I can do the rest," said the Belgian. "I have a small pocketknife which they overlooked when they searched me," and in this way he succeeded in ridding himself of the ape-man's attentions that he might find and open his little knife and cut the thong which fastened the pouch about Chulk's shoulder, and transfer it from his waist band to the breast of his shirt. Then he rose and approached Tarzan.

Once again had avarice claimed him. Forgotten were the good intentions which the confidence of Jane Clayton in his honor had awakened. What she had done, the little pouch had undone. How it had come upon the person of the great ape, Werper could not imagine, unless it had been that the anthropoid had witnessed his fight with Achmet Zek, seen the Arab with the pouch and taken it away from him; but that this pouch contained the jewels of Opar, Werper was positive, and that was all that interested him greatly.

"Now," said the ape-man, "keep your promise to me. Lead me to the spot where you last saw my wife."

It was slow work pushing through the jungle in the dead of night behind the slow-moving Belgian. The ape-man chafed at the delay, but the European could not swing through the trees as could his more agile and muscular companions, and so the speed of all was limited to that of the slowest.

The apes trailed out behind the two white men for a matter of a few miles; but presently their interest lagged, the foremost of them halted in a little glade and the others stopped at his side. There they sat peering from beneath their shaggy brows at the figures of the two men forging steadily ahead, until the latter disappeared in the leafy trail beyond the clearing. Then an ape sought a comfortable couch beneath a tree, and one by one the others followed his example, so that Werper and Tarzan continued their journey alone; nor was the latter either surprised or concerned.

The two had gone but a short distance beyond the glade where the apes had deserted them, when the roaring of distant lions fell upon their ears. The ape-man paid no attention to the familiar sounds until the crack of a rifle came faintly from the same direction, and when this was followed by the shrill neighing of horses, and an almost continuous fusillade of shots intermingled with increased and savage roaring of a large troop of lions, he became immediately concerned.

"Someone is having trouble over there," he said, turning toward Werper. "I'll have to go to them — they may be friends."

"Your wife might be among them," suggested the Belgian, for since he had again come into possession of the pouch he had become fearful and suspicious of the ape-man, and in his mind had constantly revolved many plans for eluding this giant Englishman, who was at once his savior and his captor.

At the suggestion Tarzan started as though struck with a whip.

"God!" he cried, "she might be, and the lions are attacking them — they are in the camp. I can tell from the screams of the horses — and there! that was the cry of a man in his death agonies. Stay here man — I will come back for you. I must go first to them," and swinging into a tree the lithe figure swung rapidly off into the night with the speed and silence of a disembodied spirit.

For a moment Werper stood where the ape-man had left him. Then a cunning smile crossed his lips. "Stay here?" he asked himself. "Stay here and wait until you return to find and take these jewels from me? Not I, my friend, not I," and turning abruptly eastward Albert Werper passed through the foliage of a hanging vine and out of the sight of his fellow-man — forever.

Chapter XXIV

HOME

*A*S TARZAN OF the Apes hurtled through the trees
the discordant sounds of the battle between the
Abyssinians and the lions smote more and more distinctly upon his sensitive ears, redoubling his assurance that the plight of the human element of the
conflict was critical indeed.

At last the glare of the camp fire shone plainly
through the intervening trees, and a moment later the
giant figure of the ape-man paused upon an overhanging bough to look down upon the bloody scene of
carnage below.

His quick eye took in the whole scene with a single
comprehending glance and stopped upon the figure of
a woman standing facing a great lion across the carcass
of a horse.

The carnivore was crouching to spring as Tarzan
discovered the tragic tableau. Numa was almost beneath the branch upon which the ape-man stood,
naked and unarmed. There was not even an instant's

hesitation upon the part of the latter — it was as though he had not even paused in his swift progress through the trees, so lightning-like his survey and comprehension of the scene below him — so instantaneous his consequent action.

So hopeless had seemed her situation to her that Jane Clayton but stood in lethargic apathy awaiting the impact of the huge body that would hurl her to the ground — awaiting the momentary agony that cruel talons and grisly fangs may inflict before the coming of the merciful oblivion which would end her sorrow and her suffering.

What use to attempt escape? As well face the hideous end as to be dragged down from behind in futile flight. She did not even close her eyes to shut out the frightful aspect of that snarling face, and so it was that as she saw the lion preparing to charge she saw, too, a bronzed and mighty figure leap from an overhanging tree at the instant that Numa rose in his spring.

Wide went her eyes in wonder and incredulity, as she beheld this seeming apparition risen from the dead. The lion was forgotten — her own peril — everything save the wondrous miracle of this strange recrudescence. With parted lips, with palms tight pressed against her heaving bosom, the girl leaned forward, large-eyed, enthralled by the vision of her dead mate.

She saw the sinewy form leap to the shoulder of the lion, hurtling against the leaping beast like a huge, animate battering ram. She saw the carnivore brushed aside as he was almost upon her, and in the instant she realized that no substanceless wraith could thus turn the charge of a maddened lion with brute force greater than the brute's.

Tarzan, her Tarzan, lived! A cry of unspeakable gladness broke from her lips, only to die in terror as she saw the utter defenselessness of her mate, and realized that the lion had recovered himself and was turning upon Tarzan in mad lust for vengeance.

At the ape-man's feet lay the discarded rifle of the dead Abyssinian whose mutilated corpse sprawled where Numa had abandoned it. The quick glance which had swept the ground for some weapon of defense discovered it, and as the lion reared upon his hind legs to seize the rash man-thing who had dared interpose its puny strength between Numa and his prey, the heavy stock whirred through the air and splintered upon the broad forehead.

Not as an ordinary mortal might strike a blow did Tarzan of the Apes strike; but with the maddened frenzy of a wild beast backed by the steel thews which his wild, arboreal boyhood had bequeathed him. When the blow ended the splintered stock was driven through the splintered skull into the savage brain, and the heavy iron barrel was bent into a rude V.

In the instant that the lion sank, lifeless, to the ground, Jane Clayton threw herself into the eager arms of her husband. For a brief instant he strained her dear form to his breast, and then a glance about him awakened the ape-man to the dangers which still surrounded them.

Upon every hand the lions were still leaping upon new victims. Fear-maddened horses still menaced them with their erratic bolting from one side of the enclosure to the other. Bullets from the guns of the defenders who remained alive but added to the perils of their situation.

To remain was to court death. Tarzan seized Jane Clayton and lifted her to a broad shoulder. The blacks who had witnessed his advent looked on in amazement as they saw the naked giant leap easily into the branches of the tree from whence he had dropped so uncannily upon the scene, and vanish as he had come, bearing away their prisoner with him.

They were too well occupied in self-defense to attempt to halt him, nor could they have done so other than by the wasting of a precious bullet which might be needed the next instant to turn the charge of a savage foe.

And so, unmolested, Tarzan passed from the camp of the Abyssinians, from which the din of conflict followed him deep into the jungle until distance gradually obliterated it entirely.

Back to the spot where he had left Werper went the ape-man, joy in his heart now, where fear and sorrow had so recently reigned; and in his mind a determination to forgive the Belgian and aid him in making good his escape. But when he came to the place, Werper was gone, and though Tarzan called aloud many times he received no reply. Convinced that the man had purposely eluded him for reasons of his own, John Clayton felt that he was under no obligations to expose his wife to further danger and discomfort in the prosecution of a more thorough search for the missing Belgian.

"He has acknowledged his guilt by his flight, Jane," he said. "We will let him go to lie in the bed that he has made for himself."

Straight as homing pigeons, the two made their way toward the ruin and desolation that had once been the center of their happy lives, and which was soon to be restored by the willing black hands of laughing laborers, made happy again by the return of the master and mistress whom they had mourned as dead.

Past the village of Achmet Zek their way led them, and there they found but the charred remains of the palisade and the native huts, still smoking, as mute evidence of the wrath and vengeance of a powerful enemy.

"The Waziri," commented Tarzan with a grim smile.

"God bless them!" cried Jane Clayton.

"They cannot be far ahead of us," said Tarzan, "Basuli and the others. The gold is gone and the jewels of Opar, Jane; but we have each other and the Waziri — and we have love and loyalty and friendship. And what are gold and jewels to these?"

"If only poor Mugambi lived," she replied, "and those other brave fellows who sacrificed their lives in vain endeavor to protect me!"

In the silence of mingled joy and sorrow they passed along through the familiar jungle, and as the afternoon was waning there came faintly to the ears of the ape-man the murmuring cadence of distant voices.

"We are nearing the Waziri, Jane," he said. "I can hear them ahead of us. They are going into camp for the night, I imagine."

A half hour later the two came upon a horde of ebon warriors which Basuli had collected for his war of vengeance upon the raiders. With them were the captured women of the tribe whom they had found in the village of Achmet Zek, and tall, even among the giant Waziri, loomed a familiar black form at the side of Basuli. It was Mugambi, whom Jane had thought dead amidst the charred ruins of the bungalow.

Ah, such a reunion! Long into the night the dancing and the singing and the laughter awoke the echoes of the somber wood. Again and again were the stories of their various adventures retold. Again and once again they fought their battles with savage beast and savage man, and dawn was already breaking when Basuli, for the fortieth time, narrated how he and a handful of his warriors had watched the battle for the golden ingots which the Abyssinians of Abdul Mourak had waged against the Arab raiders of Achmet Zek, and how, when the victors had ridden away they had sneaked out of the river reeds and stolen away with the precious ingots to hide them where no robber eye ever could discover them.

Pieced out from the fragments of their various experiences with the Belgian the truth concerning the malign activities of Albert Werper became apparent. Only Lady Greystoke found aught to praise in the conduct of the man, and it was difficult even for her to reconcile his many heinous acts with this one evidence of chivalry and honor.

"Deep in the soul of every man," said Tarzan, "must lurk the germ of righteousness. It was your own virtue, Jane, rather even than your helplessness which awakened for an instant the latent decency of this degraded man. In that one act he retrieved himself, and when he is called to face his Maker may it outweigh in the balance, all the sins he has committed."

And Jane Clayton breathed a fervent, "Amen!"

Months had passed. The labor of the Waziri and the gold of Opar had rebuilt and refurnished the wasted homestead of the Greystokes. Once more the simple life of the great African farm went on as it had before the coming of the Belgian and the Arab. Forgotten were the sorrows and dangers of yesterday.

For the first time in months Lord Greystoke felt that he might indulge in a holiday, and so a great hunt was organized that the faithful laborers might feast in celebration of the completion of their work.

In itself the hunt was a success, and ten days after its inauguration, a well-laden safari took up its return march toward the Waziri plain. Lord and Lady Greystoke with Basuli and Mugambi rode together at the head of the column, laughing and talking together in that easy familiarity which common interests and mutual respect breed between honest and intelligent men of any races.

Jane Clayton's horse shied suddenly at an object half hidden in the long grasses of an open space in the jungle. Tarzan's keen eyes sought quickly for an explanation of the animal's action.

"What have we here?" he cried, swinging from his saddle, and a moment later the four were grouped about a human skull and a little litter of whitened human bones.

Tarzan stooped and lifted a leathern pouch from the grisly relics of a man. The hard outlines of the contents brought an exclamation of surprise to his lips.

"The jewels of Opar!" he cried, holding the pouch aloft, "and," pointing to the bones at his feet, "all that remains of Werper, the Belgian."

Mugambi laughed. "Look within, Bwana," he cried, "and you will see what are the jewels of Opar — you will see what the Belgian gave his life for," and the black laughed aloud.

"Why do you laugh?" asked Tarzan.

"Because," replied Mugambi, "I filled the Belgian's pouch with river gravel before I escaped the camp of the Abyssinians whose prisoners we were. I left the Belgian only worthless stones, while I brought away with me the jewels he had stolen from you. That they were afterward stolen from me while I slept in the jungle is my shame and my disgrace; but at least the Belgian lost them — open his pouch and you will see."

Tarzan untied the thong which held the mouth of the leathern bag closed, and permitted the contents to trickle slowly forth into his open palm. Mugambi's eyes went wide at the sight, and the others uttered exclamations of surprise and incredulity, for from the rusty and weatherworn pouch ran a stream of brilliant, scintillating gems.

"The jewels of Opar!" cried Tarzan. "But how did Werper come by them again?"

None could answer, for both Chulk and Werper were dead, and no other knew.

"Poor devil!" said the ape-man, as he swung back into his saddle. "Even in death he has made restitution — let his sins lie with his bones."

11-19-19

LEADERS
FOR LIFE

To Weston,
a champion and Kingdom
builder.

1000X Blessings
+ Favor,

LEADERS FOR LIFE

Creating Champions through the
NOW Leadership Process

WILL MEIER

FOREWORD BY DR. BRUCE COOK

First printing May 2019. Printed in the USA.
Published by Kingdom House Publishing, Lakebay, Washington, USA.
ISBN (print): 978-1-939944-47-4
ISBN (kindle): 978-1-939944-48-1
ISBN (ePub): 978-1-939944-49-8
Library of Congress Control Number (LCCN): 2019941072
Editing by Dr. Bruce Cook.
Cover design and interior formatting by Wendy K. Walters.

Contact the Author:
Website: www.leadersforlife.global
Email: info@leadersforlife.global

ACKNOWLEDGMENTS

I want to thank the friends and team who contributed and supported us through the Leaders for Life journey. We honor those spiritual fathers and mothers that invested in us to allow us to become who we are today and pass on our legacy to others.

Thank you to those who provided stories, feedback and contributions:

John Anderson, Tyler Beckwith, Erlinde Beliveau, Sylvia Blair, Dr. Bruce Cook, Dr. Michael Evans, Edgar Hernandes-Ramos, Anna Jackson, Jeff Johnson, Candace Long, Clive Mather, Anna T. Meier, Donna Meier, Jonathan Meier, Luke Meier, Dr. Chinekwu Obidoa, Darrel Qualls, Dr. Iris M. Ramos, and David Schmid.

Special thanks to Dr. Bruce Cook who activated and empowered destiny.

ENLIGHTENED LEADERSHIP IS
SPIRITUAL IF WE UNDERSTAND
SPIRITUALITY NOT AS SOME KIND OF
RELIGIOUS DOGMA OR IDEOLOGY
BUT AS THE DOMAIN OF AWARENESS
WHERE WE EXPERIENCE VALUES
LIKE TRUTH, GOODNESS, BEAUTY,
LOVE AND COMPASSION, AND ALSO
INTUITION, CREATIVITY, INSIGHT
AND FOCUSED ATTENTION.

DEEPAK CHOPRA

DEDICATION

To Donna: the best life partner and friend for her encouragement, feedback and the immeasurable investment of love and listening.

God's marvelous grace imparts to each one of us varying gifts and ministries that are uniquely ours.

So if God has given you the grace-gift of prophecy, you must activate your gift by using the proportion of faith you have to prophesy.

If your grace-gift is serving, then thrive in serving others well. If you have the grace-gift of teaching, then be actively teaching and training others.

If you have the grace-gift of encouragement, then use it often to encourage others.

If you have the grace-gift of giving to meet the needs of others, then may you prosper in your generosity without any fanfare.

If you have the gift of leadership, be passionate about your leadership.

And if you have the gift of showing compassion, then flourish in your cheerful display of compassion.

Rom. 12:6-8, TPT, author's emphasis

CONTENTS

ENDORSEMENTS FOR LEADERS FOR LIFE

The NOW Leadership model is an authentic, multi-dimensional look at the age-old subject of leadership. The timing of this book is significant as it clearly meets the needs of a generation of leadership that is in crisis. Global and local leaders seem to have lost their way in the morass of spiritual, ethical, moral, social, political and personal indecision. There are too many dots to make sense of a world that is rapidly changing in the Fourth Industrial Revolution.

Will Meier is a leader at a Fortune 50 company who writes with both insight and precision. He provides leaders from every level of life with the three signposts of Perspective, Provision and Process. He suggests 12C's that give the reader practical tools to connect the dots and to make sense of our world.

This book is both reflective, as it looks at case-studies of what has been, and then inspirational as it points us to the future of what can be. Seasoned and emerging leaders will find this book a tool that they will often refer to. I suggest that you don't simply skim read the contents of this book but rather actively engage in the Process, reflect on the Takeaways and put the NOW Action into practice. Every sector of society is in urgent need of NOW Leaders – I encourage you to be one.

GRAHAM POWER
Chairman, Power Group
Founder of the Global Day of Prayer and Unashamedly Ethical
www.powergrp.co.za | www.unashamedlyethical.com
Cape Town, South Africa

I have read many books on leadership over the years. *Leaders for Life* stands above them all. It weaves biblical truths with practical life stories and takeaways. Will doesn't shy away from the challenges of being a leader. Accessible, witty and wise are words that I would use to describe the book. The title says it all: an essential read to help us all be both leaders for life and in every area of life.

DEEPAK MAHTANI
Managing Director, Winning Communications Partnership, Ltd.
Chair of the Board, City Gateway
www.citygateway.org.uk
Carshalton, Surrey, United Kingdom

The book *Leaders for Life* lives up to its title. One of my personal goals is to be a lifelong learner. Another goal is to encourage as many leaders as I know on the same journey, learning and being leaders for life. This book gave me practical, understandable tools to apply and teach. I took pages of notes on the first read and am excited to reread the book and answer the questions and use the knowledge to assist others to become the best leaders we can be.

AL CAPERNA
Chairman, CMC Group of Companies
www.cmcgp.com
Founder, called2business
Bowling Green, Ohio

We are living in a time of unprecedented global transformation. Amid chaos and uncertainty lie amazing potential and opportunity. This book is a gift to our world in such as time as this. It is a practical guide for all aspiring or functioning leaders, a road map, a companion's guide on how to become the type of leader our world so desperately needs. It's one of the best leadership books I have read!

CHINEKWU OBIDOA, PH.D.
Author, Award-winning Researcher, and Global Health Professional and Activist
https://cla.mercer.edu/global/faculty/chinekwu-obidoa.cfm
Atlanta, Georgia

As a graduate education professor for over 32 years I have seen and used a lot of books on leadership theory but none like the one you have in your hands. This unique read integrates biblical revelation, anointed apostolic perspective, and contemporary case studies that give us benchmarks to raising leaders that last. Because the author models what he presents, I have full confidence that you will refer to these chapters as one of your most underlined and applied books in your own development, and your mandate to multiply quality leadership in your vocation.

DR. JOSEPH UMIDI
EVP, Regent University
www.regent.edu
CEO, Lifeforming Leadership Coaching
www.lifeformingcoach.com
Virginia Beach, Virginia

Will Meier has created something rather unique and quite spectacular in this remarkable new book *Leaders for Life*. He turned a book about the Apostle Peter into a coaching guide for the corporate world and for leaders in life. His NOW (New Operating Wisdom) leadership approach and the grid of 12 leadership attributes, each beginning with the letter "C", provides a genius structure to evaluate and facilitate the leadership process. Enriching the whole reading experience are both case studies and intriguing stories of remarkable individuals from Alexander the Great to George Washington and from Florence Nightingale to William Wilberforce and Winston Churchill. A MUST READ!

DR. BERIN GILFILLAN
Founder and CEO of ISOM – World's Largest Video Bible School
with Media and Curricula in 85 languages and over 150 nations
www.isom.org
San Bernardino, California

In *Leaders for Life*, Will Meier presents a thorough, thoughtful process for becoming a Champion. I especially appreciate his call to 'authentic servant leadership', emphasizing the power of listening and asking transformational questions to help others discover deeper levels of self-awareness as they grow in their own leadership.

PAUL WHITE, PH.D.
Psychologist
Co-author of the best-selling, *The 5 Languages of Appreciation in the Workplace*
www.drpaulwhite.com
Wichita, Kansas

Leaders for Life offers thought-provoking encouragement along the road to becoming a leader. Not just another "how-to" book on leadership, *Leaders for Life* takes you on the journey, showing how God intentionally prepares each of us for leadership. The book offers the perfect blend of tried-and-true business principles coupled with timeless biblical truth.

BILL HIGH
CEO, The Signatry
www.thesignatry.com
Overland Park, Kansas

Leaders for Life offers readers of all kinds a real shot at taking their leadership up several levels. Beginners and those of limited specific interest can pick and choose nuggets of wisdom, put them into practice, and reap the benefits NOW. Those committed to leadership mastery will find a long-term companion for their journey. If coupled with an expert NOW coach like Will, *Leaders for Life* may be the last leadership book you will need.

JOHN ANDERSON
President
GDP Group Ltd SPC
www.gdpgrp.com
Gig Harbor, Washington

In my 40+ years as a corporate executive, two things have always amazed me. The first is just how quickly an organization recognizes the presence or absence of real leadership. The second is how fast an organization will come together to support good leaders, and how fast that begins to show up on the bottom-line.

This inspiring book proposes that New Operating Wisdom (NOW) is the foundation for successful leadership. But the reader is not left wondering how to do this. A well-constructed framework for this process is clearly and ambitiously outlined in way that, at least for me, stirred a fresh passion to further develop in my life!

The process of walking in NOW will challenge each of us, and will likely require fresh doses of metanoia – changing our perspective and way of thinking about leadership. NOW requires a servant's heart and leaning upon our all-wise Heavenly Father who promises wisdom and His favor for those who love Him. All we have to do is ask! James 1:5 says, "If you need wisdom, ask our generous God, and He will give it to you."

MIKE HARDEGREE
Vice President, Strategic Business Development
Tietex International, Ltd.
www.tietex.com
Spartanburg, South Carolina

Through a blend of personal narrative, biblical accounts and sound leadership principles, Will leads readers through a reflective study to increase personal impact and kingdom advancement. Will fearlessly challenges young and old alike to remember who they are in Christ and sharpen leadership skills and ability. Romans 12:8 (TPT) says, "If you have the gift of leadership, be passionate about your leadership." Will provides a framework to walk in passionate leadership. Great for individual work, families or small groups and teams, this roadmap towards increased kingdom effectiveness is a must read for today's leaders.

MICHAEL EVANS, PH.D.
Adjunct Professor, Urban Studies Program, Eastern University, Pennsylvania
Director of Academic Advancement, Lincoln Leadership
Academy Charter School, Allentown, Pennsylvania

This book by Will Meier is a must read for all who have ever aspired to be in leadership. It is a delightful read in truly breaking down terminology and language helping the reader to better understand the entire book. I was definitely blessed by the pertinent Scriptures which provided support and strength to this wonderful leadership module that God has given him. The 12C's that are presented in this book are such a new, innovative and revolutionary teaching module that can be utilized in all Seven Mountains of Culture. Readers will enjoy reading this from cover to the end as they are able to apply real life situations to each chapter.

DR. SHARON BILLINS
CEO, Palm Tree International Ministries
www.sharonbillins.org
Columbus, Georgia

I've been in the trenches together with Will Meier for over a decade. Will knows what it's like to be down and looking up for the path forward. He is an experienced guide who will lead you into the new era of your life with the unerring truth of the Word of God. Don't waste your battles, your pain, your hard lessons learned in life! Will lays out clear direction for transformation using all of the elements of your own life – the good stuff and the hard stuff. In these pages you will see God's path forming in front of you. Step into the fullness of all that God has for you through *Leaders for Life*. Your destiny awaits!

SYLVIA BLAIR
Business Leader/Worship Leader/Psalmist
Foundations Prime Ministries
Hamden, Connecticut

This is a wonderful book on leadership through a new lens and perspective. There are so many great nuggets in here that we can grab hold of and walk out in our lives every day. I love the analogy of NOW, which stands for new operating wisdom; that is a great revelation in itself. I often talk about the NOW of God and being in the NOW, walking out our lives real-time with the Lord. This analogy brings much depth and clarity to the NOW of God.

Will does a great job of bringing his coaching techniques into the book and interacting with the reader as their coach, so that at the end of the book we have arrived at a new place with God, a deeper place with God. It's not just a read but an adventure with the Holy Spirit as Will graciously guides us through some new territory to help us tap into more of who we are in Christ and how we can help others do the same.

I believe this is part of the new wineskin and acceleration the Lord is releasing where we can engage and learn and mentor all at the same time as we are discovering more of God with each other and within each other. This is an on time book for this kingdom age and is one of those books you can refer back to regularly for navigating the times we are in.

WENDE JONES
President, KCIA
www.kcialliance.org
CEO, Agile Business Services
www.agilenw.com
Beaverton, Oregon

Leaders for Life is written so simply, but bears such weight in truth. Stepping into relationship with the Father requires sonship and sonship requires surrender and sacrifice. From this foundation, God can start the process to reshape and rebuild who we are in Him, reforming and refining us into His image, creating champions for change. It is only through relationship, with our Creator Yahweh, that we will truly grasp who we are and what we are to walk out.

Will Meier brings to light the responsibility we carry as sons and daughters, calling us to align with the Father and His plan. It is up to us to step into our calling and use what we have at hand, right NOW. He will be with us in every step we take, guiding us, protecting us, showering on us extreme favor, loving us, encouraging us, even carrying us when we grow weary. But ultimately, He needs our yes.

Leaders for Life will equip you with practical steps and bring you to the realization of the process, to not only becoming, but growing great leaders. Outlining key points such as perspective and that our trials are opportunities for growth, God wants to bring us to maturity. All callings need to be associated with a deep sense of responsibility and therefore require discipline and maturity from the one choosing to walk it out.

For too long we have forfeited our seats of government, in our respective mountains and God is calling us back, to be rulers and stewards over our dominion. *Leaders for Life* may only take you a couple of sittings to read. I exhort you to engage with its contents, spending time in prayer, deeply reflecting on how it relates to you and applying it to your life. This book overflows with ripened wisdom and understanding that has evidently been aged and tested with time.

I commend Will for his walk with the Lord, from which the words of this book clearly stem. When you interact with this book it does not simply go to your head. Rather, it flows straight from Will's heart and showers over yours, sinking into the depths of who you are, calling your inner being to rise up and be in the fullest extent of its creation. I connected with this book and a piece of Will's heart on a profound level, as I hope you do, too.

Leaders for Life is a book that you will keep on the "frequent reads" section on your bookshelf, to be revisited time and time again.

MICAH SANCHEZ
Millennial Entrepreneur
Calgary, Alberta, Canada

Will Meier's prophetic voice breaks through the complications of leadership development to call kingdom people into kingdom action. With clear focus and mission, Will leads readers through a personal process as they learn to hear and respond to the voice of God. Leadership rooted in relationship with God yields fruitfulness that will push back darkness and usher in greater kingdom realities. Both emerging leaders and those of us who have been leading for a long time can benefit from this clarion call to righteous leadership.

DAN EVANS
Pastor, Mount Zion Christian Fellowship
Bolton, Connecticut

Thank you for the invitation to read *Leaders for Life* and the chance to immerse myself in the rich tapestry of leadership from a biblical perspective. It is a tour de force that weaves together the heroes of our faith and civilization through history. I recognize in Will's work an immense amount of research and biblical authority. It is remarkably comprehensive and logically written.

CLIVE MATHER
President & Chair, Relational Peacebuilding Initiatives
www.relationalpeacebuilding.org
Chair, Tear Fund USA
www.tearfundusa.org
Worplesdon, Guildford, United Kingdom

Will Meier is a great example of an emerging apostolic leader and his book, *Leaders for Life*, is a game changer and raises the bar for all leaders globally. Will has given us a blueprint for leadership that all leaders can use and benefit from.

DR. MARK KAUFFMAN
CEO, Butz Flowers and Gifts
www.butzflowers.net
Apostle, Jubilee Ministries Intl.
www.jubileeministriesint.com
Board Chair, Kingdom Congressional International Alliance (KCIA)
www.kcialliance.org
Author, *The Presence Driven Leader*
New Castle, Pennsylvania

There is a lot of talk about leadership, and with good cause as each of us has some kind of influence over at least one person. That makes us a leader at some level. This book by Will Meier will help you to become the leader that God wants you, and has called you to be. In fact, in addition to the excellent material, Will also adds very specific tools at the end of each chapter that will allow you to incorporate these concepts quickly in your life. I have found that great leaders never stop learning. This book is a great tool to enable you to become the leader you aspire to be.

RICH MARSHALL
Author: *God@Work; God@Work II*; and *God@Rest*
Host of God@Work on GodTV
www.god.tv
Castle Rock, Colorado

Leaders for Life gives practical and relevant information that can help any leader go to the next level in their career. Like any great book, there will always be a need to change the way in which we think if we are going to improve in leadership. I have found in over 20 years of leadership that we grow the most as we are being stretched. Read this book and implement its principles. You will be stretched and also glad that you did.

CHAD NORRIS
Lead Pastor, Bridgeway Church
www.bridgewaychurch.org
Author of *Mama Jane's Secret: Walking in Friendship with God*
Greenville, South Carolina

As a senior manager of an engineering consulting firm and a youth pastor, there is one thing I want my young professionals and youth to know—their IDENTITY. Ephesians 2:10 says, *"We are God's Masterpiece; He has created us anew in Christ Jesus, so we can do the good things He planned for us long ago."*

Leaders for Life is a great start to finding out what awesome, fantastic miracles and mountain-moving things God has planned for you to do in bringing heaven on earth. The 12C NOW Model is an incredible, dynamic, simple way to understand your leadership strengths and weaknesses. God's kingdom is dynamic, and we are also just as dynamic because we were created for heaven in God's image long ago.

More than just another book on Christian leadership, Will Meier does not just teach you how God created you to be a leader, but you learn how to encourage and lift others to be leaders as well. After reading, you won't just be the best you, but a loving, living, purposeful, heavenly known leader for God.

DAVE DORMIER, P.E.
Professional Engineer, Youth Pastor,
KCIA Director & Treasurer
www.erlandsen.com
www.kcialliance.org
Quincy, Washington

Engineer, leader, and long-haul learner, Will Meier, gives us fresh, innovative insights to decipher ways to cooperate with God as Master Gardener as He tends and grooms us.

Will's constructs help tie down the loose ends, flights of fancy, fresh joys, and puzzling pieces that come up when we are freed to look up after an arduous, daily "calling" journey. He supplies tools to address the leadership vacuum. I will use his wise perspective to study my garden plots that have become acreage!

JANE VANDERPLOEG
Co-Founder and Corporate Officer/ Community Relations
Flightcom, Firecom, & Sonetics Corporation
www.flightcom.net
www.firecom.com
www.soneticscorp.com
Executive Director, Encouragers, Inc.
(Serving as an alongside trustee, campus minister, encourager, poet and friend)
Lake Oswego, Oregon

Please do not read this book merely for a fresh theory or theology of leadership. Though it provides both, it also provides much more—practical strategies and spiritual exercises to implement personal and corporate transformation. It is rare for an author to have the experience and expertise necessary to deliver on such broad and ambitious objectives.

This book demonstrates that Will Meier has all the multiform gifting required. The thoughts and actions of leaders in every sphere of life will greatly benefit from reading, marking, inwardly digesting and applying what they read between these covers.

DR. PETER S. HESLAM
Director of Transforming Business and Senior Fellow, University of Cambridge
www.cam.ac.uk
Cambridge, England, United Kingdom

Leaders for Life is worth reading slowly. Will Meier unpacks leadership perspectives from a variety of common, professional and faith resources to make an exciting journey into what NOW Leadership looks like. Mixing personal, anecdotal and apostolic insights into practically applicable leadership practice, Will thoughtfully guides the journey to assist leaders to discover where they fit into the leadership spectrum, where they can access fresh perspectives, and how to improve their leadership as men and women of God.

By inserting practical exercises to improve understanding and response to God's call to leaders, Will makes *Leaders for Life* more than a book. He presents a course of leadership development principles to help readers understand apostolic, fivefold ministries and seven mountains of influence leadership perspectives and practice. His NOW Leadership Model benefits the leadership development of those responding to the call of God to dive deeper and live fuller lives.

Will's coaching background comes through in powerful and dynamic fashion as he guides readers through each chapter and each exercise with the intent and desire to see each person become the best leader they can be and respond to God's call to them as leaders in His kingdom. Every page is a commitment to Spirit-led leadership development and a deeper life experience of that leadership through a full surrender to Jesus Christ.

Your leadership, life and ministry will benefit in every area of application as you determine to embrace each truth and challenge, NOW and into the future. Read slowly. Drink deeply. Reflect honestly. Submit fully. Harvest abundantly.

DR. D. L. (DOUG) ATHA
Assistant Professor of Graduate Studies
& Christian Ministry/Non Profit Stream Director
Master of Arts in Leadership
Trinity Western University
Langley, British Columbia, Canada

Will Meier's book, *Leaders for Life,* is a beautiful blending of principle and practicality to bring transformation. As a Ph.D. in Organizational Leadership, I have read my share of books on leadership, many of them faith-based. *Leaders for Life* is more than faith-based; it is a masterful integration of biblical basis, kingdom perspective and contemporary theory with corporate application. Meier includes historical case studies and action steps based on his 12C's for New Operating Wisdom. I encourage all leaders or would-be leaders to read *Leaders for Life.*

TIMOTHY HAMON, PH.D.
CEO, Christian International Ministries
www.christianinternational.com
Santa Rosa Beach, Florida

FOREWORD
BY DR. BRUCE COOK

The success of any organization rises or falls on the effectiveness, strength, wisdom and health of its leadership. This has been true through the ages and remains so today. Defining leadership is another matter. A vast body of knowledge on the subject of leadership exists, and entire departments, schools, colleges and/or curricula of universities are devoted to and focused on the study of leadership.

Several theories of leadership have been postulated, including the Great Person theory that the best leaders are born great, and the Developmental Theory that the best leaders become great over time through life experience. This has been referred to as Nature versus Nurture. Then there are the Organizational and Environmental theories that Circumstances, Crises and Cultures necessitate and produce great leaders when the time is right, and cause them to emerge, step forward, rise to the top, or come to the forefront. These are referred to as Situational Leaders. Finally, there are hybrid theories that combine elements of each of these.

The Bass Handbook of Leadership: Theory, Research, and Managerial Applications by Bernard M. Bass is a standard academic textbook on this subject that has been used since the 1970s, and other well-known contributors to this field are Fred Fiedler, Warren Bennis, and John Maxwell, among many others.

Yet, with all of this knowledge, research and a vast, rich literature; personality assessments and profiles; and psychological tests available today, leadership success and effectiveness remains somewhat elusive, difficult to define, measure, and predict, and an enigma shrouded in a mystery – in short, a mixture of art and science. However, most people can recognize when it's present, and when it's not (absent). And obviously, some groups like military organizations, have a more defined and standardized process for training, evaluating and promoting leaders.

I have had the privilege of studying, observing and practicing leadership for over 40 years, and have served in Board governance for some 20 organizations, and in management and/or senior leadership for several other organizations, both for-profit, nonprofit and governmental/political. This includes businesses and corporations in several different industries and sectors, investment firms, banks, universities, political parties, churches, and para-ministries, and a wide variety of nonprofits with different missions and foci.

My conclusion from a lifetime of learning and practice on the subject of leadership is that the key focus or primary outcome for any organization in regard to leadership must or at least should be to develop, grow, nurture, incentivize, reward, compensate, promote and reproduce great leadership teams throughout the organization, in every division and department, rather than just focus on one Chief Executive Officer or Executive Director to lead the organization by themselves. The best leaders recruit, recognize, reward and develop great teams at all levels of an organization.

Natural charisma, intelligence, respect for authority, and a strong work ethic can be great tools for leaders, but sustainable leadership for the long term must go far beyond natural endowments and general principles. It must also include vision, mission, systems, processes, goals, objectives, benchmarks, strategy, tactics, measurement, metrics, monitoring, margins, service, character, culture, communication, capacity, competency, teamwork, innovation, profitability and more.

Will Meier has authored a seminal work and added an important new contribution to the literature on leadership, and filled a gaping void by writing on leadership process – not just from an organizational or environmental perspective, but also from a personal and interpersonal framework. His book and writing style are clear, concise and eloquent, and each chapter includes in-depth content on one of the 12C's, a case study of a famous historical figure, as well as one or more stories from current leaders.

The 12C structure and architecture for the NOW Leadership model includes Calling, Connection, Competency, Capacity, Convergence, Catalyst, Champions, Culture, Collaboration, Creativity, Communication and Compassion. Within these main chapters are additional subset topics such as Character, Constraints, Correction, Community, Covenant, Compensation, Courage, Context and Celebration. There are also several tables, figures and diagrams included to help illustrate key data points to the readers.

I commend Will for his effort and accomplishment, and lead the chorus of applause that will no doubt follow the release of this brilliant, inspired book by saying, "Thank you." I would have benefited many times over from having read and applied this NOW Leadership process much earlier in my career, but it's never too late to learn and practice the NOW Leadership model. So why wait? I encourage you to take action and start today. This book is destined to become a classic, and I encourage you to read it and apply it to your own leadership role, situation, journey and legacy, and become one of the many "Leaders for Life" globally.

BRUCE COOK, PH.D.
Chairman, VentureAdvisers, Inc.
Chairman, Kingdom House Publishing
Chairman Emeritus & Global Ambassador, KCIA
Co-founder, 8thMountain.com

THE BEST LEADERS RECRUIT, RECOGNIZE,
REWARD AND DEVELOP GREAT TEAMS
AT ALL LEVELS OF AN ORGANIZATION.
THEY DO THIS NOT JUST FROM AN
ORGANIZATIONAL OR ENVIRONMENTAL
PERSPECTIVE, BUT ALSO FROM A
PERSONAL APPROACH AND WITHIN
AN INTERPERSONAL FRAMEWORK.

DR. BRUCE COOK

PREFACE

For many years I contemplated writing a book. I had many false starts and hit roadblocks along the way. But, when the appointed time comes to step into your assignment, God will make it abundantly clear. A series of events took place that catapulted me into my calling that I could not have imagined. I was in a meeting at the beginning of this year with a spiritual father who is an author, editor, publisher, entrepreneur, businessman and more. At the end of the meeting, he prayed for an impartation of his anointing upon his Right-Hand Prayer Team.

Well, the next morning I woke up and heard a very clear directive. It did not originate in my thinking. It came from outside of myself. I heard, "Write a book about Peter." My initial response was, "Well, I have not thought much about Peter. I have always gravitated to Joseph, Jeremiah, Isaiah, and Abraham." The impact of the directive carried a momentum I could not ignore, so I began to embrace it. As I was reflecting on this, I felt relieved that the assignment did not originate with me, and that the request was not unreasonable. This was something I could do. So I said, "Yes."

In that yes, I realized that the genesis of this book was birthed through my pain, struggles, frustrations, and setbacks to gain a healthy way to interpret my life circumstances. Our interpretive process can create life-long, repeating scripts that either empower or disempower our future. An empowering script my friend told me is that "Your pain is pregnant with purpose." God wants to use our pain redemptively to create solutions and teach us new wisdom. Nothing has to be wasted in life.

When I was reviewing this book and getting feedback from a friend, I wrote that this manuscript was written as a result of my pain, passion and purifying to create new positive outcomes in others. The refiner's fire is the backdrop of this book. The words you are about to read have the potential to weld the pieces of your life together through that refiner's fire.

One of my passions, gifts and strengths lies in activating and actualizing the blueprints of heaven given to each of us from the Father. Some call them the scrolls written about your life (Psa. 139:16); others refer to them as the dreams God has given you, and the word destiny. We need the breaker anointing to set the captives free from their confinement to bring people into the fullness of Christ (Isa. 42:6-7). By this I mean the fullness of their purpose, calling, destiny and potential.

This does not happen automatically. Since I believe all followers of Christ are leaders, I am writing this book to "leaders". You are a leader if Christ is in you, who is the hope of glory.

THE PROCESS IS DESIGNED TO PERFECT YOU

This book is about the process by which we become leaders, grow and raise up other leaders. There are literally hundreds if not thousands of books written on different leadership models and principles of leadership. Principles are important, but learning the process of leadership is for the most part overlooked. Embracing the process will bring you into proven principles that work for you based on your gifts, talents, skills, abilities, personality, personal history, culture, education, work experience, personal constraints, organizational resources, and the people that you lead.

By way of definition, a principle is a fundamental truth or proposition that serves as the foundation for a system of belief or behavior. A process is a series of actions or steps taken to achieve a particular end. As we embrace the process, foundations will fall into place and remain.

The construct of this book is about the leadership process which will enable you to connect the dots so you understand where you are in your journey. The transitions between phases in the process are perhaps our most insecure time with the greatest potential for anxiety and vulnerability. The lines between these different stages may not always be clear to us; therefore, at times we may experience feelings of instability, insecurity, and/or uncertainty. Finding your point of reference and learning to recognize, navigate and integrate the different phases of the process, are perhaps the most important outcomes you may receive or experience by embracing NOW Leadership.

Whether you are the chief operations officer (COO) of your family, a mom, engineer, nurse, care giver, secretary, business owner, or CEO of a large corporation, church or ministry in any vocation or profession, we are ambassadors of the King of Kings who have a commission to bring the kingdom of heaven into our spheres of influence. The steps to becoming a leader are multifaceted, as are the steps to maintaining and advancing as a leader.

I have a particular heart to see C-level entrepreneurs, intrapreneurs, inventors, creatives, collaborators, innovators, facilitators, revivalists, awakeners, reformers and the like to find their place, platform and voice. We are in a season where God is assembling a great army for the next great harvest. Individuals as well as organizations, businesses and nations require kingdom re-engineering and overhaul to upgrade and orient them to this new season. If not, they will rapidly experience obsolescence, and disruptive innovators will take the new spaces. Kingdom leaders and enterprises that embrace the acceleration of heaven will nullify the impact of deceleration.

Beyond that, there is an emergence of apostolic and prophetic marketplace champions who will arise and impact their areas of influence. This book lays out a construct, or railroad tracks, that you can follow and utilize. Peter will be our key focus in this journey primarily through the "Acts" of the apostles as an extended case study of someone utilizing the 12C's in different seasons of their journey and development as a leader, and so Peter's life and the 12C's are the common thread through all of the chapters.

By no means is this book exhaustive in its scope; it is just touching the tip of an iceberg and scratching the surface. What is recorded in the book of Acts is the history of the new now – what God is doing presently in the earth. We see the birthing and emergence of the Church ("ecclesia") that has since been used by God to help equip, edify, empower and transform billions of lives to impact, influence, shape and transform the history of nations.

NEW LANGUAGE FOR LEADERSHIP INNOVATION

We have called this construct of new language to describe aspects of leadership development, NOW Leadership. The NOW stands for: **N**ew **O**perating **W**isdom.

God is in the business of downloading wisdom to those who seek Him. To be clear in this definition, there is only One who has ALL wisdom who is the Ancient of Days (Dan. 7:13; Prov. 8). There is nothing new that can be added, but I believe there are dimensions of wisdom which are yet to be unveiled at this time in history (Jas. 1:9).

"By me kings reign, And rulers decree justice. By me princes rule, and nobles, All who judge rightly. I love those who love me; And those who diligently seek me will find me. Riches and honor are with me, enduring wealth and righteousness." (Prov. 8:12-14)

The benefits of engaging wisdom will produce a lasting leadership legacy which includes justice, doing right, riches, honor and enduring wealth. Every leader needs wisdom to lead. A wise leader will ask for godly, divine wisdom (Jas. 3:13-18).

Therefore be careful how you walk, not as unwise men but as wise. (Eph. 5:15)

The word wise in the Greek is *sophos*. The Greeks derived this word from the Hebrew word *sophim* which refers to watchmen who used to ascend the mountains to gain perspective and understand the motions of the heavens. How apropos. If you are going to ascend the 8 Mountains of the Lord, you will need this wisdom to gain kingdom perspective! The basic meaning of sophos is one who knows how to regulate one's course in view of the heavens or relationship with God! Wisdom is skillful, expert, prudent, sensible, and judicious.

The New Operating Wisdom carries and conveys the kingdom of heaven perspective.

We need wisdom's perspective to build according to the blueprints given from heaven. The apostle Paul built according to the grace given him as a "wise" master builder. We need to do the same in every area we touch in the mountains of culture. It is not just relegated to the four walls of the Church but must expand into every facet of our society. Our business plans and ventures need New Operating Wisdom to compete in today's ecosystem with Jesus being the Chief Executive Officer.

According to the grace of God which was given to me, like a wise master builder I laid a foundation, and another is building on it. But each man must be careful how he builds on it. (1 Cor. 3:10)

The NOW also refers to the immediacy of the kingdom. Jesus said, "Repent for the kingdom of heaven is at hand." We don't want to live in the past, or park ourselves at futuristic prophetic words. We need to be positioned to receive the kingdom *now* by being aligned in the right direction. Right now God gives His children wisdom in every age to provide solutions to the problems. Most simply put, wisdom is knowing what to do and knowing that it works from heaven's perspective.

NOW Leadership defines the leadership process with the 12C's model (see Chapter Four) and redefines the purpose and goal of leadership as being to impact culture by creating and implementing solutions to earthly problems from heaven's perspective.

Now is the time to step into the future. My prayer is that you would be encouraged not to give up or lose hope, but to stay the course and run your race. You are a work in progress. God is forming each one of us as His diamonds through the pressures and difficulties of life. He is cutting and polishing every facet. When the light shines on our lives, it will reflect the beauty and majesty of our God as we are made in His likeness and image.

WILL MEIER
April 19, 2019

CHAPTER ONE

LEADERSHIP:
Principles, Process, and Power Produce Profitability

Therefore, since we have so great a cloud of witnesses surrounding us, let us also lay aside every encumbrance and the sin which so easily entangles us, and let us run with endurance the race that is set before us. (Heb. 12:1)

In God's kingdom ecosystem of life, there are two railroad tracks that run throughout Scripture. We are commanded to keep God's word and obey his voice, embrace the Law and the Prophets and the Truth (or Word) and the Spirit. Truth grounds us in the foundations and Spirit is the inspiration of application to run the race before us to keep us balanced so we can handle the curves and ups and downs of life!

The Holy Spirit is the one that brings leadership Principles into daily application of our lives through the agency of Process and He gives us Power. We need the illumination from the Holy Spirit and also the ability for accomplishment. And, while there are a plethora of books written on leadership Principles, there are very few in comparison written on leadership Process. This book seeks to remedy that imbalance in the literature and body of knowledge.

The definition of power is the ability to do something especially as a faculty, quality or capacity. Power comes from the Latin meaning "to be able". If you put God in the equation, the end result is the power or ability to accomplish your objectives and mandates at hand.

Deut. 8:18 says, "And you shall remember the Lord your God, for it is He who gives you power to get wealth, that He may establish His covenant which He swore to your fathers, as it is this day." The Hebrew word used for power here is *koach,* meaning strength or power (Strong's H3581). In the New Testament, the Greek word used for power is *dunamis,* which is the root word for dynamite. Another word which is sometimes translated as power is *exousia,* which means authority.

The convergence of Principles, Process and Power will result in having the foundations, railroad tracks to run on, and the Power to get to your destination. This will result in being a profitable servant and wise steward (Matt. 25:14-30) as well as being financially and relationally profitable. (Author's Note: Purpose is subsumed within Process under the Calling chapter, and Performance and Productivity are subsumed within Process under the Capacity, Competency, Connection, Convergence, Communication and Compassion chapters.) I therefore postulate the following equation for leadership:

WE NEED TO GROW UP IN HIS POWER TO MAKE AN IMPACT.

PRINCIPLES x PROCESS x POWER = PROFITABILITY

As my friends from the Jesus movement era would say, "If all you have is the Word (principles) you will dry up. If all you have is the Spirit (process) you will blow up, but if you have the Word and Spirit, you will grow up". And from that same movement, the popular song was sung, "There is Power in the Name of Jesus".

We need to grow up in His Power to make an impact. Applying the Principles, Processes, and Power to Leadership will cause you to grow in the manner to run your race and not fall short. The process of growth requires pruning for increased fruitfulness (John 15:2). If growth is not realized, the consequences are not favorable (Matt 3:3-11; John 15:6).

Embracing the Principles, Process and Power will give you the added stability, fruitfulness, effectiveness, thrust to catapult, and will accelerate you into your destiny to create sustainability and legacy, impacting the generations to follow.

CALLED TO RUN THE RACE

It was the Wednesday before a long vacation that my wife and I watched the movie *Secretariat*. It is an award-winning film about a horse of the same name that won the Triple Crown of horse racing against all odds. Although the story ends well, the beginning was dismal. The horse racing farm which owned Secretariat was on the verge of bankruptcy. The entire family except one person, Penny Chenery, wanted to see the enterprise close because it was bleeding money. As I watched this movie, something moved deeply within me and I wept.

> *Deep calls to deep at the noise of Your waterfalls; all Your waves and Your billows passed over me.* (Psa. 42:7)

This story evoked a heart cry within me, that it is time to stand against the odds and go for it. It started with faith by one person, the heroine, in the potential of a horse breeding outcome. Her faith was in the power of their legacy's greatness that the genetics and bloodline would create a winning horse. Her faith was in the power of potential, which is in the seed!

Peter talks about being born again of imperishable and incorruptible seed which is the living and enduring word of God (1 Pet. 1:23). That seed nurtured will become a kingdom enterprise of life, a tree where God's word, life, and presence flow (Matt. 13:30-32).

There was a leader who had faith in Secretariat's future and destiny. Chenery hired a great trainer, and together they nurtured and trained this horse so he could exercise his God-given assignment to run like a champion. What was it about this movie that director Randall Wallace had captured and expressed in this story about a great horse, his trainer and owner? Something deep within me began to resonate louder and louder, and clearer and clearer.

In one scene, the father and owner of the horse estate shared a lucid moment together with his daughter, "Let him run his race". These words became the racetrack for Secretariat to fulfill his destiny. Just as Peter was called forth into greatness with his failures and successes, there is a cry and hunger in every human heart to fulfill their destiny.

The word destiny does not occur in the Bible, but there is an antonym we would like to unpack. It's the Greek term *hamartia*, which means to miss the true end and scope of our lives in God. This word is translated "sin". It is the antithesis of destiny. Destiny is reaching our destination and fullness in Christ (Eph. 4:13). The voice calling us forward resonates deep within us to bring forth the greatness and beauty within – the fullness. In Secretariat's case, it was the father's daughter who carried out the vision with impetus, sacrifice, commitment and dedication to forge a Champion.

THE POWER OF BELIEF

Champions need people to believe in them. This perhaps is the greatest gift we can give to emerging leaders: Simple belief. It provides the often needed perspective. Secondly, they need people to invest resources into them. This can look many different ways based on what people value. I made a deal with my two sons when they were younger and told them, "As long as you get your school work done, if there is anything you are interested in, I will invest in it." I put a caveat on it, that if it was super expensive, we would split the cost 50/50.

Well, my sons took me up on that and as a result, they followed their passions, interests, and curiosity. My wife and I influenced them to become continuous adult learners and successful young professionals. By the way, I never had to employ the 50/50 rule. Investing in my sons became a catalyst for their growth and their desire for learning is still a fire in their belly. If we strengthen and build according to the blueprints God put in us, the momentum will continue throughout our lives.

As parents, it is sometimes hard to find things you think you did well. Putting your money where your mouth is in this instance had big paybacks by saying loud and clear, "I believe in your passion and interests." It is not just about investing, but could also be your love and the words you use, or your hugs, prayers, affirmation, praise and encouragement. The expressions of nurture can take on many different forms.

WHEN WE CONNECT WITH THE FATHER'S PURPOSES THERE IS A SOUND THAT BEGINS TO REVERBERATE WITHIN US.

After Peter denied the Lord, Jesus used words to call him back to his assignment to feed His sheep. Jesus nurtured Peter back to health and right relationship. Another major contributor to anyone's success is the nurture you receive in the formative years when those seeds of destiny are germinating. Perhaps women have played more pivotal roles in creating heroes because of their strong influence of mothering their children. Secretariat had an owner that believed in him, and invested in him. Penny Chenery found the right trainer for this future Triple Crown horse. Her belief and investment paid off many times over, making world history.

The nurture from heaven to facilitate the growth of God's kingdom comes in many ways. The "sounds of His waterfalls" speaks to hearing His voice time and time again in the closeness of intimacy. In this place, alignment takes place within us. When we connect with the Father's purposes and design for our lives, there is a sound that begins to reverberate within us. Some people refer to this as being at the resonance of heaven.

The years of refinement and walking with the Father through the trials that have matured and perfected us, make it all worth it. It is the place where Connection causes the current of heaven to begin flowing in us through our uniqueness. Heaven and earth meet in Convergence. We move beyond Convergence to becoming change agents in the earth – Catalysts who make things happen. At the end of this process, we sense the Father's great joy and pleasure as we move in our God-given destiny and purpose.

THE SEASON OF DIVINE ACCELERATION

We are in a season where the seeds of destiny are coming to maturity in the kingdom age. When God's favor and His presence fell on Aaron's almond rod, it blossomed and bore fruit overnight to confirm his authority (Num. 17:18). This is a biblical example of supernatural growth from God's presence that many believers are experiencing today around the globe. Acceleration is when your speed keeps increasing and it does not remain constant.

Air Force pilots experience extreme accelerations of 9G's. They require special equipment so they don't black out during these extreme maneuvers. This perhaps is not the case from a spiritual perspective, but it can feel intense at times. That which took 10 years, may take 10 months, and that which took 10 months, may take 10 days. Just as fighter pilots need special equipment to maneuver, we need new spiritual technology or measures of agility to adapt to change that is coming at a faster pace than ever before.

The force of heaven has been released in the earth for the advancement of the kingdom age. There has been a great shift that has taken place. The seeds, scrolls, destinies, gifts, and storehouses that were dormant are being activated by the Holy Spirit. Advancing through the stages of NOW Leadership will create an inner spiritual flexibility to yield at every turn. God is preparing an army of Champions. The firstfruits of this company will be a first wave of harvesters who will be trained, educated, and developed to be sent into the global harvest. The gates of hell will not prevail against this great army.

This apostolic movement will not be limited to the confines of the four walls of the church. There will be apostolic hubs, resource centers, and revival centers birthed across the nations to equip, empower, and engage these hungry, radical, sold out lovers of Jesus. We see the saints of the Most High God gathering together under a convening and gathering umbrella where the atmosphere of God's presence is growing.

Apostolic and prophetic governance will be released to equip the saints for a massive end time harvest. They will be sent with a sending anointing as select arrows into every sphere of culture and society. This book is just one of many which will provide a construct for kingdom spiritual advancement for leaders.

In our weekly gatherings at Awakening Destiny Global fellowship, we are experiencing God pouring out His grace in this kingdom age. We have by no means tapped into the depths of what God is doing but are experiencing the flow of His grace. We are seeing people set free from the spirit of religion, destinies are being activated, dreams are being reconstituted, family relationships are being restored, and the new wine of innovation and new language is being poured out.

There is divine acceleration taking place, ushering us into new seasons, and there are healings, cleansings, salvations, deliverances, joy, and much more. God is bringing forth His army to confront the darkness and release the light. The forerunners and pioneers God is developing will lead this charge in the NOW.

Next, we will turn our attention to Chapter Two.

CHAPTER TWO

ACCELERATION:
Building a Strong Foundation

Therefore, since we are surrounded by such a huge crowd of witnesses to the life of faith, let us strip off every weight that slows us down, especially the sin that so easily trips us up. And let us run with endurance the race God has set before us. (Heb. 12:1, NLT)

This book is designed to facilitate leadership awareness, understanding, acceleration, transformation and empowerment in your journey. There are some basic ideas, concepts and terms about coaching and transformation we would like to introduce to you now to build a solid foundation. This includes some basics to the coaching and transformation process. The genesis of all personal and professional development is facilitated by growing in self-awareness. You cannot change that which you are not aware of. Awareness is the beginning point. Follow these steps:

1. You must first find your reference or your starting point.

2. Process new ideas, thoughts, and approaches in the context of relationships, followers, and community both personally and professionally.

3. Continuously ask powerful questions, and seek feedback to adjust your approach to grow in your self-awareness.

4. Finally, take action by developing strategy and plans for your next steps.

Transformation takes place when we grow in our self-awareness as it relates to our values and beliefs. If we understand our values, we can better understand and predict our behavior. Our beliefs can either be empowering us to advance forward into destiny, or disempowering us, which may sabotage our efforts, thus creating constraints or unwanted, self-imposed limitations, delays, hindrances, and/or blockages.

Understanding our values and beliefs as they relate to our relationships and behaviors, will enable us to change. This provides opportunity to introduce new operating wisdom! We all need resets, sometimes reboots, and even reformats to address the new challenges that face us in a dynamic, changing, global landscape.

Each chapter presents some ideas to give you a frame of reference on the topic. Included are some examples about the particular topic from leaders my friends and I know, or else they were taken from history. The stories are intended to increase your understanding of the application of the 12C process to increase your directional visibility. At the end of each chapter, there is a list of Takeaways for those of you who like the bottom line summary.

To assist you in finding your starting point, there is a short inventory you can take to get a sense of where you are in your journey. In order to move forward and create plans for the future, you need to know your starting point.

There are at least two NOW Actions assigned for each chapter. These are typically journaling exercises designed to help you grow in your awareness of yourself and others. There also is a prayer point designed to strengthen your spiritual journey.

COACHING CONVERSATION BASICS

There is a list of NOW Coaching questions that you can answer by yourself, or with a peer(s), or in a group setting. The intent is to work together with peers and teams to provide support, encouragement, and accountability.

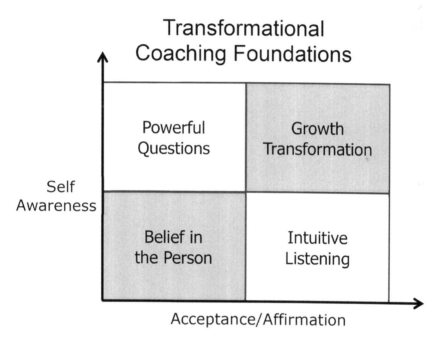

FIGURE 1.
Transformational Coaching Foundations.

TRANSFORMATIONAL COACHING FOUNDATIONS.

The NOW Coaching Process includes four key principles we encourage you to practice in your discussions. They are as follows:

1. We believe in the person we are engaging with. This is a way we honor others in their uniqueness, personal history, gifts, talents, special abilities, assignments, calling, mandates, etc. In other words, we always believe the best and give our friends and associates the benefit of the doubt.

2. In every conversation, we are not necessarily the experts and may not know the full story. We need to "tell" less, and be in the habit of asking powerful questions to help people grow in their self-awareness, dig deeper, and discover, and even uncover their blind spots to advance forward. Powerful questions create queries to bring forth the knowledge within which we can create powerful results.

3. Examples of Powerful Questions:

Non–Powerful Questions		Powerful Questions
Where are you moving?	vs	What are you moving toward?
What did you think about the project?	vs	What did you learn from the project?
How much weight do you want to lose?	vs	What does being fit mean to you?
What has changed recently?	vs	In what ways did you experience change?
What are your next year goals?	vs	What needs to happen to move to the next level?

4. The other side of powerful questions is intuitive listening. When we listen to others, we communicate affirmation, acceptance, and create a positive relationship space. People feel "heard" in this safe place. In this context, we can read between the lines, observe body language, and listen to our intuition about what is being

said. From this place we can ask more powerful questions. We want to move away from self-centered, autobiographical listening to purposeful and intuitive listening.

By growing in self-awareness through asking powerful questions and practicing intuitive listening in the context of a safe environment, you are able to grow, experience "aha" moments, and have breakthroughs that will lead to growth and transformation.

MOVING TOWARDS GREATER AUTHENTICITY —A MODEL FOR GOING DEEPER

There is no question that in order to lead more effectively, we need to develop and maintain effective interpersonal relationships and trust. There is a tool that was developed by Joe Luft and Harry Ingham in 1955 called the Johari Window. It is a model which describes interpersonal relationships based on the simple fact that any relationship is comprised of things known and unknown.

The importance of their model is this: We often get into problems when we don't know what we don't know. When people see themselves as others see them, they function better with those around them and are in alignment or congruence. When our behavior, perception, status or identity differs from that of others' view of us, it can open up opportunity for misunderstanding, dissonance, offences, and conflicts.

WHEN PEOPLE SEE THEMSELVES AS OTHERS SEE THEM, THEY FUNCTION BETTER WITH THOSE AROUND THEM.

On the following page, you will find a "Johari Window" which can help us to understand some of the dynamics of inter and intra personal relationships. The interaction of what is known or unknown to us, with what is unknown to others, leads to four areas that impact on the relationship.

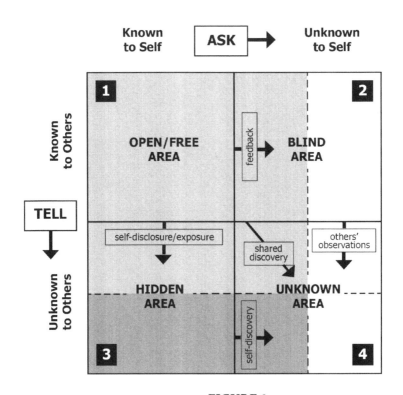

FIGURE 2.
The Johari Window.
Copyright © 1955 by Joe Luft and Harry Ingham.

FOUR AREAS THAT IMPACT RELATIONSHIPS

What Everyone Knows – Open Area

This consists of information mutually known and shared by both people in the relationship. It includes those things which others see in us, and which we see in ourselves – e.g., strong work ethic, values, love your family, etc.

Our "Blind Spots" – Blind Area

Unlike the open area, this area contains those things that others know about us of which we are unaware. This is often referred to as our "blind spots." These are things people know about us, but we don't know about ourselves. There are also things God may know about us that we do not acknowledge or see.

Through verbal and non-verbal interactions, we convey messages that allow other people to know us. A slip of the tongue or a facial response may reveal to others our thoughts, motives, etc. while we remain unaware of them having been communicated nonverbally. For example, we may think we are doing a great job at solving a problem, but we may leave people behind who have different perspectives and approaches. This could create a space for misunderstanding, thereby potentially impacting the team. To move deeper into the aspects of yourself that are unknown to yourself, feedback will minimize the blind area.

Our Private Space – Hidden Area

This area includes those things we know about ourselves, but which we choose to keep private from others, or information, thoughts and feelings that we choose not to share with others. For example, we may put up a front or a facade to mask how we really feel or what we really believe. Ideally, we can reduce this space by being appropriately open or transparent with those we trust. Self disclosure is the driver that reduces this hidden area in our relationships and community.

Unseen Potential – Unknown Area

This is the undiscovered aspect of a relationship and as such it forms the "potential" area. One member of a relationship may discover something new about the other. This information may enter the blind or hidden area of the relationship or it could be mutually shared and become a part of the open area – e.g. this could be a latent talent, something hidden from your history that is impacting your perspective, or from a kingdom of heaven standpoint, a treasure or resource that has not been unveiled.

Whenever we go through trials and conflicts, the unknown area grows smaller as you grow in awareness. Many of us do not fully comprehend what we really value. Our perceived values and actions do not always line up. There may be buried, disempowering scripts hidden in our bruises and wounds from our past. These belief systems create demand for fulfillment and create atmospheres about us. We want to be attracting heaven in our lives.

Jesus said in John 14:30 that the ruler of this world is coming, and has nothing in me. Reducing the unknown area eliminates the opportunity for the enemy to inflict his chaos and pain in your life. There will be nothing that Satan can use to pull your strings and sabatoge your future. The enemy of your soul does not play fair and will wait for the most opportune time to derail, sabotage, and minimize you.

SELF-DISCLOSURE AND FEEDBACK ARE KEY TO GREATER AUTHENTICITY

The importance of the Johari Window for NOW Leadership is that we must continuously be self-disclosing and obtaining feedback. We can close the gap on the unknowns to create knowns. Feedback is the breakfast food of champions. It provides mirrors in which to see ourselves in the way others we relate to do.

We can receive feedback from our direct reports, followers, networks, the Word of God, the Holy Spirit, coaches, mentors or even social media. What are people saying about you? If we do not get feedback through the normal channels of Connection, Communication, and Collaboration, we may get it during the Capacity phase. This will surely reveal the areas we may need to change in or great opportunities for advancement and growth.

All feedback needs to be properly filtered, weighted and adjusted so we can respond to it accordingly. You may find that you can't see some of the things you do really well because you think it is "normal."

And, on the other hand, you may find that you are doing things you were not aware of. Either way, as leaders we need to take ownership and responsibility and decide how to improve.

Self-disclosure is another term for being authentic and transparent. As leaders migrate toward being "real" and take off the masks and facades, you will develop improved relationships, rapport, respect, and credibility. This is where developing Connection and Communication is of vital importance. This practice can potentially eliminate misunderstandings.

We are living in an age where people do not have much tolerance for fakes. It takes courage to be yourself and be comfortable in your own skin, and not allow rejection, insecurity, and fear to derail you. The greater confidence you convey in being true to yourself and others, the more effective you will become as a leader. People are more apt to accept you for being you versus trying to be something that you are not.

The powerful part of getting feedback by asking for it, and self-disclosing by telling, is it creates an opportunity to move you into new potential. You may discover things about yourself you didn't know. Or through prayer – asking and self-disclosure or telling – having conversation with the Lord or a group of believers, God may show you a key or give you wisdom, or a strategy that was not realized.

This whole process can help you understand why you have conflicts with people. Many people do not understand what they value and how it predicts your behavior. The unknown dimensions, especially around values, are spaces where misunderstanding can take place.

This short chapter is provided to give you a brief introduction to coaching practices to implement and practice while doing the NOW Actions and NOW Coaching Questions. In the end it is all about relationships. Develop them as best as you can for as long as you can. They are worth it and will pay rich dividends.

Next, we will turn our attention to Chapter Three.

CHAPTER THREE

C-LEVEL CHAMPIONS: The Problem and Solution

It will become a sign and a witness to the Lord of hosts in the land of Egypt; for they will cry to the Lord because of oppressors, and He will send them a Savior and a Champion, and He will deliver them. (Isa. 19:20)

THE PROBLEM: CHAMPIONS IN GREAT DEMAND

Champions are in great demand in every generation, including today, due to their scarcity and the issues and challenges of the day. The prophet Isaiah had a powerful revelation of the coming Messiah King centuries before the time of His birth. Most of us have an understanding of Jesus as our Savior. He is the loving and understanding One. But, Isaiah also had insight into the fact that Jesus was a Champion.

This word champion means a person who has surpassed all rivals. Synonyms include chief, captain, chief officer or leader. It is the highest rank. It is also of the greatest importance and influence. Jesus is our chief of the C-level leaders and the Champion who conquered sin and the grave. That DNA of Jesus is given to His children and we are made in His likeness and image and told by Jesus that we will do even "greater works" (John 14:12).

I believe our forefathers in the faith were Champions, and that David's mighty men were in that same league. Many of them are listed in Hebrews chapter 11. These are those who are recorded in history, but there are myriads today who are like them, prepared and positioned, many of whom are still undiscovered, unnoticed or unrecognized.

The Lord is looking to raise up dread Champions of the faith in both the marketplace and ministry. For too long we have limited ourselves about what this looks like. Our religious paradigms need to shift to realize that there are Champions emerging to impact our Culture and society beyond the Church's four walls.

> But the LORD is with me like a dread champion; Therefore my persecutors will stumble and not prevail. They will be utterly ashamed, because they have failed, With an everlasting disgrace that will not be forgotten. (Jer. 21:11)

There is another dimension to these Champions. At the beginning of 2019, I attended an international kingdom marketplace summit in Denver, Colorado. At the summit, Bridgette Marx from South Africa shared about five major movements taking place in the earth currently. As I reflected on this discussion, I realized the movements were really about God raising up a new generation of leaders. They are movements led by leaders.

Before we share these five movements, we should introduce the five ascension gifts Jesus gave the Church to equip and prepare her to walk in the fullness, unity and maturity of the saints. These are the gifts of the apostles, prophets, teachers, pastors, and evangelists.

> But to each one of us grace was given according to the measure of Christ's gift. Therefore it says, "When He ascended on high, He led captive a host of captives, And He gave gifts to men." (Now this

expression, "He ascended," what does it mean except that He also had descended into the lower parts of the earth?) And He gave some as apostles, and some as prophets, and some as evangelists, and some as pastors and teachers, for the equipping of the saints for the work of service, to the building up of the body of Christ; until we all attain to the unity of the faith, and of the knowledge of the Son of God, to a mature man, to the measure of the stature which belongs to the fullness of Christ. (Eph. 4:7-9, 11-13)

Walt Pilcher has written an excellent book on this subject titled *The Five-fold Effect: Unlocking Power Leadership for Amazing Results in Your Organization.* His book applies each of the fivefold gifts to optimal functioning in the marketplace—corporate positions, team dynamics and results. These spiritual gifts help facilitate and touch on Connection, Creativity, Collaboration, Capacity, Competency and Communication. Each of these fivefold gifts can be more effectively recognized, discerned, developed and stewarded through practice and usage over time.

My wife quotes often a statement her divinity professor spoke. "Anything worth doing is worth doing poorly." This was said to break through procrastination, the fear of failure and thinking we need to arrive at perfection instantaneously. Growth is a process. We are in a season of accelerated growth for Champions to emerge and come forth from hiding.

At the summit, Bridgette shared that the five movements taking place in the earth today are the following:

1. **The reformation of the Church** - This is about building the culture of heaven and honor where God's presence is stewarded in the dynamo of the word and spirit.

2. **True apostles** – These are the authentic ones that will walk in humility and stand up in the Government Mountain that will bring the government of Jesus to the earth in the nations. They will establish the sheep nations versus goat nations. They will be

selfless servant leaders supporting from the bottom up and not top down and endued with power to accomplish God's mandates in the earth.

3. **New breed of prophets and teachers emerging** – These folks will be the catalysts and a pivotal force in the earth for releasing a global tsunami of His Spirit in the earth.

4. **Marketplace leaders that create kingdom ecosystems** – These leaders will innovate, invent, create, build, trade, store, release, harvest, and transform through the marketplace.

5. **Great Harvest** - This is the work of the evangelists and the season of the saints. Multitudes will come into the kingdom and the saints will indeed do the work and not just a few men and women.

ADVANCEMENT IN THE NOW: THE INTERNATIONAL CULTURE SHAPERS SUMMIT

There are numerous movements emerging that are mobilizing leaders and strategic partnerships. Champions from every area of culture are gathering in a great army to transform our society. One movement to impact our Culture was birthed over 43 years ago in 1975 as a result of God speaking to Loren Cunningham and Bill Bright. Both of these men were fully engaged with the younger generation of believers, YWAM and Campus Crusade for Christ, respectively. Interestingly, they both recognized there was a need to impact the Culture through the emerging generation. Francis Schaeffer also received and helped to pioneer this revelation of the Seven Mountains of Cultural Influence.

The progress of embodying this word seems to have taken some time. Some seeds perhaps take a longer time to mature. New positive narratives are being created. In many cases, emerging leaders are being trained for their assignments through men and women who are laying down their lives to raise up Champions in the earth.

At the Culture Shapers Summit March 28-31, over 350 leaders from around the globe with over 40 speakers joined the continuum to evaluate, create, unify, and implement strategies and create kingdom cohorts. Leaders from every sphere of influence shared their learning, stories, insight and wisdom.

Some of those leaders included Os and Pamela Hillman, Lance Wallnau, Bruce Cook, Joseph Mattera, Del Tackett, James and Anna Kramer, Steve Green, Stephen Kendrick, Roma Downey, Franklin Santagate, Hugh Hewitt, Pat Asp, Tony Perkins, Ford Taylor, Patrice Tsague, Ken Blackwell, Chad Merrill, Mike Sharrow, Greg Leith, Robert Watkins, Doug Spada, Joe Battaglia, Chris Conant, Charlie Lewis, Lonnie Gienger, Guy Rodgers, Karen Covell, Gordon Pennington, A.R. Bernard, Chris Purifoy, Kathy Branzell, Lea Carawan, Randy Powell, Chuck Stetson, Grant Skeldon, Gabrielle Bosche and Rich Marshall.

This was a catalyst to developing Creativity, Communication and Collaboration, which are key to God's strategy. God has been preparing this company of Champions over the decades for such a time as this.

WE NEED THE REAL DEAL – TRUE CHAMPIONS

The nations are in need of Champions who will develop and lead special teams that will crack the tough nut problems (social, political, financial, economic, environmental, medical, cultural, infrastructure) that have stymied nations. They are "sent" (apostolic) and are "inspired" (prophetic). They are "grounded in truth" (teachers) and have a "voice" (evangelists). They "love and nurture people" (pastors). They will uniquely fulfill their assignments and not fit into any mold made by man.

We need to connect the dots and create the linkages between the sacred and the secular by breaking down the dividing walls. In other words, God is raising up apostolic and prophetic leaders along with teachers, pastors and evangelists who will rock the landscape of our world and what we know as normal in every dimension of culture. These men and women will disruptively innovate and will cause the common to become uncommon, and the uncommon common. They are the Catalysts who will Communicate, Create, and move in Compassion to create new Culture.

We need Champions who know their God, and will do exploits in His name (Dan. 11:32). They will know their strengths and limitations and will run their race fully engaged with passion and vigor. It is not about running in our own strengths, but about being empowered. Peter, as a fisherman, I am sure was not a weak man but was strong physically since he was in the fishing trade which required heavy manual labor. He appears to have had a strong personality as well, and was impulsive at times.

After Peter was restored to Jesus, he received his assignment to "tend my sheep and feed my lambs". Jesus gave Peter this significant operating instruction.

> *"Truly, truly, I say to you, when you were younger, you used to gird yourself and walk wherever you wished; but when you grow old, you will stretch out your hands and someone else will gird you, and bring you where you do not wish to go." Now this He said, signifying by what kind of death he would glorify God. And when He had spoken this, He said to him, "Follow Me!"* (John 21:18-19)

God is going to gird us, not in our own strength, but in His strength! It will cause us to lay down our own agendas and serve kingdom agendas. We need to die faster to see divine acceleration. It will cost us everything. We need to activate these Champions and not hold them back or frustration and messes will ensure which may have been avoided. There are signposts along the race track with milestones along the way. We need to provide them the perspective, provision and the process.

PERSPECTIVE - PROVISION - PROCESS

We need perspective that we would see ourselves with God's insight from His vantage point. In order to discern the forest from the trees, we often need to see through the eyes of another. When leaders get perspective and can connect the dots, there is a divine energy released through the understanding and vision that comes from heaven.

NOW Leadership provides a construct for that perspective to emerge. I have had countless conversations with leaders who have either confirmed or told me the NOW Leadership process is relevant. They all had "aha" moments and were encouraged, and found their reference so they could get unstuck and advance in their assignment, their destiny, and their race.

Secondly, we need to see that God is in the pro-vision business. God is "pro" - for us and the vision He has given us to steward. We need to surround ourselves with men and women who believe in that vision. God wants to provide for us and teach us to live in the place of abundance versus scarcity.

Scarcity has its roots in the spirit of poverty which declares that there will never be enough, drives us to be stingy and causes stagnation. God loves joyful generosity and blesses it with increase and overflow. When we live in the provision of heaven, we will approach our calling, assignment, and relationships with greater joy and confidence.

God's favor is upon our assignments and with that favor comes provision. We may need to believe for it by faith for a season, but the resources will come. I believe that resources that have assignments connected to them carry God's favor. We may even be called to supply resources for the emerging generation to fulfill their assignment.

GOD'S FAVOR IS UPON OUR ASSIGNMENTS AND WITH THAT FAVOR COMES PROVISION.

David provided the resources for Solomon to build the temple for God's presence. David's investment was extravagant. What if there was a storehouse like the Bill and Melinda Gates Foundation available to fund kingdom initiatives and enterprises? For every problem there is a solution, and that solution has provision attached to it. God pays for what He orders.

And lastly, this book is about process, and creating a construct or model for your leadership journey. Sometimes we need to not take ourselves so seriously. Why? Because we are going to make mistakes, especially if you are pioneering something new. We must embrace the process by which we are being perfected. Peter wrote about his personal process in 2 Peter chapter 1.

In Peter's reflections, diligence, faith, moral excellence, knowledge, self-control, perseverance, and godliness were the construct for spiritual development. This list of items perhaps indicates that Peter was a continuous learner, always seeking to improve. We need to quickly take ownership of our mistakes and blunders. We can never stop being reminded of those elements of process that keep us grounded, relevant, and effective as leaders, parents, marketplace leaders, and servants of the Most High God.

RECOVERY FOR THOSE BURNED OUT

The prophet Jeremiah calls us to assess where we are in our journey as it relates to our strength to run the race. Jer. 12:5 says, *"If you have run with footmen and they have tired you out, Then how can you compete with horses? If you fall down in a land of peace, How will you do in the thicket of the Jordan?"*

There are many in the race who have been taken out because perhaps they were not equipped for the race. Pioneers and innovators experience the torrent of the upstream forces that can be very draining and taxing. There are not-so-well-meaning people that may also have contributed to your pain and wounds through treacherous behavior including betrayal, character assassination, sabotage, rebellion, accusation, slander, stealing intellectual property and the like. There are no easy answers, many feel trapped, and some have fallen prey to becoming the "victim".

For those in the race who are burned out and broken, you are not out of the game. Remember that burnt embers have the potential to start uncontrollable fires. I do not believe that the fire ever really goes out! And remember that diamonds are made out of carbon that has undergone great pressure over long periods of time. The formation process comes in ways we do not expect.

There is a path to restoration to get back into the race – the place of communion, where waiting and worship eventually give way to a reset and reboot. If you have run in your own strength and failed, then you are a prime candidate for reentry and resynchronization. The power of the spirit of adoption will bond and bandage you back together to heal.

> *Do you not know? Have you not heard? The Everlasting God, the Lord, the Creator of the ends of the earth does not become weary or tired. His understanding is inscrutable. He gives strength to the weary, And to him who lacks might He increases power. Though youths grow weary and tired, And vigorous young men stumble badly, Yet those who wait for the Lord Will gain new strength; They will mount up with wings like eagles, They will run and not get tired, They will walk and not become weary.* (Isa. 40:28-31)

This book is written for the Champions who have gone before us, to those who are in process, and to those who are yet to emerge into greatness. This is the story about the process of being perfected as sons and daughters and about being supernaturally engaged in the Father's business, moving with His strength and knowing the Father's good pleasure.

THE SOLUTION: LEADERS FOR LIFE – THE 12C NOW MODEL

NOW Leadership is for leaders who want to advance the kingdom of heaven and build for future generations. It is a leadership construct and continuum for lifetime development which is scalable to any institution, enterprise or people group. We develop and train kingdom-minded leaders to impact the marketplace and bring spiritual and cultural transformation. Our interactive and strength-based approach facilitates transformation to understand your kingdom purpose, your identity and assignment. Leaders gain and develop clarity, self-awareness, leadership agility, greater resilience, and they learn to live in kingdom career convergence.

At the core of this leadership reformation is the convergence of the royal (kingdom) and priesthood functions that John speaks of in Rev. 1:6 and 5:10 and that Peter refers to in 1 Peter 2:9. We see the practical outworking of the kingly and priestly functions in the rebuilding of the walls of Jerusalem with Nehemiah. Both Joshua the high priest and Zerubbabel the governor worked collaboratively to rebuild the walls of Jerusalem with prophetic support from Zechariah and Haggai.

> *But you are a chosen race, a royal priesthood, a holy nation, a people for God's own possession, so that you may proclaim the excellencies of Him who has called you out of darkness into His marvelous light;* (1 Pet. 2:9).

> *... and He has made us to be a kingdom, priests to His God and Father—to Him be the glory and the dominion forever and ever. Amen.* (Rev. 1:6)

We need both the royal (kingdom) and spiritual relationship dimension to effectively build with prophetic encouragement. The kingly, priestly, and prophetic is a triad that effectively builds in resilience. This triad is available to all believers. The priestly function provides us with relational insight with spiritual and emotional intelligence. Believers have a 10X advantage because of the Holy Spirit working in their lives. The royal function can be translated kingdom or leadership. The kingdom leadership dimension is the rule and reign of Jesus from the mountain of the Lord.

Those leaders that walk in the government of heaven as leaders will carry authority, decrees, establish atmospheres, create systems, policy, and laws to govern their sphere of influence. The end result of this triad is a positive belonging and sonship – identity, legacy, excellence, light, sustainability of that leader effectiveness, and resounding glory that is consequently released. God gets the Glory! Leadership priests rule from the mountain of the Lord. One does not become a kingdom priest overnight. There is a process involved.

We will explore your Calling, empower strategic Connections, and provide a framework to develop your Competencies and Capacities, enabling you to live in your sweet spot of Convergence and become a change agent – Catalyst. The end goal is to produce Champions who will release God's presence and kingdom-transforming communities and Cultures around the world.

C-SUITE LEADERS ARE WELCOMED

The original intent of the "C" process was for C-level or C-suite leaders. C-level leaders have a number of acronyms that describe their multi-functioned roles. The list includes: CEO, CFO, COO, CTO, CIO, CCO, CSO, CDO, CXO, CGO, CKO, CLO (executive, financial, operation, technology, information, compliance, security, digital, experience, green, knowledge, learning respectively) of business. The C stands for Chief, which are high ranking officers in a company or entity who have influence to shape the enterprise, direct others, and make decisions.

If you are in one of these roles, the end game to be successful in NOW Leadership will require that you give your enterprises over to the CHIEF, the Lord Jesus Christ. We could easily use the synonym for chief as Champion! I realized that the C-level distinction was scalable in every direction and consequently arrived at the 12C's.

FORESEEING THE FUTURE AND SEASONS

Twelve is the number for government and the "C" stands for seeing into your future and is linked to becoming a C-level leader – a champion-level leader! Seeing into the future through one lens will cause us to be myopic in our leadership approach and style. We must see through the many different facets of our experience to manage the breadth of complexities and ambiguities we face as leaders. Going through some of the 12C seasons and understanding the process, will cause our leadership to be more seasoned and effective.

There are seasons that we need to go through in the process. The apostle Paul described his life as a drink offering that was being poured out through sacrifice and service. When wine is made, there are byproducts from the fermentation process. The sediments left behind are called dregs, which are made of yeast cells and leftover grape solids. They are not necessarily bad, and some winemakers (vintners) keep some in the wine for taste. When they are in the bottom of a barrel they are called "gross lees".

The wine needs to be separated from the byproduct of wine making. In some instances wines are intentionally aged with "lees" to add to the wine's complexity to white wines like Chardonnay, Muscadet, and Champagne. This is done through the decanting process. The wine is allowed to settle and then it is poured out from one container to another. The sediment is left behind during the process to provide clearer wines.

This metaphor or analogy depicts the seasons or stages we go through, and this process will likely produce a unique combination of the 12C's that is being developed in each of us. There are byproducts we will want to leave behind so we can be poured out into our next season. It may take several decanting operations to get the wine to the level of clarity for the winemaker's or vintner's approval and satisfaction.

Similarly, God is working in our lives in such a way to produce NOW Leaders who are the new wine being poured out in the earth. It is a process and there are seasons, and sometimes the 12C's get blended together. You will see this emerge as we review different leaders' stories and case studies. It is all good. God is saving the best wine for last. It will be good, tasteful, and impactful.

We need the government of Jesus to impact every facet of our lives. His government flows from having a revelation of who the Son of God is and being in proper relationship with one another (Matt. 16:18-20, 18:15-19). Those relationships are constituted by God's family and are keys to our spiritual authority. It is all about relationships.

The Scriptures exhort us to those relationships. When we abide in Him and His word abides in us, we can ask for anything by the Spirit and it will be given to us. God desires us to release the government of heaven to loose and bind so that we see His kingdom released. The goal is that it would bear fruit and bring him much glory (John 15:7-8). We need to bear fruit in every season, like the tree in Psalm 1.

> **GOD DESIRES US TO RELEASE THE GOVERNMENT OF HEAVEN TO LOOSE AND BIND SO THAT WE SEE HIS KINGDOM RELEASED.**

John writes in Revelation about the tree of life that bears fruit in every season and that the leaves were for the healing of the nations. God's government, in His seasons, will bear fruit that will impact the nations.

> *On either side of the river was the tree of life, bearing twelve kinds of fruit, yielding its fruit every month; and the leaves of the tree were for the healing of the nations.* (Rev. 22:2)

Imagine that the leaves have the capability to heal the nations! The fruit must be even more extraordinary. The NOW Leadership 12C's is a model and microcosm of possibility regarding how we can grow into our intended fullness as leaders. That fullness involves reclaiming, releasing, being relevant and creating revolutions that lead to sustainable, life-giving reformations that will ultimately create renaissances.

Working in a Fortune 50 company for several decades, I have experienced many leaders all having different styles and levels of experience as well. I have seen companies grow top heavy with leaders and intentionally begin promoting younger leaders into positions of executive responsibility. Many of these leaders are very gifted, talented, and perform well; however, there is simply no substitute for going through the seasons and stages of development.

Working for well-seasoned leaders versus younger executives is often like night and day. Emerging leaders often lack the experience, humility, empathy, "ears to hear", and bandwidth to deal with people and complex problems. They can often lack confidence and their insecurity often drives them to surround themselves with teams like themselves because that is what they are comfortable with.

My point here is there is no substituting the leadership development process. There are seasons and experiences that cannot be replaced by a conversation or a Google lookup.

If you skip a step, you will surely and eventually get to retake the test in one way or another. It is best to embrace the 12C's proactively than to learn the hard way. If we want to be catapulted into excellence and C-level leadership in the mountains of culture, then I recommend you engage in the governmental process of heaven through the 12C's.

Leadership is not for wimps. It takes courageous men and women to embrace the process. It is a dynamic process and requires pioneering, role playing, facilitating, communicating, negotiating, mentoring, coaching, disciplining and adapting. There are often many twists, turns, and surprises. To be at the C level, you certainly need eyes to see. It is not necessarily a linear process. So, let us explain each term so you have a reference and context for the meanings as we discuss the process.

This process is not limited to individuals, and it is scalable. The NOW Leadership technology can be applied to teams, families, churches, businesses, communities, states, and nations. Any entity with a mission and assignment that needs to develop, steward or accomplish a task or assignment can benefit from applying the NOW Leadership process.

Next, we will turn our attention to Chapter Four and the 12C's.

CHAPTER FOUR

THE 12C's: Key to Your Leadership Blueprint

"Surely the Sovereign Lord does nothing without revealing His plan to His servants, the prophets." (Amos 3:7)

A blueprint is an architectural drawing that explains the details of a project. The blueprints represent what needs to be built and the architect includes the plans for all the parts and their placement. Everyone who is going to work on that project needs to know how to read the blueprint, so every blueprint comes with a key to explain what all the symbols mean. The key eliminates the confusion of personal interpretation that might muddy the architect's original intent.

Following is the key to the blueprint for the 12C NOW Leadership Model. We all need to be on the same page about what things mean and how they go together, and this graphic diagram will help us to do that.

LEADERS FOR LIFE - NOW MODEL DEFINITIONS

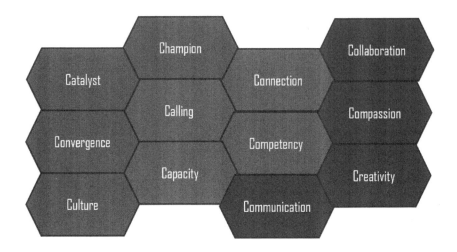

FIGURE 3.

The 12C's of NOW Leadership – Multi Dimensions and Interconnectivity.

- **CALLING** is about understanding your potential and beginning your journey with the end in mind. You have a unique DNA that God put in you as a result of creating you in His likeness and image, which dovetails with dreams God has put in you.

- **CONNECTION** is about your relationships with God, yourself and others. The most critical connection is developing your bond with your heavenly Father and understanding your identity and the deep love He has for you.

- **COMPETENCY** is about developing your talents (raw natural ability) and skills needed for you to fulfill your destiny or assignment. On a deeper spiritual level, there are spiritual resources available including the spirit of wisdom, understanding and knowledge that enhance your natural abilities.

- **CAPACITY** is the crucible in which deeper transformation takes place where we are refined, aligned and strengthened. This often shows up in our lives through adversity, trials, tribulations, difficulties, extreme complexities, challenges, conflict, betrayal, tests, and significant obstacles and hindrances to overcome. Personal character and emotional, spiritual and relational maturity are a big part of Capacity.

- **CONVERGENCE** is about your engaging your sweet spot where you enter into your flow (Heaven comes to earth), and where everything seems to come together with purpose. It is where all your understanding of your purpose and assignment-Calling, preparation and character-Capacity, developing skills-Competency, growing in your identity and relationship-Connection come together in God's perfect timing. Convergence can happen over the short term or can build through a lifetime.

- **CATALYSTS** identify, initiate, and deliver meaningful change while often not being seen or recognized, and remaining in the background. They facilitate growth and activate initiatives and people's callings, development and destinies. They are at times idea people and at other times encouragers and networkers and team players who bring positive energy to their roles.

- **CHAMPIONS** are mature, life-tested leaders who are making an impact in the areas they have been called to. They engage emerging leadership in the development process and invest in the generations through their encouragement, coaching, mentoring, instructing, and providing resources to build.

- **CULTURE** is the summation of a people group's or organization's thoughts and actions including their values, beliefs, creative expression, industry, and relationship. Leaders are called to influence culture and bring transformation for the greater good of society. In organizations, culture is the internal environment or atmosphere that employees work in and relate to. It includes systems, policies, rules, codes, perks, benefits, incentives and rewards, organizational history and philosophy, and more. It provides the context for employees to work and perform in and plan their lives around, and is a reference to understand organizational identity and expectation.

- **COLLABORATION** is when leaders come together in an interlocking manner to support one another regarding a larger goal to create synergies and extraordinary results. The more complex the problem, the greater the collaboration is required. Collaboration and cooperation are the opposite of competition. Individuals, teams and organizations must have confidence, security, maturity, resources and trust to collaborate successfully and effectively.

- **COMMUNICATION** is the imparting or exchanging of information on various levels. Developing communication mastery is a key to leadership success because it requires connecting the dots from numerous dimensions – the emotional, mental, spiritual, physical, relational, and communal – to influence, inspire and accomplish God's purposes and build/ lead teams.

- **CREATIVITY** comes from the word create, which means "to cause to exist; bring into being". It is the fundamental element in our spiritual DNA given to us by our Heavenly Father who is the Creator and Sustainer of the universe to solve problems, create beauty, and more. We are created in His image and we are fearfully and wonderfully made. In Him we live and move and have our being. He is the Author and Perfecter of life, all creation, and the cosmos. Literature, music, art, dance, design, invention, innovation and more all originate from and find their source in God.

- **COMPASSION** is identifying with others on a deeper level and being moved to alleviate or provide solutions to their need or situation. It is a pure force that can activate heaven from which generosity flows and the reaping of numerous benefits occurs. Eph. 4:32 says, *"Be kind and compassionate to one another, forgiving each other, just as in Christ God forgave you."* Prov. 19:17 adds, *"Whoever is kind to the poor lends to the Lord, and he will reward them for what they have done."* It pays to show compassion to others.

Compassion is also part of God's nature. Psa. 145:8-9 says, *"The Lord is gracious and compassionate, slow to anger and rich in love. The Lord is good to all; he has compassion on all he has made."* Psa. 86:15 adds, *"But you, Lord, are a compassionate and gracious God, slow to anger, abounding in love and faithfulness."* Psa. 103:13 notes, *"As a father has compassion on his children, so the Lord has compassion on those who fear him."* And Psa. 116:5 writes, *"The Lord is gracious and righteous; our God is full of compassion."* When we act with compassion, we are acting according to God's nature at work within us.

NOW LEADERS ARE:

- Courageous about their CALLING to develop their potential

- Alive in their identity and authentic in their relationships to make CONNECTIONS

- Passionate about excellence and develop their COMPETENCIES

- Transformed and Uncompromising in their Integrity and Character – They developed CAPACITY

- Intentional about kingdom flow and live in CONVERGENCE

- Engaging culture and being CATALYSTS

- Building synergistically as COLLABORATORS

- CHAMPIONS who engage the whole process for kingdom impact

- Aware and intentional about developing organizational CULTURE

- Developing and leveraging COMMUNICATION to build new language and vision for the future in positive ways

- Embracing CREATIVITY beyond their five senses and natural gifts (finite, natural realm) to tap into the supernatural realm through the Word and Spirit

- Embracing COMPASSION for people and nations to build their operating system for maximum impact and sustainability

THE 12C'S AND THE 3 WHEELS

The 12C's NOW Leadership process can be expressed as a wheel within a wheel like in the vision Ezekiel had. The first 4C's are the seasonal cycle of preparation. Calling is like Spring, Connection and Competency are like Summer and Fall, and Capacity is like the winter. The seasons of development will create desirable outcomes which will include planting, germination, growth, fruitfulness, pruning, and needed dormancy – rest. The focus of this cycle is transformation integrated with practical and spiritual skill creation. We must learn to lead from the inside out, not the outside in.

Authentic servant leadership must originate from a healthy identity and deep self-awareness of what you are and what you are not. Otherwise, you may become "religious" which involves having an outward form without the inner realities and substance of life. People will quickly see through you and see the incongruities. The day you try to be something that you are not, your leadership effectiveness will be quickly diluted.

FIGURE 4.
12C NOW Leadership Model–Wheels within Wheels.

As you advance in higher levels of leadership, the grey space (less black and white) increases and there are many more intangibles to manage. The complexities will increase. The second wheel includes more abstract concepts – Convergence, Catalyst, Culture, and becoming Champions – but these are very important to understand. They are designed to bring clarity and simplicity to the complexities leaders face.

These four dimensions integrate your inner world and your outer world. It is where the clutch is engaged to provide horsepower from the engine to drive forward. They are the forces by which we work to model excellence, influence, working in integrative ways, and making the clarion call to our mission and mandate. This is most often felt and seen in terms of leaders leading the way!

The third wheel is the fruit or benefit of the first two sets of wheels, and expresses our impact, influence and effect on the world around us, including the organizations we serve and lead. These four dimensions include Collaboration, Creativity, Communication, and Compassion. These four dimensions are elements of Competencies that leaders need to develop. NOW Leaders who have become Champions, will have mastered these four elements.

These wheels can and are intended to be counter rotating so that you can see the diversity and complexity of how you may be in different seasons of growth and leadership at the same time. If you take 3 samples (or combinations) out of the 12C's, there could be a total of 220 different combinations of 3C's at any time in a different sequence. You could be in Convergence while in the crucible of Capacity. Or, you could be serving as a Catalyst and your Calling could be redefined.

As a Champion, you may have gotten promoted and now need to learn new Competencies. While all of this is happening, you may be in a place where you are faced with challenging problems that require Creativity and the ability to Communicate or Collaborate. Or, perhaps you are moving into a new level of Compassion and generosity toward those that you lead. Or, you may need to influence Culture.

As you can see, this 12C NOW Leadership model is fluid, dynamic, interactive, integrated, continuous and multi-dimensional rather than being static or seasonal. It is not a list of dos and don'ts or best practices. It is not one-dimensional, but has been developed from a lifetime of real-world, time-tested, results-oriented, hands-on, personal experience and practice.

The NOW is the innovative momentum, awareness and connectivity to create new outcomes in life and leadership. The C-levels in the 12C process provide the railroad tracks for the NOW to operate effectively just as a train with all the horsepower in the world, cannot create locomotion without railways to run on. Wisdom by definition requires a point of focus where sound action or decisions are made with application of experience, knowledge, and good judgment. Wisdom creates, builds, flows, assists, navigates, discerns, accesses, evaluates, loves, and acts intentionally and creates desirable results. The 12C's provides a construct for advancing in C-levels through the creative process of leadership innovation and application to take place.

> **WISDOM REQUIRES A POINT OF FOCUS WHERE DECISIONS ARE MADE AND SOUND ACTION IS TAKEN WITH THE APPLICATION OF EXPERIENCE AND GOOD JUDGMENT.**

The application of the 12C's also requires NOW because the subject of leadership and life is so vast, complex, and multi-dimensional in life's time domain. The interdependency between them is absolutely essential. The C-level thought structure provides clarity and an element of simplicity to chisel away at life's complexities.

This book may cause you to feel exhilarated and overwhelmed from one chapter to the next. We need the NOW to provide our location in the process, and then apply the concepts we are learning to advance through the stages. You may wish to consider working with an experienced coach who can serve as a catalyst and guide. We all have our own unique journeys and stories and it is best that you don't do it alone as you integrate New Operating Wisdom and the 12C process in your life and leadership.

On the following page, we will explore how Joseph, David, Daniel, Mary, Paul, Esther, and Jesus demonstrated the first 7C's—Calling, Connection, Competency, Capacity, Convergence, Catalyst and Champion. By studying how these dimensions of leadership applied to their lives, you will better understand how these can apply to anyone's life, including yours.

PERSON	CALLING	CONNECTION	COMPETENCY	CAPACITY	CONVERGENCE	CATALYST	CHAMPION
JOSEPH	Dream— sheaves, moon/sun	Father's Joy— robe	Shepherd, project manager	Betrayal, Potiphar's house, prison	Saved two nations from starvation	Restoration of family	Provided for his family— legacy, father to Pharoah
DAVID	Anointed shepherd boy	Worshipper, man after God's own heart	Shepherd, killed lion & bear, warrior	Saul's insanity— honoring authority, Absalom's rebellion	Goliath, various war victories	Initiated new order of worship— tabernacle of David	Provided materials for next generation to build the temple
DANIEL	No clear calling other than king's decree	Favor at a young age	Skillful in learning, knowledge, dreams, government admin.	Thrown in a furnace for not bowing down to false gods, the den of lions	Dream interpretation, revelation, favor with kings	Provided significant revelation about the end times	Mentor and leader to the most powerful leaders of the day for several successive kings
MARY	Birth mother of Jesus	Highly favored, connected to Gabriel & Joseph	Obedience & humility	Shame of being pregnant but not married	Jesus' birth	Facilitated the growth of the Messiah	Stewarded the gift to raise up the Champion— Jesus
PAUL	Road to Damascus	Skillfully connected with people, intimate exchanges with Jesus	Pharisee— skilled at the Law, tent maker	Wilderness, thorn in the flesh	Preached to the Gentiles, established churches	Ingnited regions on fire for God, transformed cities like Ephesus	Mentored and coached Timothy, established elders, planted churches
JESUS	Angelic entrance	"This is My Son in whom I am well pleased."	Carpenter, versed in the Word '	Wilderness, Gethsemane	Preaching, teaching, healing ministry	Transformed culture, activated twelve leaders	Reproduced disciples, apostolic fathers
ESTHER	Selected to be the king's wife	Connected with Mordecai	Able to communicate teacher	Orphan, removed from family, death sentence of the Jews	Intervened by entreating the king	Saved people through her influence	Preserved the people and future generations

TABLE 1.

Examples of Biblical Leaders using the first 7C's.

THE GOAL IS WALKING IN THE TRUTH

We are creating a construct or model to process your leadership journey. Peter wrote about his personal process in 2 Peter chapter 1. In his inspired reflections and exhortation, diligence, faith, moral excellence, knowledge, self-control, perseverance, and godliness were the construct for his development. Peter's list of virtues and character traits came from his lessons learned while growing through the school of hard knocks.

In the end, in spite of his ups and downs, Peter remained in continuous learning mode, keeping his eyes on the prize. The exploits and pages of history in Acts were Peter's sandbox to learn valuable leadership lessons. We can identify with his love, faith, enthusiasm, passion, boldness, audacity, and sensitivity. We can never afford to stop being reminded of those elements in the process that keep us grounded, relevant, and effective as leaders.

God is raising up leaders – spiritual fathers and mothers – to mentor and coach a generation to walk in their greatness. They will impact every facet of our culture and society. There is no greater pleasure than to see God's children walking in the Truth, according to 3 John 1:4: *"I have no greater joy than this, to hear of my children walking in the truth."* There is a great reward for those who persevere in the promises God has given us. The end goal is to see the expression of Jesus' love and power working uniquely in us –- not in a cookie-cutter mold or an image of another person -- but Jesus' image and likeness shining through and demonstrated by you and me.

A STORY ABOUT CREATING SOLUTIONS NO MATTER WHO GETS THE CREDIT

Commander Groth greeted me as I entered his office, and came to attention. "Sit, Lieutenant. You did an excellent job restacking barracks administration. Over the last six months, we've reduced the number of hours wasted on extra military instruction (EMI) by over 20,000, and the Master at Arms reports that the barracks have never been in better material condition. This is due to your leadership."

My thoughts wandered back to a year ago, when my goat locker (Chief Petty Officers) complained daily about our students being placed on EMI because of failed barracks inspections attributable to roommates failing to maintain cleanliness of a shared room, or mold growing near leaking faucets. We all complained, but no one did anything about it.

The barracks belonged to another command, and our 2,500 students were simply residents. The Master at Arms assigned rooms randomly, and the finger-pointing crossed several command structures. A failure by any resident resulted in 16 men being assigned 2-4 hours of close order drill, calisthenics, or other extra-military instruction details. The cost to morale was high, and the cost to the Navy Nuclear Power School's mission was palpable. Every hour counted for our students, and EMI was draining energy and diluting focus.

I threw the challenge back to my management team (nine Chief Petty Officers). The next week, they presented a plan that, if adopted, would solve the problem. The challenge was that it required the agreement and participation of the other class directors and their goat lockers, as well as the Command Master At Arms. I gave the go-ahead, and asked that they report back when the implementation schedule was set.

The plan would require that every resident pack their gear and clean their room after duty on Thursday. Friday after duty, they would assemble in their rooms, turn in their room key and get a new room assignment. At their new room, they would receive a new room key. A thorough inspection of the condition of the new rooms was conducted, and signed off by a Chief Petty Officer. The report, together with new room assignments, was delivered to the Master At Arms, together with a new set of procedures for assigning students to rooms, coordinated by a member of my staff. Savings were immediate, and morale took a big jump.

The results continued to benefit our students, our staff and even the barracks themselves. I submitted proposals nominating Chief Stone, Chief Resch, and Chief Tessier for promotion to Limited Duty Officer. In peacetime, and as the result of shore duty, this was rare. Six weeks later, a ceremony was held, and we pinned Ensign's bars on my three Chiefs. Afterward, I was summoned to meet with the Commanding Officer. As I sat before him, Cdr. Groth concluded, "Just remember, Lieutenant, there is no limit to what can be achieved if you are not concerned about who gets the credit. Getting your Chiefs promoted was the right thing to do. Your men will follow you anywhere now!"

JOHN ANDERSON
Founder and President, Global Development Partners (GDP) Group, Ltd. SPC

CASE STUDY: ALEXANDER THE GREAT – A CHAMPION WHO IMPACTED CULTURE

This is the story about Alexander the Great who demonstrated many of the 12C's throughout his leadership journey as he lived his life through natural gifts and culture. The point here is even without a God relationship, these principles are still an effective metric for assessing a person's development. He matured in his Competencies, he embraced the Call to conquer through his father's legacy, he experienced Convergence at a young age through his military genius, and he was Champion and commander of armies.

Alexander was thrust into prominence when his father, King Philip of Macedonia, was assassinated, but his preparation began in early childhood. The Greeks of Alexander's time eschewed the luxuries often associated with wealth and position. To prepare him for his future as a military leader and king, he had learned as a boy to sleep on the ground and to endure long exposure to cold, heat, hunger and thirst. Through this training, he developed an intuitive sense about the need for preparation – the development of Capacity.

He developed his Competencies as well and was trained in the use of the weapons of his day, but he was also trained to use his mind by the great philosopher Aristotle. He experienced Convergence at a young age when he demonstrated his military genius at the age of 18 by playing the decisive role in the battle of Chaeronea.

When King Philip died, Alexander began to make plans to fulfill his father's dream of conquering the Persian Empire. He carried in his heart the dream from his father. I am not sure it was the heavenly Father's dream, but the principle is there. Persia was the greatest empire of Alexander's day. The Persian army outnumbered Alexander's army by as much as 100 to 1; however, they were easily routed by Alexander's much smaller army. So began a campaign in which Alexander's army repeatedly defeated the Persian armies, until Alexander ruled the entire Empire.

Once Alexander ruled all of Persia, he began to live as the Persian emperors had lived, in feasting, drinking and wild living. It seemed that after he accomplished his father's dream, he never connected to the dream within himself. In drunken rages, he at times had loyal followers and advisors put to death. He lost the respect of his men. Alexander, this great military leader, experienced a convergence and even was a champion as a military leader, but did not have a vision for leadership beyond his identity as a commander, and, in these later years, failed the tests of Compassion and Character.

Eventually, he assembled an army to attack and gain territory in India. But, when his army reached the Hyphasis River, they refused to go further. They had been away from Greece for years and wanted to go home. So, Alexander reluctantly turned for home. He died in Babylon at only 32 years old. His empire was divided among his various generals. He was buried in Alexandria in Egypt, a great city which he himself had designed and built.

In his short life, Alexander changed the known world. Greeks began to settle in what had formerly been the Persian Empire, bringing their Culture and their great learning. The Greek language became the lingua Franca of all the varied people groups in Greece and Asia Minor. This impact was demonstrated in countless ways, but one that further changed the world was the New Testament, written primarily in Greek.

The City of Alexandria, Egypt was also a great legacy. It was known for centuries as a center for learning and arts. It is here that 70 Jewish scholars gathered to translate the Hebrew Scriptures into Greek. This translation is known at the Septuagint, which means 70. It was used in all the known world to reveal the Old Testament Scriptures. *(Source: Wikipedia)*

Although the example above models some of the 12C's, there is a great shortfall because Connection with the Creator was not made and the value system of heaven was not embraced. Alexander developed his Competencies, walked in Convergence, and was a Catalyst and Champion of his Armies as a commander. God still used this great man to pave the way for leaving a great legacy where the Hebrew Scriptures and New Testament were translated into Greek!

Our legacy may impact Culture and the generations that follow. As we experience life and leadership, the ultimate goal is transformation that has a reference to the Truth. In the end, Alexander's life indirectly impacted Communication – the truth of the Word in Greek. We need to experience transformation that is Truth based on the great eternal reference – Elohim, El Shaddai, Yahweh, Jehovah, the Ancient of Days.

What NOW Leadership competencies were demonstrated in these two stories?

TAKEAWAYS

- We are all leaders if we are followers of Christ. We are called to run the race with poured out passion, strength, and ability.

- NOW Leadership is a construct or framework for our leadership journey.

- NOW Leadership is about working with a new operating wisdom – knowing what to do and knowing that it works with kingdom perspective.

- The 12C's are interactive, multi-faceted, seasonal, and scalable.

- With new perspective, provision will come, grace and abundance for the process.

- There is recovery for those who are burned out or have been burned.

- The goal is to reach our full potential as leaders and to be conduits, facilitators and/or funnels for the creative, innovative and breakthrough solutions for the world's perplexing problems.

NOW ACTION

1. After reading this chapter, journal or talk to a friend about what you learned about the NOW Leadership process and what your takeaways are.

2. Create a list of all your leadership successes, failures, and what you have become as a leader. How do you see your successes and failures in light of the NOW Leadership process?

PRAYER

Lord, help me to understand and activate the NOW Leadership Model in my life. I will faithfully engage in the intentional development of greater self-awareness and the necessary skills to increase my capacity to lead. May I grow in knowledge, wisdom, and grace as I become courageous about my Calling, make meaningful Connections, develop my Competency, enlarge my Capacity, live in Convergence, become a Catalyst, build synergistically as a Collaborator, live as a Champion, develop solid organizational Culture, Communicate in positive ways, explore my Creativity, and demonstrate Compassion for people and nations.

NOW COACHING QUESTIONS

1. What are the 12C's in the NOW Leadership process?

2. In what ways have any of the attributes of a NOW Leader impacted you?

3. Are there any of them that stand out?

4. Explain how any of the dimensions are relevant to your experience or that of others?

5. In what ways have you been discouraged, burned out, wounded or hurt?

6. What actions are you taking to find healing and recovery?

7. In what ways is there a desire, passion or fire burning in you to make a difference to impact the Seven Mountains of Culture in your sphere of influence?

8. In what ways are you pursuing and taking action to advance?

CHAPTER FIVE

CALLING
Your Potential

"Follow Me, and I will make you fishers of men." (Matt. 4:19)

BEGINNING WITH THE END IN MIND

One of Stephen Covey's habits in his best-selling book, *The Seven Habits of Highly Effective People,* is to "begin with the end in mind." It is an important starting point for everyone, but is often overlooked. Believe it or not, if you don't have a picture about your future, then someone else will create it for you. You may look back after a period of time and wonder what happened, and you may feel regret.

Simply put: Leaders know where they are headed. In order for followers to follow – leaders need to lead!

Vision is seeing at a new level – seeing what others don't see.

Pointing to the future and connecting it with your passion, is a very powerful motivator. Leaders who can activate their future and fuel the passion, will have followers on fire – fully engaged.

The word "calling" in the Bible means "to summon." It refers to a vocation, an occupation to which a person is especially drawn or for which they are suited, trained, or qualified. We see from Scripture how men and women were called to be solutions to problems in the earth. Peter was called by Jesus and given a spoken promise that he would become a fisher of men.

Our Calling transcends us. It comes from above; it is heavenly, holy, and speaks to our identity, purpose and potential. We cannot earn it, nor do we receive it because of our special status. It is a call to one body, one Spirit and one hope. We are to walk worthy of that Calling and be diligent about it. God's gifts and Calling are irrevocable. God won't take it away, nor can people take it from you. People may try to take it away or thwart your call but it still remains. The seed within you is resilient to such attacks. If nurtured, it will grow; if ignored, it will haunt you.

Your calling creates a space for you to walk into, and we should be free enough to play in different sandboxes to discover it. The call of God does come at an appointed time and space.

In a dream I had, the Lord revealed something to me about our Calling. Embedded in our Calling are dreams and God-given desires. When we dream with God and connect with our identity, there destiny emerges. The Lord showed very clearly that the dreams He has put in you are blueprints for your life. The dreams and desires that are percolating in you very well could be connected to your Calling. God wants to connect those dots in your life.

DISCOVER YOUR BLUEPRINTS
THROUGH YOUR DREAMS

That blueprint reveals insights and plans for your future. It is not intended to limit you, but to provide you with a construct for building your future. It isn't static; it will grow as you grow. Dreaming is not just for while we're sleeping; dreaming is about finding inspiration for life and painting a desirable future. Learning to awaken your dreams is vitally important. There is a great likelihood that God may show up in the intersection of your dreams, desires and your calling.

So, why is dreaming important? It connects us to the creative muscles within. Hope emerges as we think imaginatively about our future and connect to our inner desires. Whether we dream with God or have a clear call like Noah, Abraham, Isaac, Jacob, Joseph, Isaiah, Jeremiah, Daniel, David, Moses, Joshua, Deborah, Esther, or Mary the mother of Jesus, I believe there is purpose for all of us to fulfill in God's ecosystem.

Some get there by pursuing their God dreams, and others through divine encounters. Either way, if we know where we want to go in the future, we can commit our ways to the Lord and create plans to get to that end rather than wasting time and resources. The worst thing we can do, is do nothing. Everyone's journey is unique. There are no formulas that fit each person. We can't compare one another in the process. There is space we need to fill that only we can uniquely fill.

THE LEADERSHIP VACUUM

There is a great leadership vacuum in the world we live in. If that void is not filled through our intentionality, something else will fill that void. For example, on a very practical level, if a parent does not provide direction and guidance to their children, they will be parented by other means. It may include their peers, the spirit of the age through social media, or perhaps a coach or teacher.

If parents are not deliberate about their children's dormant or latent potential, it will never come to fruition. Potential not activated and developed has little or no value in the end game. The obstacles of fear, procrastination, and scarcity are just a few of the reasons we do not invest. We can see in the Parable of the Talents and Minas that strategy, planning, and taking risks are a part of God's intent for His servants.

We also can see in the life of Peter that he was a man who stepped out and took risks. In one instance he was rebuked by Jesus for opposing God's plan, and at Pentecost he hit it out of the park. What we appreciate about Peter is that he did not sit on the sidelines waiting for God to do something. In this kingdom age that is upon us, there is an invitation to move forward; it's a green light unless you get the red light. Without God's children taking initiative, the leadership vacuum will prevail.

The U.S. Army orginated this term which describes the leadership vacuum that needs to be brought into order using the acronym VUCA. It stands for **V**olatility, **U**ncertainty, **C**omplexity, and **A**mbiguity. It describes a chaotic system that requires leaders to bring order into it; otherwise, disorder will reign. Similarly, any relationship, team, organization, or nation that is not attended to intentionally, will atrophy.

> **WITHOUT VISION, PURPOSE, HOPE, FAITH AND INTENTION, PEOPLE WILL LOSE HEART AND DRIFT NEEDLESSLY.**

Without vision, purpose, hope, faith and intention, people will lose heart and needlessly drift. We see in Genesis that God spoke into the chaos and created order. In chaos there is complexity and blurred lines and distinctions. It is easy to be confused and disheartened in chaos. This is the leader's greatest opportunity. Why? It's quite simple; order dispels chaos and confusion, creating clarity. We have been made in the likeness and image of our Creator (Gen. 1:27), who is a God of order and clarity. Our Commander-in-Chief's intent is clearly defined.

- **Cultivate** - be fruitful and multiply.

- **Name all things** - that which you name you have authority over.

- **Rule and take dominion** - when you name, you instill identity.

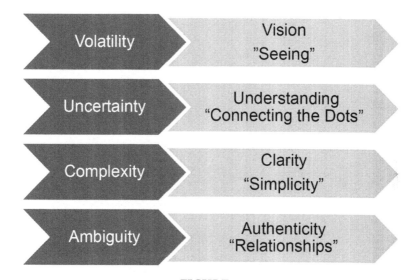

FIGURE 5.
The VUCA Challenge and Strategy Solutions.
VUCA was developed By Gen. Dennis Reimer (Ret.), former U.S. Army Chief of Staff.[1]

With this DNA from our heavenly Father, we take joy in bringing Jesus' government and order into our world to solve problems and be the solution! Through our leadership, God calls us to bring vision to a highly unpredictable, volatile world. The 12C's will allow us to develop vision to "see" at the right level into our futures. We can bring understanding amid uncertainty by "connecting the dots" to see how the puzzle pieces come together.

This perhaps is a place of the greatest impact. In a complex world where chaos wants to win through self-perpetuating entropy, we are able to gain clarity so that we can simplify our perspective and approach. And lastly, we can do nothing without relationships. In a world where there is ambiguity, where there are many interpretations and a sense of inexactness, sometimes we simply need relationship to get through it. Authenticity provides an avenue to connect relationally with our constituents. Relationships are often the reference and glue that hold everything together.

Your calling as spiritual and marketplace leaders, parents, or business leaders will in some way impact the world that is described in the VUCA model. Albert Einstein is quoted as saying, "You cannot solve problems at the same level they were created". It's time to bring solutions at a new level.

PETER'S CALL

How does that call come to us? Well, in the case of Peter and Andrew, it was pretty clear and concise. There was little complexity in their call. Simply put:

> *Now as Jesus was walking by the Sea of Galilee, He saw two brothers, Simon who was called Peter, and Andrew his brother, casting a net into the sea; for they were fishermen. And He said to them, "Follow Me, and I will make you fishers of men." (Matt. 4:18-19)*

Peter was at work one day tending to the family fishing business with his partner, his brother, and Jesus showed up on the scene. While they were casting their nets, Jesus called to them: "Follow me, and I will make you fishers of men." These guys were hard-working, rugged, strong fishermen. They earned their keep and livelihood by fishing to feed their families.

Jesus' words created a paradigm shift in Peter's and Andrew's thinking and perception. They were being called to another, higher reality. For two guys to give up their business because of ten words – well, there had to be something going on in that exchange. There had to be power and substance in that invitation. Put yourself in their shoes. Would you have left your livelihood, family, houses, land, friends, children and more (Matt. 19:29) based on a few words? I would have had a hundred questions. Jesus' words carried power and impacted these two emerging leaders.

From two of Paul's apostolic prayers we see a linkage between calling, inheritance, and God's will and knowing His power (Col. 1:9-10; Eph. 1:18-19). Something more powerfully had to be working for this transition to take place. How did Elisha so quickly slay his six oxen and destroy his plow to follow Elijah? (see 1 Kings 19:19-21). The power of God's word somehow impacted them in the moment of that decision and they perhaps understood how the reward outweighed the cost.

RESPONDING TO CALLING

The words that Jesus speaks to us have power to move us to make these life-changing decisions. Beyond that, those words need to connect to something deeper in us. They have to resonate with something about our spiritual DNA. They have to ignite or spark a sound or energy, perhaps a desire to become something and accomplish something beyond ourself. There has to be a deeper hunger working in us creating dissatisfaction and deeper surrender to create the tipping point to forsake it all.

Calling will launch us on a new journey that is fueled by our dreams mingled with our desires of making a difference, impact, or adding value in some way. Peter and his brother were promised they would become fishers of men. What they had learned to do in the natural, they would learn to do with people in their new spiritual vocation as apostles.

Accomplishing something of significance brings value, but what we become through the process is of equal or greater importance. Jesus' call will ultimately transform us. Jesus does not make empty promises without reward. The call made a connection for Peter and Andrew. The call likewise ignites something to propel us to follow Him to receive the prize.

Whether you are in the ministry or in the marketplace, or both, God can interrupt your life with His call. I believe there are calls being broadcast right now from the throne room. God is surfing to and fro over the spiritual internet, looking for a responder – for someone to click "yes." There are many who have not responded to call(s), and God is looking for willing vessels. Is there a "yes" in you?

As the Lord pours out His grace and anointing in this kingdom age, it is the "yes" that will bring us into the place of His choosing us. Those who have not embraced the preparation process will potentially be disqualified. To be chosen, after we have been called, means that we have satisfied or met the training and development requirements to fulfill our assignment or commission. The greater the call, the greater the preparation. Are we willing to invest and make the plans needed to walk out our calling to fulfillment to impact the spheres of influence in the earth?

IMPACTING THE MOUNTAINS OF CULTURE

Dr. Bruce Cook, in his book, *The 8th Mountain*, describes how everything flows from the 8th Mountain, which is God's kingdom. It is referred to as Mount Zion in the book of Hebrews. The intent is to impact the Seven Mountains of Culture – religion, education, business, family, media, government, arts and entertainment. God is looking for leaders – influencers who will bring the government of Jesus, including His righteousness, peace and joy – into these spheres or sectors. It involves making disciples in all disciplines to disrupt the world with divinely-inspired solutions.

We need higher level leaders in the Seven Mountains, but we need boots on the ground in all levels of the mountains in order to be salt and light. We cannot disqualify ourselves because we are not at the top. We need to start somewhere. When was the last time you heard a conversation with a junior or senior in high school who was planning their career to impact any of the seven spheres of influence? We need to begin training leaders at every stage of development.

We have a friend who did plan his education. He felt his assignment was to impact the business/technology mountain in food technology.

He went to school to become a food scientist and eventually got his PhD degree. I asked him, "Why are you investing so much in education?" He said, "God is sending me as a missionary into the marketplace to impact the food business for the kingdom!" We need to invest in our raw talent through training and education especially if it has a divine purpose connected to it. Our response to the call, and whatever the preparation, the ideal answer is, "Yes, Lord."

CREATING CLARITY IN CALLING

The calling in your life is about something bigger than you, and comes from another source; it comes from above. It originates in heaven, and is somehow communicated to you in a love language you can understand. In most instances, if you are connected to your desires and dreams, there will be a connection. If it is obscure or unintelligible, then we need greater clarity.

THE CALLING IN YOUR LIFE IS ABOUT SOMETHING BIGGER THAN YOU AND ORIGINATES IN HEAVEN.

God wants to release the knowledge – knowing regarding His will and calling – so that you know how to pursue it. That is the spiritual wisdom and understanding we need to take action and connect the dots so that our hearts are enlightened and we can get a visual on the rich inheritance within us.

The bottom line is, inherent in the call, there is a connection to your divine inheritance, purpose and assignments that God wants to reveal and fulfill. In one way or another, they will solve a problem and be or bring a solution.

Isaiah was a statesman who responded by a deep call in the Spirit in a time of loss and grief to be a prophetic voice to a nation and decree words regarding the coming Messiah. David was a shepherd boy tending his sheep as a worshipper when he was anointed to be king to rule a nation.

David's call contradicted the patriarchal family protocols – he was the youngest son.

Peter and Andrew were fishermen who collaborated with heaven to birth the New Testament church. Joseph was his father's favorite and a dreamer when God gave him the blueprint to save a nation in a time of famine. By his obedience, foresight, planning and administration, other nations were saved (fed and supplied) as well during the famine.

Abraham was longing for a son and legacy, and God interrupted his life with a promise that would change the nations through his seed. Matthew was a tax collector getting rich off of the Jewish people who later became one of the gospel writers. The apostle Paul was a Pharisee and a persecutor of Christians before he encountered Jesus and wrote the majority of the New Testament. The call will come and we need to be diligent to tend to it, regardless of the time or circumstances.

THERE IS POWER IN THE SEED

Your calling is like a seed that is planted in you that will eventually sprout, grow, and bear fruit. There is an inherent tenacity in that seed to germinate. It has a preprogrammed script which includes the gestation, water and light requirements to create a tipping point to mature. Peter says we were not born again of seed that is perishable, that which will decay.

> For you have been born again not of seed which is perishable but imperishable, that is, through the living and enduring word of God. (1 Pet. 1:23)

Within the seed that is planted in us is enduring faith, hope, and love which were planted within us when we were born again. We carry something that is living and eternal because of the word of God working in our lives. In Heb. 4:12, the Word of God is referred to as powerful, living, quick, effective, effectual, full of power, operative and energizing.

Within that seed is the code for our destiny. Respectively, Jeremiah and Paul wrote about how our lives carry the destiny of heaven with the following language:

> *"For I know the plans that I have for you," declares the Lord, "plans for welfare and not for calamity to give you a future and a hope."* (Jer. 29:11)

> *For by grace you have been saved through faith; and that not of yourselves, it is the gift of God; not as a result of works, so that no one may boast. For we are His workmanship, created in Christ Jesus for good works, which God prepared beforehand so that we would walk in them.* (Eph 2:8-10)

And David had the revelation that God formed each person uniquely and that there are scrolls in heaven that have been written concerning our lives. This passage below is a sister text to Eph. 2:10.

> *My frame was not hidden from You, When I was made in secret, And skillfully wrought in the depths of the earth; Your eyes have seen my unformed substance; And in Your book were all written The days that were ordained for me, When as yet there was not one of them.* (Psa. 139:15-16)

These scrolls refer to the plans and destiny God has encapsulated in the seed of our calling. The nice thing about this is that God's calling does not change. He is the same "yesterday, today and forever." From Rom. 11:29, we understand that "God's gifts and calling are irrevocable". He will not take them back! God has planted in you a powerful seed of destiny that is intended to grow and mature. It is not reversible but it can be delayed. It is the kingdom of God within you (Luke 17:21). Jesus spoke about this kingdom seed attribute in the Parable of the Mustard Seed.

> *And He said," How shall we picture the kingdom of God, or by what parable shall we present it? It is like a mustard seed, which, when sown upon the soil, though it is smaller than all the seeds*

that are upon the soil, yet when it is sown, it grows up and becomes larger than all the garden plants and forms large branches; so that the birds of the air can nest under its shade." (Mark 4:30-32)

God's intention is to grow that seed and mature us into a huge tree to become a place of refuge, healing, transformation, and shade representing the ability to influence our culture. We are called to be oaks of righteousness (Isa. 61:3) so that our lives will display His splendor!

GOING BACK TO THE BASICS OF CALLING

If you do not have insight into your calling, you can lean into the Word to embrace the foundations of your calling. This is a God space we can grow into regardless of where we are in our journey.

- Called according to His purpose (Rom. 8:28)

- We are called to one hope (Eph. 4:4)

- We are called to be holy (1 Pet. 3:9; 2 Tim. 1:9)

- God has called us to peace (1 Cor. 7:15)

- Called to freedom (Gal. 5:13)

- Called to sanctification, not impurity (1 Thess. 2:4)

- Called to receive the promise of eternal inheritance (Heb. 9:15)

- Called out of darkness into His marvelous light (1 Pet. 2:9)

- Called you to eternal glory in Christ (1 Pet. 5:10)

- Called you by His own glory and excellence (2 Pet. 1:3)

- Called to be children of God (1 John 3:1)

God is releasing His call into the earth. We need to absorb and synthesize what God is communicating through His Word and personal promises to us. For some, Calling will emerge over a longer period of time, for others, it may solidify in one God encounter. If you have gotten off track, there is spiritual technology available to restore, reset, and re-align. The Lord promises us a hope and future with a plan. The plan is the vision of the future. As Kim Clement would sing, "I am somewhere in the future, and I look a lot better than I look right now!"

- Embrace your call.

- Cultivate your God-given desires and dreams.

- Steward the seeds of kingdom leadership.

- Envision your desirable future.

VISION INVENTORY

Here is a short Vision Inventory to think about your future:

- What is the vision for your life?

- Where are you going?

- What will happen if you don't have vision?

- How does this make you think and feel?

- Who influenced this thinking about your future?

The NOW Leadership process will align you to begin with the end in mind and connect to the potential and future within you. Understanding your call, your dreams and the blueprints that are within you are the road map to your destiny. Jesus said that many are called but few are chosen. We want to be those who have been chosen because we have embraced the preparation. The following pages of this book will provide insights to help you get grounded and advance in the plans and purposes God has for you.

CASE STUDY: FLORENCE NIGHTINGALE – FOUNDER OF MODERN NURSING AND REFORMER

Florence Nightingale (1820-1910) was the mother of the nursing movement and revolutionized the profession. She took her calling seriously. She prayed incessantly for God to give her a life-defining task or assignment. Nightingale became very tenacious in her pursuit. She was a member of the Church of England and also developed significant relationships with congregational ministers in the U.S., which caused her to develop a deeper relationship with Jesus.

Florence volunteered in the Crimean war and assisted wounded soldiers. As a result of her experiences where many men lost their lives because of sanitation rather than war wounds, she worked to bring about medical reforms around hygiene in Army hospitals. She was an avid communicator working to improve the treatment and care of wounded soldiers. She was also a strong advocate for laying the foundation of nursing as a profession.

The Victorian age was cruel towards women pursuing any type of vocation and she felt nursing required intelligence and knowledge. She changed the perception of nursing. She reformed the nursing profession and the role of women in that role in society.

"She would just not rest until she would seize hold of that for what she had been called. She just would not rest until she had taken hold of that for which Christ had taken hold of her. She did finally attain that and took it to heart, and she revolutionized nursing," stated Filmmaker Cristóbal Krusen. She also became a very significant communicator as a writer and much of her published work concerned spreading medical knowledge.

Florence, through her Connection with Jesus, and personal Capacity, Competency, and Compassion, did not rest until she took hold of what Christ had apprehended her for. She was tenacious and her life transformed the medical system and Culture through her Creativity and Communication. Her legacy lives on as a Champion, forerunner and pioneer in the medical field of nursing.

A STORY ABOUT HOW CALLING EMPOWERS US TO STAY THE COURSE

Calling visited my life when I was five years old. We had recently moved into a new home and across the street were dirt mounds of gravel. We had just gotten a puppy and I took him for a walk in the gravel beds on a beautiful spring morning. I looked up into the deep blue, cloudless sky and had a moment in eternity. With great clarity, I knew that God had created the heavens and the earth, and somehow I was a part of that great plan. As quick as that "aha" moment came, it vanished like a vapor.

Thirteen years later I had a second significant encounter with Jesus and His presence through the working of the Holy Spirit. I was radically transformed and began my Christian walk my senior year in high school. Deep in my heart, the Lord planted a deep sense of purpose in my life, and that my life would count for something. Jer. 1:5 became a favorite verse; God called me from the womb. Through all the transitions and turbulence that life can bring you, this seed remained in me. Whenever I wanted to give up, He would always encourage me and provide opportunities and open doors to not give up or quit.

Later, in my 20's, I received some significant promises about my future. I remember a significant encounter where the Lord revealed Himself to me as the refiner's fire. It was all-consuming. I did not know what it meant. The Lord was asking me to cross the line into apostolic ministry. I had no clue what that word even meant. These types of events would happen and I would tuck them away in my heart. I realized that the Lord was building foundations and expectations for the future to keep hope alive. All the words were signposts God was creating to demonstrate His love and faithfulness toward me.

In the latter part of my life, I am seeing these promises come to pass. I did not realize the preparation process to walk out my Calling could take decades. Because of the Calling, I was able to go through the cleansing process so that the commissioning could take place. There was much fire that brought about that cleansing.

In each step of the journey, there would be events that would put the previous words and promises into context. The words and promises created a railroad track that allowed me to walk in obedience to the call. The commission is the place where you are chosen and God's favor rests upon your life to fulfill your assignment and destiny. Each person's journey is unique. Calling called me at a young age and I believe it will serve us if we submit to God through the process and are willing to pay the price. I believe saying "yes" along the way made a big difference.

TAKEAWAYS

- Leaders know where they are going.

- Calling speaks to potential – beginning with the end in mind.

- Your potential is not just about what you accomplish, but what you become.

- Dreaming with God can connect you to your desires and point you to your Calling.

- Dreams and Calling often intersect and will emerge through the seed.

- God's Calling is a powerful seed within each of us that is irrevocable.

- There is a great need/vacuum that demands solutions.

- Allow Calling to serve you through the cleansing to get to the commission.

- You can pray to get clarity about your Calling.

- Your Calling in God has great bandwidth of opportunity to grow into.

- A part of our Calling will bring solutions in the earth.

CALLING — SELF-ASSESSMENT

- I have great clarity about my Calling and purpose (assignment).

- I know how to prepare and develop in my Calling.

- I am not frustrated but feel empowered about my future.

- My sense of destiny comes from my dreams and deeper desires.

- I know that there is provision for my Calling.

Rate the above statements on a scale from 1 to 5:

> 1 - strongly disagree

> 2 - disagree

> 3 - neither agree nor disagree

> 4 - agree

> 5 - strongly agree

If your score is 1-8, you have opportunity to grow in Calling.

If your score is 9-17, you are making progress and should continue in your forward momentum.

If your score is 18+, you have a good handle and grasp on Calling.

NOW ACTION

1. Make a list of 50 things that you want to do in your life. Review the list with a friend and look for common threads and focus. At the end of the exercises, distill the common theme or thread in one sentence.

2. Take some time to write about what you think your Calling is. Reflect on any life Scriptures, prophetic words, dreams, or things that people have said about you. Share these findings with trusted friends and get their feedback.

3. Find a healthy and gifted prophetic presbytery to pray for you regarding your Calling (1 Tim. 2:14; 1 Thess. 5:16-20).

4. To get deeper clarity about your Calling, spend a month praying the following Scriptures and write or share with a friend what you learn.

    For this reason also, since the day we heard of it, we have not ceased to pray for you and to ask that you may be filled with the knowledge of His will in all spiritual wisdom and understanding, so that you will walk in a manner worthy of the Lord, to please Him in all respects, bearing fruit in every good work and increasing in the knowledge of God. (Col. 1:9-10)

    I pray that the eyes of your heart may be enlightened, so that you will know what is the hope of His calling, what are the riches of the glory of His inheritance in the saints, and what is the surpassing greatness of His power toward us who believe. (Eph. 1:18-19)

PRAYER

Lord, we pray that you would enlighten us so that we would know the hope of our calling and the riches and treasures that are found in our calling. Fill us with the knowledge of your will in all spiritual wisdom and understanding. Give us a download of our calling and potential so that we can walk in a manner that is pleasing to you in all respects. Give us the endurance to go through whatever cleansing we need to fulfill our calling, so that we can be commissioned as champions in your great army. As we connect with your purpose and plan for our lives, empower us to bear fruit in all that we do so that we would increase in the knowledge of Christ. Amen.

NOW COACHING QUESTIONS

1. Describe in a few sentences what your Calling is.

2. In what ways do you see God's Calling in your life based on God's promises regarding Calling?

3. In what ways do you have clarity about your Calling?

4. How could you gain greater clarity?

5. How could you gain greater confidence about your Calling?

6. What really "bugs" (irritates or frustrates) you?

7. What problem(s) do you want to fix in the world?

8. What is holding you back from pursuing your calling, desires or dreams?

9. How would you go about overcoming those obstacles?

10. In what ways are you learning new things through these obstacles?

11. What are some of your dreams?

12. In what ways could your dreams be connected to your Calling?

13. What are your next steps?

— — — — — — — — — — — — — →

ENDNOTE

1. https://chiefexecutive.net/5-key-strategies-success/

CHAPTER SIX

CONNECTION
Your Identity

He predestined us to adoption as sons through Jesus Christ to Himself, according to the kind intention of His will. (Eph. 5:1)

We often think about Jesus' Great Commission and relegate the gospel to just getting people saved so that they can go to heaven. Jesus preached the kingdom of heaven and said that we should align ourselves with the new order and system of spiritual life. In that kingdom, Jesus gave us a mandate to teach and make disciples of nations. The scope is huge! To be a disciple is to submit yourself to someone greater than you as a follower, student, or pupil. It is a transformational relationship. The kingdom works through these relationships.

The Father's intention and passion is to create sons and daughters made in His likeness and image. It is the "kind intention of His will" that we be connected to Him. Connection is about your relationships with God, yourself and others. The most critical Connection is developing your bond with your heavenly Father and understanding your identity and the deep love God has for you.

REVELATION OF YOUR IDENTITY

Peter is an interesting character. He is either revered because of his boldness and faith or looked down upon because of his shortcomings and failures. You might conclude that Peter lacked the intimacy with Jesus that John seems to have had. I think Peter was a kinesthetic learner who learned by doing rather than relating or thinking things through.

I love Peter because he was willing to try new things – stepping out in faith from the boat onto the water. He failed Jesus and denied him and later recovered, and he also did some extraordinary things, in spite of having a limited education. He preached one of the most eloquent sermons in history which helped birth the New Testament church on the day of Pentecost, and he became an extraordinary and exemplary, strong leader.

In order for Peter to be successful, and for any leader to be successful, having a Connection with the Lord is critically important. At the core of Connection is identity. As leaders, we have to be located at our true north and know who we are and how God views us. If not, we will drift, and possibly make decisions to get involved in things that may dilute, distract, dissolve, and possibly destroy us. Peter had a life-changing Connection which unfolded as a foundational revelation of who Jesus is. From that Connection was birthed a mandate that governed his relationship and ministry as a bondservant.

> Now when Jesus came into the district of Caesarea Philippi, He was asking His disciples, "Who do people say that the Son of Man is?" And they said, "Some say John the Baptist; and others, Elijah; but still others, Jeremiah, or one of the prophets." He said to them, "But who do you say that I am?" Simon Peter answered, "You are the Christ, the Son of the living God." And Jesus said to him, "Blessed are you, Simon Barjona, because flesh and blood did not reveal this to you, but My Father who is in heaven. I also say to you that you are Peter, and upon this rock I will build My church; and

the gates of Hades will not overpower it. I will give you the keys of the kingdom of heaven; and whatever you bind on earth shall have been bound in heaven, and whatever you loose on earth shall have been loosed in heaven. (Matt. 16:13-19)

Connection requires that we have a revelation of who Christ is, and it will determine how we relate to Him. Peter had a revelation that Jesus was the Son of God. He is the first person to have had this revelation that is documented in the New Testament. This was huge and has become a revelation the Church builds upon even today.

Moments after that, the enemy tried to sabotage that revelation with a distracting thought Peter spoke in haste as an alternative agenda and scenario about the future of Jesus. The seed of that divine revelation obviously did not have time to permeate Peter's thinking and behavior and settle in his subconscious. It takes time for the value system of heaven to shift our values in our identity so that our actions and agendas are aligned with heaven and settled in our subconscious.

THE BATTLE AGAINST IDENTITY THEFT

The battle for identity is one of the greatest battles raging in the world today. The air waves through the media are filled with messages influencing us to sell our birthright and inheritance for temporal satisfaction. The lust of the flesh, the lust of the eyes, and the pride of life are major blinders (Gen. 3:6; 1 Sam. 13:11-12; 1 John 2:15-17).

Seeking pleasure, leisure, and treasures are distractions that will choke the growth of our God-given identities. In addition, the fear of man, rejection, loss, abandonment, and preserving our reputation like the Pharisees did, are culprits. If the enemy can steal, distort, conceal, shift, confuse, or manipulate the identity of an individual or nation as it relates to their Creator, dilution and chaos will ensue.

The battle of identity has partners: individuation, isolation, and intimacy. As we dither on our true identity, we often need to individuate from parents, authority figures, and communities to break from cruches, dysfunctional relationships, and systems that have limited or constrained us. During that time, we often can feel isolated and alone as we learn to embrace the new creation in Christ.

During the process we are hopefully engaging in new levels of intimacy and truth so that the formation of what God is birthing grows healthily. We advocate as you grow into the new, you do so with grace and honor with both the old and the new to perpetuate God's blessings.

Identity is the foundation or true north by which we build kingdom value systems that are the foundations for impacting the mountains of culture. You will not be able to hold your place on your mountain of influence if you are easily allured by the power of pop culture through pleasure, leisure, and treasures or be sabotaged by fear. The greatest battle for identity is often related to the battle of who you give your affections to. Your affections will affect what blossoms and grows within you.

What we nurture will grow. We need to train our senses to discern good and evil through practice. The saying that, "He who rocks the cradle, rules the world" is more significant than we realize. What is nurtured in our hearts as natural or as spiritual children will become the railroad tracks our train runs on. If the programming and code is grounded in truth and love in the spirit and the word, the fruit will be sweet and everlasting.

For some of us, because the structures of truth were not built correctly at an early age, we have spent years reprogramming our thinking to realize transformation. We are uprooting contrarian thinking, and God is empowering us to plant the seeds of truth in our identity about who we are. It is a daily process of prayer, meditation, decrees, reflection, worship, and walking out our salvation with fear and trembling.

Peter had a revelation of who Jesus was which established a cornerstone in his life. It would become the foundation for the authority he would walk in. This cornerstone was key to building Connection with the

Lord. It was the reference to enable Peter to reach a tipping point in his affections to willingly lay down his life for His Savior.

AFFECTION IS LINKED TO CONNECTION

When Peter's Connection was tested during Jesus' trial with the pressure of persecution and the threat of his life and loss, he did not fare so well. The weakness in his character leaked out in denial. He was later restored when Jesus drew him back to Calling to feed Jesus' sheep (John 21:15-19). Peter was restored through a shift in his affections to a deeper love relationship with Jesus.

Jesus had the keys to Peter's heart to reconnect his heart to his assignment of feeding His sheep. Peter needed more than one encounter to keep the Connection. Jesus is a master at managing the inner workings of our inner lives regarding how we see and value ourselves, and how we relate to our inner and outer world.

Where your treasure is, there your heart is also. Your heart is the repository of your affections and what you value. Those affections will empower your self-talk, or scripts, behaviors and decisions. They are either both connecting and firing on all cylinders or there are disconnections that cause interruptions and disturbances in our relationships.

Your affections will influence your Connection. Your Connection will determine your direction. Your Calling and Connection will create commitment. That commitment and direction will determine your destiny.

Connection is central to who you are at the core of your identity. Paul the Apostle indicated in Eph. 3:14-19 that we are to be strengthened in the inner person through faith and in the depths of God's love. The depths of God's love impacts our values and affections so much more than the largest body of knowledge that you can imagine. It is through this construct we interpret life, events, and history through the lens of your identity to validate your existence. You will rationalize your behavior, interpret events and either be grounded in the truth and reality or live a lesser life in the shades of grey and uncertainty.

Those inner scripts of self-talk will empower or disempower you, cause advancement or erode your sense of wellness and identity. Jesus was able to reconnect the dots for Peter after there was a break in his connection with Jesus through the restorative force of love. Peter's self-worth was restored, his affections were aligned with Jesus to love, tend, and feed His sheep to the degree that he was willing to lay down his life in service. When our inner person is made strong through Connection, then we are positioned for exponential growth and advancement.

THE BONDING PROCESS—THE DIVINE ACCELERATOR OF HEAVEN

Beyond these deep moments of revelation, there is another Helper that will come to assist us in our journey. The Holy Spirit is characterized as our counselor, the spirit of truth, the paraclete, and in Paul's writing we see another expression of the Spirit's work. He is revealed as the One who brings about the adoption as sons and daughters. It was important enough that Paul wrote about it in three of his epistles.

For you have not received a spirit of slavery leading to fear again, but you have received a spirit of adoption as sons by which we cry out, "Abba! Father!" And not only this, but also we ourselves, having the first fruits of the Spirit, even we ourselves groan within ourselves, waiting eagerly for our adoption as sons, the redemption of our body. (Rom. 8:15, 23)

So that He might redeem those who were under the Law, that we might receive the adoption as sons. (Gal. 4:5)

He predestined us to adoption as sons through Jesus Christ to Himself, according to the kind intention of His will. (Eph. 1:5)

The workhorse of heaven in your life that will empower you to run your race is the Spirit of Adoption. When we are yoked with this Spirit of Adoption, we will advance from being children and orphans to become spiritual sons and daughters. It is this working of God's Spirit that forges and refines our identity. This force of heaven comes to us, washing us relentlessly with God's love and truth about who we are, and catapults us into C-level living. The intention of heaven is that you bond with your heavenly Father so you can call him Papa (Abba). In addition, He reveals our uniqueness, strengths, experiences, natural and spiritual giftings, desires, passions, and talents in light of our Calling.

You can accomplish great things as a leader, move in powerful gifts, impact nations, and do all the more, but if you do not get this Connection, you will struggle with orphan thinking. You will continue to compare, need validation, and there will always be a missing piece. It will never be enough. Some will be in constant competition with their peers. If you are trying to be the best, there will always be someone better.

Whether in the marketplace or ministry, these people will behave as if it is a big game to succeed and try to get a bigger piece of the pie. For businesspeople, it is competing in the red ocean, fighting for a bigger piece of the finite pie, rather than creating new markets and solutions through the blue ocean strategy. This thinking is rooted in a mindset of scarcity versus abundance. This orphan thinking will erode your sense of healthy identity in Christ

ORPHAN THINKING WILL ERODE YOUR SENSE OF HEALTHY IDENTITY IN CHRIST.

Bonding with your Father in heaven will create an unprecedented security. It won't matter if people praise you or abase you. That confidence will enable you not to grasp and strive but to release and trust God for the results enabling you to stay focused on what you are to build and create. It is a place where intimacy forges the plans and purposes of heaven. In that place we get connected to our Father's intention for our lives, in building and walking out our calling.

WHAT DOES RELATIONSHIP BUILDING AND BONDING LOOK LIKE?

Everyone is created uniquely and has their own love language. God knows how intricately we are made and knows how to connect the dots within us. Some of the smallest and most insignificant things to one person may mean something totally different to others.

God's love is relentless, washing over us time and time again. In a sense it is almost painful because it positions you to receive. His love washes over our pain and hurts, and re-defines who we are. It is probably the most uncomfortable thing I have experienced at times because it requires a commitment to transparency and authenticity. But, at the same time, it has also been the most empowering and exhilarating. From the overflow of that love, flows the basis for loving others. Each person will experience this bonding with God in a different and unique way.

A key enabler for advancing in kingdom matters is turning from things that Jesus does not value, and valuing the things He values. When Jesus began His preaching, he taught His disciples to repent because the Kingdom of God was at hand (Matt. 4:17). The kingdom is NOW – new operating wisdom. When one repents, one turns away from something and turns toward something else. The immediacy of the supernatural kingdom is at hand. We stand at the gates to receive when we make that shift in our will, mind and emotions.

This is not a dry and drawn out process. In Rom. 2:4, God intercepts the repentance process with His goodness. It is God's goodness that leads us to repentance, not by self-will, good works, or feeling ashamed or guilty. When we are in the now, we turn away from self-driven interests and distractions to reorient our inner compasses toward God.

Instead of being a performance and programs-driven people, we become a presence-driven people, relationally based in solid Connection. Instead of looking through a lens obscured by worldly filters, we begin to look through a lens colored by God's love and will for this world.

The word repent for some has many religious connotations associated with it. Some may fall into performance through self-effort to make the change. "Perhaps, if I only try harder, things will change." The wonder and beauty in Jesus' command is that we are to shift our thinking and take on the mind of Christ so that we can experience the kingdom. This trade is HUGE! Isa. 61:1-3 sets the precedent for these trades.

We make shifts resulting in trades through Connecting. Some of those benefits are as follows:

- Darkness to light

- Orphans to sons and daughters

- Victims to victors

- Unrighteousness to righteousness

- Sin focused to Jesus focused

- Fear to Love

- Insecurity to security

- Striving to rest

- Heaviness to praise

- Mourning to joy

- Shame and humiliation for a double portion

- Scarcity to abundance

- Surviving to success

- Success to significance

- Consumer to producing

- Problem-focused to solution-oriented

- Lose-lose to win-win-win

SHIFTING OUR FOCUS

If we simply change what we focus on, and shift our focus onto God, and our God-given identity, we can tap into the eternal power of the Almighty! Focus is a driver creating shifts so we can Connect! We shift from our limited ability, resources and wisdom, to His unlimited measure. There's alignment that takes place when one is in the now. Shifts occur in our identity.

When we are aligned with heaven, we are able to live in the now and are able to let the now flow in us so that God's presence and power, His purpose, provision and pleasure, are released in us and through us. Kingdom resources are released to bring transformation and influence our culture. This simple awareness can change atmospheres and reverse negativity in the spaces and spheres we influence. It will change you, as well as families, communities, industries, sectors, regions and nations.

WHY CONNECTION IS IMPORTANT — INTENT WILL DETERMINE OUTCOMES

A year or so ago, I had a picture where I saw two leaders standing in an elevated spiritual space. Their influence was very significant and here is why. Whatever they thought seemed to materialize. I wondered how this could be. Then I was reminded of the following Scripture:

For as he thinks in his heart, so is he. (Prov. 23:7)

As leaders ascend the heights of influence, they become very influential. In fact, I believe they become gatekeepers to what kind of spiritual atmospheres they release. Leaders become spiritual lightning rods that attract either good or evil, God's Spirit or the contrary. Jesus' command to repent for the kingdom of heaven at hand is really about a gatekeeper function which permits the kingdom of heaven to be realized.

What was also fascinating about this picture was the power of a thought. It was very clear that in an instant, God could think a thought and humble one of these leaders and make them like King Nebuchadnezzar. The power of thought or the heart's intent is very powerful.

Leaders have the ability or authority to release the kingdom of heaven through their intentions. As leaders spend time with the Lord in intimacy or Connection, ideas and initiatives are incubated. When that divine intention is released, it creates agreement with the realms of their origin. The genesis of that thought and where it was incubated is key. Fathers and mothers are known for developing original thoughts and ideas. In the Scripture below, note how mature leaders are described.

> *I have written to you, fathers,* **because you know Him who has been from the beginning.** *I have written to you, young men, because you are strong, and the word of God abides in you, and you have overcome the evil one.* (1 John 2:14, author's emphasis)

Fathers know God who was from the beginning. They have an innate ability to focus on the origin of things. Fathers have the divine authority to release the intentions of heaven, the divine seed, dreams and destiny because they are acquainted with the ageless One, the Ancient of Days, who has been from the beginning.

Working with leaders, I have found that the higher the level of the leader, the easier it is to convey intent. Leaders synthesize intent quite rapidly. I received feedback from my boss for a presentation I had made to senior management. He said, "You emphasized these items too much. You did not properly perceive the leadership space you were working in. All the information you shared could have been done with less words." I realized that in this meeting, I did not perceive the leadership space I was speaking to, and that they would capture the intent of the presentation more quickly than I had estimated.

Effective leaders read intent quickly and efficiently. It is a necessary skill for survival and effectiveness that helps leaders discern character, motives, and abilities. For the leader without the Holy Spirit, you could say they are operating in the five senses. With **EFFECTIVE LEADERS READ INTENT QUICKLY AND EFFICIENTLY.** the Holy Spirit, you can add a sixth sense to discern and understand leadership intent and leadership operating spaces you are working in. In an ideal world, business leaders that are operating in kingdom dimensions, should have better trained ears because they have practiced the art of effectual listening.

The higher levels of responsibility you walk in require higher levels of accountability, especially with your words. What you speak will either resonate with heaven or hell, the flesh or the devil. When those intentions on the inside become words and then actions, the consequences could be significant. One could release witchcraft and the powers of darkness through gossip or slander or curses. Moses, when God commanded him to speak to the rock, struck it instead, and it prevented him from entering into the Promised Land. Similarly, there could be high costs to our actions as we grow in responsibility and accountability.

Every leader needs to spend energy building the connection to God. In the incubator of intimacy, bonding takes place and we can understand the Father's intentions. From that place of intimacy, intention is developed which facilitates the birthing of the kingdom of heaven through what we speak and think. Connection will be the life source of your success so you can end well and impact your spheres of influence. It will enable you to endure the testings that come in the Capacity phase, and perhaps the rigors of training in developing Competency, or learning how to deal with successes when Convergence emerges and you become a Catalyst.

The end result of Connection is that you will be comfortable in your own skin. You will trust who you are at your core and not try to be something that you are not. Connected leaders are confident and content in who they are at their core. Their Connection empowers them in their affection, direction, intention, identity, and ultimately destiny. They are in touch with their true north; that is, they have a reference to their identity.

NO SUBSTITUTE FOR DEVELOPING RELATIONSHIP TO PREPARE FOR CAPACITY

I worked with a young man in his teens that had a strong leadership gift. I would often encourage him to invest in his relationship with Jesus so that when the stresses and pressures came, he would be prepared. It was simple stuff like spending time in prayer and reading God's Word. I said this because it was evident that there would be many stressors, challenges, and temptations that would come his way. They were well meaning words that fell on ears that could not hear at the time.

Events came up later and we had to deal with tough issues. I believe if there had been a stronger foundation of prayer and the word, the outcomes of some of the behaviors and decisions made would have been far different. He would have had strength to handle the difficulties and storms differently if he had developed a deeper relationship. To have this foresight is challenging at a young age, and even when you are older and have learned some hard lessons, it can be something we do not embrace.

When Jesus was in the Garden of Gethsemane, and he was doing business with the Father regarding the last part of his assignment on earth, his three friends Peter, James and John were nearby. In that moment they were under great pressure and distress. Temptation was knocking at the door in this difficult transition and Jesus exhorted his disciples to pray.

> *And He was saying, "Abba! Father! All things are possible for You; remove this cup from Me; yet not what I will, but what You will." And He came and found them sleeping, and said to*

Peter, "Simon, are you asleep? Could you not keep watch for one hour? Keep watching and praying that you may not come into temptation; the spirit is willing, but the flesh is weak." Again He went away and prayed, saying the same words. And again He came and found them sleeping, for their eyes were very heavy; and they did not know what to answer Him. And He came the third time, and said to them, "Are you still sleeping and resting? It is enough; the hour has come; behold, the Son of Man is being betrayed into the hands of sinners. Get up, let us be going; behold, the one who betrays Me is at hand!" (Mark 14:13-42)

This passage is tough to read because Jesus came to his three friends three times and each time they could not resist the pressure and they slept. They failed three times in a row – they struck out. Their best friend was going through the hardest time in His life, and they were not there for Him. He was processing his betrayal and impending death by crucifixion. Jesus looked to his leaders and exhorted them to pray because He did not want them to fall prey to temptation and He needed the moral support!

Just as Jesus had to deal with the temptation at hand, He needed his team to do the same. Prayer would have strengthened the team of three to stand in the difficult hour and also prepared them for the downstream fallout. Maybe Peter's denial would have looked different if he had been strengthened with Jesus in that hour. We cannot underestimate the power of prayer that builds deep relationship so that we are prepared for difficult times and seasons in our lives. We need to build our Connection day to day so that our foundations stand strong when the storms come.

CONNECTING THROUGH COVENANT AND COMMUNITY

From that place of confidence and contentment, empowered leaders are able to Connect with others, Communicate in healthy ways, Collaborate when appropriate, serve as Catalysts for others, develop Competencies and Capacity, and become Champions. Connected leaders know how to build and create Community, and a sense of group belonging and corporate identity, similar to a family or tribe.

Healthy communities are safe places, and include rules of conduct and engagement, governance, policies, boundaries, order, authority structure, opportunities for rest and recreation, Creativity, Communication outlets and channels, celebration, contribution, Collaboration, Compassion, initiative, shared goals and mission for teamwork and productivity, accountability, sharing, training, performance review and feedback, rewards, penalties, mechanisms for discipline, and screening or eligibility criteria for joining and leaving the Community.

Some relationships by their nature are short-term, seasonal or transactional, such as casual acquaintances, distant friends and one-time customers, while others are longer term with more frequent contact and greater levels of trust and intimacy. These would include close friends and some family members; and possibly authority figures such as coaches, teachers, pastors, priests, chaplains, doctors, dentists, chiropractors, and other professionals, as well as repeat or long-term clients.

THE HIGHEST FORM OF CONNECTION IS COVENANT

The highest form of Connection is Covenant and God modeled that for us repeatedly and perfectly with Noah, Abraham, Isaac, Jacob, Moses, Joshua, David and Solomon, among others. Jesus willingly (voluntarily) laid down His life for us to take on the sins of the world and offer Himself as a spotless sacrifice, fulfill the law, and usher in the New Covenant or Testament of grace (see Heb. 9:11-28).

In ancient times, to "cut covenant" meant that two parties would cut an animal in half, hang the carcass dripping with blood on two poles, and walk between the two poles to swear their oath or Covenant of loyalty and allegiance to one another and their families. It was a serious commitment with a penalty of death for violating such a bond, and the Covenant might be in force for multiple generations.

Ruth made a Covenant with Naomi and then Boaz, and Jonathan made a Covenant with David. God made a Covenant with Israel and renewed it on multiple occasions after Israel proved unfaithful and violated the Covenant. God even said in Isaiah 28 that He was annulling their Covenant with death and through several Old Testament prophets such as Isaiah, Jeremiah, Ezekiel and Hosea, that He was betrothing Himself to Israel.

Similarly, His disciples today are betrothed to Christ in a spiritual sense as the bride of Christ (Matt. 22:2, 25:1-13; 2 Cor. 11:2; Rev. 19:7-9, 21:2, 22:17). Covenant relationships are rare but worth identifying, pursuing, developing, and maintaining.

In today's modern world, there are many types of legal agreements or Covenants, including: Marriage Certificates or Licenses, Letters of Agreement, Letters of Intent, Consulting Agreements, Intellectual Property Agreements, Noncompete Agreements, Nondisclosure Agreements, Licensing Agreements, Confidentiality Agreements, Noncircumvention Agreements, Mineral Rights Agreements, and Royalty Agreements.

Also, there are Lease Agreements, Title Transfer Agreements, Employment Agreements, Severance Agreements, Settlement Agreements, Memorandum of Understanding, Compensation Agreements, Stock Purchase Agreements, Stock Transfer Agreements, Shareholder Agreements, Joint Venture Agreements, Publishing Agreements, Visitation Rights Agreements, Joint or Sole Custody Agreements, Irrevocable Trust Agreements, and much more.

God says that all things were made by and are held together through His Son by the power of His Word (Col. 1:15-17; Heb. 1:3). His Word is the glue that binds or connects every level together from the atomic level to the universe. And of course, Jesus is called The Word (John 1:1-5, 14).

The realization of His Word is made through the power of Connection through Covenant.

The agreements above are expressions of those forces that unite us so God's life can flow in our relationships and communities. God commands a blessing on unity (Psa. 133). In verse 3 the Lord commands the blessing – life forever. The blessings of God's Covenant leave a lasting legacy.

A STORY ABOUT HOW CONNECTION BECAME A THREAD TO SUCCESS FOR DAVE

From a young age I knew that I wanted to make a positive difference. The odds were definitely stacked against me for doing so. Growing up the youngest of three children with a father who was a teacher and a stay at home mom, we were what I would later identify as an upper lower-class family. My 12 years of Catholic School upbringing led to some significant rebellious tendencies in my late teens, resulting in my walking away from my faith.

I was to find faith again through business. At an early age just out of college, I met a group of people for whom I had great respect and admiration. They were marketplace ministers and my wife and I were led back to Christ through this association. I was a hardworking young man with endless energy, an optimistic point of view, a generous spirit and a desire to succeed.

It would take 18 years for me to discover the source of my driven-ness through a Christian men's book group and with the help of my friend Will Meier. By the time I was around 40 years old, the Lord had led me to what the world would consider an initial level of outward success. God significantly transformed my understanding of His will for my life, broke off the old reasons for my passionate pursuit of "excellence", and allowed me to become self-aware and brutally honest with myself.

The past 10 years have been ones of discoveries with setbacks and successes. During this time, I have worked very deliberately on myself coming to understand and realize that it is the Lord who brings opportunity according to His will despite the shortcomings of the object (me) implementing the opportunity. Surrender, time for prayer and meditation, association, discernment of seasons and generosity have led me to an understanding in my business and personal life.

We need to work on ourselves so that when the timing and opportunity of the Lord presents itself that we recognize it, act upon it and have faith that we are prepared to execute even when the challenge seems bigger than our capacity because we have a heavenly partner helping us over the finish line.

DAVE SCHMID
Entrepreneur, Chief Investment Officer & Managing Partner

In my friend's journey, Calling did not capture his heart, but the concept of Calling as it related to the Church as he knew it detracted him from making significant Connection. This was not an unreasonable response for someone longing to do things with excellence and know the truth. God was faithful to draw him back to Himself through his passion, desire for excellence and success.

Dave's Competencies seemed to lead the way for him in his journey. Dave recognized and leveraged his Competencies at a young age and experienced Convergence in the business world. He became very successful as a "parallel" entrepreneur. Dave has started many ventures and businesses simultaneously. Through the times he spent in Capacity, he also developed deeper Connection which facilitated significant shifts in his understanding of the source of his success. Dave's Convergences, combined with his Calling, Connections and Capacity, have enabled him to be a marketplace Catalyst and Champion to many as he has learned to co-labor with the Lord.

CASE STUDY: A WOMAN WHO HAD THE CONNECTION WITH GOD TO BE A DELIVERER

Harriet Tubman was an American abolitionist who was born into slavery in the eastern part of Maryland and as typical in that time period, slaves were beaten and abused by their masters. Her life did not begin well by any means. In an unfortunate and tragic event, a slave owner threw a heavy metal weight trying to hit someone else, and hit Harriet. As a result of the wound, she suffered a traumatic head injury that caused her pain, dizziness and hypersomnia throughout her life.

In 1849 she escaped and reached the North, traveling 90 miles to Pennsylvania to freedom. When she arrived, she said, "When I found I had crossed that line, I looked at my hands to see if I was the same person. There was such a glory over everything; the sun came like gold through the trees, and over the fields, and I felt like I was in Heaven."

Harriet had a close relationship with God. Her friends would often say of Tubman that the source of her strength came from her faith in God. God gave her a heart of a deliverer and protector of the weak and this was integral to her identity. There was no ambiguity. Out of her Connection with God, she was able to become one of the most famous "conductors" of the Underground Railroad that brought many slaves to freedom and safety. She earned the nicknamed "Moses" as a deliverer.

It is estimated that she helped at least 700 fellow slaves to freedom and made over 19 trips and boasted that she never lost a passenger. At one point, slaveholders put a $40,000 bounty on her life for capture. She was protected and never caught. Harriet lived a fearless life and often said, "I can't die but once". After attaining her freedom, she likewise began bringing others to freedom. Slowly, she brought her relatives out of state into freedom.

None of this could have happened if she had not developed an intimate relationship with Jesus first. Harriet said that as she was leading slaves to the North, that she would carefully listen to the voice of God and would only go where she felt God was leading her. Fellow abolitionist Thomas Garrett was quoted as saying, "I never met any person of any color who had more confidence in the voice of God."

Another outworking of Connection was her ability to connect with others to build a coalition of support for the Underground Railroad. After slaves were freed, slave owners would put up wanted posters. Harriet hired men to take down the signs. She built trust in her relationships and with sympathizers to be able to be effective as a "conductor". She also became friends with many of the best known abolitionists of the day for her bravery. John Brown was quoted as saying Tubman was "one of the best and bravest persons on this continent – General Tubman as we call her." She was able to Connect.

Later she served the Union Army as a laundress, nurse, and even a spy along the coast of South Carolina. After the Civil War ended she settled in Auburn, New York and was involved in the women's suffrage movement, working with Elizabeth Cady Stanton and Susan B. Anthony. She died and was buried in 1913 with military honors at Fort Hill Cemetery in Auburn, New York.

For Harriet, who walked in her identity as a deliverer, it meant successfully fulfilling her assignment avoiding harm and delivering every passenger safely. She became a Champion bringing freedom to others because she was focused and on point in her Connection. Without a Connection to God and to a network of others, the Champion could not have succeeded in her assignment and mission.[1]

A STORY FROM LUKE ABOUT FINDING YOUR IDENTITY AS A MILLENNIAL

As I began to try to build relationships in my late teens, I noticed that people would identify me by my intelligence and humor. Having found an open seat at the table, I started identifying myself the same way and placed my identity in my abilities. My identity in strengths matured into an identity propped up on others' weaknesses. It evolved into a fragile patchwork of self-negativity, envy, perfectionism, and half-hearted self-affirmations.

I dealt with the different symptoms of my broken identity instead of the causes. For self-negativity, I practiced self-compassion for a few months. With feelings of inferiority, I would assure myself I'm superior in some area, or if that failed, work until I was. I would take these small steps to suppress the underlying issue that I had made a poor choice in basing my self-worth on myself and my success.

I decided I wanted to be "grounded," knowing who I am independent from my environment. To me, "grounded" means integrity, honesty, and love regardless of the social consequences. In order to be stable and grounded, I needed to find a solid foundation. This is my big area in which to grow, because I know that foundation lies in my connection with God. So, I am seeking to grow in my knowledge and relationship with God's love. It is not easy at times, but I know that I am moving in the right direction.

LUKE MEIER
Software Engineer

TAKEAWAYS

- Connection is about your relationship with the Father.

- Understanding your identity is key to who you are at your core.

- Living in your identity in Christ (revelation) will sustain you in leadership.

- Your identity is likely under constant attack; it takes work to maintain it.

- Orphan thinking is a saboteur of identity.

Peter had a revelation of the Son of God that transformed and empowered him.

- Connection builds the power of intent to release the kingdom.

- There is no substitute for preparing and building Connection for our future.

- Connection is a conduit for Creativity to flow.

- Understanding your Maker's intent will impact your leadership effectiveness.

- Connection often leads to Covenant relationships.

CONNECTION — SELF-ASSESSMENT

- I know that I am loved by my Father in Heaven.

- I celebrate God's goodness on a regular basis.

- I feel secure and do not compare myself to others.

- I can articulate my identity in Christ with clarity.

- I love who I am and have great relationship skills.

Rate the above on a scale from 1 to 5:

1 - strongly disagree

2 - disagree

3 - neither agree nor disagree

4 - agree

5 - strongly agree

If your score is 1-8, you have opportunity to grow in Connections.

If your score is 9-17, you are making progress and should continue in your forward momentum.

If your score is 18+, you have a good handle and grasp on Connections.

NOW ACTION

1. Pray through the following Scriptures for a month asking the Lord to increase your understanding of your adoption as sons and daughters.

    For you have not received a spirit of slavery leading to fear again, but you have received a spirit of adoption as sons by which we cry out, "Abba! Father!" And not only this, but also we ourselves, having the firstfruits of the Spirit, even we ourselves groan within ourselves, waiting eagerly for our adoption as sons, the redemption of our body. (Rom. 8:15, 23)

    So that He might redeem those who were under the Law, that we might receive the adoption as sons. (Gal. 4:5)

    He predestined us to adoption as sons through Jesus Christ to Himself, according to the kind intention of His will. (Eph. 1:5)

2. Just as parents, teachers, or coaches talk about their children, students, or team members respectively, write as if they are talking about you and your identity. What do you think they would say? Or simply have a conversation with the Lord and ask him how He sees you.

PRAYER

Lord, we ask you for the spirit of adoption to fill our lives. We renounce and disassociate with all fear and bondage to slave thinking, and ask that you wash us with your love so we can identify with you as Papa, (Abba) Father. Reveal your goodness and kind intention toward us. Continue to wash me, heal me, and wash me in your love so I am totally connected and identified with you. Bring me to the place where I have the sense and security that I am the Father's joy. Amen.

NOW COACHING QUESTIONS

1. In what ways do you feel you are bonded with your heavenly Father?

2. What are obstacles that keep you from knowing you are loved?

3. In what ways do you understand your identity in Christ?

4. What experiences have built your understanding of your identity?

5. In what ways do you understand the Father's intent for your life?

6. What actions can you take to go deeper in your relationship with God?

7. How could you influence others to go deeper?

8. How will you know you have made a deeper Connection?

9. What are your next steps?

ENDNOTE

1. Sources for Harriet Tubman excerpt:

   • https://www.christianitytoday.com/history/people/activists/harriet-tubman.html.

   • https://www.womenshistory.org/education-resources/biographies/harriet-tubman.

   • Wikipedia.

CHAPTER SEVEN

COMPETENCY
Developing Excellence

Do not neglect the spiritual gift within you, which was bestowed on you through prophetic utterance with the laying on of hands by the presbytery. Take pains with these things; be absorbed in them, so that your progress will be evident to all. Pay close attention to yourself and to your teaching; persevere in these things, for as you do this you will ensure salvation both for yourself and for those who hear you. (1 Tim. 4:14-16)

If anyone thinks they will achieve greatness or excellence without applying themselves with discipline, they are mistaken. One of the great misconceptions some Christians believe is that because God has established the work of the cross and we are saved by faith through grace, we think God is going to do everything else for us. I know countless people who are still waiting on God for Him to do things. Sadly, nothing is likely to happen until they step out and apply themselves to develop.

God calls us to co-labor with Him (John 15). Competency is about your development and requires your participation. Competency is about developing your talents (raw natural ability) and skills needed for you to fulfill your destiny or assignment. On a deeper spiritual level, there are spiritual resources of the spirit of wisdom, understanding and knowledge that enhance your natural abilities.

Peter started his journey as an uneducated laborer and after three and a half years with Jesus, he emerged as a voice to launch the New Testament church. His training was spending time with His Master. The Connection he developed empowered him to preach one of the most profound sermons in history. It became the launching pad for demonstrating his Competencies. Peter learned how to preach!

In his later years, he wrote two powerful epistles. Peter found his voice in the context of the Holy Spirit being poured out. I believe Peter remained teachable throughout his life. 2 Peter chapter 1 gives us insight into the continuous learning he embraced. He was not afraid to remind people of his journey on how to stay true.

> *Therefore, brethren, be all the more diligent to make certain about His calling and choosing you; for as long as you practice these things, you will never stumble; for in this way the entrance into the eternal kingdom of our Lord and Savior Jesus Christ will be abundantly supplied to you. Therefore, I will always be ready to remind you of these things, even though you already know them, and have been established in the truth which is present with you.* (2 Pet. 1:10-12)

THE EXCELLENCE OF GLORY

Beyond these reminders, we see Peter also referring to the excellencies of glory in his first epistle. Excellence refers to an eminent endowment, property or quality. There was a revelation of God's excellencies imparted to Peter, and he shared that with us.

But you are a chosen race, a royal priesthood, a holy nation, a people for God's own possession, so that you may proclaim the excellencies of Him who has called you out of darkness into His marvelous light. (1 Pet. 1:9)

Today, God is calling a generation to move into the area of excellence. There is restoration taking place. Leaders are calling their followers to live in excellence. This is not perfection or performance; it is an attribute of identity. We possess it, and then live from that place. Daniel carried this excellence and was considered 10 times better than all of his peers. His gift brought him before great men. He served as an administrator and counselor to four kings without compromise! And, in the times when he shared bad news with the kings he served, he grew in favor. We need to see this competency restored to believers!

TODAY, GOD IS CALLING A GENERATION TO MOVE INTO THE AREA OF EXCELLENCE.

As for every matter of wisdom and understanding about which the king consulted them, he found them ten times better than all the magicians and conjurers who were in all his realm. (Dan. 1:10)

There were other men in the Scriptures who carried that same excellent spirit. Bezalel was a master craftsman and possessed the spirit of Wisdom, Understanding and Knowledge (WUK). He had artisans from every trade working with him to build the tabernacle. The Fear of the Lord was their reference and starting point.

Through wisdom they developed application of their technologies, methodologies, and integrated systems to build the temple masterpiece. They knew how these technologies would corroborate and fit together by connecting the dots. Through the process they applied their knowledge, expertise and discernment. As a result, Bezalel and his team were recognized as renowned craftsmen who built the tabernacle of Moses.

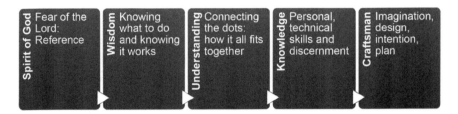

FIGURE 6.

Advancing in Supernatural Dimensions to Create Solutions.

Some of the Bezalels of today are the marketplace entrepreneurs transforming our digital and media landscape, and creating now economic ecosystems. God wants to give the WUK Factor so we can be 10x better.

We can see how Peter was transformed by spending time with Jesus. Acts 4:13 says, "Now as they observed the confidence of Peter and John and understood that they were uneducated and untrained men, they were amazed, and began to recognize them as having been with Jesus."

The mark on Peter's and John's life was that others could see they had spent time with Jesus! And, apparently Jesus was a master teacher, since previously they were uneducated and untrained. In Jesus we have the fullness of understanding, including wisdom and knowledge.

> *My goal is that they may be encouraged in heart and united in love, so that they may have the full riches of complete understanding, in order that they may know the mystery of God, namely, Christ, in whom are hidden all the treasures of wisdom and knowledge.* (Col. 2:2-3)

The Jesus WUK Factor will not only transform us but accelerate us into kingdom dimensions that will set us apart by orders of magnitude. His treasury is infinite.

EXCELLENCE IN ACTION

Every call has a preparation to develop our competencies in practical ways. This is not just limited to spiritual development. It takes hard work and devotion to become good at something. Every one of us has been given a measure of faith, talent, and gifts. We are made in God's likeness and image and by design, we express a dimension of who God is to the world.

I have heard that there are about seven critical skills one needs to learn to take on in any vocation. If you are changing jobs, or moving into something new or want to move, can you identify those skills? And, if you are thinking about becoming an expert at something, research suggests that it takes about 10,000 hours of work to become an expert at something. I am not sure if this can be accelerated under certain situations or in special circumstances, but the point here is, know what skills you need to develop and know that it will take a considerable time investment to achieve mastery.

Getting an education will teach you vocabulary, concepts, and the ability to think creatively so that you develop knowledge construct around a body of knowledge. Degrees are credentials that let people know that you have an ability to learn and grasp the concepts of a particular body of knowledge. Learning to apply that knowledge takes wisdom – knowing what to do and knowing that it will work. And it requires understanding – the ability to know how that knowledge fits together and wisdom to get things done in the proper context.

Unfortunately, our education system often leaves people high and dry with regards to developing wisdom and understanding. There are education institutions that employ internships, and practicums that empower the applications process. Learning work and life skills are not often taught in many schools. Not everything can be Googled or found on YouTube or Vimeo!

We need to disciple the generations to cultivate a spirit of excellence and challenge them to embrace the WUK Factor, and spend time with Jesus who holds the keys of wisdom, understanding and knowledge! The bandwidth of heaven is far greater and more powerful than any smart phone technology or microchip processor.

We need to be comfortable in this Competency phase to apply ourselves to continuous learning whether it is in education, on the job training, certifications, or developing excellence. Developing our raw talent, spiritual gifts, and turning them into valuable skills and abilities with the spirit of excellence will bring us before great men and women. God's favor is upon excellence and is easily recognized. With this in hand, we can face new challenges. As continuous learners, we access the resources to develop solutions in a complex world.

PERSONALITY INVENTORIES

Beyond skills, there are aspects about your personality that are helpful to know. This will help you to grow in self-awareness and develop and improve your relationship skills and effectiveness. There are many great tools available for you to learn more about how you are wired. I have found some of the following tools very helpful and insightful.

- Strengthsfinder™

- Myers-Briggs Type Indicator®

- DISC Assessment

- Hogan Personality Assessment

I have used Strengthsfinder™ with teams both in the marketplace and in ministry. It is very helpful to understand peoples' strength orientation and where they are motivated to make contributions. My wife and I have used the Myers-Briggs Type Indicator® (MBTI®) to help us understand each other and how we communicate, collect information and make decisions.

This has been an invaluable tool to enable us to grow in our understanding of each other and to diffuse conflicts. We also have found it a helpful tool to interpret our relationship during stressful transitions. Whatever tool you use, be positive and constructive with it and develop language and mutual understanding on which to build.

KNOW YOUR UNIQUE GIFT MATRIX

Each one of you is created uniquely based on your DNA, personal history, personality type, strengths, gifts, skills, and talents. This list gives you distinctions. God gives us these resources so that we can develop them and prove ourselves to be faithful, productive contributors to society. Oftentimes your gift matrix is related to your calling and assignment. At some point, you should take the time to reflect on your distinctions that make you unique. Here is a list of categories that I suggest you take an inventory of:

- What are your natural talents?

- What is your personal history? How has this helped you?

- What skills seem to be easy to develop or come natural to you?

- What is your personality type? (Myers-Briggs®, DISC, etc)

- What are your spiritual gifts? (fivefold, motivational or charismatic gifts) (see Eph. 4:11; Rom. 12:1-8; 1 Cor. 12:1-11, 27-31; and 1 Cor. 14:1-33)

- What skills have you developed?

- What do people come to you for help with?

- What do people say you are good at?

Take the time to develop a working understanding of your uniqueness and learn how to communicate and further develop your gifts, skills and talents.

This section is perhaps one of the most important with regards to getting grounded in your unique identity as it relates to your Calling, Competency, Connection, Capacity, and Compensation. When these dimensions come together, it is a place where kingdom career convergence takes place which is more than just having a professional career, but a destiny. As we connect with our passion, skills, abilities, unique identity, character, and adding value, our work will take on new meaning.

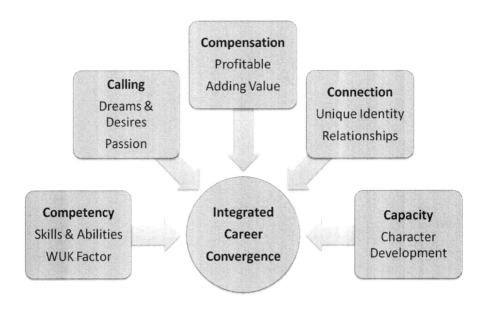

FIGURE 7.
Creating an Integrated Career Convergence.

When our dreams, desires, passions, skills and abilities are integrated with our identity, which was formed through the crucibles, we are positioned to bring forth the greatest value in our lives. When heaven comes to earth in our work, there is a great fullness and fruitfulness that will abound. In the following chapters of this book, we will unpack these realities in more detail.

DOES THE MONEY MATTER?
—YOUR COMPENSATION

Part of organizational Culture is reflected in how we reward and honor various members – staff or labor, management, shareholders, trustees or directors, donors, volunteers, and/or owners – for their contributions of time, talent and treasure. Money, while important, is not the only motivator or reward for employees. In God's kingdom ecosystem, there is a law of cause and effect or reaping and sowing, and the law of multiplication – the measure you give is the measure you receive and still more is given to you.

In other words, what you invest will create returns. You will reap what you sow plus more. One of those returns comes in the form of compensation, which is money received by an employee as salary, wages, commissions or bonuses, as well as benefits.

Benefits can include annual vacation, medical leave, sabbatical, health insurance, life insurance, disability insurance, retirement plan, dental insurance, membership to a health club or gym or YMCA or country club, scholarships or tuition and books for education, professional training, certifications, licenses and industry conferences, etc.

Compensation from God's perspective includes both earthly and heavenly rewards and benefits. Your perspective on compensation and investing will ultimately determine your true wealth both in the natural and spiritual dimensions and honor is a key constituent to create positive outcomes.

From a heavenly perspective, we should invest in the things that God values. There are two things that are eternal, the Word of God and the souls of people. We are commanded to store up our treasures in heaven by doing things God cares about and not seeking personal recognition or attention. This could include prayer, giving alms, fasting, serving others and giving generously. There is great reward for those who have laid down their agendas and self-centeredness to become God-centered in their mindset and actions.

Similarly, if we provide valuable service or skill by serving others and providing a solution, we should be compensated. The workman is worthy of his wages (Matt. 10:10; Luke 10:7; 1 Tim. 5:18). If you are gainfully employed, the laws of economics will establish the reward you receive for your work. If you are aligned with God's purposes and following His plan for your life, assuredly, you will be compensated by your heavenly Father.

UNDERSTANDING TRUE VALUE

What God orders, He pays for. He is not a cheap, impoverished, miserly, stingy, greedy Father, but a loving, generous Father of unlimited resources and abundance who gives good gifts to His children (Matt. 7:9-11; Luke 11:11-13; Jas. 1:17) and promotes those who are faithful and wise stewards (Matt. 25:14-30; Luke 19:11-27). God is a lavish, extravagant and cheerful giver. And He expects that from us as well.

Those who have a scarcity mindset do not understand kingdom economics because they are blinded by their perceived need and lack. They believe if they compensate someone fairly for a good or service, they will not have enough so they are always seeking a deal. In reality, they seek a deal to steal from others. Jas. 5:4 says, "Look! The wages you failed to pay the workmen who mowed your fields are crying out against you. The cries of the harvesters have reached the ears of the Lord Almighty."

There is a place for being prudent and shrewd to protect from excesses and greed, but not at the expense of fair value. When we do not properly evaluate the value of a good or service, then we rob others of the value that is due them. We are not creating a return on our investment, but a return of debt upon our lives.

Our work ethic should be pleasing to the Lord, and so should our compensation, *"And whatsoever ye do, do it heartily, as to the Lord, and not unto men; Knowing that of the Lord ye shall receive the reward of the inheritance: for ye serve the Lord Christ."* (Col. 3:23-24)

Champions understand value and will invest to bless and create a return on their investment whether it is in the natural or spiritual dimension. And, whether it is a product, service, spiritual gift, assignment, mandate, treasure, business, asset, education, or financial investment, they will steward those resources with honor. Embracing honor will enable us to properly appraise value and then respond with deference and generosity. Applying honor, the law of sowing and reaping, and the law of multiplication, to our organizations will bring about a blessing empowered by heaven.

DON'T SABOTAGE YOUR FUTURE SUCCESS

Probably one of the worst thought structures around is to think that, because Jesus is coming back really soon, we should not invest in training, development, mastery, and education. If we are going to be relevant and impact our culture, we need the social currency and credentials to do so. Some of us have a deterministic world-view of fatalism. Its voice cries, "Why bother? The world is going to end soon." Jesus calls, trains and equips marketplace people. Often our first love response to the Lord when He saves us is to go into ministry. Seminary is not the only solution for service or training.

Dr. Bruce Cook, in his book, *Aligning with the Apostolic, Vol. 1*, states that only about 2-3% of the Christian population globally is engaged in full-time ecclesiastical (vocational ministry) work. The remainder of the saints are in the marketplace. Perhaps acquiring an advanced degree could give you credentials to impact one of the Seven Mountains of Culture. Don't sell out because you think the end is coming. Occupy until Jesus returns. Develop your gifts and talents to train you in stewardship and faithfulness so God can reward you.

Invest in your future. Pray for an excellent spirit so that the WUK Factor allows Christ to shine through you with His preeminence. Evaluate your calling and understand what training and development and/or licensing or credentialing is necessary for your success.

Leaders know their abilities and limitations. Their limitations become the building blocks for creating great teams. In addition, every great leader should be a continuous learner. They are not intimidated by their lack of skills, resources or Competencies because they will either develop them as rapid, continuous, adult learners or they will find others to assist them. Developing your Competencies will catapult you into greatness.

STORY ABOUT TWO TRANSFORMATIONAL WORDS THAT DEVELOPED A NEW COMPETENCY

During my career as an advancing leader in a large organization, one of the executives I worked for gave me some feedback about a personal growth opportunity. There was power and simplicity in a two-word phrase. It was hard to hear at the time, but I am glad I received this counsel and did not discard it.

After the performance review, the feedback I received was, "embrace chaos." The executive proceeded to unpack this statement by saying, "If you want to manage people and organizations, you cannot analyze everything. You have to be willing to live in the grey space of chaos. If you don't," he continued, "your brain will likely explode."

I got his point! I listened to that feedback and realized it was a Competency that I needed to develop. I did not know how I would do this. At that time, we had children and I realized that raising small children provided an opportunity. With my high need for order, when I looked at the house sometimes, I would gently remind myself that my need for organization was not more important than my family and that I should embrace chaos.

It took time to synthesize those two words as I continued in my career progression and raised children. I thought that if I embraced chaos, my life would get more stressful. The opposite actually happened. I became less stressed out, because I realized that there were many things I could not control, and I needed to embrace the grey space where things were not black and white. The new Competency of embracing chaos was exactly how chaos theory works. Small inputs or changes can create significant outcomes.

To this day, when I am faced with complex problems, especially relationally, embracing chaos is a pressure relief valve. I can't fix everything all at once, and sometimes incremental changes and leveraging influence go a lot further. Two words had the power to build a life-long Competency which has become a cornerstone for addressing complexities in leadership.

What phrase do you need to embrace to unlock the keys of your leadership success?

CASE STUDY: ALBERT EINSTEIN'S RAW TALENT DEVELOPED AND HE IMPACTED THE SCIENTIFIC COMMUNITY

Albert Einstein was a German-born physicist who developed the general theory of relativity. He won the Nobel Peace prize for Physics in 1921 for explaining the photo elective effect. He is most known for the equation $E = MC^2$, the precursor to the development of atomic energy. He had raw talent and it emerged at a young age. He managed to develop this Competency with the help of his parents to become a world renowned scientist.

Albert Einstein was born on March 14th, 1879 at Ulm, Wurttemberg, Germany. During his younger years he attended elementary school at Leopold Gymnasium in Munich. During those years he struggled with the rigidity and regime of that competitive school and his grandparents reported that he was a droll young child.

In 1889 their parents invited Max Talumd, a Polish medical student, to visit Albert to tutor him, and Talumb introduced him to philosophy and mathematics. At age 12 Albert was given a geometry book and mastered it. He then started teaching himself calculus at 12 years old. Two years later he said he had mastered integral and differential calculus. He also studied Kant's *Critique of Pure Reason*, synthesizing it with ease, and he became his favorite philosopher at age 13. He became convinced that nature could be understood through a "mathematical model".

Eventually Einstein entered the Swiss Federal Polytechnic School in Zurich due to his genius math and physics score. He did not do well on the first exam on the standard section. Consequently, he had to take a detour based on the recommendation of the principal to complete his secondary school in Switzerland. During his journey, he ended up renouncing his German citizenship with his father's permission to avoid the German military draft.

At age 16, Albert explored the question of what would light look like if you run alongside of it, and wrote his first scientific article about the paradox of the light wave on whether it was a light wave or particle - "The Investigation of the State of Ether in Magnetic Fields." He studied James Maxwell's nature of light and discovered that the speed of light was constant which was in opposition to Newton's Law of motion, and this became the basis for his formulation of the principle of relativity.

For his doctorate at Polytechnic Academy, he published in 1905 *The Photoelectric Effect, Brownian Motion, Special Relativity, and the Equivalence of Matter and Energy E=mc2*. He continued his research and was the director of the Kaiser Wilhelm Institute for Physics from 1913 to 1933.

In December of 1933, Albert made a decision to leave Germany because of the emerging Nazi movement. He accepted a position at the Institute for Advanced Study at Princeton, New Jersey in 1933 and taught there until his death. He became a U.S. citizen in 1940. Because he was a displaced person from Europe, he worked with organizations working with refugees arriving from Germany in the United States.

In 1939, Roosevelt invited Einstein to meet with him to discuss Germany's progress in developing fission of the Uranium atom to create a possible atomic bomb. Roosevelt invited him to be part of the Manhattan Project, and he accepted. Einstein made significant contributions to the development of the atomic bomb during WWII.

In the latter years of his career, he researched and developed various topics in physics and continued teaching. On April 17, 1955 he died of an abdominal aortic aneurysm at the age of 76.

Because of Albert's genius, he did not fit the mold or standard education system model. His parents were influential in the decisions he made and the opportunities he pursued for education. Their family worked collaboratively to develop Albert's talent. Raw talent sometimes comes with constraints and adjustments need to be made to develop those Competencies. The world would have looked like a very different place if Albert had not developed that raw talent and made the choices that he did. *[Source: Wikipedia]*

CASE STUDY: MARIE CURIE OVERCAME POVERTY AND PREJUDICE AGAINST WOMEN BY UNIVERSITIES, OBTAINED AN EDUCATION, DISCOVERED RADIOACTIVITY AND MORE

Marie Skłodowska Curie was born Maria Salomea Skłodowska on November 7, 1867 and died July 4, 1934. Curie was a Polish and naturalized-French physicist and chemist who conducted pioneering research on radioactivity. She was the first woman to win a Nobel Prize, the first person and only woman to win twice, and the only person to win a Nobel Prize in two different sciences. She was part of the Curie family legacy of five Nobel Prizes. She was also the first woman to become a professor at the University of Paris, and in 1995 became the first woman to be entombed on her own merits in the Panthéon in Paris.

She was born in Warsaw, in what was then the Kingdom of Poland, part of the Russian Empire. She lived there until she was 22. At the age of 10, her sister Zofia died. Her mother died two years later. Marie Curie was the fifth child in her family. Her father was a math teacher. He died when she was 11. As a young girl, she was interested in physics. She was at the top of her high school class. She graduated at 15.

Marie taught school so she could earn money to go to school in Paris, France. She also went to an unaccredited college in Poland. She studied at Warsaw's clandestine Flying University for several years and began her practical scientific training in Warsaw. In 1891, aged 24, she followed her older sister Bronisława to study in Paris, where she earned her higher degrees and conducted her subsequent scientific work.

She graduated first in her class in 1893. One year later she earned a master's degree in mathematics. Later, she met her husband, Pierre, at the Municipal School of Industrial Physics and Chemistry. They were married in July 1895. They also started to work together on scientific discoveries. She shared the 1903 Nobel Prize in Physics with her husband Pierre Curie and physicist Henri Becquerel.

Marie and Pierre had their first daughter, Irene, in 1897. Their second daughter, Eve, was born in 1904. Pierre died on April 19, 1906, after he was hit by a horse-drawn wagon. Marie also won the 1911 Nobel Prize in Chemistry.

Her achievements included the development of the theory of radioactivity (a term that she coined), techniques for isolating radioactive isotopes, and the discovery of two elements, polonium and radium. Under her direction, the world's first studies into the treatment of neoplasms were conducted using radioactive isotopes. She founded the Curie Institutes in Paris and in Warsaw, which remain major centers of medical research today. During World War I she developed mobile radiography units to provide X-ray services to field hospitals.

While a French citizen, Marie Skłodowska Curie, who used both surnames, never lost her sense of Polish identity. She taught her daughters the Polish language and took them on visits to Poland.

She named the first chemical element she discovered polonium, after her native country.

During the 1920s, Curie and many of her colleagues began to suffer from symptoms of cancer. Curie began to lose her sight. Cataract surgeries to try to bring back her sight did not help. In the early 1930s, Curie's health started to quickly get worse. Doctors diagnosed her with pernicious anemia. It is a condition that occurs when the body cannot make enough red blood cells due to the lack of vitamin B12 in the system.

Marie Curie died in 1934, aged 66, at a sanatorium in Sancellemoz (Haute-Savoie), France, of aplastic anemia from exposure to radiation in the course of her scientific research and in the course of her radiological work at field hospitals during World War I.

She was a pioneer in women's education and science, developed her Capacity and Competencies, and became a Champion for medicine and healthcare, science, research, technology and chemistry. *[Source: Wikipedia]*

TAKEAWAYS

- Competency is about developing your talents (raw natural ability) and skills needed for you to fulfill your destiny or assignment.

- Leverage personality profiles to understand your strength orientation.

- Develop excellence in your work; it will bring you before great people.

- Understand the skills and abilities you currently have, and their limitations.

- Identify the skills and abilities you need for your next assignment.

- Invest in yourself and your future and develop new skills and abilities for your next assignment.

- On a deeper spiritual level, there are spiritual resources of the spirit of wisdom, understanding and knowledge that enhance your natural abilities.

- Get prepared: The marketplace will be one of the greatest harvest fields ever.

COMPETENCY – SELF-ASSESSMENT

- I can clearly identify my talents, skills, and natural abilities.

- I can clearly identify the supernatural gifts I walk in and steward.

- I know what skills and knowledge I need for my next assignment.

- I know how to engage heaven in my work.

- God gives me creative ideas and solutions.

Rate the above on a scale from 1 to 5:

1 - strongly disagree

2 - disagree

3 - neither agree nor disagree

4 - agree

5 - strongly agree

If your score is 1-8, you have opportunity to grow in Competency.

If your score is 9-17, you are making progress and should continue in your forward momentum.

If your score is 18+, you have a good handle and grasp on Competency.

NOW ACTION

1. Pray through the following Scriptures for a month, asking the Lord to grow in the creative force of the spirit of wisdom, understanding and knowledge.

   As for every matter of wisdom and understanding about which the king consulted them, he found them ten times better than all the magicians and conjurers who were in all his realm. (Dan. 1:10)

   See, I have called by name Bezalel, the son of Uri, the son of Hur, of the tribe of Judah. I have filled him with the Spirit of God in wisdom, in understanding, in knowledge, and in all kinds of craftsmanship, to make artistic designs for work in gold, in silver, and in bronze, and in the cutting of stones for settings, and in the carving of wood, that he may work in all kinds of craftsmanship. (Exo. 31:2-5)

   ... that their hearts may be encouraged, having been knit together in love, and attaining to all the wealth that comes from the full assurance of understanding, resulting in a true knowledge of God's mystery, that is, Christ Himself, in whom are hidden all the treasures of wisdom and knowledge. (Col. 2:2-3)

2. Take a personality inventory and review it with people you live or work with. Get their feedback.

PRAYER

Lord, please fill us with a spirit of wisdom, understanding and knowledge. Reveal to us all the hidden treasures and wisdom that are in Christ. Fill us with your insights and perspective so that we are 10x better than our peers in all that we do. Give us grace and ability to develop our skills, talents, and abilities so we can stand before great men and women. Let your Name be glorified in all that we do. Amen.

NOW COACHING QUESTIONS

1. What do people say you are good at?

2. What do people come to you to get help with?

3. How do you see the spirit of excellence working in your life?

4. How could you grow in excellence?

5. Identify the skills you use in your current vocation.

6. What sphere of influence have you been called to?

    a. religion, education, business, family, media, government, arts and entertainment

7. What skills and abilities do you need for your next assignment?

8. In what ways are you investing in developing or improving your Competencies?

9. In what ways do you think a lack of Competency would impact your career or destiny growth?

10. In what ways would you invest differently in your Competencies in light of what you could lose if you do not invest?

11. What are your next steps?

CHAPTER EIGHT

CAPACITY
Character
Development

"Lead us not into temptation but deliver us from evil." (Matt. 6:13)

We define the Capacity part of our leadership journey as the time when God refines our character through adversity, trials, difficulties, betrayals, misunderstanding, lack, abundance, and more. We need to be delivered from temptation and evil, but there are some things we need to walk through. It is a season in our lives where God tests us to reveal to us what is in our hearts and mind so that we can connect with him more deeply to experience transformation. As we are refined in the fire, we become conduits of fire to ignite and transform our landscapes.

Peter seemed impetuous, and often spoke before he thought it through. I believe Jesus loved his audacity, boldness, faith and willingness to obey and step out. Peter wanted to emulate His master and be pleasing to Him in every way. He had passion. There is nothing harder than working with someone who has not engaged their passion because they are not internally motivated.

I would love to have had Peter on my team. It would be satisfying to see him develop, but it would also challenge everything in me as a father and leader to learn how to coach, mentor, and develop him. As leaders, we cannot be afraid of the diamonds in the rough that need to go through the refiner's fire as well as be put on the diamond cutter's wheel to get cut and polished. Capacity is the place where carbon – the natural things we have – are pressured and sanctified to be turned into diamonds. Those diamonds become conduits to reflect the Son's light in us in its multifaceted colors and beauty.

I believe Peter had insight into the process when he penned the following verses. Through the trials Peter experienced, he realized that he was being refined and that the evidence of success came through his precious faith worth more than gold.

> *In this you greatly rejoice, even though now for a little while, if necessary, you have been distressed by various trials, so that the proof of your faith, being more precious than gold which is perishable, even though tested by fire, may be found to result in praise and glory and honor at the revelation of Jesus Christ.* (1 Pet. 1:6-7)

Malachi spoke of the refiner's fire. Daniel's friends Shadrach, Meshach and Abednego literally stepped into the fire and survived. And, John the Baptist spoke of the promise of the Holy Spirit and fire. You don't get one without the other. As we are moving into the kingdom age, experiencing God's fire is a part of the package in God's timing and sequencing of events.

In one of my God encounters where the Lord called me to the apostolic, Jesus revealed himself as the refiner's fire. In the revealing of the fire, I literally curled up into ball and fought to escape its intensity. He and an apostle were standing on the other side of a line that I needed to cross. It was a decade and half later that I crossed that line. Events eventually lined up to confirm that I had crossed that line into the calling and purposes God had predestined. There are many testings and trials we may need to go through to create the needed formation of Christ's character in our lives.

There are three critical events in Peter's relationship with Jesus that we want to explore. He denied knowing Jesus, fell into the water when stepping out in faith, and was sternly rebuked by Jesus. I believe Peter loved Jesus deeply and that he had succumbed to fear and perhaps loved his life and reputation more than Jesus. Perhaps he was overconfident about his loyalty and pride and perhaps inadvertently or unknowingly opened the door to these events.

WHEN THINGS GO BAD: PETER'S DENIAL

But he said to Him, "Lord, with You I am ready to go both to prison and to death!" And He said, "I say to you, Peter, the rooster will not crow today until you have denied three times that you know Me." (Luke 22:33-34)

If any of us think we stand, we need to pay attention because we may be about to fall. Many of the trials and adversities that come our way are linked to things that need to change in us. They are the things we don't know about ourselves. In the Johari Window it is what we don't know that gets us into trouble – the unknown area.

There are areas of our lives that only the fiery heat will expose. We are often the root cause of or a contributor to them. Our strengths often need tempering. For a person who has a strong value for loyalty and honor, experiencing betrayal and denial are perhaps the most difficult to endure. One thing is clear: If you are working with men and women in a fallen world, difficulties will come.

You may be in circles of people and teams where people deny they know you or even worse, they may betray you. Betrayal can be a deeper preparation for acceleration and promotion. The way up is sometimes down. Overconfidence, pride, and impetuousness may blind us to weaknesses and faults in the foundations of our character.

How we respond to the unknown areas is critical to outcomes. When we are the victim, it takes a different resource to forgive, release and walk free and clean without accusation and vengeance. But, when we are the ones doing the betraying of those we love, the guilt, shame and self-hatred or self-condemnation could overwhelm us. The good news is that Jesus is greater than that shame and embarrassment. He brought transformation to Peter's heart and restored him, just as He did with Doubting Thomas. He can do the same for you.

Jesus allows us to walk through these fires to overcome rejection, self-pity, hatred, revenge, the party spirit, dissensions, bitterness, resentment and strife. These are all ugly expressions of the less desirable nature. We can go to Jesus and make an exchange at the cross and receive love, acceptance, affirmation, self-control, longsuffering, unity, and tolerating one another in love. They are the best trades you will ever make as a leader.

However, they come with a cost of dying to yourself at the cross. It is the only place to stop the chaos and nonsense so that personal transformation is realized. All of these circumstances are designed to cause us to change from the inside out. We trade the negative at the cross to embrace life!

There is one thing for sure about walking through the Capacity phase: If we have any areas of self-sufficiency, overconfidence, pride, or wrong perceptions about who we are, the Lord will bring His instruction to bring us into alignment. It is one of the great promises of our Father, that He will not leave us as orphans - fatherless. He will work and develop us to become sons and daughters so we reflect His likeness and image. Hebrews chapter 12 has a life-long passage we must engage and invest in all of our lives.

> *It is for discipline that you endure; God deals with you as with sons; for what son is there whom his father does not discipline? But if you are without discipline, of which all have become partakers, then you are illegitimate children and not sons. Furthermore, we had earthly fathers to discipline us, and we respected them; shall we not much rather be subject to the Father of spirits, and live?*

For they disciplined us for a short time as seemed best to them, but He disciplines us for our good, so that we may share His holiness. All discipline for the moment seems not to be joyful, but sorrowful; yet to those who have been trained by it, afterwards it yields the peaceful fruit of righteousness. Therefore, strengthen the hands that are weak and the knees that are feeble, and make straight paths for your feet, so that the limb which is lame may not be put out of joint, but rather be healed. (Heb. 12:7-12)

Jesus will bring us into alignment with His purposes. Working through our character flaws and weaknesses is part of the program. It is not to punish us but to develop us as sons and daughters. I would not trade anything for it. It will forge an intimacy and bond that no person can break. It is the most priceless aspect of your relationship with the Father – that intimate Connection and deep trust.

It is unfortunate that the working of the cross must be applied to those things that are out of alignment in our lives, but that is how He heals what is lame. The joy of being the Father's delight, walking in His holiness, and being strengthened, is the end game. That makes all of the pain, suffering, tears, testing, trials, and sacrifice, worth it.

WALKING ON THE WATER BUT SINKING

When Peter was called to step out of the boat, he had the initial faith, but not the sustaining faith, to water walk. There was a faith-filled boldness to be just like His master. In my opinion, Peter was just responding in his love language to Jesus. I think he was a kinesthetic believer. He did not want to talk about stuff; he wanted to do it.

In this instance, he unfortunately took his eyes off of his assignment to "come", and succumbed to fear. As a fisherman on the stormy Sea of Galilee, he knew the risk of drowning was real. There is no walking out of faith without facing and overcoming fear. There is no prophesying without the exercising of faith. To be a creative force or agent in the earth, we need to overcome our fears.

Peter said to Him, "Lord, if it is You, command me to come to You on the water." And He said, "Come!" And Peter got out of the boat, and walked on the water and came toward Jesus. But seeing the wind, he became frightened, and beginning to sink, he cried out, "Lord, save me!" Immediately Jesus stretched out His hand and took hold of him, and said to him, "You of little faith, why did you doubt?" (Matt. 14:28-31)

I believe this experience prepared him for the day of Pentecost. Peter learned the lesson not to look at the circumstances around him. The faith in Peter to preach and decree the launch of the Church was greater than the fear of the crowds, the opposition, and persecution. Peter was trained to keep his focus. Peter passed the test! Instead of sinking, he arose to the occasion as a Champion of the Church, breaking down the barriers between Jews and Gentiles and uniting the nations.

MOVING TOWARD GREATER ALIGNMENT THROUGH REBUKE

And lastly, we will take a look at Peter's misfortune of taking Satan's bait. Right after Peter had a profound, foundational revelation about the Son of Man, he thought he had this mastered. Perhaps pride entered in immediately and Satan began to exercise his agenda. God needs to deal with our blind spots and agendas that are not consistent with God's interest.

But He turned and said to Peter, "Get behind Me, Satan! You are a stumbling block to Me; for you are not setting your mind on God's interests, but man's." (Matt. 16:23)

Jesus, remarkably in one moment, commended one of his most vocal and strongest leaders, and then an instant later, rebuked him. Ouch! Peter got humbled, from the mountain top to the valley in a blink. That is some serious acceleration in the wrong direction. I am sure he had to go back to the ancient scrolls Solomon had written to interpret and embrace the experience. Peter had to work through this harsh rebuke.

A rebuke goes deeper into one who has understanding than a hundred blows into a fool. (Prov. 17:10)

We really are not ready for the big leagues if we cannot receive a rebuke and process it. Some of the self-talk scripts I have to employ to ensure that I don't get trapped when I need alignment are: "You need to get over yourself", "Don't take yourself too seriously", "You are not perfect," and "It is okay to make mistakes, as long as we learn from them and don't repeat them".

I don't know if Peter employed those, but I guarantee you that our forefathers like Joseph, Moses, David, and Jeremiah, had to develop internal truth scripts to get them through the tough times of getting aligned, instructed, and corrected. Instruction from our Father will result in the peaceable fruits of righteousness, including humility.

THE POWER OF HUMILITY

Here is one last statement about capacity development pertaining to Peter. I believe Peter learned the power and grace released through humility and how to wait on God to exalt him. He learned how to let God exalt him, rather than trying to do it in his own strength. Most of Peter's failures came when he stepped out in his own gumption.

Therefore humble yourselves under the mighty hand of God, that He may exalt you at the proper time, casting all your anxiety on Him, because He cares for you. Be of sober spirit, be on the alert. Your adversary, the devil, prowls around like a roaring lion, seeking someone to devour. But resist him, firm in your faith, knowing that the same experiences of suffering are being accomplished by your brethren who are in the world. After you have suffered for a little while, the God of all grace, who called you to His eternal glory in Christ, will Himself perfect, confirm, strengthen and establish you. To Him be dominion forever and ever. Amen. (1 Pet. 5:6-11)

This text reveals his understanding of how pride or self sufficiency and anxiety are brother and sister. Pride and anxiety will blind us for spiritual discernment and insights that we need to overcome the enemy. Humility will cultivate spiritual awareness and sensitivity to heaven's operating of wisdom. It will keep you in the NOW. With this perspective, we can see how in suffering, or the Capacity development phase, God will perfect, confirm, strengthen and establish us. This brings a high return on your investment. What we seek most – to be established – is often found through the maze of trials and adversities we encounter.

Going through the Capacity phase in your life as a leader, may often encompass very dark and difficult seasons. Those times either make or break us. Fortunately, we get to take retests until we get it right because God is the God of second chances. If we don't despise these times of testing and embrace them the best we can, acceleration will take place. Our attitude through the process will determine the aptitude we develop. As we become more like our Father and we connect with His kingdom purposes for our lives, His favor will be poured out to accelerate our destinies.

The crucible of Capacity will give you the confidence as a leader to embrace trials and adversity to prepare you for positions of preeminence and promotion.

ARE YOU LIMITED BY YOUR CONSTRAINTS?

Have you ever hit an invisible wall that keeps you from your objective? No matter what you do, the results are the same. You may be bumping into one of your constraints. They can be internal or external. Constraints are often a means to keep us walking in humility. Perhaps you have a great strength, gift, or ability. Did you realize that on the flip side of your strength could be lurking a constraint? Visionaries often forget to celebrate the small successes.

Highly technical and detailed individuals cannot often see the forest from the trees. Your success may not be limited by your strengths but by other governing limitations whether conscious or unconscious that must be addressed. The word constraint is a state of being checked, restricted, or completed to avoid or perform a certain action. A constraining condition is an agency or force that resists you.

The Theory of Constraints was developed and prolifically communicated by manufacturing expert Eliyahu M. Goldratt in 1984 through his book, "The Goal." Goldratt defines a Constraint as anything that limits a system from achieving a higher performance versus its goal. A positive way to look at constraints could be "A thought process that empowers people to create simple solutions to seemingly complex problems."

In terms of leadership, leaders must deal not only with personal constraints, but also organizational constraints and environmental constraints. Often, our personal constraints are either unknown, unrecognized or unheeded by individuals, ala the Johari Window we discussed earlier.

Personal Constraints has to do with Capacity and character development, emotional maturity and interpersonal behavior. Often, Personal Constraints can be a limiting factor in how a leader is perceived or accepted by others. We cannot become any greater than what the most important person in our life thinks about us. We will be either empowered or disempowered.

Organizational Constraints has to do with reputation, goodwill, resources, people, history, Culture, brand awareness, systems, processes, mission, technology, morale, safety record, competitive advantage, assets, intellectual property, and other factors.

WE CANNOT BECOME GREATER THAN WHAT THE MOST IMPORTANT PERSON IN OUR LIFE THINKS ABOUT US.

Environmental Constraints has to do with political and regulatory environment, tax policy, other government or industry policies or regulations that affect organizational mission and ability to operate, suppliers, distributors, manufacturers, and the ecosystem in which organizations must function and operate.

Identifying your Constraints – whether personal, organizational, or environmental – is the first step. That positions you to begin exploiting the Constraints and non-constraining elements begin to serve the Constraints. Then, you need to determine if the output will meet your market demand or need. We need to focus, follow through and be productive.

If we are able to address our Constraints as leaders, it will lead to breakthroughs and improved productivity, both relationally and in every arena of life and business. Don't let your Constraints limit or restrain you, but leverage them to personal and professional growth.

A PRICE TO PAY IF YOU SEEK GREATNESS

And there arose also a dispute among them as to which one of them was regarded to be greatest. And He said to them, "The kings of the Gentiles lord it over them; and those who have authority over them are called 'Benefactors.' But it is not this way with you, but the one who is the greatest among you must become like the youngest, and the leader like the servant. For who is greater, the one who reclines at the table or the one who serves? Is it not the one who reclines at the table? But I am among you as the one who serves.

"You are those who have stood by Me in My trials; and just as My Father has granted Me a kingdom, I grant you that you may eat and drink at My table in My kingdom, and you will sit on thrones judging the twelve tribes of Israel. Simon, Simon, behold, Satan has demanded permission to sift you like wheat; but I have prayed

for you, that your faith may not fail; and you, when once you have turned again, strengthen your brothers."

But he said to Him, "Lord, with You I am ready to go both to prison and to death!"

And He said, "I say to you, Peter, the rooster will not crow today until you have denied three times that you know Me." (Luke 22:25-34)

Whenever there is a conflict about greatness, position or control, you can guarantee there will be a price to pay in one way or another. Alignment will come through fire, testing, purifying, and realignment because pride, ego, insubordination, rebellion, and mutiny open the door to give Satan permission to ask to sift us in the circumstances.

Jesus' senior leadership team had a heated argument about who would be greatest among them during the Last Supper (Luke 22:24-38). His team was jockeying for position and security in the future. Their hearts were in the wrong place. He set things in order by setting the precedent that greatness is achieved through servant leadership. Phil. 2:1-11 states this powerfully and eloquently. He demonstrated that for them by taking a towel and a basin of water and washing their feet. These words and actions were designed to shift their self-centered thinking.

I am not sure what all transpired in that heated discussion between the apostles, but Jesus did have some poignant words to share with Peter during the debrief. Jesus shared that all the apostles would forsake Him, then told Peter he was going to be sifted by Satan, and would disown Him three times that very night, but that He already had prayed for him that he would return and strengthen his brothers.

The crucible of Capacity may include seasons of sifting. When wheat is sifted the purpose is to loosen the shaft from the wheat. Then the wheat is threshed to remove the chaff from the edible part. So, when Satan received permission to sift Peter like wheat, he wanted to loosen him up with the intention to destroy him or the fruit. Jesus prayed and was able to prophesy Peter's success. Peter became our main character to learn from through the Capacity phase because of the sifting process.

ARE YOU A CHARACTER OR WALKING IN CHARACTER – INTEGRITY?

The crucible in the end is intended to develop your character. Gifting and talent may bring you success, but character is what will enable you to sustain your success over the long term. The word integrity means to have the quality of being honest with strong moral principles and grounding. It is the state of being whole, undivided, cohesive, together and congruent. It is an homogeneous state of virtue.

Synonyms for this powerful word include: honesty, rectitude, honorableness, upstandingness, ethics, righteousness, nobility, right mindedness, noble mindedness, decency, fairness, scrupulousness, sincerity, truthfulness, trustworthiness. There is a baseline of truth imbedded in this attribute. It is not relativistic where you choose what the moral code is for each situation, but it is immersed with Truth. This is a tall order for any person to attain. King David understood something about the process.

> God arms me with strength, And he makes my way perfect [blameless, complete, secure or having integrity]. He makes me as surefooted as a deer, enabling me to stand on mountain heights. He trains my hands for battle; he strengthens my arm to draw a bronze bow. (Psa. 18:32-34, NLT, author's emphasis)

The crucibles of Capacity must deepen our Connection and are necessary to yield desirable outcomes. When we invite God into the process, He strengthens and transforms us. Character development comes through the transformation of our mind and beholding His glory (Rom. 5:1-5, 12:1-2; 2 Cor. 3:18). In addition, through the transformation process, we become more agile and flexible.

David said that God made his feet like hinds feet. Hinds' feet can traverse the high mountain places – kingdom heights and dimensions. The maneuverability attained by walking in integrity paves the way for training that will give us strategic advantages in the battles we face in taking the Seven Mountains of Culture. Strengthening, integrity, agility and being teachable will make a way for us to win these battles and wars.

There are very direct benefits in processing integrity. It provides inherent advantages of security, protection, guidance, access, peace, and posterity.

- He is a shield to those who walk in integrity (Prov. 10:9).

- He who walks in integrity walks securely (Prov. 11:3).

- Integrity provides an internal guidance system, it will guide you (Prov. 19:1).

- Those who walk in integrity will minister to God and keep his position (Psa. 101:5-7).

- A blameless or integrous person will have peace and posterity (Psa. 37:37).

- And lastly, although not a benefit initially, you may become a target of testing (Job 1:8, 2:3).

The antithesis of integrity is disrespect, dishonesty, deception, unreliability, manipulation, lying, deceit, fraud, theft, breaking or violating a covenant or agreement, and obstructing or perverting justice; these things can cost people their life savings, fortunes, careers, and reputation. Both individuals and companies have acted in non-integrous ways, and some are infamous. We will not take up space here to list the numerous corporate failures of not doing business ethically. Just Google "ethical failures." At the time of the writing of this book, there were 31.8 million results.

In the United States, The Standards of Conduct Office of the Department of Defense General Counsel's Office has compiled an *Encyclopedia of Ethical Failure* of real examples, which is used as a training tool. The Bible does not mask us from the same, but provides transparency into those that have gone before us. The Scripture exhorts us in 1 Cor 10:1-13 to learn from their example and to let their stories instruct us.

When we try to become successful by leveraging illegitimate means, it leads to failure. The essence of that failure can be distilled to having the wrong focus. It is called idolatry. When we focus on the wrong things, and do not fix our eyes on Jesus, we perhaps have made one of the worst trades ever – multiplying sorrow.

> *As for the saints who are in the earth, They are the majestic ones in whom is all my delight. The sorrows of those who have bartered for another god will be multiplied;* (Psa. 16:3-4)

We need to do a rapid risk assessment when shortcuts are presented to us and evaluate the short-term benefits versus potential irreversible down stream consequences. This is when we really need to pray, "Lead us not into temptation, but deliver us from evil!" Leaders that choose God's operating system, which embraces integrity, will have a lasting legacy and avoid much heartache, disaster, and regret.

THE POWER OF FOCUS

There is something powerful about running your race unencumbered (Heb. 12:1-2). Because we have such a great cloud of witnesses – that is, there are many who are watching us and rooting us on in our journey -- we are exhorted to lay aside every weight and sin that can entangle, hinder and destroy us. Sin, which is missing your mark and potential, is a destiny destroyer and separates us from God.

We are called to run our race, fixing our eyes on the Truth who is the author and perfecter of our faith. Jesus is the best trainer and is writing a story about us becoming Champions – those who have been perfected in their beliefs and behavior. We are empowered to accomplish great things by embracing the "joy factor". Through this joy, we can endure the training to create desired outcomes leading to a life well lived.

Character development and joy are inseparable. Don't attempt taking the mountains of culture without the joy factor of heaven or it will be impossible (Jas. 1:1-3; Rom. 5:1-5). Joy is the creative force that facilitates transformation and the ability to overcome (Neh. 8:10; Col. 1:10; Psa. 20:5). The joy of the Lord is our strength.

CHARACTER DEVELOPMENT AND JOY ARE INSEPARABLE.

The next phases we will discuss are Convergence and Catalyst, which are part of the preparation process to becoming Champions. I believe for leaders to become Champions, we need to embrace the Capacity phase with great passion, energy and focus. It will accelerate your advancement and bring you into the place of Convergence – your sweet spot. Capacity will prepare you so you can sustain the seasons of great success and promotion. It will also strengthen you so you can walk through your darkest hours. The joy in the end will catapult you into your Convergence. Enjoy the ride!

A STORY ABOUT ALLOWING GOD TO REFINE, REMODEL AND REINVENT YOU

It was early in 2008, and I was crying out to the Lord in prayer and feeling a bit frustrated. I had been attending Christian marketplace conferences and apostolic conferences since 2005 and was telling the Lord that business people need to hear more than concepts, theories, principles and rhetoric at these conferences. They need working models, strategies, actual case studies, practical demonstrations of the Spirit and personal testimonies of God at work in scenarios beyond the confines of a church setting. They also need genuine heart transformation if they are to be able to align with the kingdom in practical rather than theoretical terms.

One day, perhaps a month or so later, as I was praying, the Lord spoke to me and said, "Bruce, I want you to convene a World Economic Forum type of gathering for the body of Christ. Most of my marketplace leaders don't know each other, and the ones who do are not cooperating or collaborating with each other. I need for this to change. I also want you to help expose and eliminate the poverty mindset and spirit in the Church, and replace them with biblical prosperity and stewardship. The Scripture I am giving you as a commission is Ezekiel 37:1-14" (The Valley of the Dry Bones).

I was shocked that the Lord would speak to me this way and I needed to try and grasp what He was saying before I could even wrap my imagination around it. The Lord had called me once before into the financial arena in early 1995, and I knew what that meant. More death. So, I had at least learned to count the cost when God speaks to me.

As I reflected on what God had said to me, I realized it contained something more than a prophecy to ancient Israel. God gave this Scripture to me as a commission for my assignment in the marketplace and Seven Mountains of Culture. I knew it carried great significance for the mission He was now directing me to accomplish.

In addition, He said, "I also want you to create an immersion environment." I understood this to mean such a forum was not a typical conference, where people come to be taught a few new ideas and spend time visiting with old friends. This was to be a setting which plunged leaders into a truly spiritual environment, filled with worship and intercession and angels and God's presence, as well as practical, functional, effectual, applicable strategies and methods which could be put into practice in every circumstance of life.

This forum would provide marketplace leaders who are also committed Christians with genuine opportunities to connect—bone to bone—and establish effective, meaningful, useful collaborations, business associations, and alliances to strengthen, encourage, and empower the body of Christ in the marketplace.

To be honest, I was not all that enthusiastic about doing something like this. This was way out of my league, or so I thought, and I protested to the Lord in no uncertain terms: "Lord, you have asked the wrong person. No one knows me and I have never hosted a conference before. I'm not a public speaker, I'm not rich, and I attend a small church."

My excuses were as numerous as you can imagine, but the Lord was not impressed with my reluctance. His response to my resistance was simply, "No, I don't have the wrong person, but you have the wrong God." More precisely, you have God wrong. God is not in the habit of choosing the wrong people to accomplish His purposes.

Once I got past my initial shock at what God was requesting, and that He actually wanted me to convene and host this event, I decided I was willing to be ready to move forward. Still, I was shaken to the core of my being and I spent the next several days in prayer and fasting, trying to wrap my head and heart around the magnitude of the assignment. After three days I told God, "Yes."

At that time, I was a financial consultant and church elder, making a six-figure income, and was comfortable. Immediately, God began to strip away some of my identity and comfort, and He gave me divine favor for the assignment, and miracles began to happen. Over the next six months, as I surrendered to Him and His process and plan for my life, God reinvented me and gave me a new, vastly expanded identity that was how He saw me and who He said I was.

The first KEYS summit took place Sept. 3-6, 2008, and was an overwhelming success. All of the details came together and seven churches in my city gave me 200 volunteers to help organize and staff the event. Over a thousand people from 15 nations attended, the Spirit of God moved, and financially we finished in the black even after giving love offering honorariums to 40 speakers with a $250,000 budget and no corporate sponsors.

Since then, I have been privileged to help convene, host, and/or co-host over a dozen more summits for KEYS and KCIA, with well over 10,000 alumni in aggregate attendance. God developed and increased Capacity within me for His glory and purpose.

God showed me and proved to me how big and faithful He is, and how He can use anyone to accomplish His purposes if they will say "yes." My life was radically transformed and God helped me birth an international marketplace ministry to steward. I also served as an Advisor for the inaugural European Economic Summit during 2013-14. God has given me a writing ministry and publishing company as well, and I have authored, edited and/or published many books over the last 10 years.

DR. BRUCE COOK

Chairman, VentureAdvisers, Inc. and Kingdom House Publishing;
Global Ambassador & Chairman Emeritus, KCIA;
Author, Speaker & Co-founder, 8thMountain.com

In this story, we see how Competency paved the way for success, but through a divine interruption, which tested all Bruce's comfort zones. Through Bruce's process of saying "yes," God yielded a great harvest of impact which he could not have achieved had he stayed in the momentum of that which was merely good. New doors are transitions where the crucible of Capacity is experienced so we can let go of our traditions and limited identity.

CASE STUDY: CORRIE TEN BOOM– FROM THE CRUCIBLE OF CAPACITY TO COMMUNICATOR IMPACTING CULTURE

Corrie ten Boom was born on April 15, 1892 in Amsterdam, the Netherlands. Shortly after her birth, her father, Casper ten Boom inherited the family watch shop at 19 Barteljorisstraat in the Haarlem. Her family grew up in the Christian faith and were strict Calvinists in the Dutch Reformed Church.

They carried a family value system in which they believed they should be a solution to society by offering food, shelter, and money to those less fortunate. They also had an honor for the Jewish community in Amsterdam. They considered them "God's ancient people." This, I believe, was influenced by Corrie's great grandfather who started prayer meetings for the Jewish people in 1844.

In 1922 Corrie's mother died and, after a breakup of a romance, Corrie decided to train as a watchmaker. She broke new ground and became the first woman watch maker in Holland. She worked in her father's watch shop for the next decade and also established a youth club for teenagers, equipping them with knowledge of the Bible and life skills.

In May of 1940, the Germans invaded the Netherlands, and everything changed. The ten Boom family became a safe haven for Jews, students, and intellectuals. They innovatively used their watch shop as a means to hide refugees in their home through a secret room no larger than a clothes closet. The whole family became a part of the Dutch resistance, risking their lives and using their strengths to save those who would perish. There were an estimated 800 people saved through their activities until they were imprisoned in a Nazi concentration camp in 1944.

In prison, Corrie lost first her father and then her sister Betsie. It was a grievous time of loss and abuse. After the death of Betsie ten Boom, Corrie was released from the infamous Ravensbruck camp due to a clerical error in late December 1944 and returned to Holland. What Corrie suffered in prison was an intense crucible of adversity. It is hard to say that "capacity" was developed during this season of her life since it was so gruesome.

As soon as World War II ended, she began her travels around the world. In each country she visited, she told anyone who would listen that there is no pit so deep that the love of God is not deeper still. As she left one church after speaking about forgiveness and reconciliation, a man came up to her to tell her how much her words of forgiveness meant to him. Corrie instantly recognized him as one of the soldiers from the concentration camp she had been in. He was one who had, along with the others, mocked and ridiculed the women as they were made to stand naked while waiting to be processed.

Painful memories flashed in her mind of herself, and her dear sweet Betsie being humiliated by him. He was holding out his hand to shake hers. She cried to the Lord to help her. The Lord responded, "I died for this man's sins. Do you demand more?" As she reached out and shook the man's hand, she felt electricity going through her body, and all the pain and anguish was replaced with God's peace. For 33 years she shared the message about God's redemption and forgiveness in over 64 nations.

What the enemy intended for evil, God redeemed through Corrie's life because she was determined to do things God's way and on His terms. She chose God's operating system and not hers. Corrie developed her gifts and talents, and applied them to equipping the younger generation, and eventually risked her life to save people during World War II. This crucible, as painful as it was, God used redemptively through forgiveness. Corrie went on to Communicate the powerful message of forgiveness, and impacted Culture with her story. Her powerful stories inspired and have impacted Culture for decades.

CLEANSED FROM PRIDE: A STORY ABOUT JEFF TAKING A FALL TO FIND FAVOR

This is a story about Jeff, who was well educated, very ambitious and working for a large corporation in the USA. He took every opportunity possible to advance his career. One day in his early career, the Lord spoke to Him and said that your job situation is going to change. A day later he was invited into the office of his executive. The executive asked him to be his assistant to help shape and build the new organization. In a moment, Jeff was now the 2nd most powerful person in a very large organization.

Jeff was excited about the new role and felt like this new role could lead him up the career ladder. Jeff and his boss bonded and there was great synergy, intuitive dialogues, and creative ideas and solutions flowing to bring about organizational change and improvements.

When it came to implementing some of the new initiatives, Jeff did not leverage his influencing and communications skills, and instead requested a lot of the work to be done out of his positional authority, rather than through influence and relationships. There was one instance where Jeff asked someone to do something, and the person resisted, and he said, "You need to do it because our executive said so." The person responded and said, "You are off base and you can't treat people like that."

Jeff took those words and reflected on them and realized that the osmosis of pride had settled into Jeff's purview and thinking because of his power and position. He did not like what he had become. He asked the Lord to change his heart and take away the toxicity from that power when he was not secure in his identity and own skin.

In a few months, a new executive came on board the company to join the team. Jeff was asked by this new executive to leave and find another job in the company. The new executive wanted to clean house and get people out of the way so they could have the existing executive to themselves.

Jeff took a new manager's role in a new division and for the first year or two it was a little bumpy. Jeff had to stand on his own two feet, and the organization was not used to his communication style. Then there were some shifts in leadership, and Jeff ended up in a role that he was not well fitted for, and ended up working with a team that did not really like him.

The next three years were brutal. Jeff ended up being the bad guy on the team and could not do anything right. He was doing work not well suited for his skill sets and strengths. It was humiliating and demoralizing, and it took sheer discipline to go to work everyday.

But, the Lord's mercy was toward Jeff. The Lord sent a manager to help him. That manager had compassion on Jeff and worked with him to recover his value and sense of self-worth. Jeff stood on a Scripture from Micah and took responsibility for his attitude and actions. This and other Scriptures became the lifeline for Jeff in this season that brought him hope.

Do not gloat over me, my enemy! Though I have fallen, I will rise. Though I sit in darkness, the Lord will be my light. Because I have sinned against him, I will bear the Lord's wrath, until he pleads my case and upholds my cause. He will bring me out into the light; I will see his righteousness. Then my enemy will see it and will be covered with shame, she who said to me, "Where is the Lord your God?" My eyes will see her downfall; even now she will be trampled underfoot like mire in the streets. (Mic. 7:8-10)

After this season and there was a settling, Jeff applied for some jobs back at the main division, and got two job offers. He took a new role and in the first week he felt like he was home. Over the next several years, the Lord's favor allowed him to advance his career. He received several promotions, and is now doing a job that he loves. The Lord answered Jeff's prayer to change his heart and remove the pride that had blinded him.

It took being in a job where he was not appreciated or valued and was misunderstood to get cleansed of the toxicity of pride. He had to go low to be able handle the high places. The process to bring Jeff into alignment in this area of life took five plus years. Some adjustments to our foundations and inner life take time with difficulties to bring about the desired change. In the end it is worth it, and Jeff will testify today that it was all worth it to prepare to walk in new levels of greatness free from pride and insecurity. *[SOURCE: JEFF JOHNSON]*

TAKEAWAYS

- Capacity is part of our leadership journey as the time when God refines our character through adversity, trials, difficulties, betrayals, misunderstanding, conflict, tests, lack, abundance and more.

- Capacity is the inward work of reconstruction and transformation.

- As sons and daughters, your Father is committed to your Capacity development. Capacity gives you confidence to lead in adversity as well as in promotion.

- Your failures are your greatest learning opportunity.

- Capacity will prepare you for Convergence and promotion.

- Humility and integrity are two treasured Capacity outcomes.

- Constraints are an opportunity to create new solutions.

- Character is subsumed within Capacity. It is a byproduct or outcome of Capacity.

- The benefits of integrity far outweigh the short-term benefits of taking shortcuts to success.

- Seeking greatness by inappropriate means has consequences.

CAPACITY – SELF-ASSESSMENT

- I embrace the preparation for my next promotion.

- I have learned many lessons through trials and adversity.

- Failures have become stepping stones for my success.

- I am not afraid of difficulty because God is with me.

- I can make sense of my difficult experiences in light of my future.

Rate the above on a scale from 1 to 5:

> 1 - strongly disagree
>
> 2 - disagree
>
> 3 - neither agree nor disagree
>
> 4 - agree
>
> 5 - strongly agree

If your score is 1-8, you have opportunity to grow in Capacity.

If your score is 9-17, you are making progress and should continue in your forward momentum.

If your score is 18+, you have a good handle and grasp on Capacity.

NOW ACTION

1. Pray through the following Scriptures (Heb. 12:7-12; Jas. 1:2-8; Rom. 5:1-5; I Pet. 5:6-11) for a month, while asking the Lord to show you about how He is developing your Capacity.

2. Write about three difficult things you have been through in your life. What did you learn from these experiences? Were they repeat experiences? Comment if there were any themes or patterns.

NOW COACHING QUESTIONS

1. In what ways have you experienced Capacity development?

2. What did you learn from these experiences?

3. What were some of your greatest failures?

4. What did you learn about yourself from your failures?

5. How did they prepare you for your future?

6. In what ways to do you feel like you are taking the test over and over again?

7. In what ways do you share authentically about your difficulties?

8. If you are repeating the same difficulties, what do you need to change?

9. In what ways has this discussion helped you to connect the dots to make sense of your experiences?

10. What are your next steps?

CHAPTER NINE

CONVERGENCE
Your Sweet Spot

"Your kingdom come. Your will be done, On earth as it is in heaven." (Matt. 6:10)

Convergence, from the Latin, comes from two key words, "together" and "to incline." Based on this definition, it is the inclination for things to come together, and the state of being or conditions or timing when things come together. Some of the synonyms include to meet, intersect, cross, connect, link up, coincide, join, unite, and merge. So, what does this have to do with our leadership and spiritual journey?

Convergence is about heaven coming to earth through you.

Convergence is about you engaging your sweet spot where you enter into your flow. It is a space in time when everything seems to come together with purpose. It is where all of your understanding of your purpose and destiny, assignments, preparation, skill development, growing in your identity and relationships, influence, and resources come together in God's perfect timing. Convergence can happen over the short term or can build through a lifetime. It can occur in the natural as well as in the supernatural realm or dimension.

Convergence can take on many expressions. For the leader, it is when your Calling, Connection, Competencies, and Capacity development come together. What makes it your sweet spot is that God's favor is in your Convergence because it is related to your assignment. This is a place where time does not seem to exist and you are in your created element and purpose.

It is characterized as the place of "flow". It carries the elements of the Creator's Creativity. Whether it is releasing healing, deliverance, transformation, freedom, building, restoring, reviving, awakening, impacting children, adults, churches, communities, or nations – it is a place, a state and/or a time where and when heaven shows up in you and through you.

Peter hit his sweet spot when the new wine was poured out upon the Church on the day of Pentecost.

But Peter, taking his stand with the apostolic team, raised his voice and declared to them: "Men of Judea and all you who live in Jerusalem, let this be known to you and give heed to my words. For these men are not drunk, as you suppose, for it is only the third hour of the day; but this is what was spoken of through the prophet Joel." (Acts 2:14-16)

Convergence will engage your personal history, the gifts, talents, passion, and skills you have developed. All of Peter's life paid off for this moment in history. Peter was able to speak into the vacuum and articulate what God was releasing in the earth. He turned the volatility, the perceived uncertainty, the tension of awkward complexity, and ambiguity into a moment of great vision, understanding, clarity, and authenticity!

Convergence also includes moving in the supernatural. Peter had numerous experiences where he flowed with heaven's rhythm. Here are just a couple.

But Peter said, "I do not possess silver and gold, but what I do have I give to you: In the name of Jesus Christ the Nazarene—walk!" (Acts 3:7)

And behold, an angel of the Lord suddenly appeared and a light shone in the cell; and he struck Peter's side and woke him up, saying, "Get up quickly." And his chains fell off his hands. (Acts 12:7)

Peter brought heaven to earth through his faith and the intercession of the saints!

FAVOR

God's favor is in your Convergence because of the process you have been through in Connection, Competency, and Capacity. Noah found favor because he walked with God, was righteous and blameless – this is referring to how he walked in integrity.

But Noah found favor in the eyes of the Lord. These are the records of the generations of Noah. Noah was a righteous man, blameless in his time; Noah walked with God. (Gen. 6:8-9)

Noah found his voice by building the ark and made a profound statement that solved a predicament that God had with mankind. What is interesting is that Noah's solution involved a product – an ark. The product had a voice that spoke to the multitudes of the day! He stood his ground as a Champion obeying the Lord's voice. That word and the force of favor had to have been a fire in his belly to persist over the years and not lose heart to build the ark.

The favor of heaven came upon Peter in powerful ways in the book of Acts. When the favor of God hit his life in Convergence, he was able to begin to fulfill his assignment in the earth. I believe fire and favor are spiritual accelerators of our purpose. The shaping and chiseling, molding and modeling that took place during Capacity was worth it. The cleansing and purifying positioned him, and will position us, for godly and good success. Favor without the refining fire of heaven may produce self-centered outcomes. We need the purifying fire for the force of favor to create the combustion in the Connection.

PERPETUAL ENERGY

There is something very attractive about Convergence. In this sweet spot all of your personal history — the good, bad, ugly, training, preparation, and challenges — all seem to make sense. The scripts often get rewritten in this place. There is a grand alignment that takes place in God's perfect timing. This can happen on many different levels, whether in moments, days, weeks, or longer periods of time. It can feel like all the dots are connecting.

In that sweet spot, leaders will talk about having a lot of energy they feel which is connected to your creative flow. In this space, people often report that there is "a sense of timelessness". I believe this happens because God put eternity in our hearts. When you are doing what God created you for, there is a divine connection that is realized. Everything within you resonates at the frequency aligned with heaven.

Proverbs 13:12b states that, *"A desire fulfilled is as a tree of life."* Perhaps Convergence has the flow of divine energy because it is also linked to the deepest desires in our lives. The Connection, the timing and alignment tap into the deepest rivers in our being. This is where the strength of Champions finds its source to run the race with all their heart, mind, will and strength.

Those rivers make a sound and have a frequency associated with them. It is like a combustion process. There is a combustion of heaven that resounds in the hearts of Champions. The energy impacts spheres and mountains, and manifests in the glory of God being released through them.

FINDING YOUR VOICE

It is often in the place of Convergence where our voice emerges, as with Peter. During an encounter I had with the Lord, Jesus expressed the importance of connecting our voice with His voice. When that Connection is made through the process steps of understanding your Calling, developing your Competencies, and then allowing God's fire (Capacity) and favor in Convergence, your story and voice will emerge. It is a natural byproduct of the process.

In a dream that I had, I was speaking to a group of 30+ clients. At the end of the day, I asked if there were any questions. One person asked the following question: "If you had one thing to tell someone for their lifetime, what would you tell them?" To my surprise, the answer hit me: *"The most important thing anyone will ever do in their life is to find their voice".*

When you find your voice, everything that you are aligns and works together to be vocalized and to impact your world. What you value – your strengths, passion, abilities and relationships – all positively converge. It is a sweet spot where the truth of who you are resonates.

I like the way best-selling, award-winning author John Grisham explains it: *"In life, finding a voice is speaking and living the truth. Each of you is an original. Each of you has a distinctive voice. When you find it, your story will be told. You will be heard."*

There were numerous companies launched during the Great Depression when many were experiencing financial failure and loss. During that time men and women found their voice to provide goods and services in a difficult economy. The hardship is the hammer, fire and anvil to forge the trumpet of inspiration and solutions to make the sound.

Convergence is a NOW word creating shifts in the kingdom age. There is a worldwide acceleration taking place around the globe. God has been preparing His servants for such a time as this. The momentum on Convergence will increase and many will be in the flow of heaven. All the preparation and training is worth it. Lord, let your kingdom come, on earth as it is in heaven.

CAREER CONVERGENCE

The end game of Convergence is value contribution and can come in many different forms. We are designed to be creators like our Father who is a Creator. Understanding our identity and value through Connection, and developing our Competencies contributes to our value proposition individually and collectively. The creative process works itself out through how we live, learn, and love.

A primary expression of the value comes through our work which is also an act of worship. Your work is spiritual (Rom. 12:1; Eph. 6:5-7). Work and worship are not disconnected. Convergence is not disconnected from value contribution either. Ideally, we want to be in our sweet spot which may practically express itself through your career which is an occupation for a significant period of time in one's life with opportunities for progress.

If it just pays the bills, then perhaps there needs to be a shift in perspective to a kingdom mindset. Our career, which really is a destiny, is the place for creativity to express itself through Competency development and Convergence. It is a place for continuous learning, growth, expansion, development, teamwork, Collaboration, Communication and contribution. Your gifts will cause you to stand before great people, as Jesus' greatness is actualized in you.

Here are some practical steps to turn your day job into a God job. God wants to redeem your work.

- Give the work of your hands and mind to the Lord.

- Invite God into your work.

- Thank God every day for the work you have and your ability to contribute.

- Ask the Lord to continue to reveal the value you carry within.

- Ask the Lord to bless your work and that you would be a blessing to others.

- Seek opportunities be the solution to problems.

- Take every opportunity for personal and professional development where possible.

- Ask the Lord to show you and give you opportunities to walk in Convergence.

- Ask God to direct your steps and to shine His light on your path.

One question that often arises is, "How do I get into the place of Convergence or sweet spot?" There is no simple answer to this question because God works uniquely in every person. The NOW Leadership process points to nuances for each individual and community. Joseph did not choose to be thrown into a pit to be positioned for the palace. The apostle Paul didn't book a meeting with Jesus to have a transformational calling and encounter with Jesus.

However, there are road signs that God gives us along the way allowing us to understand who we are, so through preparation and wise counsel, you can make decisions to move toward Convergence. The desires God puts in your heart are big indicators. There is a combination of providence and thoughtful planning needed in a Collaborative mindset. We are called to co-labor with Christ. You will need to trust in the Lord, listen, obey, yield, and work together.

If it was as simple as using a formula, then we just traded our intimate relationship for the spirit of religion – rules, performance, and tyranny. If you need help or feel stuck, I suggest you find a mentor or a coach to work with. We provide coaching services for C-level executives and other leaders through Leaders for Life Global (www.leadersforlife.global).

God is for your Convergence and is developing you in relationship so you will become a reflection of His glory!

A STORY FROM DONNA ABOUT HOW SPIRITUAL MOTHERS ARE NEEDED

When I was growing up, I loved school. I loved learning, being with my friends, and all the related activities. I was particularly good at math and science, and was encouraged to study engineering after high school. I didn't really know exactly what an engineer was, but I liked math and science. I was good at it, and I was told it was a very marketable career. So, I studied chemical engineering.

The major I was in was considered the hardest at my university. It was hard, but there was no way I would quit, lest someone think I couldn't handle it. I went through college saying to myself, "I don't know if this is what I want to do with my life. But I don't know what I do want to do with my life, so it makes sense to continue with something that will allow me to earn a good income."

The summer before my senior year, I worked at a Christian camp. This was a completely new world to me. The landscape was stunning, the activities were really fun, and the kids were great! Besides the regular activities, the counselors would lead their cabins in devotions every morning. It was a chance to share with them on a meaningful level, and to learn of their hopes, dreams, fears and disappointments. I had the amazing privilege of touching these children's lives! I was hooked and there was no turning back! I went into my senior year of engineering with a longing to be in full time ministry!

I did graduate as an engineer and worked for a short time in engineering while I started seminary on a part time basis. I eventually went to seminary full time while I began to work with a local high school ministry. I learned to mentor the young students in my small group, even as I was mentored by the youth pastor. This was a dream come true for me! From high school ministry, I moved to college ministry. I was doing what I was made for—loving, mentoring, encouraging, supporting and strengthening young people!

As I got a little older, I began to long for my own family. I was approaching 30 and I was still single. A traumatic experience brought my longing for a family into sharp focus. I went to the emergency room with severe abdominal pain. The medical diagnosis indicated I might never be able to have children.

At that moment, I came face to face with how very desperately I wanted to have children. I cried out to the Lord in my distress. With my inner hearing, I heard as clearly as can be, "At about this time next year ..." I knew the reference was to Abraham's encounter with God in Genesis 17:21 where God revealed that the promised heir would be born at about that time the following year. I talked back to God: What? Am I going to have a baby next year?

Exactly a year later, I went on my first date with my future husband, Will. It was some time before God gave us children, but I can truly say that raising and home-schooling my kids has been by far the most meaningful thing I have done in life. That desire I felt at camp to love on those kids was just a nascent longing to mother young people.

I have come to understand that, even now that my kids are launching out on their own, being a Mom is not just something I did. It is the core of who I am. It is what I bring to all of my relationships. Now that my kids are on their own, it is for me to discern where and with whom God wants to use this powerful gift, which is just a reflection of the Holy Spirit, the paraclete, who comes alongside to help. I am a spiritual mom!

DONNA MEIER
Wife of the Author

CASE STUDY: WILLIAM WILBERFORCE – HE FOUND CONVERGENCE AND FACILITATED THE ABOLITION OF SLAVERY

William Wilberforce, a son of a wealthy merchant, was born in 1759 in Hull, Britain. When Wilberforce was a teenager, English traders raided the African Continent and captured 35,000 to 50,000 Africans and transported them across the Atlantic, selling them into slavery. He was well educated, studying at Cambridge University. At the University, he developed a lasting friendship with the future prime minister, William Pitt the Younger. Wilberforce became a member of Parliament in 1780.

For several years he experienced gloom and sorrow, and in 1786 during a church service, he had a spiritual conversion. Through his deep relationship with God, he began to see his assignment in the earth. He stated, "My walk is a public one. My business is in the world, and I must mix in the assemblies of men or quit the post which Providence seems to have assigned me."

Later in 1790 he became a part of a leadership group known as the Clapham Sect—a group of devout Christians of influence in government and business. This is where he began his journey in social reform. He first began advocating to improve working conditions for factory workers in Britain.

Thomas Clarkson, an abolitionist, influenced Wilberforce and others campaigning for the end of the slavery trade. Over the next 18 years, Wilberforce would lobby for the abolition of the slave trade. He was supported by many members of the Clapham Sect to communicate awareness. They used several means including their relationships, books, rallies, pamphlets, and petitions.

With great perseverance and persistence, a tipping point was reached and in 1807, the slave trade was abolished in Great Britain and throughout the British Empire. He had introduced 12 resolutions against the slave trade and was outmaneuvered with the bills he introduced in 1791, 1792, 1793, 1797, 1798, 1799, 1804, and 1805.

Wilberforce took on many more social causes over his lifetime and was a successful advocate and social reformer. (*Source: Wikipedia*) His legacy to the nations was freedom. He built Connection to build coalitions and influence a government and nation over many years. Through his Competencies, Communication, Compassion and Capacity, he became a Catalyst and Champion for global transformation through Convergence and Culture.

TAKEAWAYS

- Convergence is about you engaging your sweet spot where you enter into your flow (heaven comes to earth), where everything seems to come together.

- Convergence is often connected with purpose and assignment.

- God's favor is upon your assignment in the place of Convergence.

- Convergence can express itself through the natural or the supernatural. Convergence can happen over the short term or can build throughout your lifetime. Your voice will emerge through Convergence.

- Your voice will create a sound that reverberates through creation.

- In Convergence there is often no sense of time and an intense energy flow.

CONVERGENCE – SELF-ASSESSMENT

- I am fully engaged in my passion and assignment.

- I have experienced my sweet spots and love them.

- There is no sense of time when I am in Convergence.

- God's favor rests on my Convergence experiences.

- I see God expanding His Kingdom through Convergence.

Rate the above on a scale from 1 to 5:

> 1 - strongly disagree

> 2 - disagree

> 3 - neither agree nor disagree

> 4 - agree

> 5 - strongly agree

If your score is 1-8, you have opportunity to grow in Convergence.

If your score is 9-17, you are making progress and should continue in your forward momentum.

If your score is 18+, you have a good handle and grasp on Convergence.

NOW ACTION

1. Write about three experiences you had when you were a child, in high school or college, and then later in life. Include what you were proud of accomplishing and what you did specifically. Review what you wrote with someone to find the themes where you experienced Convergence.

2. Pray through the following Scriptures for a month, asking the Lord to give you insight to spiritual Convergence.

   Your kingdom come. Your will be done, On earth as it is in heaven. (Matt. 6:10)

   For this reason I bow my knees before the Father, from whom every family in heaven and on earth derives its name, that He would grant you, according to the riches of His glory, to be strengthened with power through His Spirit in the inner man, so that Christ may dwell in your hearts through faith; and that you, being rooted and grounded in love, may be able to comprehend with all the saints what is the breadth and length and height and depth, and to know the love of Christ which surpasses knowledge, that you may be filled up to all the fullness of God. (Eph. 3:14-19)

PRAYER

Lord, we thank you for the preparation process. We align ourselves with your plans and purposes for our lives. We honor you as our Father and thank you that we have been adopted into your family. Strengthen us so we would be filled with the depths of your love so we can walk in divine Convergence with you! Bring about all the aspects our lives need so you can fulfill your good and perfect will. Let the heavens open and let time seem to stop as we enter into your divine purposes and assignments. Be glorified in all that we are and what we accomplish. Let our lives bring joy to your heart as we walk in the sweet spots you created for us. Amen.

NOW COACHING QUESTIONS

1. What did you learn from your assignment about writing about three things you were proud of doing? Did you find any common themes?

2. In what ways did you see your assignment emerging or did you identify places of Convergence?

3. Do you know what your assignment is? (That which you have been called to do that only you can do because of your uniqueness, identity, gifts, talents, passion, personal experience.)

4. In what ways have you experienced Convergence?

5. How did you feel about those experiences?

6. What unique contribution did you make?

7. What do you think needs to happen to find your sweet spots?

8. What are your next steps?

9. In what ways have you found your voice?

10. What area do you want to change by your voice?

11. What are the next steps to finding or amplifying your voice?

CHAPTER TEN

CATALYSTS
Influencing Change

Yet more and more believers were brought to the Lord—large numbers of both men and women. As a result, people brought the sick into the streets and laid them on cots and mats, so that at least Peter's shadow might fall on some of them as he passed by. Crowds also gathered from the towns around Jerusalem, bringing the sick and those tormented by unclean spirits, and all of them were healed. (Acts 5:14-16)

Catalysts identify, initiate, and deliver meaningful change, oftentimes not being seen. A catalyst in chemistry either accelerates or slows down a chemical reaction and often is not detected. It is an agent that makes something happen sooner or perhaps may have never happened without its interaction. Catalysts are change agents and activate change in others or in systems, processes and cultures to advance the kingdom of heaven. They may impact individuals, communities, and nations by activating initiatives, callings, development and destinies. In the above text, Peter's shadow released healing. That is a high-level, indirect influence where power was released to bring healing. Healing was accelerated and we would say, "This is 'crazy, catalytic activity.'"

Peter had a huge Convergence experience at Pentecost and many turned to the Lord as recorded in the book of Acts. Repeated Convergences will build your confidence and mastery as a leader. Through the process you will come to understand what you carry regarding Jesus' kingdom deposit in you. However, there comes a time and place that you will find that you will want to do more. Just as you experienced the joy of Convergence, you will begin to realize that others need to experience the same thing. The apostle John had this insight into the spiritual maturing process. We need to mature from walking as children, to becoming sons and daughters, to becoming spiritual mothers and fathers.

> *I am writing to you, little children, because your sins have been forgiven you for His name's sake. I am writing to you, fathers, because you know Him who has been from the beginning. I am writing to you, young men, because you have overcome the evil one. I have written to you, children, because you know the Father. I have written to you, fathers, because you know Him who has been from the beginning. I have written to you, young men, because you are strong, and the word of God abides in you, and you have overcome the evil one. (1 John 2:12-14)*

Sons and daughters use all of their spiritual strength and resources to be successful, whereas fathers and mothers use all of their resources and strength to make sons and daughters successful. In this instance, we move from wanting to live in convergence all the time, to enabling others to find their sweet spot. We want to awaken, activate and develop others. This is what being a Catalyst is all about.

The power of being a Catalyst lies not just in the doing but in what we become and what we possess. The growth and lessons of Connecting serve us well in this phase. There are either two modalities we are engaged in: "doing" or "being". The transactions associated with "doing" can become addictive. The tangible nature of "doing" gives us a sense of accomplishment and may anesthetize your inner voice. "Being" is more challenging because the reward and recognition system changes and is invisible. The hallmark of being a Catalyst has its foundations in "being." Influence is empowered by the atmosphere we carry as well as in the words we speak.

As mentioned, a Catalyst is a chemical that can accelerate or decelerate a chemical change without changing its substance. There is a divine energy that works in Capacity, Convergence and in the Catalyst phase which is powerfully directional, creating different outcomes. The catalytic phase will require some tempering at time and temperature, just as a fine wine is decanted and aged. The responsibility is often far greater because the focus is more outward to impact others, whether it be for an individual, organization, community, industry, sector, region or nation.

Peter became a Catalyst for advancing the gospel through a trance he had. Up until that time the Jews had lost sight of the promise in Isa. 55:5, that God would call forth nations we know not, that is, the Gentiles would come to the Lord. Through a supernatural revelation, Peter became an agent or Catalyst to bring forth God's purpose to an entire new people group. Acts 10 is an incredible story which I recommend that you take the time to read and study.

> *Opening his mouth, Peter said: "I most certainly understand now that God is not one to show partiality, but in every nation the man who fears Him and does what is right is welcome to Him"* ... *While Peter was still speaking these words, the Holy Spirit fell upon all those who were listening to the message. All the circumcised believers who came with Peter were amazed, because the gift of the Holy Spirit had been poured out on the Gentiles also. For they were hearing them speaking with tongues and exalting God. Then Peter answered, "Surely no one can refuse the water for these to be baptized who have received the Holy Spirit just as we did, can he?" And he ordered them to be baptized in the name of Jesus Christ. Then they asked him to stay on for a few days.* (Acts 10:34-35, 44-48)

With another prolific sermon, he became a Catalyst for transforming the landscape of nations and initiated the beginning of fulfilling Jesus' commission to go into all the nations. A spiritual exchange took place by Peter being a Catalyst, activating a chain of events that would change history.

As leaders learn how to be change agents, this can be very public or it may be hidden. The heart of an effective leader is to activate positive change and express it through various ways. They are flexible, adaptable, strategic and relational. You may be influencing someone's thinking, providing opportunity, or having a cup of coffee and investing some time, or launching a new global movement.

IT IS AMAZING HOW MUCH CAN HAPPEN IF YOU ARE NOT WORRIED ABOUT WHO GETS THE CREDIT.

The key is that you "do" and "be," not worrying about who gets the credit. One needs to co-labor with what God is doing in their life. It is amazing how much can happen if you are not worried about who gets the credit. Be the change agent to bring about God's purposes and Convergence in someone else's life. In doing so you will accelerate and catapult others to become history makers.

On a practical level, Catalysts influence using a variety of tools and here are a few to consider.

PROVIDE FEEDBACK

A Catalyst will provide feedback for your personal, professional, and spiritual development. Feedback is the breakfast food of Champions. It will give insight into the areas where we need to grow. On a deeper level, it will reveal our blind spots that could be sabotaging our efforts, helping us move into the unknown areas on the Johari Window. These are things we do not see that often impact our leadership. It takes courage to face these areas with humility and an open mind.

MENTOR

A mentor guides, provides insight, and assists others so they avoid pitfalls and mistakes. Mentors can accelerate your development and provide you the encouragement you need to walk through transitions, new initiatives, or perhaps help you close something down. They provide a wealth of knowledge, wisdom and experience but do not do the work for you. Mentors will partner with you through the process to help you meet your objectives and desirable outcomes. They will touch your life periodically, depending on your relationships and circumstances.

COACH

A coach asks powerful questions, engages in intuitive listening, and facilitates the creation of strategies and plans. Coaches will not necessarily give you the guidance and wisdom of a mentor, but will draw upon the resources that can assist in solving your problems. They can provide perspective, connections, support, belief in you, accountability, feedback, and nurture growth.

INSPIRE

A Catalyst can provide insights and draw out your greatness by connecting with you to motivate you to act. There is an intuitive element to being a Catalyst by encouraging, creating perspective and vision about your potential and future. It should ultimately ignite your passion.

ACTIVATE

Your dreams, desires, and calling often need an extra turbo boost to pursue your passions and strengths. Catalysts will activate you by igniting the fire within. They will pour fuel on the combustion working in your life.

Here are some further distinctions to consider between a traditional leader versus a catalytic leader.

C- Category	Traditional	Catalytic
Calling	Career	Purpose & Destiny
Competency	Skills & Abilities	Excellence & WUK Factor
Connection	Relationships	Bonding & Identity
Capacity	Get Over Hardship	Character Development
Convergence	Success & Compensation	Sweet Spot & Transformation
Champion	Winning & Achievement	Family & Leadership Legacy
Culture	No Broad Impact	Influence & Impact

TABLE 2.
Traditional Versus Catalytic Leaders.

CASE STUDY: NELSON MANDELA — HOW A MAN OF CONVICTION AND COMPASSION BECAME A CATALYST TO TRANSFORM A NATION

Nelson Rolihlahla Mandela was born in Mvezo, South Africa on December 05, 2013. Nelson was the son of Henry Mandela who was the chief of the Madiba clan of the Tembu people. When his father died he was raised by the regent of the Tembu but Nelson renounced his claim to the chiefdom to become a lawyer. In 1944, at age 31 Nelson joined the African National Congress (ANC), a black liberation group, and became a leader of its youth league. Mandela held several leadership positions in the ANC and infused and reenergized the organization in opposition to the apartheid policies of the majority National party.

In 1952, Mandela held a significant role in defiance against South Africa's pass laws which mandated that non-whites carry documents to authorize their presence in "restricted" white only areas. Mandela traveled extensively throughout South Africa attempting to build support for non-violent strategies to challenge the discriminatory policies of the government. In 1955, Mandela participated in the drafting of the "Freedom Charter" which called for non-racial social democracy in South Africa. Mandela's activism made him a frequent target of government authorities and he was officially banned periodically by the government from traveling and speaking publicly. In 1956, Mandela was arrested for treason along with 100 others. Mandela was acquitted of the alleged crime in 1961.

At Sharpeville in 1960, police forces were involved in a massacre of unarmed black South Africans who were protesting against pass laws. Sixty-nine people were killed and hundreds wounded in this affair. This action influenced Mandela to abandon his non-violent protest convictions and was a catalyst toward his promulgating acts of violence and sabotage toward the government. Mandela "went underground" and was one of the founders of the "Umkhonto we Sizwe", a military wing of the now banned ANC. In 1962 Mandela was caught at a roadblock and subsequently sentenced to five years in prison.

In 1963, police discovered weapons at the Umkhonto we Sizwe headquarters in the Rivonia suburb of Johannesburg. Mandela and others were put on trial for treason, sabotage and violent conspiracy in what came to be known as the Rivonia trial. Mandela used the opportunity to claim some of the charges against him and publicly spoke against tyranny and the defense of liberty. Mandela narrowly avoided the death penalty and was sentenced to life imprisonment.

Mandela was finally released from prison in 1990 after spending 27 years in prison. During his imprisonment, the government offered Mandela his release most notably in 1976 and 1985 by offering conditions for his release that were unacceptable to him. Mandela maintained that "only free men were able to engage in such negotiations and, as a prisoner, he was not a free man"[1].

After his release, Mandela was made the deputy president of the ANC and then became president of the party in July 1991. Mandela led the ANC in negotiations with the South African government under Jan de Klerk to end the government's policy of apartheid and to forge a non-violent and peaceful transition of the country to a nonracial democracy. Mandela and de Klerk were jointly awarded the Nobel Peace Prize 1993.

In April 1994, Mandela was elected (in free elections) to be the first president of the new multiethnic South African government. Mandela worked throughout his presidency to improve the quality of life for black South Africans by improving housing, education and economic policies. After leaving the presidency in 1999, Mandela retired from active politics but became an international catalyst for the advocacy or peace, reconciliation and social justice. He established the Nelson Mandela Foundation in 1999 to champion these ideals.

Undoubtedly, Mandela had a Compassion theme of social justice and advocacy coursing through his veins, and he was willing to endure the crucible of Capacity, enduring 27 years in prison. During that time he did not waiver in his convictions. Through continuous learning he did alter his methods to create the desired tipping point to change a nation. In this case study, we draw your attention to how he was a Catalyst to transform a nation to embrace democracy and improve the quality of life for black South Africans.

Biographical sketch provided courtesy of Tyler Beckwith.

CASE STUDY: JOSHUA CHAMBERLAIN – HE BECAME A CATALYST AND CHAMPION

Joshua Lawrence Chamberlain was an unlikely hero. Chamberlain was born September 8, 1828 in Brewer, Maine. Chamberlain's mother imbedded a religious devotion in young Joshua (he grew up in the Congregational Church with Puritan beliefs and values)[2] and his father taught him an interest in the military. His mother felt that he should go into the ministry and Joshua being a studious young man set his sights on entering Bowdoin College in Bath, Maine.

While studying at Bowdoin, one of his contemporaries was Calvin Stowe, the husband of Harriet Beecher Stowe who was writing *Uncle Tom's Cabin* at the time. Chamberlain participated in reading groups where Mrs. Stowe read some of her manuscript. Chamberlin developed "very strong feelings" in regards to the issue of slavery through this influence[3].

During the years preceding the Civil War Chamberlain was distressed about the secession of the southern states and the outbreak of the conflict in 1861. His wife was against his entering the war but despite his wife's objections, Chamberlain wrote the Governor of Maine offering his services. Chamberlain wrote at the time; "I have always been interested in military matters," he wrote "and what I do not know I am willing to learn"[4].

In August of 1862, Chamberlain found himself a Lieutenant Colonel, second in command of the 20th Maine Volunteer Infantry Regiment. The 20th Maine found itself at the battles of Antietam and Fredericksburg where it drew first blood assaulting Marye's Heights[5]. Losses at Chancellorsville elevated the position of Ames, and Chamberlain found himself in command of the regiment just before the next great battle. The battle of Gettysburg was fought on July first, second and third in 1863.

The battle of Gettysburg was the turning point of the War. Up to that time Robert E. Lee and his Army of Northern Virginia had defeated the larger Army of the Potomac in each conflict. But this time the Union Army grabbed the heights on Cemetery Ridge and forced the Confederates to fight on ground of Union choosing. Gettysburg was the first major victory for the Union and much sought after by President Abraham Lincoln[6].

By the end of the first day of battle it was one of the bloodiest days of the war but the worst was yet to come[7] On July second, the 20th Maine found itself on the extreme left of the Union line. They were told they must hold that line or the Confederates could roll up the exposed rear of the Union Line. Confederate General James Longstreet hurled wave after wave of Alabama and Texas soldiers against the union left under General John B. Hood[8] and were repulsed time and time again.

It is unclear if Chamberlain's soldiers were nearly out of ammunition or not but nonetheless, Chamberlain ordered a bayonet charge against the oncoming Confederates after continuous battle and the threat against the Union left was all but over. Thirty years later, Chamberlain was awarded the Congressional Medal of Honor for "conspicuous gallantry" at the battle of Gettysburg.

Chamberlain later became the Governor of Maine for four terms and President of Bowdoin College[9]. What caused this man to withstand such pain (he dealt with severe pain for the rest of his life) and stand in honor and respect to his enemies? What caused such valor in the face of death and continuing, single mindedness of duty to his nation and to his God?

Chamberlain said, "This is the great reward of service, to live, far out and on, in the life of others; this is the mystery of Christ. – to give life's best for such high sake that it shall be found again unto life eternal".

It could be ventured that Chamberlain's and the 20th Maine's stand on Little Round Top that day in July 1863 was the catalyst for a Union victory and the forthcoming Gettysburg address by President Lincoln in November 1863 for the dedication of the Soldiers' National Cemetery for the Union soldiers who died there. These words ring just as true today as they did then when again we are faced again with a divided nation. We can only hope that Champions of such stature will again arise and reign true.

Biographical sketch provided courtesy of Tyler Beckwith

TAKEAWAYS

- Catalysts identify, initiate, and deliver meaningful change, oftentimes not being seen.

- Learning to influence others comes from the place of being more than doing.

- Catalysts facilitate growth and activate initiatives and people's callings, development and destinies.

- Catalysts will influence others by providing feedback, mentoring, coaching, inspiring and activating.

- You will be surprised how much can get accomplished if you don't worry who gets the credit.

CATALYSTS — SELF-ASSESSMENT

- I am comfortable with not having to be known or seen.

- I am just as comfortable "being" as "doing".

- I gain great satisfaction influencing others to create new outcomes.

- I am mentoring and coaching others to create solutions.

- I am influencing culture by inspiring and activating people's greatness.

Rate the above on a scale from 1 to 5:

> 1 - strongly disagree
>
> 2 - disagree
>
> 3 - neither agree nor disagree
>
> 4 - agree
>
> 5 - strongly agree

If your score is 1-8, you have opportunity to grow as a Catalyst.

If your score is 9-17, you are making progress and should continue in your forward momentum.

If your score is 18+, you have a good handle and grasp on being a Catalyst.

NOW ACTION

1. Target a problem and develop a strategy to influence change and be a Catalyst to create a solution. Pray for insight how to influence the people or organization. Identify how you can achieve your goal and then assess if you accomplished it. Comment on how you went about doing this and how long it took to accomplish.

2. Pray through the following Scriptures for a month, asking the Lord that you would grow through "being" so that you can influence others and be a Catalyst to ignite heaven's atmosphere whereever you go.

> *... and let us consider how to stimulate one another to love and good deeds, not forsaking our own assembling together, as is the habit of some, but encouraging one another ...* (Heb. 12:24-25)

> *If you abide in Me, and My words abide in you, ask whatever you wish, and it will be done for you. My Father is glorified by this, that you bear much fruit, and so prove to be My disciples.* (John 15:7-8)

> *This is My commandment, that you love one another, just as I have loved you. Greater love has no one than this, that one lay down his life for his friends. You are My friends if you do what I command you. No longer do I call you slaves, for the slave does not know what his master is doing; but I have called you friends, for all things that I have heard from My Father I have made known to you.* (John 15:12-15)

PRAYER

Lord, fill us with your Spirit so we can be Catalysts who bring about positive change and transformation. Empower us to spur one another on to love and good works. Teach us how to abide in you and your word, so that through that inner connectedness, we can influence others to pursue their greatness. Bring us into the secret places and give us the keys to unlock people's hearts, callings, and destinies. Teach us your ways so that in all that we do, we would facilitate growth so fruit would be borne and that it would remain, impacting the generations to follow.

NOW COACHING QUESTIONS

1. How have you been influenced by a change agent?

2. In what ways was your experience positive or negative? Explain how you have learned to influence people?

3. In what ways have you been a Catalyst to advance the kingdom?

4. Where would you like to influence change as a Catalyst?

5. In what ways are you influencing Culture?

6. What are your next steps?

ENDNOTES

1. Encyclopedia Britannica; Nelson Mandela: President of South Africa, https://www.britannica.com/biography/Nelson-Mandela.

2. Civil War General: Joshua Chamberlain (Documentary), https://www.youtube.com/watch?v=LeTKMM8DD9g&t=2s.

3. Civil War General: Joshua Chamberlain (Documentary), https://www.youtube.com/watch?v=LeTKMM8DD9g&t=2s.

4. Biography, "Joshua Chamberlin, Military Leader (1828 – 1914)", https://www.biography.com/people/joshua-chamberlain-090815

5. American Battlefield Trust, "Joshua Lawrence Chamberlin", https://www.battlefields.org/learn/biographies/joshua-lawrence-chamberlain.

6. Williams, T. Harry, *Lincoln and His Generals* (New York, Alfred A. Knopf, 1952).

7. Gettysburg: Animated Battle Map, https://www.youtube.com/watch?v=vUKreep2P1M.

8. American Battlefield Trust, "Joshua Lawrence Chamberlin", https://www.battlefields.org/learn/biographies/joshua-lawrence-chamberlain.

9. Biography, "Joshua Chamberlin, Military Leader (1828 – 1914)", https://www.biography.com/people/joshua-chamberlain-090815.

CHAPTER ELEVEN

CHAMPIONS
Empowering the Next Generation

But the Lord is with me like a dread champion. (Jer. 20:11)

Champions are mature, life-tested leaders who are making an impact in our culture based on their mandates and assignments. By definition, a Champion is a person who fights or argues for a cause or for someone else, a warrior, fighter, one who battles for the rights of others with honor. They are defenders, sponsors, advocates, promoters, standard bearers, torch bearers, resolute protectors, prime movers, pioneers, and apostles. They engage emerging leadership in the development process and invest in the generations through their encouragement, coaching, mentoring, instructing, and providing resources to build. It is through the agency of these leaders, that I believe we are able to see the last part of the Lord's prayer fulfilled (Matt. 6:13).

"For Yours is the kingdom and the power and the glory forever."

There is legacy embedded in the word "forever". God requires leaders in every generation to ensure the baton is passed and that each successive generation is prepared for their assignments. There is a tremendous need for preserving our sense of identity from the past, to the present and for the future. Isaiah referred the Israelites back to Abraham from which the blessing flowed.

"Look to the rock from which you were hewn and to the quarry from which you were dug. Look to Abraham your father and to Sarah who gave birth to you in pain; when he was but one I called him, then I blessed him and multiplied him." (Isa. 51:1-3)

Champions know their beginning and reference. Israel was exhorted by Isaiah to look to their point of origin. Fathers and mothers know Him who has been from the beginning (1 John 2:13). In addition, they know the place from which they started, whether it started in the negative or positive. They understand that it has been God's enabling grace that has caused them to advance, strategize, lead, follow, change, impact, transform, help, nurture, build, restore, pioneer, tear down, pluck up, and plant.

CHAMPIONS KNOW THE PLACE FROM WHERE THEY STARTED AND APPRECIATE GOD'S GRACE.

Therefore, there is a deep sense of positive indebtedness cultivated in the heart. Honor is due to those in authority that have gone before us. This practice of honor paves way for the multi-generational blessing and the transfer of inheritance. Peter spoke about the importance of honoring authority. In the verse below, he talks about how those who have humbled themselves will be exalted.

Likewise you younger people, submit yourselves to your elders. Yes, all of you be submissive to one another, and be clothed with humility, for "God resists the proud, But gives grace to the humble." Therefore humble yourselves under the mighty hand of God, that He may exalt you in due time, casting all your cares upon Him, for He cares for you. (1 Pet. 5:5-7)

Exaltation can take many forms including promotion, preeminence, recognition, sitting in the place of honor, and remuneration. The outcomes will depend on the seeds of humility and honor that were sown. We need to sow these seeds in the generational, relational and cultural interfaces where there are complexities, challenges, volatility, tensions, chaos, ambiguity, uncertainty, polarities, juxtapositions, fears, judgments, bias, and opposition. The power of humility clothed in honor will release God's grace!

This is where the kingdom of heaven needs to take root to bring life and solutions. Champions are courageous in throwing themselves into these interfaces that are crying out for resolution. They are courageous and fearless, and are willing to serve in whatever capacity is needed. Champions have gone through the process, have paid the price, and are laying the foundations for the future generations.

CHAMPIONS:

- Invest in the Callings of others

- Identify and facilitate the development of Competencies

- Catalyst for releasing the Spirit of adoption to create Connection

- Strengthen and guide leaders through the crucible of Capacity

- Celebrate Convergence

- Use their influence to develop influencers

- Champion the NOW Leadership Process

Within this construct they carry a treasure trove of:

- Total unconditional acceptance

- Facilitating the Culture of joy and honor

- Unwavering perseverance

- Intestinal fortitude

- Fearlessness and courage

- Resilience in times of difficulty

- Integrity

- Lovingly providing instructions, guidance, counsel and correction

- Compassion

SELF-SERVING LEADERS OR SERVANT LEADERS

A key attribute of Champions is servant leadership. Servant leadership requires large doses of humility. Humility is best defined as knowing who you are, and who you are not, and who God is in relationship to yourself. In other words, it is the proper estimation of who you are in light of your relationship with God. In that place, God will enable you to see others in the correct perspective, and you will be able to lead them into their greatness.

Servant leaders are willing to lay down their greatness to develop the greatness in others. They use every strength they have to develop the strength in others. And when required, they will lay down what is necessary, adapt, flex, and improvise to help others. It is not about us but others. It will cost us our lives in one form or another. Paul so clearly articulated this attitude and approach in all that he did.

> *Do nothing from selfishness or empty conceit, but with humility of mind regard one another as more important than yourselves; do not merely look out for your own personal interests, but also for the interests of others. Have this attitude in yourselves which was also in Christ Jesus, who, although He existed in the form of God, did not regard equality with God a thing to be grasped, but emptied Himself, taking the form of a bond-servant, and being made in the likeness of men.* (Phil. 2:3-7)

This approach will create great leaders. Companies that focus on serving their customers and adding value will succeed. Businesses that lose sight of their customers and become self-centered will lose those customers. The crazy thing about pride is, it creates a powerful skewed focus that blinds its possessor from reality. It is not dynamic and locks you into the wrong thinking about who you really are by either overestimating or underestimating your value. In the kingdom, self-centeredness is a viper that will poison and stymie kingdom growth. Choose servant leadership instead of top down leadership.

CHAMPIONS ARE FORMED

"Remember these, O Jacob, And Israel, for you are My servant; I have formed you, you are My servant; O Israel, you will not be forgotten by Me!" (Isa. 44:21)

Jacob was known as the supplanter or deceiver. After the Lord dealt with him over the years, he got to the place where he wanted God more than doing it his way. He wrestled with God, and his name was changed from Jacob to Israel ("May God prevail. He struggles with God. God perseveres, contends"). In the end, God formed something new in Jacob. His new name represented the inner transformation that had taken place. God saw the potential in Jacob, the Champion inside. Do you see the potential in those emerging leaders who are still trying to make it in their own strength and conniving?

We can be saved in a moment, but to be changed into the image of Jesus takes formation over time. We often joke about how some people need more time and temperature in the oven to get tempered. Peter, our role model, had that experience. God forms Champions who are servant leaders in the crucible of life. And yes, there are many life lessons to be learned along the way. Champions are familiar with the process and can serve other leaders to navigate their process without being controlling, manipulative, or trying to create leaders in their own likeness and image.

We need eyes to see the end from the beginning. Our Father sees the diamonds in the rough and knows the intricate cuts and extensive polishing, for the gemstone to reflect the image of His Son. Champions get the download or the blueprint regarding the process and required pursuit. They are not intimidated by the formation process, but are at work with individuals to navigate the process. It requires patience, persistence, and faith! They honor the DNA and blueprint, to build using God's word and solid foundations.

FAMILY IS THE INCUBATOR FOR KINGDOM LIFE

For many of us, we did not come from healthy families where we received a rich inheritance of love, affirmation, and support. In order for this to happen, we need healthy parents. In God's house, it requires spiritual fathers and mothers to steward and facilitate growth. Perhaps it was quite the opposite or somewhere in between for you. The family unit, which was intended to be an incubator to cultivate your potential and greatness, actually may have created the inverse in some cases.

Somewhere in the process, we need to break the cycle of scarcity, poverty, victimization, fear, orphan thinking, destabilization, and the like. We need transitional leaders to stand in the gap and change the tide! To raise up a generation of Champions, it requires Champions. At some point, someone needs to stand up and say it is enough. We are going to shift the negative momentum and turn it positive. Champions will accept that challenge with courage and tenacity, and they will persevere until headway is made.

Jesus' government is disruptive. It changes the status quo and we are the facilitators of that disruptive innovation. Jesus' government is meant to be actualized in the family. Family is God's ordained business unit to nurture and build according to the God blueprint in each one of us individually and collectively.

THE GOVERNMENT OF JESUS IS MEANT TO BE ACTUALIZED IN THE FAMILY.

I believe one of the reasons Jesus told His disciples to wait for the Holy Spirit was to form family. The several days they prayed, broke bread and shared life together, created a bond – a bond of unity. Jesus' new government was poured out by the Holy Spirit in a family. Through the process, they developed personal and family identity. They became a mini tribe where the foundations of heaven's culture were being formed. They shared stories, values, and inevitably learned to love and accept others in new ways.

When we look into our identity in Christ - the point of origin in the Father's heart - and mix this with the Father's goodness regarding His plans and purposes for our lives, it creates an equation that shouts out: We don't have to live in the past, but we can recreate our future together, by changing the way we think about ourselves and others. We don't do it alone. We can partner with others. All the phases in the NOW Leadership process serve us by preparing us for greatness in the context of family!

We need to honor those who have paid the price to live true to their values and convictions as facilitators nurturing the seed of the kingdom in others. For example, I have seen countless mothers champion the cause for children, orphans, the needy, broken marriages, political issues, and taking a strong stand and voice against injustice. I am often humbled by listening to women who live true to their values and integrity regarding hard issues. They are fearless in the face of opposition, especially if it has to do with their children.

We need to mature beyond being children spiritually. Building upon our yieldedness, we need to embrace sonship, where we live in our identity, take responsibility, and demonstrate faithfulness. Beyond sonship, we need to build further and take initiative, cultivate dreams in others, and learn how to co-labor.

Champions are not waiting for God to move; they are advancing the kingdom through their relationships. They are making things happen. They live in the world where everything is a green light to advance the kingdom of heaven until God gives you a yellow or red light. They do not ask permission to take the land; they are taking the land because they know it is theirs for the taking.

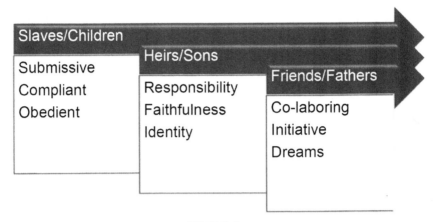

TABLE 3.
Advancing Spiritual Maturity Spectrum.

Shifting your thinking about who you are will shift the atmosphere that surrounds you. This is the Law of Attraction. If you agree with what the Father says about you, you will attract the power of the source behind that thinking. That power will change the atmosphere around you from negativity, to God's presence, and unlimited possibility.

LEAVING A LEGACY

Champions are not myopic but have the ability to see across the generations. They take time to reflect and capture multi-generational life messages and learning. It is part of the Communication process. As we honor each generation and what they carry, we build upon their learning and experiences. A 19-year-old young man who is wise beyond his years said this, "We need you (the older generations) because where you leave off, is our starting point. If you don't end well, we can't start well. We need you."

Peter, our case study here, took time to pen two powerful epistles that were written on the signature of his life. The gospels were written with the goal to transfer the Jesus legacy to His followers. We need to tell the stories of God's goodness to the generations. Psa. 45:17 says, *"I will make*

Your name to be remembered in all generations; Therefore the people shall praise You forever and ever."

In order to create legacy, there are three key contributors which when combined can create powerful outcomes. Back in the chapter on Competency, the spirit of excellence that was upon Daniel and his friends created a 10X advantage because of the Spirit of wisdom, understanding and knowledge which we refer to as the WUK Factor. There was an Old Testament account where Isaac experienced a 100X increase in one year in Gen. 26 when sowing in the land. This was a sign of God's covenant, favor and presence generating accelerated growth and abundance. In the New Testament, Jesus speaks about 100X believers who have the rich soil in their hearts for God's word to grow (Mark 4:1-25). In addition, He promises a 100X increase to those who surrender homes and families for the kingdom of God (Mark 10:29-31).

THE 1000X FACTOR

Recently, the Lord shared with me His thinking about what I pray for. He said, "You pray for the 10X and 100X increase, but I am looking for 1000X leaders." I thought this was a big ask. In Deut. 7:9 a generational blessing is pronounced to the 1000th generation. This implies an impact, a legacy that is limitless or infinite. God was and is looking for 10 x 100 = 1000X champions. These men and women would possess the WUK Factor, cultivate a rich soil of heart for the Word of God to grow and take root, and would live totally surrendered lives.

GOD WAS AND IS LOOKING FOR 10 X 100 = 1000X CHAMPIONS.

Deut. 1:11 says, *"May the Lord, the God of your fathers, increase you a thousand times and bless you as he has promised!"* If Moses, speaking by inspiration of the Holy Spirit, had faith to speak and write this in his day, how much more should we today have such faith. Isaiah, writing centuries later by inspiration of the same Holy Spirit, said, *"The least of you will become a thousand, the smallest a mighty nation. I am the Lord; in its time I will do this swiftly"* (Isa. 60:22). The Lord's intent and purpose is clear, having been established at the mouth of two or three witnesses.

WUK FACTOR x (FERTILE HEARTS x SURRENDER) = GENERATIONAL CHAMPIONS

A.E. Winship, an American educator (Jukes-Edwards – *A Study in Education and Heredity*, written in 1900), traced the descendants of Jonathan Edwards, who was a preacher, revivalist and author of the 1700's during the First Great Awakening and later became President of Princeton University. The brilliance of the Lord's blessing on his 1400 descendants over a century and a half is remarkable. It is reported that Jonathan Edward's legacy included: 1 U.S. Vice President, 1 Dean of law school, 1 dean of medical school, 3 U.S. Senators, 3 governors, 3 mayors, 13 college presidents, 75 Military officers, 80 public office holders, 100 lawyers, 100 clergymen, and 285 college graduates.

This perhaps sounds ridiculous to the average person. The original 12 disciples transformed the world and did not come from families of distinction and education. Regardless of your background, the potential is there. Champions will pass on the spiritual blessings with encouragement, prophetic words, and the testimony of Jesus in ways that far exceed our understanding. The generations will praise the Lord forever.

THE DEMAND FOR CHAMPIONS

When we think and pray about awakening and revival in the nations, we need leaders to be thinking from a systems perspective. We need systems and strategies to impact Culture. In the Bible, God raised up governors in the land to execute God's will and mandates. People like Nehemiah, Daniel, and Joseph were innovators that put systems and policies in place to administer a kingdom.

Nehemiah rebuilt a broken city. Daniel ruled under several different kings and empires in a foreign land, and Joseph implemented a food program to save at a minimum two strategic nations, Egypt and the Israelites, from the disaster of mass starvation. Gen. 41:57 records, "And **all the countries** came to Egypt to buy grain from Joseph, because the famine was severe in **all the world**." (author's emphasis)

Ezekiel's prophetic word in his time domain still resonates with heaven's cry for leaders. God is investing His divine energy in leaders to prepare them to fulfill their destinies for the nations.

> *I searched for a man among them who would build up the wall and stand in the gap before Me for the land, so that I would not destroy it; but I found no one.* (Ezek. 22:30)

There is demand for leaders to move into vertical leadership development versus horizontal. Horizontal leadership development is about adding more skills and Competencies but might not change your thinking or the construct within you. It enhances Competencies without transformation or creating greater bandwidth.

On the contrary, vertical development is about developing thinking Capacity to embrace more challenging problems. It is the gap where new thinking and solutions are required. It brings you into the space of thinking into more complex problems from a systemic and interdependent perspective. In the end, horizontal leadership development is about transferring information – business as usual - versus vertical development which is about bringing about leadership transformation that leads to game changers.

NOW Leadership defines some of the elements of the preparation process. The goal is to move beyond information and embrace transformation to become the solution. There is no skipping of any steps in the process. We will re-take the same test until we pass. Developing Competencies is good, but it is not enough. If you ever wondered why complex problems keep coming your way, it is because God wants to get your attention to change the way you think about yourself and the solution. The goal is to create faithful, effective, creative, and innovative leaders and collaborative teams who can steward and sustain what God desires to be manifested in the earth.

CHAMPIONS NEED COURAGE TO BRING OTHERS INTO DESTINY

There would be no Champions without courage. Courage is the ability to do something that we are afraid of or the ability to face pain or difficulty. Peter exhibited great courage when he stepped out in faith to boldly preach as well as when he stepped out to walk on the water and brought about miraculous healings. Every leader needs to draw from the reservoir of strength of relationship for courage to flow in our lives.

> *Be strong and courageous! Do not tremble or be dismayed, for the Lord your God is with you wherever you go.* (Jos. 1:9)

Joshua was the first apostolic leader of the Old Testament to take a people into their destiny. It is interesting that Joshua was in need of encouragement to be courageous to take the land on the other side of the Jordan River. He was commanded to not listen to his feelings of fear and dismay! God's presence was with him. The Levites led the way with the Ark of the Covenant. He had one of the best spiritual fathers a man could have. Moses was a man who talked face to face with God. (Deut. 34:10).

Even with the very best, as pioneers, leaders, parents, entrepreneurs, executives, grandparents and teenagers, we need courage to face the challenges of our generation. The battle is dynamic and is unique for each one of us. Courageous agility is required for the battle. Champions are not afraid of the fear, difficulty, pain, and hardship. Taking the land is the prize and Champions will do whatever it takes to dispossess the land of its giants so that it can be possessed by the generations to follow. Facing your giants will take courage. God will give us the courage we need to face and conquer the impossible.

DEVELOPING AND RESTORING CHAMPIONS

In a recent leadership collaborative initiative, I was offended through a misunderstanding which arose because of differences in gift orientation and personalities. Through this process, I learned some things I did not like about myself. At the time of the writing of this book, I began to understand why the Lord instructed me to write about Peter. The lights went on as a result of some encounters I had with the Lord.

My eyes were opened to see that I was a lot like Peter in some ways. I was mortified. He showed me I was strong, focused, independent, and self-reliant at times. In order for the Lord to move me into the next level of leadership responsibility, he needed to bring a new level of breaking.

Looking into the past, I wondered, "How could You have used me when I was like that?" I felt unworthy and embarrassed. Then the Lord brought me to Peter's restoration with Jesus and my eyes were opened.

> So when they had finished breakfast, Jesus said to Simon Peter, "Simon, son of John, do you love Me more than these?" He said to Him, "Yes, Lord; You know that I love You." He said to him, "Tend My lambs." He said to him again a second time, "Simon, son of John, do you love Me?" He said to Him, "Yes, Lord; You know that I love You." He said to him, "Shepherd My sheep." He said to him the third time, "Simon, son of John, do you love Me?" Peter was grieved because He said to him the third time, "Do you love Me?" And he said to Him, "Lord, You know all things; You know that I love You." Jesus said to him, "Tend My sheep." (John 21:15-17)

I realized that strong leaders run hard and with all their strength, passion and energy. It's a green light until it is yellow or red. I believe the Lord saw this in Peter and that He tapped into it. It was Jesus' belief in Peter, and the potential yet to be released, that drew Peter out of his own negative self-perceptions and muck. Jesus restored a man so he could run his race by believing in him and restoring his confidence and place of leadership.

Similarly, the Lord through Connection drew me out through His love. He reminded me of my Competencies in the secret place. He showed me that the crucible of Capacity was the only place safe enough to show me my character strengths and flaws. It was the only place where He could humble me to open my eyes. I was walking in Convergence, but I needed greater refinement and alignment for my next assignment.

God is raising up Champions and there is a strong fire burning in His heart toward you. It is relentless. He knows all about my failures and shortcomings - and yours - and He still loves us. God's love is what ultimately forms us into master Champions. It will wreck you at your core to build you into His prize. Words cannot capture the intensity, the intimacy, the grief, the weeping, the dying, the letting go, the loneliness, the comfort, the pleasure, the joys, the camaraderie and more.

Jeremiah, in a dark hour in his life, had the revelation that God was like a Dread Champion. Jer. 20:11 says, *"But the Lord is with me like a dread champion."*

It may just be that you are being formed to join this great company of Champions at this time. Some of you may have been taken out, others may have thrown in the towel, or perhaps you are just waiting for some help, or holding on to the knot at the end of your rope. I pray that this NOW Leadership process will be a companion, guide and resource for you. God in this hour is breathing upon the dry bones and is restructuring old and broken systems and people.

That breath of life has the divine energy that Peter talked about to raise you up and develop you. The winds for awakening and revival are here. Catch it. Embrace it. Let it take you places you would have never been before. It is not just for you but is for your family and family's families and beyond. The generations are crying out for these leaders to fill the leadership vacuum to bring vision, understanding, clarity, and authenticity.

Run your Race as a dread champion! You will never be the same! The world will never be the same! And there will be no greater joy!

It's time for us to become the Champions God intended us to become.

CASE STUDY: WILLIAM BOOTH – A CHAMPION FOR THE LOST

William Booth was an English-born evangelist who was born near Nottingham in April of 1828. As a young man, he apprenticed to be a pawn broker, but God intercepted his life at a young age through a conversion experience to Christ. He immediately began preaching for the Methodist Chapel. In 1849 he moved to London to work as a pawnbroker for three years, but then decided to go into ministry and became a full-time preacher in 1852. He married Catherine Mumford, who became a life partner in ministry and she was ordained in 1858. As a unified team, they worked together to bring the gospel to the lost.

One of the hallmarks of their ministry was they abandoned the standard church model and reached out to the poor, engaging people on the streets of London. They were known for their singing in the streets and sharing testimonies in the streets. They loved the homeless, destitute, unlovely, and uneducated.

They did not shy away from the industrial slums and there was brokenness, misery and suffering in the groups where they engaged: thieves, prostitutes, drunkards, and those bound in addiction. They offered them an opportunity for repentance. They broke the mold of conventional Christianity of the day and brought the power of the Gospel to the poor and broken-hearted.

When persecution from the Church came because of their unconventional methods, they took refuge in the Lord, turning inward to develop leaders. This was a brilliant response to the resistance from the traditional "church". Their compassion drove them to equip and deploy more evangelists for the lost. Within 10 years, their organization which was initially called the "The Christian Mission", had over 1000 workers and evangelists. Booth felt that women were the best soldiers in Christ.

In 1878 Booth started to use military terms and called his organization an army of volunteers. This language turned the name to what is now called the Salvation Army. The Booths "took the land" in spite of the resistance from organized religion, and between 1881 and 1885, they had over 250,000 converts.

They slowly built social programs for food, housing and community which they are still known for today. Booth's goal was to use the social programs to be the hook that leads to salvation. The word of the Lord went forth to the nations from there, and today the Salvation Army is in over 100 countries worldwide and serves millions of people annually.

This couple pioneered a new model to reach the lost and minister to the disenfranchised and downtrodden members of society. The love of Christ compelled them to reach those who would be otherwise overlooked. He championed the cause for the lost through the Booths' Compassion. The end result of their actions and motives were evangelistic and humanitarian. A lasting impact and legacy were made by bringing healing, salvation and relief to those who were suffering. This is an example of Compassion in action and being a selfless Champion for others who are in need.

CASE STUDY: GEORGE WASHINGTON – A GENERAL, FOUNDING FATHER, AND PRESIDENT WHO BECAME A CHAMPION FOR FREEDOM

George Washington was born on February 22, 1732 on his family's plantation in the British colony of Virginia. Washington's father died when he was 11 years old. George's father left most of his income to George's older half-brothers, leaving George to help his mother manage the plantation where they lived. It was then that George learned to rely on hard work and efficiency to get tasks accomplished.[1]

Washington's education ended around age 15 and he was never to go to college. Washington was known for his aptitude in mathematics and as a teenager became a successful surveyor. He surveyed much of the Virginia wilderness and thus earned enough money to begin purchasing land.

In December 1752 with no prior military experience, he was made a commander in the Virginia militia. Washington gained experience commanding militia in the French and Indian Wars. In 1755 Washington was a volunteer aid to General Edward Braddock who led an expedition to "… drive the French from the Ohio country."[2] Washington's "conspicuous bravery" led to the eventuality of his being named commander of all Virginia militia forces.

In 1759 Washington returned to Mount Vernon which he had previously inherited from his brother Lawrence who had died in 1752. There he was elected to the Virginia house of Burgesses and married Martha Dandridge Custis, a widow with two children in 1759. He became a devoted stepfather to Martha's children but George and Martha had no children of their own.[3]

Washington served as a delegate of the First Continental Congress at Philadelphia in 1774. In 1775 the war for independence from England had started and Washington was named Commander in Chief of the Continental Army. His brilliance came in his ability to motivate a rag tag army of farmers together through much adversity including defeat by the hands of the British and lack of food, supplies, ammunition and even shoes for some of his troops. The Continental Army under Washington's guidance and heartfelt conviction kept fighting against the preeminent army of the day.

Finally, in 1781, with the help of the French who had come to the aid of the Americans, the Continental Army trapped the British under Lord Cornwallis at Yorktown, Virginia and forced their surrender. Washington became a national hero at the momentous defeat of the British under Cornwallis. A peace treaty with the British was signed in 1783 and Washington returned to Virginia to farm.

In 1787, Washington was asked to attend the Constitutional Convention in Philadelphia and lead the group of statesman crafting a new constitution. His leadership in this endeavor led to the belief that Washington should become the young nation's first president. Washington resisted the request initially but gave in to the pressure and agreed to participate. America's first presidential election was held on January 7, 1789 and Washington became the nation's first president. Washington diligently pursued an attitude of fairness, prudence and integrity[4].

Washington died in 1799 after serving two terms as the nation's president. One of Washington's greatest gifts to the United States is something he did not do. He did not set himself up as a military dictator of the young nation but sought to unite leaders with different beliefs and felt that divergent views were necessary to have successful government.

What George Washington "… had was a confidence in our dream and our purpose and he had confidence in his fellow citizens. That if you want freedom, this is what it's going to take" (General Colin Powell).[5]

Biographical sketch provided courtesy of Tyler Beckwith

TAKEAWAYS

- The Lord is our Champion and we need to rethink what greatness looks like.

- Champions are not born but formed.

- God's love toward champions is relentless.

- Champions do not quit, but persevere.

- Courage is a necessity to possess your future – your destiny.

- Champions need periodic restoration.

- Build according to the heavenly pattern and blueprints.

- Champions are servant leaders that traverse and impact the generations.

- Champions assist others through the NOW Leadership process.

- God is seeking leaders who have a generational vision – 1000X.

CHAMPIONS – SELF-ASSESSMENT

- I understand the numerous steps in NOW Leadership.

- I can coach and mentor leaders and organizations through the process.

- I am aware that developing people is important to my assignment.

- I am comfortable in being a servant leader across generations and cultures.

- Leaving a legacy is important.

Rate the above on a scale from 1 to 5:

1 - strongly disagree

2 - disagree

3 - neither agree nor disagree

4 - agree

5 - strongly agree

If your score is 1-8, you have opportunity to grow as a Champion.

If your score is 9-17, you are making progress and should continue in your forward momentum.

If your score is 18+, you have a good handle and grasp on being a Champion.

NOW ACTION

1. Make a list of your heroes or Champions. Take time to describe the characteristics that made them great and effective. What traits are there to admire and gravitate toward? These perhaps are ones God wants to develop in you.

2. Pray through the following Scriptures for a month, asking the Lord to develop an understanding of what a Champion is and how a Champion could pioneer change in the earth through the NOW Leadership Process.

    In that day there will be an altar to the Lord in the midst of the land of Egypt, and a pillar to the Lord near its border. It will become a sign and a witness to the Lord of hosts in the land of Egypt; for they will cry to the Lord because of oppressors, and He will send them a Savior and a Champion, and He will deliver them. Thus the Lord will make Himself known to Egypt, and the Egyptians will know the Lord in that day. They will even worship with sacrifice and offering, and will make a vow to the Lord and perform it. (Isa. 19:19-21)

    But the Lord is with me like a dread champion; Therefore my persecutors will stumble and not prevail. They will be utterly ashamed, because they have failed, With an everlasting disgrace that will not be forgotten. (Jer. 20:11)

PRAYER

Lord, raise up Champions after your own heart who will advocate and develop the next generation of leaders. Bring us through the fires, successes, failures, and relationships so we will release our inheritance to the generations. Put the resolve of heaven in us to stand in the gap until we see your solutions being realized. Let us stand, advocate, impart, heal, restore, develop, fight, and resolve to see godly leaders equipped to bring us into the future, for your glory. Amen.

NOW COACHING QUESTIONS

1. Who are some of your Champions?

2. What are the most important traits of a Champion?

3. How have you been a Champion to others?

4. In what ways was your experience positive or negative?

5. In what ways have you been a Champion to advance the kingdom?

6. Where do you think we most need Champions?

7. Where would you like to Champion?

8. What are the benefits of having Champions in the faith?

9. What are your next steps?

— — — — — — — — — — — — — →

ENDNOTES

1. George Washington's Mount Vernon, *Biography of George Washington*, https://www.mountvernon.org/george-washington/biography/.

2. Ibid.

3. History, George Washington. https://www.history.com/topics/us-presidents/george-washington.

4. Ibid.

CHAPTER TWELVE

CULTURE
Defining Atmosphere

The God who made the world and everything in it is the Lord of heaven and earth and does not live in temples built by human hands. And he is not served by human hands, as if he needed anything. Rather, he himself gives everyone life and breath and everything else. From one man he made all the nations, that they should inhabit the whole earth; and he marked out their appointed times in history and the boundaries of their lands. God did this so that they would seek him and perhaps reach out for him and find him, though he is not far from any one of us. "For in him we live and move and have our being." (Acts 17:24-28)

When you travel to a new nation or visit a new city, when your feet touch the ground, what are your first impressions? What perceptions flood your natural and spiritual senses? When you attend a meeting in a company or visit a family, what do you observe? When you join a network or online community, what attracts you to them?

Whenever we engage with any people group, whether it is a family, community, corporation, or nation, we will be impacted by their Culture. The signposts of Culture are written in numerous ways including the atmosphere, relationships, music, art, infrastructure, language, traditions, stories, films, history, geography, weather, architecture, business, education, religion and the like. Culture is everywhere.

Culture is the way of life of a group of people and is the way they do things and live life. It is the summation of all their thoughts and behavior along with all that they own and produce. It includes a people group's beliefs, dreams, desires, values, social behavior, material goods, folkways, mores, oral traditions, history, identity and more. It is expressed through their behaviors, art, music, literature, relationships, how they solve problems, create and enforce laws and policies, spend money, administer justice, educate, innovate, trade money, and how and with whom they do business.

WHO IS IN CHARGE?

Whoever controls Culture will control the world. Culture creates an atmosphere over people groups and nations. Those who are perceptive will sense and feel what that atmosphere is announcing. In all likelihood, the atmosphere of nations is influenced by the media in democratic nations, and perhaps more by the governments in countries where leaders want to control the masses. If you want to influence a Culture, you need to influence the atmosphere. It is a leader's job to steward and influence the atmosphere of their followers.

Remember the VUCA model I shared with you earlier? In the midst of volatility, leaders speak vision, and where there is complexity, leaders bring clarity. Leaders speak to identify experiential realities as well as create new ones. If you can name what people are experiencing with empathy by identifying with them and providing hope and solutions for them with integrity, people will follow. If we embrace the challenge that we are stewarding Culture, whether it is for spiritual or marketplace vocation, we have opportunity to advance the kingdom of God in an accelerated way.

There is a movement gaining momentum to impact the Seven Mountains of Culture which includes religion, education, business, family, media, government, arts and entertainment. Over the years, I admittedly have been somewhat frustrated with all of this talk about the Seven Mountains. Only a select few are supposedly the key influencers in these domains and the chatter about making an impact on them seemed like an impossible task. How do you get to be in the top 1-3% of influencers or gatekeepers in a mountain or sphere? How do you impact these Seven Mountains?

Well, you need social currency, expertise and favor to get into a strategic position. You need a plan and strategy. One of the reasons I have written about NOW Leadership is to answer the question: How do I get to the place where I can impact the Seven Mountains of Culture? The process entails understanding your calling, developing your leadership potential and ability, creating strategies, gaining expertise, growing in favor and authority, and then executing the plan.

STRATEGIES FOR INFLUENCING CULTURE

Make no mistake; it will take hard work and commitment to influence Culture. You may work your way up the mountain, or you may get transported through divine favor by promotion, or both, or through some other means. All of this is very exciting but in essence this thinking is a bit individualistic. We may also feel that we need to displace others or take control of the existing mountains. I believe an effective strategy should have these elements in it:

1. We need to provide an alternative solution, work in teams, networks, associations, and relationships, and realize that taking or climbing a mountain needs to be accomplished by a company of people united in purpose.

2. There may also be a generational dimension to it. We may need to train the next generation to work in a collaborative way to influence these structures and spheres in society.

3. And we need to agree on a definition of what taking or climbing a mountain means and looks like. Influencing Culture may not be achieved by directly making it a goal, but may be a subsequent outcome or there may be an indirect pathway.

David had a vision to build the temple but was not able to because of some limitations created by his behavior. He was a man of bloodshed as a warrior and general of his armies. David's love and passion did not allow this roadblock to stop him. He gathered the materials and wealth necessary for his son Solomon to complete the project God had birthed in David. There was a generational connection to fulfilling the assignment that impacted Culture.

AN EXAMPLE OF CULTURAL TRANSFORMATION FROM THE BOOK OF ACTS

The apostles in the New Testament positioned themselves to impact culture as well. Their influence on Culture grew organically and out of love and relationships. I am not sure they sat down with a cultural architect to define the strategy that emerged. Their behavior inadvertently impacted Culture.

> *They were continually devoting themselves to the apostles' teaching and to fellowship, to the breaking of bread and to prayer. Everyone kept feeling a sense of awe; and many wonders and signs were taking place through the apostles. And all those who had believed were together and had all things in common; and they began selling their property and possessions and were sharing them with all, as anyone might have need; Day by day continuing with one mind in the temple, and breaking bread from house to house, they were taking their meals together with gladness and sincerity of heart, praising God and having favor with all the people. And the Lord was adding to their number day by day those who were being saved.* (Acts 2:42-47)

- They listened to apostolic teaching which Peter was likely involved in.

- They fellowshipped together - they shared life together.

- They broke bread and celebrated communion.

- They prayed together.

- God showed up in awe and with signs and wonders.

- They shared their material wealth with one another.

- Day by day they met together at the temple with one mind.

- They visited and met from house to house.

- They shared their meals together.

- God added to their numbers and there were salvations.

This is an example of transformation taking place that impacted the community and Culture of their day!

More simply put, the leaders of this movement stewarded their Culture by:

- Communicating – teaching and praying

- Collaborating – prayed and worked together, and were of one mind

- Communing – they shared the Lord's supper, their spiritual experiences, food, homes, and material goods

- Creating – they created new relationships and their numbers increased

- Converging – heaven showed up with favor and the miraculous

- Connecting – they connected with God the Father, Jesus the Son, the Holy Spirit, and with one another

- Caring – they demonstrated Compassion by distributing material goods and wealth so that all were blessed and no one was in need

The atmosphere of this community was transformed through Communication, Collaboration, Communing, Creating, Connecting, experiencing Convergence and demonstrating Compassion. This is a tall order as we reflect on this text, but it is not impossible. The momentum of this cultural transformation was inspired by the outpouring of the Holy Spirit. No leader should embark on stewarding Culture without the Holy Spirit's help or they will likely burn out and be frustrated.

> *I will ask the Father, and He will give you another Helper, that He may be with you forever; that is the Spirit of truth, whom the world cannot receive, because it does not see Him or know Him, but you know Him because He abides with you and will be in you. I will not leave you as orphans; I will come to you.* (John 14:16-18)

THE END GAME IS REFORMATION

If there is to be any advancement in nations, Culture must be in sync with its metamorphosis. If awakening and revival comes to a land or nation, if the Culture is not transformed, then the leaders of that movement have failed to steward to bring it into maturity through reformation. When a group of people rally around governing beliefs and values that are biblical and life based, that people group will walk in a measure of unity. God blesses that unity in a nation. It can become a Catalyst for God to release new wine, innovation, Creativity, provision, blessing, and protection from His hand.

We can see through the Acts how the apostles transformed nations by impacting the Culture of the day. One of the strategic advantages of spiritual leaders is they can co-labor with what the Holy Spirit is doing in the earth. As I mentioned before, Peter preached a sermon and hit it out of the park. His inspired Communication impacted the hearers. Some responded and repented, some remained open, and others violently opposed the apostles.

When you are influencing Culture, cooperating with the Holy Spirit is essential. The Holy Spirit brings conviction, draws people, releases His love, healing, deliverance, cleansing, inspiration, provision, invention, Creativity and more. How can you not want to Collaborate with Him? Initiatives birthed from the heart of the Father bring us into a place where we can exercise our faith to believe for the provision and resources. With vision from heaven, God's pro-vision will come. The strategies and resources to impact Culture should not be overlooked.

Martin Luther's 95 Theses included the disputed practice of indulgences, which was dominant among church leaders of the time, and a primary fundraising technique for raising money to build cathedrals. Luther initiated a stir that rocked the nations and shook the foundations of the religious systems. Culture needs to be continuously renewed and must experience transformation to remain relevant and healthy.

Luther challenged the status quo at the right time in history, because the peoples of those nations were ripe for change. The outcome of Luther's treatises refuting the excesses and abuses of the Catholic Church, was the Protestant Reformation.

It was not called the Protestant revival or awakening, but Reformation. Why? Most simply put, the Culture of Europe was reformed by impacting politics, economics, business, education, and religious life. This Reformation called people back to the authority of Scripture, justification by faith, and the priesthood of every believer. It addressed corruption and abuses by leadership, false doctrine and wrong theology, the immediacy of God in the present, accessibility of God and the Scriptures to everyday people, and enhanced literacy across the land. Every facet of Culture was impacted.

Looking back in history, it appears that brute force was also applied during the Protestant Reformation. This transformation took place over several years with many battles and conflicts. At least 150,000 people died as a result. The movement was not perfect by any means, and repeated some of the previous leaderships' shortfalls. In most instances, Culture is not changed by brute force but rather when incremental changes are implemented or when tipping points are reached to create cascading change. The primary mechanism for these changes comes through the Communication process backed by authentic, credible leadership.

I would suggest if you try to use a Newtonian model to transform Culture, it will fail because it will be forced. Cultural transformation follows more true to a chaos model. What this points to in chaos theory is that small inputs can create significant changes. In organizational behavior, if you can get 15% of the people to adopt a new idea, you can create a tipping point.

In Culture it is even less: 3-6% of the population can tip the Culture under the right conditions and timing (see Malcolm Gladwell's book, *The Tipping Point*). Influencing people groups and developing consensus is an art form. We need master craftsmen, or perhaps cultural architects and strategists, to engage God's wisdom to bring about cultural transformation that reflects His plan: "on earth as it is in heaven."

CULTURE MUST BE TAKEN IN CONTEXT

Culture is an internal organizational factor that impacts outward expression for an organization's or a nation's identity and values. The inverse of Culture is Context which is shaped by the environment. They are similar but different in that if we do not understand leadership context, we can misapply and misinterpret circumstances. Context is the set of circumstances that form a setting, statement, idea and/or framework so that it can be fully understood and assessed. It includes things like political, cultural, legal, factors, tax policy, regulatory environment, geopolitical environment, labor laws, risk factors, compliance requirements, and trade policy. From a human resource and interpersonal perspective, it includes things like Board dynamics, team dynamics, succession planning, levels of trust, technical competency, hiring policies, etc.

From a biblical standpoint, we interpret the Scriptures from the text based on what is written or spoken immediately before and following the verse or passage to clarify its meaning. Context also includes the book and what testament it is from, as well as historical and cultural factors of the time period in which it was written. Truth taken out of context can be misapplied which can be misleading and even damaging. This principle is easily scaled and applied to situations in leadership.

For example, the misapplication of truth in context is where Peter told Jesus: *"Never, Lord! This shall never happen to you."* This was Peter's response after Jesus told him he must suffer at the hands of the Jewish elders, chief priests and scribes, be killed and be raised again on the third day (Matt. 16:21-23). Jesus said to Peter, *"Get behind me, Satan. You are a stumbling block to Me. For you do not have in mind the things of God, but the things of men."* Peter had not perceived the spiritual context.

Another example from Peter's life was when he was on the Mountain of Transfiguration. Peter wanted to build a physical tabernacle after Moses and Elijah appeared and Jesus was transfigured before the three disciples, but Peter did not accurately or properly discern the Context and purpose for and significance of the spiritual experience he had just witnessed and observed with James and John.

I was once in a meeting with some leaders where we were reviewing our organization's tasks, priorities, and budget. I had done some pinch hitting for the last eight months for these leaders so they could address some urgent technical issues with special teams. During that time there were organizational changes which my peers were not a part of because of the technical issues. Because of this gap in perspective and experience, we were taking each other's discussion out of Context.

They were under severe pressure to meet budget requirements, and I was working to protect and develop employees and create smooth transitions. The difference in perspectives and experiences caused us to take things out of Context. We misinterpreted each other's intentions and it created some friction. I realized the difference in Context was the root cause of this problem after post-processing the conversation. Ideally, we want to engage Context while in the situation. Asking more clarifying questions will enable us to understand context more quickly, which will reduce the creation of chaos and improve our teamwork effectiveness.

It is important that we understand the internal values of the organization(s) we are part of—the Culture—as well as the external environment and special circumstances—the Context—as we interact and lead. As leaders we need to elevate our awareness of Context and Culture to healthily discriminate and eliminate waste to bring about positive outcomes.

CELEBRATION CREATES A CONNECTION

Leaders, pioneers, entrepreneurs, and task-driven people often live in the future, building to realize the vision. Their futuristic mindset can often cause them to forget to recognize the progress made in the NOW. Celebration is the action of marking one's pleasure at an important event, accomplishment, or occasion by engaging in enjoyable activity. It creates an acknowledgment to build Connection.

Celebration empowers affirmation, confirmation and recognition. It can be expressed through awards, holiday parties, group activities and recreation events, celebrating business wins, team wins, and outstanding performance or achievement wins. It is also reflected through life wins if someone we work with gets married, has a baby, gets pregnant, moves or buys a new house, becomes a grandparent, or other major milestones.

Celebrations communicate value to those you are in relationship with and inject the joy factor to brighten and enrich. It is a cement that builds teams, Culture, communities, and nations. National holidays can bring a nation together in remembrance and unity.

We need to pause to make the applause—take the time to celebrate. It provides a natural reset to bring closure to the past, and create new starts or open chapters in our lives. The investment is worth it.

A STORY OF CREATING CULTURAL CHANGE THROUGH EMPLOYEE EMPOWERMENT

Once I was involved in a special project as a manager leading an employee engagement team for a large organization. This assignment was interesting to me as a leadership coach. I was aware of Gallup studies that only 1 in 5 people are engaged in the workplace. We were also a newly-formed organization where we combined different disciplines together, so we were emerging with a new brand and identity as an organization.

This company conducts a quarterly survey. As good engineers, we analyzed the data and wanted to fix each problem one by one. The team leaders who had led previous teams used a block and tackle approach. We talked about their results and none of us wanted to be involved with the team if that would be the approach. We chose a different strategy, and the results and outcomes were very positive.

In order to influence and define our Culture, we took an appreciative inquiry approach. Appreciative inquiry identifies the strengths of an organization and begins to story tell its strengths and success rather than over-analyzing its weaknesses and trying to fix them. So, our team created quarterly strategies which involved leveraging the strength of our communications team to tell stories about engagement, work life balance, empowerment, and Communication.

The strategy was successful, and we began to see a shift in the atmosphere and prevailing attitudes through surveys. We influenced the company's Culture, created greater awareness and strengthened the organization's identity.

CASE STUDY: CHRISTIAN FÜHRER – HOW ONE MAN'S LEADERSHIP IN PRAYER CHANGED CULTURE

A man that few people may know of is Christian Führer (1943-2014). He was a pastor who at the height of the cold war in East Germany led a group of people to pray. In 1982 he started a prayer movement that met on Monday nights in the historic church of Nikolaikirche, Leipzig.

In spite of the communist regime's control over religion, they remained faithful. The movement grew from a few hundred to 70,000 by 1989. Peaceful prayer became a hallmark of protest against the communist culture. The protest grew to 320,000 which gave way to the resignation of Erick Honecker, the GDR leader. The whole government began to crumble and he influenced the collapse of the Berlin Wall, thereby ending the Cold War. Mikhail Gorbachev, the former Soviet Union President, awarded Christian the Peace Prize of Augsburg. *(Source: Wikipedia)*

The infamous Berlin Wall came tumbling down because of this man's faith. "Truly I tell you, if you have faith as small as a mustard seed, you can say to this mountain, 'Move from here to there,' and it will move. Nothing will be impossible for you." (Matt. 17:20).

Christian brought about change by mobilizing a prayer movement. Who would have imagined this was possible? The face of Europe has been changed ever since. Christian said "yes" to the Lord, and the years of prayer and intercession for the walls to come down came about through the tipping point created through this prayer movement. As a Catalyst and Champion, Culture was impacted!

TAKEAWAYS

- Culture is the summation of a people group's or organization's thoughts, identity, values and behavior.

- Those who influence Culture will rule the world.

- Transformation requires sustainability through reformation.

- Leaders are called to steward Culture.

- Celebration is the cement that can create cultural bonds.

- Whether you are a spiritual or marketplace leader, don't neglect Culture.

- God is raising up cultural strategists and architects to influence Culture.

CULTURE – SELF-ASSESSMENT

- I pray for solutions regarding my Culture's problems.

- I understand my Culture and what it values.

- I see the keys that will transform Culture.

- I am intentional about stewarding and influencing Culture.

- I think about developing leaders to influence Culture.

Rate the above on a scale from 1 to 5:

> 1 - strongly disagree

> 2 - disagree

> 3 - neither agree nor disagree

> 4 - agree

> 5 - strongly agree

If your score is 1-8, you have opportunity to grow in developing Culture.

If your score is 9-17, you are making progress and should continue in your forward momentum.

If your score is 18+, you have a good handle and grasp on Culture.

NOW ACTION

1. Write about what troubles you about the Culture you want to change. What are the problems that you see? Who do you think can solve these problems? How do you see yourself impacting these areas? What resources do you bring to solve the issues at hand? What Competencies would you need to develop in light of the situation you are addressing? Who would you want to work with to advance forward?

PRAYER

Pray the following Scripture in the context of impacting Culture.

For this reason I bow my knees before the Father, from whom every family in heaven and on earth derives its name, that He would grant you, according to the riches of His glory, to be strengthened with power through His Spirit in the inner man, so that Christ may dwell in your hearts through faith; and that you, being rooted and grounded in love, may be able to comprehend with all the saints what is the breadth and length and height and depth, and to know the love of Christ which surpasses knowledge, that you may be filled up to all the fullness of God.

Now to Him who is able to do far more abundantly beyond all that we ask or think, according to the power that works within us, to Him be the glory in the church and in Christ Jesus to all generations forever and ever. Amen. (Eph. 3:14-21)

NOW COACHING QUESTIONS

1. In what ways do you understand your Culture?

2. What is the biggest problem you see in your Culture?

3. How do you see yourself influencing change in that area?

4. What mountains of Culture do you want to influence?

5. Define the Culture of the area you want to influence?

6. What steps would you take to bring about change?

7. In what ways are you developing leaders to influence Culture?

8. What would your cultural utopia look like?

9. What are your next steps?

RECAP OF THE FIRST 8C'S

We have just reviewed the first 8C's of the NOW Leadership model. As a refresher, the first 4C's bring alignment to our inner being where the foundations are:

1. Calling – understanding your potential and future.

2. Connection – developing an unbreakable bond with your heavenly Father and growing in your identity.

3. Competency – developing clarity about your raw talent, gifts, skills and abilities that are connected to your passion.

4. Capacity – the place and space in time where the crucibles of life purify, test, strengthen, and prepare us for promotion so we can sustain success.

The next 4C's are related to the outworking of God's favor in your life in fulfilling God's destiny. They are more externally directed based on the inner compass established in the previous 4C's. They are:

5. Convergence – the sweet spot where your preparation meets God's favor, your gifts, talents, and passion to bring heaven to earth.

6. Catalysts – the place of influence emerges where you decrease and you begin to build others up to increase. It is the beginning of the transition to becoming a Champion.

7. Champions – leverage all that they are to empower and equip others into their Calling and destinies.

8. Culture – the end game for Champions is to impact our society to bring about the greater good – healing, restoration, solutions, improvements, best practices, harmony, unity, hope, health and wealth, etc.

Lastly, there are four more C's that we believe are important to leadership. They are specific Competencies that are critical to your success. Two of them will enable you to develop more effective working groups, teams, and corroborative solutions - Collaboration and Communication. The last two will fuel the generation of solutions that are based out of an upgraded operating system - Creativity and Compassion.

CHAPTER THIRTEEN

COLLABORATION
Working Together

Just as a body, though one, has many parts, but all its many parts form one body, so it is with Christ. For we were all baptized by one Spirit so as to form one body—whether Jews or Gentiles, slave or free—and we were all given the one Spirit to drink. Even so the body is not made up of one part but of many... God has put the body together, giving greater honor to the parts that lacked it, so that there should be no division in the body, but that its parts should have equal concern for each other. If one part suffers, every part suffers with it; if one part is honored, every part rejoices with it. Now you are the body of Christ, and each one of you is a part of it. (1 Cor. 12:12-27)

Our goal is to collaborate with one another in such a way to see heaven come to earth. That means we need to facilitate developing people and aligning ourselves with heaven's intention. Leaders are the movers and shakers that will make that happen. In the end, the results of Calling, Connection, Capacity, and Convergence need to pivot on the unity of the body and faith through Collaboration. We are built together – that is the body or the ecclesia – the called out ones (see 1 Pet. 2:4-5).

There seems to be a rash of denominations and divisions in the Church today beyond normal human ability. Obviously Satan is threatened by our unity and wants us to be divided. Working together is possibly the most challenging endeavor we may ever undertake or experience. The ecosystem of leadership intent is broad and requires understanding other leaders' spheres of influence and their operating space.

KEYS TO COLLABORATION

We live in a time where Collaboration is key to kingdom initiatives and stewarding the grace that is being poured out. We are seeing unprecedented shifts as foundations are being reinforced and built to sustain the emerging kingdom age. Some of the signposts along the way are the preeminence of kings and priests taking their place in the order of Melchizedek.

Leaders from every sphere are filling the leadership vacuum to penetrate the uncharted markets to take atmospheric dominance. Global initiatives and kingdom businesses are being launched. There are numerous keys to their success for which resources are required.

In the Parable of the Minas and Talents, the Lord rewards faithfulness through trusted relationships. In a sense, He is a wise investment banker looking to release resources from heaven. The Lord does pay for what He orders. If we have a plan in alignment with God's character, purposes and timing, and can demonstrate that we can steward His resources, the resources will flow. One of the key elements of demonstrated leadership and management is Collaboration, which is a key resource or ingredient to fulfilling kingdom mandates.

Unfortunately, we live in a fallen world where fragmentation and chaos multiplies with minimal effort. We perhaps are multiplying denominations more than making converts to Christ. It is perhaps the antithesis of Collaboration. In that chaos, many are chasing after their brand and market share to get a bigger piece of the pie. Many are not walking in ways that are honoring and are using people to meet their greed quotient or recognition factor or to satisfy their ego.

It is a red ocean strategy where everyone is trying to outperform their rivals to grab a greater share as the markets get crowded. In a blue ocean, the competition is irrelevant because the operating system is based on abundance rather than scarcity. Sadly, many churches and ministries have embraced the American corporate culture mentality of scarcity. I often see leaders competing and creating win-lose scenarios rather than working together and creating win-win outcomes.

It is said that when the cats are away the mice will play. This perhaps applies to the parent-child relationship in both the natural and the spiritual sense. Many working in the Lord's sandbox or vineyard are all working to be successful and often think they are the center of the universe. Perhaps they are missing the bigger picture because of the lack of apostolic fathers and mothers including the fivefold ministry teams working together.

There is a great need for leaders to emerge to help us grow beyond ourselves to serve the greater purposes of heaven in the earth. Jesus is not just pouring out His Spirit on one person or one group in this season. He is pouring out on communities, regions and nations. Jesus gave prophetic words to the churches in regions in the book of Revelation. The apostle Paul wrote letters to churches in a region.

We need to resist the temptation of self-centeredness and move toward fulfilling the Lord's mandate to be one, and to love one another. We need to embrace a bigger picture, and our paradigm of how it all fits together needs to expand.

INTEGRATING IN AN INTERLOCKING WAY

Our mandate is to work together in an interlocking way — in other words, by collaborating. Collaboration is to work jointly with others, to work together cooperatively and willingly to achieve a desired result.

Anything worth building that will have a significant impact will require Collaboration.

For example, a jet engine requires numerous teams of experts along with systems integrators to ensure that every part and system meets the desired requirements. The end product, when fine tuned, hums and sings a song of power to create thrust for aircraft lift. The hardware in these machines works together in a unified manner to keep people safely in the air.

Perhaps a more complicated system is the human body. The apostle Paul shared a metaphor that the Church is like a body which is a sophisticated, interlocking system that embodies life. When our body, soul and spirit function in a unified manner, life is good, there is harmony and the flow of life. This metaphor applies not just to individuals and churches, but to cities, regions, states, and nations. A nation with systems, infrastructure, communications, and resources will prosper in numerous dimensions.

Paul, in his epistle to the church at Ephesus, listed distinguishing characteristics of leaders who are called to build something of pre-eminence and significance that is a unified and multi-faceted expression of Jesus in the earth. In this unity, which Jesus prayed for in John 17, there is no limit to what can be accomplished (see Gen. 11:6). The signature strength of those who are to walk worthy of the calling are marked by Jesus' core DNA, which in the end produces Collaboration that ends in oneness and will ultimately multiply!

> *Therefore I, the prisoner of the Lord, implore you to walk in a manner worthy of the calling with which you have been called, with all humility and gentleness, with patience, showing tolerance for one another in love, being diligent to preserve the unity of the Spirit in the bond of peace. There is one body and one Spirit, just as also you were called in one hope of your calling; one Lord, one faith, one baptism, one God and Father of all who is over all and through all and in*

all. But to each one of us grace was given according to the measure of Christ's gift. Therefore it says, "When He ascended on high, He led captive a host of captives, And He gave gifts to men." (Eph. 4:1-8)

Paul unveils the key elements to Collaboration's success – humility and gentleness with patience and showing tolerance for one another in love. In the business world, this would look like not being egotistical, listening for understanding, understanding timing, accepting and persevering with differences, not judging others, and understanding the diversity of strengths and teams.

As leaders, we set the tone for our teams and what the ground rules are for engagement. Possessing these attributes will create a platform to work through challenges. Are we committed to bringing about the integration of one body, one Spirit, one faith, one baptism, one Lord, and one God and Father who is over all and in all? If so, we must embrace the deeper working of God in our lives.

Peter cooperated and collaborated with the Holy Spirit and the other 119 disciples in the Upper Room before and on the day of Pentecost. In Acts 10, Peter collaborated with six other believers to bring the good news of salvation in Jesus to Cornelius and his household, bringing the gospel to the Gentiles. He also collaborated with John and the other apostles in teaching about Jesus in Jerusalem in Acts 4:1-22, and Acts 5:17-42.

I can also think of an example where Peter was doing the opposite. In the Council of Jerusalem in Acts 15:1-35, there was a dispute regarding how certain of the Jewish brethren wanted to require circumcision as a condition of salvation. The apostles and elders met and Peter spoke against requiring the Gentiles to be circumcised, as did James and others. But on a different occasion, when Peter came to visit the church in Antioch, he withdrew from eating with the Gentiles, fearing man's opinion.

But when Cephas came to Antioch, I opposed him to his face, because he stood condemned. For prior to the coming of certain men from James, he used to eat with the Gentiles; but when they came, he began to withdraw and hold himself aloof, fearing the party of the circumcision. (Gal. 1:11-12)

Peter, who had the vision about all things being clean (Acts 10), was influenced by legalism and a political spirit. This was not moving toward one faith, body, Spirit, baptism and hope (Eph. 4:1-4). Even though we can be moving in the supernatural realm as Peter did, it does not necessarily mean that we may not fall prey to sectarianism, people pleasing, or demonic influences. We need to guard ourselves and develop habits that keep us true.

SIGNATURE STRENGTHS

Some of the signature strengths which should be exhibited in the fivefold (Eph. 4:11) ministry are humility, gentleness, tolerance, love, and honor. The spiritual power of these attributes becomes the glue that allows these spiritual integrators to build and link people together. The end goal will be that the sum of the whole will be greater than the parts. Linking together in an interlocking manner requires perseverance, understanding the other person's operating space, and how they will be connected to others in a complex system. The goal is to create something far greater than what we could create individually.

… for the equipping of the saints for the work of service, to the building up of the body of Christ; until we all attain to the unity of the faith, and of the knowledge of the Son of God, to a mature man, to the measure of the stature which belongs to the fullness of Christ. (Eph. 4:12-14)

God is pouring out grace for Collaboration for those called by the Lord Jesus. The solution is simple, but hard to attain at times. Stay connected to the head, and we will be of one mind, heart, and purpose.

The fruitfulness for those who pay the price for Collaboration is ever increasing. The results will be exponential in nature because every seed that falls to the ground will multiply.

> Truly, truly, I say to you, "Unless a grain of wheat falls into the earth and dies, it remains alone; but if it dies, it bears much fruit." (John 12:24)

In the throne room of heaven there are 24 elders who are worshiping the Lord. They bow down and declare a seven-fold blessing and guess what they are doing? They are laying down their crowns as a gift to the Lord. Crowns represent their authority, influence, identity, and those distinguishing characteristics of their leadership. As we lay down our rights and identity before the Lord and listen for His divine strategies to build, and as we lay down all that we are, we can then embrace Collaboration. This will attract God's heavenly charge, and the flow of Collaboration to create unified solutions will be like none other.

> The twenty-four elders will fall down before Him who sits on the throne, and will worship Him who lives forever and ever, and will cast their crowns before the throne, saying, "Worthy are You, our Lord and our God, to receive glory and honor and power; for You created all things, and because of Your will they existed, and were created." (Rev. 4:10-11)

DISCERNING THE BEST IN OTHERS

If you are going to work with leaders, the gift of discernment will be critical. This gift is intended to help you discern whether people are operating in the Holy Spirit, the soul, the devil or the flesh; that is, to determine the point of origin of intention. In addition, we need the gift of discernment and prophetic insight to understand administrations of anointing, giftings, mandates, assignments, and governances.

Without this spiritual technology activated, it will be difficult to acquire the downloads regarding the DNA of leaders. This is so vitally important. Understanding the gift and character matrices of leaders is essential to building. One needs to evaluate the resources or building materials in hand, before you can determine what you can build. If you have the blueprint, but not the proper materials, it will alter your assignment or the timing until you receive the resources.

Mature leaders who collaborate with other leaders, must learn how to step out of their leadership domain and enter into the other leaders' space. This requires setting aside all that you are. If you don't do this, you cannot evaluate if you can work with this leader. If all you have running through your mind is your vision, values, and ideas, you are not really listening. We need to be intentional about collaboration. It will not happen automatically.

If you want to collaborate with someone, it is going to cost you something. If you want to gain the power of force multipliers by working with other strongly anointed leaders, you will need to let the grain of wheat (that is you) fall into the ground and die so it can eventually multiply. Laying things down will cost you but will send out an invitation to other leaders to come and work together.

UNDERSTANDING LEADERSHIP SPACE

Entering into someone else's leadership space is important so you can understand the maturity, assignments, mandates, gifts, vision, values, personality, and character of the person you will work with. Without this, you will not understand how that person can dovetail in your assignment and the greater purpose for your business, region, or nations. This foundational work is necessary to develop alignment so that leadership intentions can gel to create a more unified solution.

There is a great demand for leaders who are sent to integrate (collaborate), that is to fill the void through their apostolic integration. There is an emerging generation of leaders who will enter into these dimensions of leadership. It is a new leadership technology that God is birthing. They are necessary for 21st Century global leadership challenges. They will understand the dimensions, systems, domains, passion, assignments, giftings, anointings, and talents to knit them together into a cohesive operating unit. If you are running with the horses in this dimension, you had better be ready for speed and acceleration because things can happen fast.

Moses is a good example of an Apostolic Integrator of the Old Testament era. There was a promise to possess the land and Moses did not have sufficiently-trained tribes to possess the land. He lacked military resources. Moses evaluated the strengths of the tribes and determined that there were 2.5 tribes that could assist in the assignment to take the land flowing with milk and honey.

Moses brokered a deal with the leaders of the tribes of Gad, Benjamin and Manasseh. If they would help the other tribes dispossess the land and establish the Culture of the kingdom in the region, they would get the land east of the river. Moses recognized that each tribe in themselves, individually, could not accomplish the assignment. It takes a group or family of tribes to possess a land and transform the Culture.

Collaboration requires the evaluation of the constituents involved. We need to complete a thorough spiritual scan. The data you acquire from those downloads will be instrumental in weaving together kingdom teams that are effective so that each person's strengths, anointings, mandates, and assignments can be leveraged to gain the maximum outcomes.

It is vital to develop a mutual understanding of who each team member is. It is a well-known fact that when teams come together and embrace the principle of honor, that unity and effectiveness will follow. If you don't know who you are working with, it is often difficult to honor someone.

Also, differences in leadership style can create opportunities for misunderstanding. You may blindly honor your team members because you do not understand them. This should be our first position. Honoring people with understanding has a much greater impact. It places a far greater demand on the resources of heaven and will encourage and validate your team members.

CLEAN UP

Collaboration is not as easy as it may sound, depending on where people are in their maturity continuum. The apostle Paul dedicated the letter to the Philippians to resolve a relationship conflict. Peter had his rough edges and his impetuous nature caused him to step out to experience some tough learning. There will always be clean up.

The manger is clean without an ox, but there is much increase with the strength of an ox. (Prov. 14:4b)

Running with the strength of horses has a fair amount of pass through. If energy is consumed, there are byproducts. I wish the process was like fusion energy – perfectly clean. It is not. We still live in a fallen and broken world. The birthing of the Church in Acts 2 was powerful and momentous, but it was laden with conflicts, misunderstandings, fallout and error. These are components that assist us in our learning today. Make no mistake; there is a high cost and maturity needed for Collaboration. The end goal is to fulfill the Lord's unity criteria.

We do not want to be those who walk in unity for the wrong motives and have the edifices we have built dispersed like at the tower of Babel. Paul admonished those preaching the gospel for the wrong reasons in Phil. 1:15-18. He also rebuked those who peddled the gospel for profit (2 Cor. 2:17). We want our language to be unified as one voice. Psa. 133 says, "How good and pleasant it is when brothers live together in unity!... For there the Lord bestows his blessing, even life forevermore."

Unity is powerful. I love the verse from Gen. 11:6 where God said that He had to confuse their language; otherwise, if they kept walking in unity, there was nothing that they could not achieve. Being "as one," working together in the context of teams means that we could be developing an unstoppable kingdom momentum. With this, we perhaps have the potential to continue Peter's journey to walk on the water and overcome the law of gravity. I believe we are entering into a time when leaders will do the unimaginable by embracing Collaboration. Collaboration is a key that enables you to solve complex problems. As one!

A STORY ABOUT CROSSING CULTURAL BOUNDARIES IN COLLABORATION

Culture is an important and determinant factor that defines how we connect to others individually and collectively. Culture is more than ethnicity, language and nationality. It is part of what shapes us into who we are, what we like, what we do, how we do it and to whom we relate. Our families of origin, our workplace, our congregation, friends, etc., all are examples of subcultures within one's Culture.

Everything we think, feel and do has traces of our cultural makeup. One of my richest experiences as a mental health consultant and provider, was to work with a multidisciplinary healthcare team in a very well-known medical community clinic when a thing now called "integrated care" was restarting on the East Coast several years ago.

This clinical team was designed to assess and treat a chronic disease. Not everyone was happy with the integration. In the medical culture, mental health was considered "not real "medicine. That being said, you can imagine how warm and welcomed I felt. To tell you the truth, I wasn't that thrilled myself. On top of that, I shared some of the cultural aspects of the served population and had lost my youngest sister a few months earlier to the same disease this team was treating.

On the positive side, I also have multicultural knowledge of the population being served and I'm very good at what I do. I am an expert in human behavior. I took the challenge, studied the disease, and was open to learn and to let others teach me about it. God has a unique way to shape us.

After my first day at the clinic, it all made sense. We were serving a disadvantaged socio-economic population, in a non-nurturing environment, from two of the most predominant ethnic minorities, different languages, with diverse religious beliefs, identities, and levels of education, but most relevantly, these were people to whom, as I call it, "life happened." All of these factors were (in one way or another) affecting their ability to fully adhere to their treatment and maintain their "healthy numbers". Crossing those barriers was key for a successful outreach and intervention.

One day a Vietnamese male patient was there for follow-up. After receiving the best treatment ever, still his numbers were a bit off. The medical team couldn't pinpoint what was the barrier. Knowing the patient's cultural background, I chatted with the man and discovered two possible cultural barriers. The man loved his rice and coffee, which he also enjoyed multiple times a day. Both are basic nutritional components of the Vietnamese cultural diet and both affected the chronic illness of this patient adversely, when consumed beyond recommended limits.

After these findings, it was easier to tailor an intervention for the client and help him to reach his healthy numbers; something simple and overlooked due to time restrictions.

From how we take our "cup of joe" or "eat our dinner", Culture influences all we do and, when we collaborate together, it is a game changer. Collaboration cannot exist without humility, love, and honor. The healthiest way to connect or reach out to others with different cultural backgrounds than ours is to inform ourselves, to respect and honor others and what they bring to the table without losing, imposing, or compromising our own identity or beliefs. This is a key to effective collaboration.

IRIS M. RAMOS, PHD, NCTTP, CTTS-M/TRAINER
Behavioral Health Network

CASE STUDY: ORVILLE AND WILBUR WRIGHT COLLABORATE TO CHANGE AVIATION HISTORY AND PIONEER THE MODERN AVIATION INDUSTRY

It was on a Saturday afternoon on December 17, 1903, that Orville and Wilbur Wright, who were from the Midwest, changed history when they developed a flying machine that transformed aviation at Kitty Hawk in North Carolina. It was the culmination of four years worth of work conducted by two very mechanical-minded men who ran a bicycle shop and tinkered with anything and everything mechanical.

Wilbur and Orville were not very good at school. Wilbur wanted to go to Yale College to be a minister. He applied and was accepted, but he never did enroll or attend classes. In March of 1889, the brothers were newspaper publishers when they took a keen interest in bicycles. They were continuously looking for improvements in everything they put their hands to. They made a counting machine for bookkeeping, they designed and manufactured new bikes, and more. Their father gave them a helicopter that sparked their interest in aeronautics. They were self taught, autonomous adult learners who pursued their interests and passions. They pursued the development of a glider, which eventually turned into the first aircraft to use a 3-axis control system.

What was the probable cause of these two men who changed the world? The Wright Brothers' father was a minister and the two boys received Jesus as their personal Savior during their youth. Throughout their lives, they were known for their Creativity and Collaboration, even though they had significant technical debates about different solutions. Their father said that his sons were positively affected by the Bible. They maintained joy even while experiencing difficulties and hardship. When fortune came their way, they did not allow prestige and fortune to derail them.

The Wright Brothers collaborated with each other and with God. They derived their insights about aircraft flight by studying God's creation, the bird. They were able to build and invent with their Creator's Creativity to impact aviation history. They used their love for learning, intelligence, experience, and ingenuity to design their witty invention – the aircraft.

TAKEAWAYS

- Our goal is to collaborate with heaven and facilitate developing people and aligning them with heaven's intention.

- In the end, the results of Calling, Connection, Capacity, and Convergence need to pivot on the unity of the body and faith through Collaboration.

- The ecosystem of leadership intent is a broad subject and includes understanding other leaders' spheres of influence and their operating space or domain.

- Collaboration will likely require cleanup activities.

- We need to commit to see the best in others to Collaborate.

- Leverage personality profiles to understand your strength orientation, especially of your teams and organizations.

COLLABORATION – SELF-ASSESSMENT

- I see the need for people to work together to be more effective.

- I understand people, organizations, and their strengths.

- I have grown [by/from] overcoming competition and differing agendas.

- I see how pieces of the puzzle fit together.

- I embrace that humility and relationship skills are needed for Collaboration.

Rate the above on a scale from 1 to 5:

1 - strongly disagree

2 - disagree

3 - neither agree nor disagree

4 - agree

5 - strongly agree

If your score is 1-8, you have opportunity to grow in Collaboration.

If your score is 9-17, you are making progress and should continue in your forward momentum.

If your score is 18+, you have a good handle and grasp on Collaboration.

NOW ACTION

1. Pray through the following Scriptures for a month, asking the Lord to make you a collaborative force in your relationships and spheres of influence.

   Therefore I, the prisoner of the Lord, implore you to walk in a manner worthy of the calling with which you have been called, with all humility and gentleness, with patience, showing tolerance for one another in love, being diligent to preserve the unity of the Spirit in the bond of peace. There is one body and one Spirit, just as also you were called in one hope of your calling; one Lord, one faith, one baptism, one God and Father of all who is over all and through all and in all. (Eph. 4:1-6)

   And He gave some as apostles, and some as prophets, and some as evangelists, and some as pastors and teachers, for the equipping of the saints for the work of service, to the building up of the body of Christ; until we all attain to the unity of the faith, and of the knowledge of the Son of God, to a mature man, to the measure of the stature which belongs to the fullness of Christ. (Eph. 4:11-13)

PRAYER

Lord, create in me a heart that embraces Collaboration and not competition. Move my frame of reference from living in scarcity to abundance, so that with joy, I can support others to be successful. I lay down my agendas, and take on your agenda and will. In my heart, I move from me, my, and our to one body, one Spirit, one hope, one calling, one Lord, one faith, one baptism, one God and Father over all. Lord, let my life be a force to be reckoned with when it comes to unity. Let us all join hands, hearts, and minds to work together in an interlocking way that brings glory to your name. In this place nothing will be impossible for us. Amen.

NOW COACHING QUESTIONS

1. What is the most important characteristic needed to collaborate?

2. How have you collaborated with others?

3. In what ways was your experience positive or negative?

4. In what ways have you been a collaborator to advance the kingdom?

5. Where would you like to collaborate?

6. What are the benefits of Collaboration?

7. What are your next steps?

CHAPTER FOURTEEN

CREATIVITY
Solution Generation

I wisdom dwell with prudence, and find out knowledge of witty inventions. (Prov. 8:12, KJV)

We need Champions who can solve the complex problems of our society. We need solutions now and not tomorrow. If we always think that the solutions are futuristic, we may miss the opportunities of the moment. We need to tune into the now dimension to be NOW Leaders. We need spiritual communicators who can ascend the Mountain of the Lord (see Mic. 4:1-2 and Isa. 2:2-3) and receive blueprints and solutions to problems that plague, perplex, frustrate, stymie and ail our culture, nation and world. (See Dr. Bruce Cook's book, *The 8th Mountain,* for a fuller discussion of this). We need God's solutions, birthed from heaven, for today's problems.

We need to go back to the genesis of our identity to bridge the gap. The gaps are the complex problems that face our society because we have not applied our birthright and created solutions as co-creators in Christ. The fundamentals are these: Since God is our Creator and we are made in His likeness and image, then His creative DNA exists within us. Proverbs states that wisdom is integral to the creative process.

When He marked out the foundations of the earth; Then I was beside Him, as a master workman; And I was daily His delight, Rejoicing always before Him, Rejoicing in the world, His earth, And having my delight in the sons of men. (Prov. 8:29-31)

This suggests that wisdom was a creative force in the making of the universe, and wisdom was rejoicing. This word for rejoicing is also "playing" which sounds like the creation process was fun! The Scriptures exhort us to seek after wisdom more than money and riches, and that if we are lacking in it, we can freely ask in faith to receive it. Wisdom along with understanding and knowledge are spiritual resources we access. So how can we obtain these downloads? We need to plug into the source which is the Spirit of the Living God.

For who among men knows the thoughts of a man except the spirit of the man which is in him? Even so the thoughts of God no one knows except the Spirit of God. Now we have received, not the spirit of the world, but the Spirit who is from God, so that we may know the things freely given to us by God, which things we also speak, not in words taught by human wisdom, but in those taught by the Spirit, combining spiritual thoughts with spiritual words. But a natural man does not accept the things of the Spirit of God, for they are foolishness to him; and he cannot understand them, because they are spiritually appraised. (1 Cor. 2:11-14)

To engage in the "spiritual realm", one has to engage in his or her intuition. Watchman Nee writes that there are three dimensions to our spirit: conscience, fellowship, and intuition. We engage with these dimensions through Jesus who is our door and gives us rightful access through His shed blood, finished work and atoning sacrifice on the cross (John 10:1-18; 1 Cor. 1:18-31; Gal. 3:6-14, 3:26-4:7; Phil. 2:5-14, 3:7-16; Col. 1:15-23, 2:9-15, 3:1-4). Our intuition is the faculty by which we can listen to the Spirit of the Lord. This requires focused and intentional listening.

In order to be effective in this area, it is necessary to turn down the dial of internal noise, so we can get in touch with the kingdom realities. Moving into the emotional realm of Compassion is the gateway for this activity. It indicates you have dialed down your self-talk, which is primarily self-centered, and shifted to other-centered listening. The ideal state is to be positioned to listen at the intuitive level, drawing from the heavenly realm to perceive new realities and solutions. Listening and creativity are linked. It may entail sharing intuitive affirmations or an insight that helps the individual connect the dots in their life, or perhaps make a connection to solve a complicated technical problem.

Connecting the dots empowers people to see how life events, experiences, ideas, solutions and potential fit together. At this juncture of heightened self-awareness is where things often "make sense". Intuitive dialogues of this nature can translate people's perceived "chaos" into something that is meaningful to assist them in moving forward. We often call these events breakthroughs or "aha" moments where something clicks inside of us and it creates a forward momentum.

In regard to Peter, how is it that he demonstrated intuitive listening and God's creativity? I have read through Peter's epistles, and it does not appear that Peter is a super creative and relational person. He is more didactic and offers numerous contrasts and instruction. I believe Peter's creativity was exhibited when God's Spirit came upon him. That is okay. We are not all "creatives".

Peter used His Creativity on Pentecost to preach one of the world's most effective sermons at the birthing of the New Testament church. It was filled with the inspiration of our Creator and became a voice for God's solution for humanity. God poured His Spirit on all flesh and broke down the dividing walls between generations, genders and ethnicities, bringing forth a supernatural unity. We also see Peter engaging the creative force of healing through His faith when he met the beggar going to the temple in Acts 3:1-10. When we are faced with the impossible, our faith can access the Creativity of heaven to bring healing into the earth. Likewise, I believe God can give us solutions to complex problems.

THE CONTEXT OF CREATIVITY AND INNOVATION

The subject of Creativity and innovation is a vast subject. Hundreds of books have been written on the subject. The word *create* means to *"to cause to exist; bring into being"*. In the context of the business domain, Creativity is key to developing products, services, and solutions to remain competitive in the marketplace. New ideas must be transformative in some way to maintain their marketplace position. The word innovate means *"to begin or introduce something new"*.

Every creative idea which survives must go through a process to be introduced. The time between when an idea is created versus the time to introduce the idea in reality can take a few days or weeks, a few months or years, or even centuries. Leonardo Da Vinci's flying machine concept did not materialize until a half millennium (500 years) later. The creative and the innovative processes require both an open mind and also discipline and perseverance to create outcomes that bring improvement.

THE ACCELERATION OF CREATIVITY TO INNOVATE

As the time between the creative and the innovative becomes smaller, we see divine acceleration taking place. When a "word" is spoken, then "manifestation" takes place, which is an accelerated creative process superseding the laws of nature or business. There is power in the authority of God's written (logos) word and His spoken (rhema) word by the Spirit.

Taking this concept into the realm of personal transformation, concepts or ideas spoken from the heart of the Father, have the potential to accelerate transformation if they are applied and embraced. These powerful thoughts have been coined as *intuitive* thoughts.

The word *intuition* means "direct perception of truth, fact, etc., independent of any reasoning process; immediate apprehension." Intuitive thinking inspired by the Spirit of Truth, has the potential to transform people's lives in powerful ways. Truth when applied produces new space for growth and freedom. In the context of a coaching relationship, truth is communicated through feedback and meaningful dialogue.

Feedback can be based on observed behaviors and it can also be intuitive in nature, reducing the space of the unknown areas in the Johari Window. We can call forth those things as though they are not and speak to the God-given potential in our lives. Talking with your peers about a project or problem and getting feedback may spark your curiosity, create connections, and reframe the problem.

Thus, when we engage in intuitive conversations that tap into the testimony of Jesus, we are engaging in the creative process that can bring about change in people's lives, thereby creating the necessary relational space for transformation to take place. It closes the gap between what is in heaven and what is on earth based on the prayer, *"Your kingdom come, your will be done, on earth as it is in heaven"* (Matt. 6:10). Intuitive dialogue minimizes the time between the introduction of the idea and its outcome, thus accelerating the release of a solution or a transformative idea.

THE CREATIVE PROCESS

Creativity is about seeing things differently. It is seeing things that other people don't see. The two primary stages of creative thinking include incubation and illumination.[1] The incubation period requires the definition of the challenge, framing the right questions. At some point during the incubation, the individual or group may experience frustration and anxiety. Experiencing frustration is a common characteristic of people who have demonstrated creative thinking.

At this point, when progress is minimal, it is easy to fall prey to black and white thinking. The best breakthrough in our thinking often comes when one perseveres in divergent views and positions. This tension creates new neural networks thinking. Embracing ideas from other disciplines to develop new associations can also be constructive.

Experts agree that putting on the mind of a child can add to developing new thinking. Healthy children have a high level of inquiry and are uninhibited by the constraints of value judgments and assumptions. The Bible has numerous juxtapositions and mysteries that cannot be explained, but only embraced in tension and faith.

During this process, challenging assumptions is important to properly frame the problem. At some point the connections begin to take place. This phase is also coined "flow," and then we enter into the next phase.[2]

In the illumination phase, the pieces of the puzzle come together and Creativity flows in Convergence. The breakthrough realization takes place and the light bulb goes on. The preparation time is essential. The greater the problem, the more energy and effort must be invested in the solution. People who are creative have a certain tenacity to keep at it until they achieve their goal. When the ideas begin to flow, there is a sorting and filtering that then takes place to refine the solutions.

Not every idea will prove to be successful or commercially viable, for a variety of reasons. Some inventors and creatives lack access to capital, teams, attorneys, engineers, branding, marketing, distribution, and other necessary resources such as strategic partners and licensing agreements. This is often an expensive and lengthy process, and sometimes an idea or invention can become obsolete by the time it is brought to market. Surprisingly, it is estimated by credible industry sources that 97% of all patents issued never make money.

The final stages of the creative act occur when it is translated into action, which is the act of innovation, followed by commercialization, which is monetizing the new service, product or process. The failure in translation between these two stages is the most common reason that some ideas or inventions are not viable, cost-effective, commercializable, or profitable. We need to persist through the creative process to the end product!

There is a growing trend by inventors, technologists and corporations to create and apply for not just one patent for an innovation or process, but an entire patent portfolio, which becomes far more valuable as intellectual property assets, and a formidable barrier to entry for other competitors. Qualcomm Incorporated in San Diego is one such example. They earn billions of dollars annually from licensing fees generated through their licensing business, QTL, which administers their vast portfolio of technology-related patents.

OVERCOMING THE VOICE OF JUDGEMENT

The process of Creativity is often stymied long before the opportunity can become a reality. Daniel Goleman in his book, *The Creative Spirit*, indicates that the voice of judgment is the primary inhibitor of creative thinking. Through the use of practicing powerful affirmations, we can learn how to squelch prohibitive self-talk. Some common excuses to engaging in Creativity are due to thinking that it is dependent on your age and intelligence. Statements such as "Only young people are creative", or "You need to have a high IQ to be creative", often squelch the flow of ideas.

Some people have an innate ability to be creative and Creativity also can be a learned skill. There are three foundational ingredients to Creativity: 1) expertise and skill mastery in an area of interest, 2) developing creative thinking skills, and 3) a passion or intrinsic motivation that is compelling and curiosity-driven to make up missing raw talent.[3] It is your attitude and approach which is likely to determine if you can engage your creative faculties more than your talent, intelligence, or age.

Einstein was able to develop his theory of relativity by changing his point of view. He positioned his thinking to being a light particle in space to develop his theory of relativity rather than applying the more traditional methods of learning through verbal and algebraic mediums. The hook-loop fastener was invented in 1941 by George Mestral, a Swiss engineer. He received the idea from the Burdock seeds which kept sticking to his clothes after daily walks in the Alps.

He connected the possibility from nature to the world of mechanical fasteners. He developed the hook and loop fastener and submitted his idea for the patent application process in 1951, which is now known as "Velcro". Translating ideas from one domain to another is a powerful method for invention. This can happen in the natural as well as in the spiritual domains.

Creative thinking is a process that takes time. The incubation period can vary based on the size of the opportunity. Developing healthy Communication and communion skills is critical to success. As a part of the Communication process, creating different journals with regards to the creative process is helpful. It also could provide assistance if there are any questions about intellectual property from a legal perspective.

Having a journal for your far-fetched ideas, one for the ideas you are processing and filtering, and another for the ideas you are innovating, is a good idea. Providing a medium for expressing the process and ideas will assist in the formation and maturing of creative ideas translated into realities.

CREATIVITY CAN BE DEVELOPED

Creativity is not limited by your emotional and cognitive intelligence. Creativity is a skill that can be developed. There are certain ways of thinking that can cultivate creative thinking, such as embracing divergent thinking techniques, changing your point of perspective, and using principles and concepts from other disciplines to expand your thinking. Holding opposing ideas in your thinking that are polarized, will pave the way to new networks of thoughts.

Apostolic and prophetic ministry often comes from two different perspectives. The two domains of thought are different but not in conflict. When held in the proper context and construct of thought, they become a very constructive force. One strategizes and plans and the other carries vision, inspires and encourages others to build with the dual goal of creating unified, coherent solutions and teams with foundational strength.

Creativity is a skill that can be learned. It is a skill that can be fostered in the context of coaching relationships. It is not dependent only on your "intelligence" as much as your affinity and persistence. George Washington Carver, a struggling botanist and agronomist in the post Civil War South, asked God for the secrets of the universe and God responded, "Let's start with the peanut." Carver went on to discover and help commercialize some 300 products and processes made from the peanut and sweet potato.

When Creativity is employed in the world of complex problems we live in, there is the potential to experience new solutions. When we engage the intuitive dimension of our Creativity, we can experience new solutions that can generate breakthrough. By tapping into the intuitive realm, we access the kingdom or supernatural realm which is filled with an abundance of resource and opportunity. The goal of engaging Creativity and intuitive processes is to accelerate the transformation process and find solutions.

CASE STUDY: MICHAEL FARADAY

A great example of a person using their knowledge in a creative way was Michael Faraday (1791-1867), a scientist. He also became known as a great communicator. He diligently pursued his faith and did not find it in conflict with science. The book of the world was not in conflict with the book of God's word. He knew there was a deeper order of nature through the Creator. He was self taught and was considered an outsider because of it. In spite of this, his major discoveries included electromagnetic induction, which is the principle behind electric transformers and power generation.

The world of electricity exists because of this man's contributions. He was not only a nationally-renowned scientist, but was also an elder in his local church and demonstrated compassion by supporting the neighboring poor and would visit the sick. Later he became a gifted communicator and held public lectures, thereby increasing the public's understanding of new scientific discoveries. Albert Einstein said of Faraday's scientific discoveries that: "He had made the greatest change in our conception of reality." *(Source: Wikipedia)*

"A CREATOR INHERENTLY POSSESSES PROPRIETORSHIP"

Since Creativity falls into the realm of the Creator, the very act of creating bears His DNA. In the 40 years I spent "paying my dues," I have observed that the act of inspired creating manifests itself with five markers, no matter what is being created and by whom. One of those markers has to do with the concept of proprietorship.

When a woman has a baby, that child is hers. It has gestated inside of her for nine months and a deep emotional bond forms between her and the baby. The same emotional connection takes place between one who births an idea and the idea itself.

Just as a woman does not typically give birth and turn the child over to someone else to raise – unless there is an adoption or surrogate contract in place – a creator should not be removed from that which he or she creates.

Recently I was asked to consult with a businessman, Ted (not his real name), who partnered in a new venture with a colleague. Ted could not wait to tell me how he was communicating the company's ideas to conference attendees. I listened as he explained each mnemonic acronym he had devised to lay out the corporate thrust. He became more animated describing each section. I knew instantly that he had already formed a *creative's* umbilical cord of proprietorship with the training material. This material was *his* baby!

I asked, "Ted, are you the one responsible for creating the instructional materials for the new organization? Do you have this in writing? Or, do each of the partners have the freedom to develop his own materials and let the company market everything for its people?" Silence.

I could tell by his non-response that this matter had never come up between Ted and his partner. I knew this was a delicate period in the development of this fledgling organization. I have seen many entities crash and burn because such matters as who does what, who gets credit, and who gets compensated for what are not memorialized in the beginning, especially among the best of friends!

Introducing the principle of proprietorship, I said, "Ted, you feel that this is your material…no one else's. And you are highly motivated about putting it all together and don't want anyone else messing with it, right?" "Yes," he sheepishly admitted. "In fact, something just happened that upset me and I don't know what to do about it." He then related that when he showed the material to his partner Frank (not his real name), Frank immediately began to change it, saying, 'This will make it better." That's when Ted's sense of proprietorship became threatened.

I advised Ted that what needs to happen in his partnership with Frank is a memorandum of understanding spelling out how they will address the training materials for the organization: Would each of them have the freedom to create his own and market it through the organization, with the entity receiving a percentage of sales? Or, is it Ted's job to do all the creating of the training materials? If so, then how is he to be compensated? Always have matters like this in writing when it comes to creating anything. Frank needs to understand that Ted's creation is his. He does not have the right to change anything unless that permission has been granted.

One solution is letting the organization be the entity that offers all training materials for sale, whoever writes them. The bulk of the sale goes to whoever expended the time and money to create them, with a percentage going to the parent organization to cover distribution costs. That corporate percentage should be commensurate with what it invests into the project. If it pays for all the printing and marketing of the materials, their percentage should reflect these costs but the copyright remains with the one who develops the idea.

Corporate Application: One of the biggest mistakes companies make is a written or unwritten policy that says whatever an employee creates is considered a "work for hire." The thinking is that since the person is on the job and receives a salary, whatever he creates belongs to the company. Nothing will destroy creativity and innovation any more than a policy like this. A creator should always be compensated in some way.

CANDACE L. LONG
Founder and President, Creativity Training Institute, Inc., Jasper, Georgia

"CREATIVITY ABUSE: TAKE CREDIT FOR SOMETHING THAT DID NOT ORIGINATE WITH YOU"

A true creator of something is very different from a "poser" – someone who appears to lie in wait for some brilliance to fall out of the mind or mouth of a true thought leader. I cannot count the times I have said or written something only to find someone close to me has taken that same thing and pretended to be its originator. In my opinion, such practices are not only disheartening; they are morally questionable.

Not long ago I was teaching a workshop on creativity and mentioned the title of one of my songs that was getting traction in the music industry. Suddenly, one of the participants got "inspired," took a line from the song and wrote a poem based on that line and proudly read it to everyone during the Q & A that followed. She couldn't wait to share her "creation!" The problem, however, was that her idea was taken from the original song belonging to me!

Many court cases have resulted from just this kind of unprofessional behavior. While it is true that no one can copyright an idea – for the tangible expression of that idea is what is copyrightable – in my mind, such work as her poem was still stealing. She took something that belonged to me and passed this new creation off as her own.

For my fellow *creatives*, please understand that whenever you are in a creative environment where ideas and concepts flow freely, there is a creatively charged atmosphere where ideas abound. Such an experience as the poem from a song can happen quite innocently, but I need to provide warning and instruction.

Being a conceptual, I know how long it takes to articulate ideas. It involves blazing a linguistic trail that has never before been charted. Thus, there is nothing more debilitating than to have worked months on something only to have someone steal part of it, write a whole other thing and beat you to the market.

Some might say, "Tough! That's just the way the world works. There are winners and losers. You just lucked out!"

Remember, true creativity is a *divine* act. God gave that idea TO that *creative* for HER to steward. Yes, it's true: you can likely steal something that originated with someone else and make a killing with it. Chances are, you might even get away with it. But, at what price to your soul?

Some years ago I was developing a multimedia product line and was particularly taken with musical sections from another composer's album. I envisioned taking certain passages from different songs and editing them together and adding a dramatic reading, thereby creating a new derivative work.

Legally, I did not have the right to do anything to his music. However, the law does allow for derivative works based on original work. I took the time and effort to contact the composer, explained what I wished to do and asked permission to create this new piece. I enclosed a copy of the new music based on his work, offered to give credit to him as well as pay him a licensing fee. He granted me that right and signed my licensing contract spelling out the terms.

When I subsequently copyrighted my piece, I registered it with the Library of Congress, put my name as the creator of this derivative piece and named him as composer of the original pieces of music from which the new work derived.

Whenever you create something for which you expect to be paid, ask yourself if you have the legal right to everything involved in that creation. If you do not, take the time and expense to seek legal help and obtain the proper licensing.

The Giver of ideas is always testing us to see how we handle the temptation to take something that did not originate with us. Scripture is very clear that we will one day give account for everything we have done, especially at another's expense.

Personal and Corporate Application: Be very careful what you portray as originating with you without giving credit or seeking permission from the originator. A true creator of something should register that copyright before going public with it. If you create something new based on someone else's expressed idea, that new work is called a "derivative work" and needs to be properly handled.

CANDACE L. LONG

Note: Candace L. Long is one of today's thought leaders on inspired creativity. Founder of Georgia-based Creativity Training Institute™. She is a 40-year veteran of the Arts & Entertainment sectors as well as a 40-year business consultant with an MBA. This excerpt is taken from her book, *The Ancient Path to Creativity and Innovation: Where Left and Right Brains Meet,* and is used by permission.

A STORY ABOUT OVERCOMING NEGATIVE SELF-TALK TO ACTIVATE CREATIVITY

When I grew up as a child, my parents were immigrants from Europe as a result of the post World War II conflict. English was their second language. I believe because people were not very receptive to their coming to the U.S. and because there was a language barrier, they often felt self-conscious about their communications. I somehow tuned into this as a child and thought that I was inferior. When I was five years old as a first grader, I exhibited some mild dyslexia. Not knowing what this was, I developed an attitude about myself that I was stupid. This cloud of darkness followed me through my entire education including college.

As you could imagine, these thoughts hindered me in many ways including my desire to step out and be creative. I often would not jump at opportunities at work because I thought people were always smarter than me. Then I started hanging around with some people who started to affirm me and call out some of my strengths. They started giving me positive feedback.

Over several years, I began to realize that perhaps I was the exact opposite of stupid and was actually intelligent. Creativity began to spring up and I found myself in conversations giving people book titles, branding ideas, and creating imaginative strategic plans and ideas. Through the exercise of my latent talent within, I realized that I am actually a co-creator, craftsman, and creator. Breaking the negative self-talk script opened the doors to a world of Creativity that I would have never known.

Although my dyslexia was minor, it did have a negative impact for a time. I later found out that there were numerous successful leaders who suffered from varying degrees of dyslexia. A few examples include Richard Branson – Virgin CEO, Real Estate mogul Barbara Corcoran, John Chambers – Cisco CEO, Charles Schwab – business icon, and Paul Orfalea, who was the founder of Kinkos. For many, learning how to overcome disabilities creates tracks of thinking, empowering you to overcome setbacks and negative circumstances.

TAKEAWAYS

- Creativity is an extension of Communication and communion.

- Creativity is not solely dependent on your intelligence but also your affinity and persistence and intuitiveness.

- Creativity is a skill that you can develop.

- Creativity can be accessed by faith through the Holy Spirit connecting with your Creator.

- Creativity is essential for NOW Leaders to solve our society's complex problems.

- Managing your self-talk and tuning into your intuitive thinking are keys to Creativity and innovation.

CREATIVITY – SELF-ASSESSMENT

- Do you spend time communing with God?

- Do you have positive self-talk?

- Do you nurture and respond to your intuition?

- Are you able to embrace two differing ideas at the same time?

- Do you find yourself following your curiosity?

Rate the above on a scale from 1 to 5:

       1 - strongly disagree

       2 - disagree

       3 - neither agree nor disagree

       4 - agree

       5 - strongly agree

If your score is 1-8, you have opportunity to grow in Creativity.

If your score is 9-17, you are making progress and should continue in your forward momentum.

If your score is 18+, you have a good handle and grasp on being creative.

NOW ACTION

1. Make a list of accomplishments in your life. Reflect on those accomplishments and determine if you solved any problems. If so, how did you employ Creativity?

2. If you don't think you are creative, make a list of the deterrents to being creative. Discuss them with a friend and figure ways to change or work around them together. Become accountability partners to foster greater Creativity in your lives.

3. Pray into the following Scripture and ask the Lord to give you a spirit of wisdom, understanding, and knowledge to grow in your craft and Creativity.

   "See, I have called by name Bezalel, the son of Uri, the son of Hur, of the tribe of Judah. I have filled him with the Spirit of God in wisdom, in understanding, in knowledge, and in all kinds of craftsmanship, to make artistic designs for work in gold, in silver, and in bronze," (Exo. 31:2-4)

PRAYER:

Lord, open up the gates of Creativity in our lives. We ask you to give us a spirit of wisdom, understanding and knowledge just like you gave Bezalel who was a master craftsman who built the tabernacle of Moses. Give us insight and understanding and the knowledge necessary to solve complex problems. Bring teams and partners together in an interlocking way to bring about robust solutions that will transform our Culture and global landscape.

NOW COACHING QUESTIONS

1. In what ways do you consider yourself creative?

2. In what ways were you creative as a child?

3. When did you see your Creativity strengthen or wane?

4. What do you think brought about this change?

5. In what ways could you become more curious and light-hearted?

6. What kind of problems do you typically solve?

7. What really bugs you and makes you think about how things would be a better place if this problem were solved?

8. Describe what your self-talk is like?

9. What actions could you take to develop the skill of being more creative?

10. What are your next steps?

———————————————————→

ENDNOTES

1. https://www.inc.com/jessica-stillman/the-4-stages-of-creativity.html.

2. Csikszentmihalyi, Mhaly, *Creativity: Flow and the Psychology of Discovery and Invention,* Harper Collins Publishing, New York, New York, 1996.

3. https://www.skipprichard.com/3-forces-of-intrinsic-motivation/.

CHAPTER FIFTEEN

COMMUNICATION
A Tree of Life

Death and life are in the power of the tongue, and those who love it will eat its fruits. (Prov. 18:21)

The quality of your Communication determines the quality of your life! What do I mean exactly by that? Well, apart from meeting our basic survival needs for food, shelter, and water, the way we interact and relate to others will be a significant determinant of the quality of life we lead. Are your relationships healthy, loving, filled with kindness, humor, honor and joy? Or, are your relationships full of argument, strife, tension, fear, hostility, and combativeness?

Based on my own experience, when my circle of relationships are filled with strife and conflict, all my energy is focused on resolving those issues because they drain me and drag me down. As I have altered my behavior and chosen alternatives, my loci of energy changes toward more positive outcomes with less stress and increased productivity.

Communication is one of the necessary Competencies required for success. It is significant enough that we will dedicate one of the 12C's to this topic. By definition, it is "the imparting or exchanging of information". If you have it mastered, things will go well with you, and you may never hear a compliment about your mastery. No news is good news. But, if you lack critical Communication skills, it may stymie your relationships, career and leadership trajectory. Most people are not familiar with their blind spots that sabotage their Communication effectiveness.

Communication is a complex process that is influenced by many variables. Our worldview, values, life experience, personality, identity, self-confidence, self-esteem, education, intelligence, health, mind, heart, lenses and filters play an important role in how we communicate. There are fundamentals to Communication that play a key role in how effective we are. They include listening, self-disclosure, expression, body language, meta messages, hidden agendas, and gender and culture. All of these items converge in the Communication process and must be sorted out and understood to grow in your effectiveness.

GOING DEEPER RELATIONALLY – THE COMMUNION CONNECTION

There is a deeper level of Communication that we call communion which is sharing or exchanging of intimate thoughts and feelings, especially when the exchange is on an emotional or spiritual level. The quality of our Communication will determine the quality of our communion with God and with others that we love and care about. We are social beings that need people. We need to share our lives with others in the context of family and community, as well as in our relationship with the Lord.

Psalm 1 speaks about how, when we choose to be different and rise above the negative influences in our lives and dig deeper roots, greater stability and fruitfulness will result. Those who meditate on God's word are managing their inner life, and will develop a reservoir of treasures to draw upon.

Blessed is the one who does not walk in step with the wicked or stand in the way that sinners take or sit in the company of mockers, but whose delight is in the law of the Lord, and who meditates on his law day and night. That person is like a tree planted by streams of water, which yields its fruit in season and whose leaf does not wither— whatever they do prospers. (Psa. 1:1-3)

Trees represent strength, stability, and fruitfulness. In Isaiah 61, those who have gone through the healing process with the Lord are called oaks of righteousness. I believe these trees refer to leaders. If a leader does not pay attention to their internal Communication skills, they will not be able to stand strong and tall in the day when conflicts and adversity arise. Champions of the faith who are prospering in their spirit will walk in some dimension of Communication excellence.

Communication is a complex process. It is fraught with opportunity to fail, as much as potential to bring about transformation. Jesus gives us insight into Communication. It is not just the exchange of information but has a substance associated with it. The Bible teaches that our hearts are the reservoir of thoughts and intentions which impacts our Communication (Heb. 4:12). Our minds generate the thoughts, but our hearts communicate a substance as well.

The good person out of the good treasure of the heart produces good, and the evil person out of evil treasure produces evil; for it is out of the abundance of the heart that the mouth speaks. (Luke 6:45)

Watch over your heart with all diligence, For from it flow the springs of life. (Prov. 4:23)

We not only exchange information but we also can "impart" from this reservoir. What we fill our treasury with will ultimately leak out of the language we use. As we mature and advance in leadership, our words become more and more important. God holds leaders to higher standards of accountability. Moses in Exodus 20:8-9, struck the rock rather than speaking to it as the Lord commanded him. Moses misrepresented God in his Communication. God was not angry with God's people; Moses was. It cost Moses the Promised Land.

Our words can either create, encourage, strengthen, build vision, and open up doors to destiny or delay, dismay, disillusion, disparagement, and discouragement, and possibly destroy new opportunities. Our words carry energy. Our focus and what we have invested in, will determine what we impart. If we are connected and intimate with Jesus, our words will carry the dew from heaven, and our words will be like honey to those who hear them.

THE POWER OF LISTENING

But everyone must be quick to hear, slow to speak and slow to anger.
(Jas. 2:19)

Listening is a key component to effecting Communication. If you cannot listen effectively, you may find yourself missing the mark and making a lot of mistakes. Being quick to listen will avert releasing words out of regret. When my wife and I were newlyweds, somehow we stumbled upon a practice, which I believe saved our marriage from many troubles and reduced the opportunities we would need to forgive one another.

One day while talking with my wife, I had this thought. When I was in grammar school, our principal would put out the "no talking" sign during our lunch period. All of the students needed to stop talking and finish their lunches. We decided that if we began to hurt one another's feelings either of us could put up the "no talking" sign. After 27 years of marriage, we still put up the sign if we are not thinking about what we are saying. It gives us time to think, to slow down, and to realize the impact our words have.

Perhaps the greatest attribute one can process is self-control regarding what you speak. You can measure a people by where they spend and invest their money, and you can do likewise based on observing their conversations.

If anyone thinks himself to be religious, and yet does not bridle his tongue but deceives his own heart, this man's religion is worthless. (Jas. 1:26)

Peter had quite a few communications mishaps in his career as an apostle. Perhaps he could have been slower to speak. Here is a list of some of them.

- He insisted that he would not deny the Lord.

- He denied Jesus three times.

- He was rebuked by Jesus for opposing God's will after receiving a revelation of the Son of God.

- He wanted to make a tabernacle during Jesus' Transfiguration – the wrong agenda.

- He got caught and corrected by Paul pulling back from associating with Gentiles in Antioch because he was trying to please Jewish brethren sent from James – works versus faith.

Peter, on the other hand, did a stellar job preaching it out of the park and listened to the Holy Spirit during the birthing of the New Testament church on the day of Pentecost and beyond.

A great factor that impacts our ability to communicate is the condition of our heart. In the Parable of the Sower there are four heart conditions that have varying degrees of results.

- If you are heart is hardened– new ideas will not stick.

- If you are shallow of heart – ideas may take root, but without depth, they cannot survive, thrive or progress when difficulty comes.

- If your heart is fertile for growth, you have to tend that garden and not allow cares and the deceit of riches to creep in, because if left untended, they will eventually choke out the fruit.

- And lastly, if your heart has good soil and is well tended, you can experience 3000%, 6000% and 10,000% growth factors.

From an agricultural standpoint, those are crazy growth factors for the farming technology used 2000 years ago. The most profound element of this parable lies in Jesus' last statement.

Take care what you listen to. By your standard of measure it will be measured to you; and more will be given you besides. (Mark 4:24)

The passage from Zechariah below connects Compassion and listening and is a great reminder and summary.

"Thus has the Lord of hosts said, 'Dispense true justice and practice kindness and compassion each to his brother; and do not oppress the widow or the orphan, the stranger or the poor; and do not devise evil in your hearts against one another.' But they refused to pay attention and turned a stubborn shoulder and stopped their ears from hearing. (Zech. 7:9-11)

IF YOU WANT TO INFLUENCE PEOPLE, THERE NEEDS TO BE A PROPER ALIGNMENT INTERNALLY WITH THE RIGHT CONNECTION!

Effective Communication flows out of how well you listen and what you do with what you hear. If your heart is in the right place with pure intentions, you are in a better place. As we progress through the NOW Leadership process, effective Communication is essential as a Catalyst. If you want to influence people, there needs to be proper alignment internally with the right Connection!

BECOME AN AUTHENTIC CONVERSATIONALIST

Real listening is about truly understanding the person or audience. We can either be other-centered and be empathic, or we can be self-centered in how we talk. Remember, our focus will ultimately determine the fruit or outcome. If we are God- and other-centered, we will have opened our radar dish to picking up the critical data for effective Communication. If we are self-centered and autobiographical, we will shut down or block the conversations very quickly.

Here are some things we tend to do that may hinder our conversations:

- Making people think you are interested but you are not.

- Listening for specifics and ignoring other information.

- Buying time to create your next comment.

- Half listening so someone will listen to you.

- Listening to find vulnerabilities to take advantage of and exploit.

- Looking for weak points so you can always be right.

- Checking for reactions so you can produce the desired result.

- Half listening because you can't get away and you don't want to offend them.

On the other hand, here are some suggestions that will improve your conversations by moving you to a higher dimension of active listening and participation:

- Maintain good eye contact.

- Lean slightly forward to demonstrate interest.

- Reinforce the speaker by nodding or paraphrasing at appropriate intervals.

- Clarify by asking questions until you understand.

- Share how you feel in a non-judgmental way.

- Be open without judging or finding fault.

- Be aware of what is really being said and what is not being said.

- Note what is being said through body language.

- Actively move away from distractions.

- Put your cell phone away.

If you really want to have a meaningful conversation, here are some things I do not recommend and strongly advise against doing:

- Evaluating: comparing yourself to others

- Mind reading: doesn't trust the person and is trying find out what they are really thinking

- Rehearsing: preparation and crafting your statement

- Filtering: selective listening

- Judging: negative labels

- Dreaming: private associations

- Identifying: always referring back to your experiences

- Derailing: changing the subject

- Projecting: inability to receive correction and needing to verbally attack or accuse or criticize the person providing correction

- Denying: refusing to take responsibility or ownership for your thoughts, words and actions

- Lying: telling a falsehood and speaking things not true

- Gossiping: speaking critically about others, tale-bearing

- Slandering: character assassination and personal attacks which are damaging, derogatory, denigrating or defaming in nature

- Violating Confidence: sharing secrets of others or facts or information pledged or labeled or marked as confidential or sensitive

OUR COMMUNICATION SPECIALIST

The above recommendations are areas we can all grow in. Effective Communication begins with growing in self-awareness about who you are. It takes courageous leaders to request feedback regardless of if it is positive or constructive for growth.

If you are a believer in Christ, you do have a powerful strategic advantage to develop your Communication skills. The Holy Spirit is described in the book of John as the following:

I will ask the Father, and He will give you another Helper, that He may be with you forever; that is the Spirit of truth, whom the world cannot receive, because it does not see Him or know Him, but you know Him because He abides with you and will be in you. (John 14:16-18)

But the Helper, the Holy Spirit, whom the Father will send in My name, He will teach you all things, and bring to your remembrance all that I said to you. (John 14:26)

The Holy Spirit is your Helper, and can teach you how to become a good communicator. If you forget and fall into old habits, He is there to remind you and prompt you to be aware, listen, share with clarity and good intent. We have at our disposal the God of eternity to assist us in the Communication process. The measure with which we listen and attend to this in our lives, will determine the levels of growth we will experience.

GAINING ALIGNMENT THROUGH CORRECTION

In an ideal world of spiritually-realized covenant, God writes His laws upon our hearts and minds, and the Holy Spirit would be our unequivocal teacher (Heb. 10:16; 1 John 2:27). Everyone would be in alignment with the Father's purposes and we would be collaborating and walking in unity fulfilling the Great Commission and our assignments. Unfortunately, there is some chaos that is introduced into the spiritual ecosystem that requires course corrections throughout our spiritual journey.

In an ideal community embracing the Culture of honor where authenticity, transparency, and the love of the truth are embraced, we might not need those course adjustments. James provided us with a voluntary solution to eliminate the need for Correction: *"Therefore, confess your sins to one another, and pray for one another so that you may be healed. The effective prayer of a righteous man can accomplish much."* (Jas. 5:16)

If everyone took responsibility for their stuff, we would likely not have to provide Correction. Imagine if we were not fault finders, but fault healers by asking for help through prayer so that we would get healed. If this were a normal part of the Culture of honor, the need for Correction would be reduced. If we are also speaking the truth in love with one another, it provides mirrors for our brothers and sisters.

The Hebrew word for Correction signifies "to instruct" and is very closely connected to word *pedagogy* which is the method and practice of teaching children. In some translations, this is translated as chastisement. The English use of the word implies there is the infliction of pain with some form of punishment. I agree with the Hebrew mind thought about the words that there is no difference between Correction, discipline and instruction. They are intertwined.

All Scripture is inspired by God and profitable for teaching, for reproof, for correction, for training in righteousness; so that the man of God may be adequate, equipped for every good work. (2 Tim 3:15-17)

Scripture is intended to bring Godly alignment into our lives so that we may be adequate and equipped for every good work. Those adjustments come through people, not just by reading the Bible. We do not want to be those who cannot accept the adjustments necessary for us to stay on track and end well. Jeremiah was one who warned God's people.

You shall say to them, "This is the nation that did not obey the voice of the Lord their God or accept correction; truth has perished and has been cut off from their mouth." (Jer. 7:28)

In order for God's government to be realized in the earth, I believe that there must be relationships established in the context of family, both natural and spiritual.

"If your brother sins, go and show him his fault in private; if he listens to you, you have won your brother. But if he does not listen to you, take one or two more with you, so that by the mouth of two or three witnesses every fact may be confirmed. If he refuses to listen to them, tell it to the church; and if he refuses to listen even to the church, let him be to you as a Gentile and a tax collector. Truly I say to you, whatever you bind on earth shall have been bound in heaven; and whatever you loose on earth shall have been loosed in heaven. Again I say to you, that if two of you agree on earth about anything that they may ask, it shall be done for them by My Father who is in heaven. For where two or three have gathered together in My name, I am there in their midst." (Matt. 18:15-20)

WE CANNOT HAVE TRUE SPIRITUAL AUTHORITY WITHOUT BEING IN PROPER RELATIONSHIP WITH EACH OTHER.

We cannot have true spiritual authority without being in proper relationship with each other. There is a governmental responsibility to address the issue of "sin." This comes in the form of Correction. We may need to assist one another in getting properly aligned. Remember that the definition of sin is not only missing the mark but missing the full scope and potential of your life in God. If our brother or sister is not entering into God's plan and is doing something that is harmful, then we need to address it.

Ideally, it would happen in a one on one interaction; if not, then with two or three people as a witness. If that does not work, then the issue needs to be addressed in the larger community. A few such issues are adultery, rebellion, violence, gossip and division. Communities must communicate and address those things that would wound or damage them. In addition, we may have blind spots we need to address. This may necessitate Correction.

As parents, my wife and I struggled to find a model to look to in disciplining our children. Donna read many books on parenting. She found the secular books to be too lenient, and the Christian books to be too legalistic. Then she read *Shepherding a Child's Heart,* by Tedd Tripp. Tripp calls the parents to focus on the heart issues behind behaviors. He reminds us that well-behaved children whose hearts have not been engaged to put their hope in God might just be little Pharisees. Our modifications to behavior create a temporary solution to social or moral problems.

Tripp encourages parents to look beyond rules and discipline to richer and more extensive forms of Communication, such as encouragement, Correction, rebuke, entreaty, instruction, warning, teaching, and prayer. And, we must never underestimate the power of listening. Applying those coaching skills to ask questions and use intuitive listening skills are invaluable tools.

When inappropriate or disobedient behaviors come from deep fears or deep wounds, no amount of correction will overcome that behavior. We must listen and ask questions to know what is going on in the person's heart. Until the heart can be brought to a place of healing and trust in Jesus, the inappropriate behaviors will continue.

The goal of instruction is transformation that leads to new behaviors. Superficial changes are not sustainable. We need to get to the root(s) and not just trim the branches or treat the symptoms.

HOW TO ADMINISTER CORRECTION

Here are some suggestions to the one administering the instruction. Some attributes include being kind, gentle, able to teach, patient when being wronged, and not quarrelsome.

> *The Lord's bond-servant must not be quarrelsome, but be kind to all, able to teach, patient when wronged, with gentleness correcting those who are in opposition, if perhaps God may grant them repentance leading to the knowledge of the truth, and they may come to their senses and escape from the snare of the devil, having been held captive by him to do his will.* (2 Tim. 2:24-26)

Here is another translation:

- Don't argue with people.

- Treat others the way you want to be treated – have compassion.

- Be poised to instruct gently and not preach or get on a soap box.

- Understand that people may fight back and hurt you.

Some additional suggestions:

- Collect the facts.

- Look for patterns.

- Interview others to ensure your perspective is accurate.

- Don't gossip and speak negatively to others. Keep the Communication clear and clean.

- Get the Father's heart for the person – see them with God's eyes.

- Ask powerful questions.

- Engage intuitive listening – listen to what is said and not said.

- Believe in the person you are speaking with.

The goal of Correction is to be aligned with the goals and objectives of those above you so that you prosper. Getting feedback for performance is much easier than working in the spiritual dimension. In the spiritual domain, it is more complicated and takes greater levels of sensitivity, intuition, and insight. You will need to pray into the situation and ask for the Lord's heart. Collect the facts to establish patterns. Be sensitive that there may be a timing associated with giving Correction.

DISCOVERING BLIND SPOTS

There may be times when we need Correction, especially if we have a blind spot or an area where we have hardened our hearts. It happens to the best of us. This is why I love the vintage Johari Window (see Chapter Two). Sometimes we don't know what we don't know, and we need others to be our mirrors and the working of the Spirit of Truth to reveal the Truth to us. As you advance to higher and higher levels of leadership, the air gets thinner and the information flow gets filtered. You are often shielded from important information.

Those blind spots will require well-meaning people who have our best interests in mind to communicate to you with Compassion and Creativity. Look for opportunities to receive feedback proactively. Don't wait until you have the conflict. I know some couples that go to counseling before they have a problem, rather than waiting until their relationship is in the mud.

Jesus exhorted us to make sure that we have listening ears. He told us to be careful how we hear. The measure we listen will determine the measure of our success. He told us to have ears that hear – not eyes that see or noses that smell, or mouths that can taste. The faculty of hearing is more critical than any other when it comes to being good communicators. When we fail to hear for whatever reason – a block, hardness of heart, stubbornness, self protection, wounds, or brainwashing – the heat is typically turned up to get our attention.

When those words and correction bring alignment to the innermost part of your being, you will have healthy foundations to live and lead your people (Prov. 20:30, 27:6). Note: *We are NOT teaching or suggesting any kind of mental, spiritual, physical or emotional abuse here in any way, shape or form.* Embrace the Correction because it is a tool and force that can save you much pain and loss. It is your friend even though it comes disguised sometimes.

Position yourself with people who are not afraid to tell you the truth. I suggest you have at least three to six people around you to tell you the truth. It is healthy to have more than one source or reference. Favor and respect will flow in those relationships where people are transparent and honest.

> *He who rebukes a man will afterward find more favor than he who flatters with the tongue.* (Prov. 28:23)

When love and trust are established and you understand the boundaries of those relationships, they can become springboards for transformation, exponential growth and lifelong friendships.

A STORY ABOUT WHAT YOU MEASURE WILL GROW – LISTEN CAREFULLY

Working for a Fortune 50 company, I was able to take advantage of their employee scholarship program. When I was pursuing a master's degree in leadership coaching, I ran across some materials on listening. One of the important aspects to experiencing growth is to measure your progress. I was challenged to improve my Communication skills, especially my listening. So, I developed some measures to track during my conversations. They included not looking at my phone, paraphrasing for greater understanding, restating key points for emphasis and clarity, having eye contact, leaning forward to demonstrate interest, and mirroring body language in a positive way.

My little experiment with the measures I created, proved to be very eye opening. I realized I was not that great of a listener. There is truth in the statement that what you measure you will value. The fact that I measured these items caused me to grow in self-awareness so I could make better in-situ listening decisions. My listening competency grew significantly through this time period and people would often give me positive feedback. I found that there are no shortcuts to effective listening communication. It takes intentionality, especially if it is not an ingrained skill you learned from childhood. If you want to grow, measure it, and you may learn some things about yourself so you can grow.

CASE STUDY: WINSTON CHURCHILL RALLIED ENGLAND THROUGH FIERY RHETORIC, UNSHAKEABLE COURAGE, AND THE DEVELOPMENT OF ALLIES

Sir Winston Leonard Spencer-Churchill (November 30, 1874 – January 24, 1965) was a British politician, army officer, and writer. He was Prime Minister of the United Kingdom from 1940 to 1945, when he led Britain to victory in the Second World War, and again from 1951 to 1955. Churchill represented five constituencies during his career as a Member of Parliament (MP). Ideologically an economic liberal and imperialist, for most of his career he was a member of the Conservative Party, which he led from 1940 to 1955, but from 1904 to 1924 he was instead a member of the Liberal Party.

Of mixed English and American parentage, Churchill was born in Oxfordshire to a wealthy, aristocratic family. Joining the British Army, he saw action in British India, the Anglo–Sudan War, and the Second Boer War, gaining fame as a war correspondent and writing books about his campaigns. Elected an MP in 1900, initially as a Conservative, he defected to the Liberals in 1904. In H. H. Asquith's Liberal government, Churchill served as President of the Board of Trade, Home Secretary, and First Lord of the Admiralty, championing prison reform and workers' social security.

During the First World War, he oversaw the Gallipoli Campaign; after it proved a disaster, he resigned from government and served in the Royal Scots Fusiliers on the Western Front. In 1917, he returned to government under David Lloyd George as Minister of Munitions, and was subsequently Secretary of State for War, Secretary of State for Air, then Secretary of State for the Colonies. After two years out of Parliament, he served as Chancellor of the Exchequer in Stanley Baldwin's Conservative government, returning the pound sterling in 1925 to the gold standard at its pre-war parity, a move widely seen as creating deflationary pressure on the UK economy.

Out of office during the 1930s, Churchill took the lead in calling for British rearmament to counter the growing threat from Nazi Germany. He was a voice crying out in the wilderness, perhaps a voice before his time. It did, however, make way for him for his future role in history. At the outbreak of the Second World War, he was re-appointed First Lord of the Admiralty before replacing Prime Minister Neville Chamberlain in 1940.

His addresses to the nation boosted morale and inspired courage. Churchill oversaw British involvement in the Allied war effort against Germany and the Axis powers, resulting in victory in 1945. His wartime leadership was widely praised, and he worked closely with U.S. President Franklin D. Roosevelt and other Allied leaders. Churchill had a season of despairing years in the 1930's, and at the appointed time, he was prepared for Convergence.

Churchill had the foresight regarding the Nazi movement, and the "iron curtain" and was able to articulate what he saw through his Communication competency. During the years of World War II, he was able to motivate and keep the morale and focus of a nation engaged. He communicated more than information but impartation to impact the nations. Churchill was awarded the Nobel Prize in Literature in 1953.

Acts like the bombing of Dresden and his wartime response to the Bengal famine generated public controversy. After the Conservatives' defeat in the 1945 general election, he became Leader of the Opposition. Amid the developing Cold War with the Soviet Union, he publicly warned of an "iron curtain" of Soviet influence in Europe and promoted European unity. Re-elected Prime Minister in 1951, his second term was preoccupied with foreign affairs, including the Malayan Emergency, Mau Mau Uprising, Korean War, and a UK-backed Iranian coup.

Domestically his government emphasized house-building and developed a nuclear weapon. In declining health, Churchill resigned as prime minister in 1955, although he remained an MP until 1964. Upon his death in 1965, he was given a state funeral. *(Source: Wikipedia).*

TAKEAWAYS

- Communication is a key Competency needed for your journey.

- Communication is more than about information and includes impartation and activation.

- Numerous variables converge to create your Communication.

- We have the Holy Spirit who is the best communicator - the Spirit of Truth, Helper and Counselor or Paraclete – that will assist us.

- We can develop and improve our communication skills.

- Feedback is essential to growth.

- Correction is a means God uses for gaining alignment.

- There is nothing easy about Correction – as giver or receiver.

COMMUNICATION – SELF-ASSESSMENT

- I listen with empathy and my mind does not wander.

- When people talk, I typically do not share my autobiographical view.

- I am quick to listen, and slow to speak.

- More often than not, I ask for feedback on my Communication.

- I use my intuition or gut when communicating with others.

Rate the above on a scale from 1 to 5:

      1 - strongly disagree

      2 - disagree

      3 - neither agree nor disagree

      4 - agree

      5 - strongly agree

If your score is 1-8, you have opportunity to grow as a communicator.

If your score is 9-17, you are making progress and should continue in your forward momentum.

If your score is 18+, you have a good handle and grasp on Communication.

NOW ACTION

1. Journal about a Communication outcome that was positive and one that did not go so well. Contrast what went well and what didn't in each scenario, compare the results, and share them with a friend.

2. Read through the following Scriptures. Select three of them to pray through and synthesize in your daily walk. I have included 50 passages that make reference to Communication as a point of emphasis. God has a lot to say about this subject through His Word.

   1. Let your speech always be gracious, seasoned with salt, so that you may know how you ought to answer each person. (Col. 4:6, ESV)

   2. If one gives an answer before he hears, it is his folly and shame. (Prov. 18:13, ESV)

   3. Let no corrupting talk come out of your mouths, but only such as is good for building up, as fits the occasion, that it may give grace to those who hear. (Eph. 4:29, ESV)

   4. Know this, my beloved brothers: let every person be quick to hear, slow to speak, slow to anger; (Jas. 1:19, ESV)

   5. A word fitly spoken is like apples of gold in a setting of silver. (Prov. 25:11, ESV)

   6. Let the words of my mouth and the meditation of my heart be acceptable in your sight, O LORD, my rock and my redeemer. (Psa. 19:14, ESV)

   7. A soft answer turns away wrath, but a harsh word stirs up anger. (Prov. 15:1, ESV)

8. Therefore, having put away falsehood, let each one of you speak the truth with his neighbor, for we are members one of another. (Eph. 4:25, ESV)

9. But now you must put them all away: anger, wrath, malice, slander, and obscene talk from your mouth. (Col. 3:8, ESV)

10. When words are many, transgression is not lacking, but whoever restrains his lips is prudent. (Prov. 10:19, ESV)

11. There is one whose rash words are like sword thrusts, but the tongue of the wise brings healing. (Prov. 12:18, ESV)

12. Be kind to one another, tenderhearted, forgiving one another, as God in Christ forgave you. (Eph. 4:32, ESV)

13. Set a guard, O LORD, over my mouth; keep watch over the door of my lips! (Psa. 141:3, ESV)

14. It is an honor for a man to keep aloof from strife, but every fool will be quarreling. (Prov. 20:3, ESV)

15. Death and life are in the power of the tongue, and those who love it will eat its fruits. (Prov. 18:21, ESV)

16. Do you see a man who is hasty in his words? There is more hope for a fool than for him. (Prov. 29:20, ESV)

17. Whoever restrains his words has knowledge, and he who has a cool spirit is a man of understanding. (Prov. 17:27, ESV)

18. I tell you, on the day of judgment people will give account for every careless word they speak, (Matt. 12:36, ESV)

19. A gentle tongue is a tree of life, but perverseness in it breaks the spirit. (Prov. 15:4, ESV)

20. Whoever keeps his mouth and his tongue keeps himself out of trouble. (Prov. 21:23, ESV)

21. Lying lips are an abomination to the LORD, but those who act faithfully are his delight. (Prov. 12:22, ESV)

22. The good person out of the good treasure of his heart produces good, and the evil person out of his evil treasure produces evil, for out of the abundance of the heart his mouth speaks. (Luke 6:45, ESV)

23. To speak evil of no one, to avoid quarreling, to be gentle, and to show perfect courtesy toward all people. (Tit. 3:2, ESV)

24. Gracious words are like a honeycomb, sweetness to the soul and health to the body. (Prov. 16:24, ESV)

25. The heart of the wise makes his speech judicious and adds persuasiveness to his lips. (Prov. 16:23, ESV)

26. Whoever guards his mouth preserves his life; he who opens wide his lips comes to ruin. (Prov. 13:3, ESV)

27. The beginning of strife is like letting out water, so quit before the quarrel breaks out. (Prov. 17:14, ESV)

28. Rejoice always, pray without ceasing, give thanks in all circumstances; for this is the will of God in Christ Jesus for you. (1 Thess. 5:16-18, ESV)

29. Therefore encourage one another and build one another up, just as you are doing. (I Thess. 5:11, ESV)

30. Let there be no filthiness nor foolish talk nor crude joking, which are out of place, but instead let there be thanksgiving. (Eph. 5:4, ESV)

31. Good sense makes one slow to anger, and it is his glory to overlook an offense. (Prov. 19:11, ESV)

32. If anyone thinks he is religious and does not bridle his tongue but deceives his heart, this person's religion is worthless. (Jas. 1:26, ESV)

33. With patience a ruler may be persuaded, and a soft tongue will break a bone. (Prov. 25:15, ESV)

34. Whoever goes about slandering reveals secrets; therefore do not associate with a simple babbler. (Prov. 20:19, ESV)

35. A brother offended is more unyielding than a strong city, and quarreling is like the bars of a castle. (Prov. 18:19, ESV)

36. Know this, my beloved brothers: let every person be quick to hear, slow to speak, slow to anger; for the anger of man does not produce the righteousness of God. (Jas. 1:19-20, ESV)

37. And let us consider how to stir up one another to love and good works, (Heb. 10:24, ESV)

38. A soft answer turns away wrath, but a harsh word stirs up anger. The tongue of the wise commends knowledge, but the mouths of fools pour out folly. (Prov. 15:1-2, ESV)

39. Whoever is slow to anger has great understanding, but he who has a hasty temper exalts folly. (Prov. 14:29, ESV)

40. For "Whoever desires to love life and see good days, let him keep his tongue from evil and his lips from speaking deceit; (I Pet. 3:10, ESV)

41. Do not repay evil for evil or reviling for reviling, but on the contrary, bless, for to this you were called, that you may obtain a blessing. (1 Pet. 3:9, ESV)

42. A man of wrath stirs up strife, and one given to anger causes much transgression. (Prov. 29:22, ESV)

43. The words of a whisperer are like delicious morsels; they go down into the inner parts of the body. (Prov. 18:8, ESV)

44. Righteous lips are the delight of a king, and he loves him who speaks what is right. (Prov. 16:13, ESV)

45. To make an apt answer is a joy to a man, and a word in season, how good it is! (Prov. 15:23, ESV)

46. Drive out a scoffer, and strife will go out, and quarreling and abuse will cease. (Prov. 22:10, ESV)

47. A dishonest man spreads strife, and a whisperer separates close friends. (Prov. 16:28, ESV)

48. A wicked messenger falls into trouble, but a faithful envoy brings healing. (Prov. 13:17, ESV)

49. You shall not go around as a slanderer among your people, and you shall not stand up against the life of your neighbor: I am the Lord. (Lev. 19:16, ESV)

50. Do not speak evil against one another, brothers. The one who speaks against a brother or judges his brother, speaks evil against the law and judges the law. But if you judge the law, you are not a doer of the law but a judge. There is only one lawgiver and judge, he who is able to save and to destroy. But who are you to judge your neighbor? (Jas. 4:11-12, ESV)

PRAYER

Lord, bring us into new dimensions of Communication that facilitate life, flow, and creativity. Break down the walls within us and between others, and soften our hearts so we can hear you more effectively in the small and large decisions. God, we submit ourselves to you and to the instruction that comes from the Holy Spirit to lead us into all Truth about what we say, how we say it, and how it impact others. Empower us to be better listeners so that we can ask more powerful questions to understand others more deeply. Increase our self-awareness in this area so we can bring forth fruit in every dimension of our lives.

NOW COACHING QUESTIONS

1. In what ways do I communicate effectively?

2. In what areas can I improve my Communication?

3. How has ineffective Communication held me back in life?

4. How deeply do you listen to people when they speak?

5. What Communication practices do you use to improve your effectiveness?

6. What is the single most important way you are going to improve?

7. In what ways do you communicate within your spheres of influence?

8. What Communications would you use with family, communities and nations?

9. What are your next steps?

CHAPTER SIXTEEN

COMPASSION
The Power of Empathy in Action

When Jesus went ashore, He saw a large crowd, and He felt compassion for them because they were like sheep without a shepherd; and He began to teach them many things. (Mark 6:34)

Compassion is the ability to feel deeply what another is experiencing with a strong desire to aid or alleviate the suffering. Empathy is the ability to understand and share the feelings of another. By these definitions, empathy will not lead you to help others but Compassion will. This is important when addressing ambiguity in VUCA (Volatility, Uncertainty, Complexity, Ambiguity). We need authentic leaders to identify with their followers when things are not clear. The leadership relationship reference is invaluable. For the purpose of this discussion, we need to move beyond empathy and apply action to it. Why? Because our Dread Champion synthesized empathy and put it into action. The New Testament has numerous instances where it was said that Jesus was moved with Compassion.

Jesus' motives were pure and He loved people. The depths of His heart are unsearchable as our Great High Priest. Jesus' ability to identify with people activated His faith to release instruction and healing. When we face problems and complexities, if we do not carry a Compassion factor, we may fall short of being a bearer of His heart and intention in the situation.

WHEN YOU CARE FOR PEOPLE, YOU GAIN HONOR AND WILL HAVE THEIR HEARTS SUPPORTING YOU.

Leaders without Compassion may be perceived as users and self-interested. If you don't care for the people you serve, then they will see this, and you may have them positionally, but you don't have their hearts. When you care for people, you gain honor and will have their hearts supporting you. Engaged followers in mind, heart, and spirit will produce and outperform others and will be a great joy. When people experience Compassion, joy will result! The seeds of joy will birth engagement and Creativity.

Shout for joy, O heavens! And rejoice, O earth! Break forth into joyful shouting, O mountains! For the Lord has comforted His people And will have compassion on His afflicted. (Isa. 49:12-14)

I believe that Compassion in essence is the deep desire to give and to eliminate suffering. In the case of Jesus, His Compassion seemed to connect Him to the supernatural realm. There was great joy when Jesus was moved with Compassion and brought forth Lazareth from the grave. When God moves through the agency of man in the supernatural, joy will result. Jesus' government brings righteousness, peace and joy. It is the fruit of heavenly interactions.

What does this have to do with the day to day of life? Every leader desires engaged followers. When you have engaged followers, they are available to give of themselves to develop and master their gifts and talents for the benefit of others. Reward, satisfaction, significance, respect, and compensation will follow.

Within the seed of Compassion is generosity. When seeds are planted they reproduce after their own kind. Compassion will create joy. Joy creates engagement. Engaged people give of themselves. The Gallup organization has done extensive research on employee engagement. They state that only 1 in 5 employees are engaged.

Gallup states that an "engaged employee is one who is fully absorbed by and enthusiastic about their work and so takes positive action to further the organization's reputation and interests." Engaged people give of themselves through their work. Industrious and generous people will prosper. Those who water others will be watered themselves! It is a positive, self-fulfilling prophecy!

The generous man will be prosperous, And he who waters will himself be watered. (Prov. 11:25)

This creates a watershed effect. This was demonstrated with Jesus when the Samaritan woman experienced Jesus' Compassion. Jesus had Compassion on this woman who was an outcast. She was getting water in the heat of the day, rather than in the cool of the morning with the other women in her community. She had a revolving door of men in her life which made her a pariah. Jesus shared a word of knowledge with her, and proceeded to introduce her to the river of living water.

Jesus answered and said to her, "Everyone who drinks of this water will thirst again; but whoever drinks of the water that I will give him shall never thirst; but the water that I will give him will become in him a well of water springing up to eternal life." (John 4:13-15)

This woman from Samaria, after experiencing a Convergence moment with Jesus at a water well, then turned and transformed her entire Community. The river of living water began to impact the Culture around her. I believe it was birthed out of Jesus' heart of Compassion, thus triggering her response to go and tell others what she had seen and heard. She became an instant evangelist who spread the good news she had experienced. Others were then converted.

Many of the Samaritans from that town believed in him because of the woman's testimony, "He told me everything I ever did." So when the Samaritans came to him, they urged him to stay with them, and he stayed two days. And because of his words many more became believers. They said to the woman, "We no longer believe just because of what you said; now we have heard for ourselves, and we know that this man really is the Savior of the world." (John 4:39-42, NIV)

CAPACITY PAVES THE WAY FOR COMPASSION

Champions of the faith do not receive "get out of jail free cards" when it comes to suffering. The crucible of Capacity can refine us and build Compassion into our inner being. Anyone following Christ, and most certainly any leader, will share in the Lord's suffering. Paul speaks to this in the book of Philippians.

But whatever was to my profit I now consider loss for the sake of Christ. What is more, I consider everything a loss compared to the surpassing greatness of knowing Christ Jesus my Lord, for whose sake I have lost all things. I consider them rubbish, that I may gain Christ and may be found in Him, not having a righteousness of my own derived from the Law, but that which is through faith in Christ, the righteousness which comes from God on the basis of faith, that I may know Him and the power of His resurrection and the fellowship of His sufferings, being conformed to His death; in order that I may attain to the resurrection from the dead. (Phil. 3:8-11)

There is a tension set before us. When we embrace the power of His resurrection, we are inaugurated into the fellowship of His sufferings. They come mingled together in the same cup. I believe this was the cup the Lord drank when He said, "Not my will but thy will be done." For men and women living in a fallen world, I believe suffering is the agency by which we stay on our knees and remain humble when the Lord does great exploits through us. It is also one of the Lord's craftsmen that conforms us to His image and likeness.

COMPASSION AND THE WIELDING OF THE SWORD

When I was in college, one of my friends said to me that my tongue could be like a razor at times. That feedback hurt, but I knew what he was saying was true and there was often no love behind my words. In my mid-20's, I hosted a church cell group in my home. A prophetic brother came to one of our meetings. He shared a prophetic word that transformed my life. At the time I did not know what it meant, but a decade and a half later, I began to understand it.

The word was quite simple. It went like this: "Until you learn Compassion, you will not be able to yield the sword. The work of Compassion must be completed in you so I can entrust you with my word."

This word set in motion a chain of events in my life that began to break off negative strongholds of thought—judgmentalism, criticism, legalism and a lack of sensitivity. It came by way of correction, difficulties and adversity, illness, and conflicts. God began to salt my life with fire to refine me, reconstruct my inner person, and soften the inner core of my being. It was a very challenging time to say the least. That grace work of Compassion is still in progress.

If the word of God is double-edged and can cut to the bone and marrow and judge the hearts and intents of men and women, it needs to be wielded in love, or we will make a really big mess!

I thought I was through in my mid-30's and that the work of Compassion was complete. Then, in 2010, we went through a very challenging 18 months where we lost three loved ones, our foster children left us to be placed in an adoptive family, and we lost our beautiful cat to coyotes. It took several years to process that grief and mourn those losses, and to adapt to our new living circumstances. I really had not experienced much loss previously. After that experience, I became much more sensitive to people's pain and suffering and changed the way I approach family, work and ministry.

Many of us have suffered losses, injustices, abuse, neglect, persecution, and have been overlooked. These are opportunities to embrace the cross of Jesus and allow His redemptive Spirit to work within us. His comfort will strengthen and nurture new spiritual health and well-being. Don't waste your trials. Learn Compassion through them, so you can be moved like Jesus to bring healing and be a solution to alleviate pain and suffering.

I believe one of the most powerful promises of the New Testament is found in the letter to the Hebrews. This is a quote from Jeremiah.

> *And the Holy Spirit also testifies to us; for after saying,*
>
> *"This is the covenant that I will make with them After those days, says the Lord: I will put My laws upon their heart, And on their mind I will write them,"*
>
> *He then says, "And their sins and their lawless deeds I will remember no more." (Heb. 10:15-18)*

God promises to write His law – His word – in our hearts and minds. He has scrolls for our lives; that is, assignments, destinies, mandates, and purposes to fulfill. If we lean into the Holy Spirit and look to the Word of God, it will transform our lives. He will change our hearts, so our hearts are filled with Compassion.

I tell myself and my sons to pray this prayer when you know your heart is not right toward someone, or if you have been offended or hurt, or have become judgmental. *"Lord, please change my heart. I know it is not what you want it to be. Impart to me your spiritual DNA so I can think and feel the way you do."* It is a simple prayer that will align you with the Lord's heart, and will take you on a journey to learn Compassion for the people who are challenging for you.

Leaders without Compassion are like clanging bells who don't carry the heart of the Father. They are very noisy, drawing attention to themselves. The work of Compassion will dampen that noise. Suffering can produce new levels of Compassion so we can make the joyful sound of heaven. There will likely not be engagement without Compassion. Where there is Compassion, joy will manifest. Joy will lead to people engaging. And if people engage, they will give of themselves and produce remarkable results.

A STORY ABOUT A NEW OPERATING SPACE BASED ON GRACE AND COMPASSION

This is a story about Jonathan who is a successful software engineer who works in New York City. In this story, we see how the chains of performance orientation were broken by leaders who endeavored to connect with Jonathan. That Connection allowed him to experience an "aha" moment which was triggered by a compassionate leader.

As a child and teenager, I always had a lot of friends who were older than me. By the time I was of high school age, I was attending a community college and my best friends ranged between 18 and 30 years old. As a consequence, I compared my Competencies relative to my peer group.

Growing up with these people around me and having a bit of a competitive streak, I frequently compared myself with them. As a 15, 16, and 17 year old, there were certain social dynamics that I simply could not master. I felt like the people around me knew more than I did and were one step ahead of me.

I considered my friends to be peers. When I could not measure up to them, I was very hard on myself. I always expected myself to be perfect. It came from a deeply egotistic view that I was actually better than everyone around me. I had fallen into the trap of pride – thinking I was something that I was not.

I brought this worldview with me through college and into my professional career. After completing my undergraduate degree, I joined a technology startup in New York City as a software engineer. I was hired onto a team where the median years of experience was close to 20, versus my two years of experience.

Just like I had at my community college, I consistently compared myself to my co-workers and treated them as peers. When I could not execute like them or produce the same quality code, designs, etc. I was very hard on myself.

Finally, after working this way for 10 months, I came close to having some kind of breakdown. I reached out to one of my co-workers for advice, and as we walked to a coffee shop near our office he told me that it was okay to not know everything. He told me that he had been doing this kind of work for 20 years, and that this experience empowered him to perceive potential pitfalls and miscommunications that I was completely unaware of. His words were filled with Compassion. He knew exactly how I felt.

These words changed my life. I realized that my co-workers would not view me as any less competent for not having an answer. They simply were mature enough to understand that I was young and would know less than them. Knowing this has empowered me to contribute to the team in a much more meaningful way. Now I can engage with them without feeling like I need to know all the answers. I can feel free to make suggestions that may turn out to be a bad idea, or to ask for implementation advice.

Most importantly of all, I no longer go through a miniature emotional crisis every time I make a mistake. I realized it was okay for me to not know things now, but that I would eventually learn them in time. If my co-workers can show me grace and Compassion, then so can I. My leaders cut me some space and helped me align my expectations.

As I'm learning to have Compassion for myself, this is slowly making its way into how I interact with the people around me as well. As I learn to cut myself space, I'm slowly learning to show it to others as well.

JONATHAN MEIER
Software Engineer

CASE STUDY: GLADYS AYLWARD – SHE OVERCAME COMPETENCY OBSTACLES FOR COMPASSION'S SAKE

Gladys Aylward had one dream: To go to China to tell the Chinese people about God's love for them. Her joy at being accepted to the China Inland Mission training school turned to disappointment when she was unable to master the difficult subjects. She had left school at age 14 to become a housemaid to help her poor and struggling family, and did not seem to have the educational foundation to learn what was needed. When she was told she would never be able to master the difficult languages of China and was therefore unqualified to go there as a missionary, she did not give up.

She deeply believed that God Himself was calling her to China. Taking service as a housekeeper, Gladys saved every penny she could, in order to pay for the expensive trip from England to China. She also read every book about China that she could find in her employer's private library. At the same time, aware that preaching experience would be needed in China, she began street preaching whenever she had the time.

Her biggest obstacle was that she knew no one in China – until she overheard a conversation about a widow who, with her husband, had spent decades in China as a missionary. The woman, Jeannie Lawson, had come back to England after her husband's death, but, finding herself bored and out of place, had returned to her work in China. Jeannie's one regret had been that she was unable to find someone to whom she could entrust the work when she could no longer continue. Gladys knew she was that person, so she obtained Jeannie's address, and by writing letters, made arrangements to meet her in Tientsin.

After seven months, Gladys saved enough for a train ticket through Europe and Russia. However, there was a war going on at the frontier between Russia and China. Gladys had to trek 30 miles back from the battlefront to the nearest town. There she was held captive by Russian authorities who, mistaking the occupation listed on her passport as "machinery" rather than "missionary," intended to send her into the interior of Russia, where she was sure she would never be heard from again, to work with machinery. She received mysterious help from strangers who enabled her to escape to a

Japanese freighter. The captain of the freighter personally brought her to the British Consulate in Japan.

Gladys' troubles were not over. Once she arrived in Tientsin, she learned that Jeannie was not there to meet her, having not really believed that she would make the journey to China. There were weeks more of travel ahead. However, with the help of the local missionaries, she made the journey and finally arrived in the village where Jeannie was working.

She then began the difficult task of learning the Chinese language. She and Jeannie opened an inn along one of the major travel routes in the area. This gave them the opportunity to tell stories about Jesus to those who passed through. Sometime later, after Jeannie had died, a law was passed throughout China ending the custom of binding women's feet. Gladys was asked to be the official foot inspector in her district.

It was considered unacceptable for a man to look on the feet of women. But what woman was there who could travel over difficult, rough country? All of the local Chinese women had bound feet and thus had difficulty walking. And what European woman could speak the local Chinese dialect? Only Gladys. The very skill that she was told she would never be able to master was the skill that opened up doors of opportunity to her. She now had the authority to travel to all the households in the district with permission to talk about her faith.

Gladys Aylward is most famous for her role in saving over 100 orphans in China during WWII. When the Japanese bombed her village, many children were orphaned. Gladys had taken in orphans before, so theses orphans were drawn to her. However, the Japanese soldiers were moving in the direction of her village. As she traveled, more orphaned children joined the group. With help from local Chinese friends, she brought the children safely through the Japanese lines to safety at an orphanage in Furfeng.

Gladys had sustained a severe head injury along the way when a Japanese soldier hit her hard on the head with the butt of his rifle. After bringing the children to safety, she fell into a coma and spent the next several months in the hospital. She went back to England for 10 years, and then spent the rest of her life ministering in Hong Kong and Taiwan, where she established the Gladys Aylward Orphanage where she worked until her death in 1970. *(Source: Wikipedia)*

Gladys did not let her lack of education or inability to speak Chinese deter her from her Calling. With perseverance she prevailed in every obstacle set before her. She was told at age 28 years old she would never master the complex language of Chinese. Now at the end of the story, they were wrong. She did possess the raw talent to master the language; it just was not expressed academically, but perhaps in relational context. Furthermore, because she was a woman and a foreigner, the deck was stacked against her. She had very good reasons to quit, but she prevailed through Compassion for the people and impacted a nation.

TAKEAWAYS

- Compassion is coming alongside and identifying with someone with the intent to help them.

- Compassion is empathy in action.

- Compassion brings forth joy and engagement.

- Engaged people give of themselves and will prosper.

- There is no way of avoiding some type and level of suffering as a leader.

- The redemption of suffering can be translated into Compassion.

- A leader will win people's hearts through Compassion.

COMPASSION – SELF-ASSESSMENT

- I understand and can articulate what people are feeling.

- People often open up to me because they feel understood by me.

- I feel people's pain and want to help them.

- I have seen God use my suffering redemptively.

- I am authentic and express my thoughts and feelings easily.

Rate the above on a scale from 1 to 5:

> 1 - strongly disagree
>
> 2 - disagree
>
> 3 - neither agree nor disagree
>
> 4 - agree
>
> 5 - strongly agree

If your score is 1-8, you have opportunity to grow in Compassion.

If your score is 9-17, you are making progress and should continue in your forward momentum.

If your score is 18+, you have a good grasp or handle on Compassion.

NOW ACTION

1. List the experiences you have had that developed a deeper sense of Compassion for people. Identify if there is a common thread or theme in them. How does this relate to your calling and assignment?

2. Pray the following Scripture to press into the Lord's heart of Compassion for people and nations.

    This I recall to my mind, Therefore I have hope. The Lord's lovingkindnesses indeed never cease, For His compassions never fail. They are new every morning. Great is Your faithfulness. (Lam. 3:21-23)

    He made known His ways to Moses, His acts to the sons of Israel. The Lord is compassionate and gracious, Slow to anger and abounding in lovingkindness. He will not always strive with us, Nor will He keep His anger forever. (Psa. 103:7-9)

    ...a renewal in which there is no distinction between Greek and Jew, circumcised and uncircumcised, barbarian, Scythian, slave and freeman, but Christ is all, and in all. So, as those who have been chosen of God, holy and beloved, put on a heart of compassion, kindness, humility, gentleness and patience; bearing with one another, and forgiving each other, whoever has a complaint against anyone; just as the Lord forgave you, so also should you. (Col. 3:11-13)

PRAYER

Lord, move us beyond empathy and into new dimensions of Compassion so that we act with your heart and faith to transform our world. We ask you that out of that godly Compassion, generosity and joy would flow so that an increase of your love and fruitfulness would abound.

NOW COACHING QUESTIONS

1. How has God's Compassion toward you impacted you?

2. In what ways has God done a work of Compassion in you?

3. In what ways do you demonstrate Compassion toward others?

4. How have you demonstrated Compassion toward the people you lead?

5. What could you do next to be a more compassionate leader?

6. In what ways do you demonstrate Compassion toward communities and nations?

7. What are your next steps?

CLOSING CALL FOR CHAMPIONS

My prayer is that NOW Leadership would encourage you and inspire you not to give up, and to press on and run your race as a Champion. It was discovered after his death that Secretariat's heart was nearly three times larger than the normal equine's. It takes a large and strong heart to overcome. Don't let your failures, weaknesses, obstacles, resistance, deterrents, objections, persecutions, lies, misfortune, misunderstanding, tragedies, mishaps, mistakes, oversights, pressure, abuse, or the like take you out. Understand it is a process God is taking you through. It is worth it, because the ROI – return on investment – is unfathomable.

Submit and give yourself to the process and let His word and Spirit have their perfect work in you. Seek out and engage with healthy spiritual fathers and mothers who see your potential and are willing to lay down their lives for you. Honor them. And then, remember to honor them as often as possible. Not all may look like Champions on the outside, but on the inside they carry the heart of the Father for you, to bring you into the fullness of God's plans, purposes, dreams and destiny.

EPILOGUE

So teach us to number our days, That we may present to You a heart of wisdom. (Psa. 90:12)

The measure of a person's life perhaps can be answered by these four simple questions:

1. Where did you start your journey?

2. What did you do with what you were given?

3. Where are you right now in the process?

4. How did you end?

The above questions enable us to measure our days and time bound our life with a measurable end. The end result is that we would present to God a heart of wisdom – something that is pleasing to Him and reflects His essence by walking in God's New Operating Wisdom. These four questions came to me when thinking about my mother's life when asking the questions, "How is it that we value life and honor those we love?" She is 90 years old at the writing of this book, and I wondered how would we measure the success and significance of a person's life?

As I surveyed these questions in light of my mother's life, I realized what a great woman she has become. These questions also transformed my perspective on my father's life as well. My mother started her life off in the negative and ended in the positive, overcoming significant odds, obstacles, rejections, betrayals, abandonment, sickness, disease, poverty, fear and loss as a WWII refugee. She overcame. She did not get bitter but got better.

I cannot compare her life to another because her life is unique, just as yours is. Where she started, and what she was given, and what she did with her life, is exemplary. I honor her as a Champion along with many others who have overcome. Don't be too quick to judge Champions by their worldly accomplishments only. She shifted the negative momentum to positive, turning the tide and becoming a transitional leader.

We cannot be measured by comparing ourselves to others or their accomplishments, whether worldly or spiritual.

For we are not bold to class or compare ourselves with some of those who commend themselves; but when they measure themselves by themselves and compare themselves with themselves, they are without understanding. (2 Cor. 10:11-12)

What we become is just as important as how we took care of what was given us. When we compare ourselves, we engage in a toxic practice because it erodes our sense of uniqueness and robs us from walking in our identity, which in the end will keep us from fulfilling our destiny. Peter wanted to compare his future with that of John, who was close to Jesus' heart – he was the one that put his head upon Jesus' chest.

So Peter seeing him said to Jesus, "Lord, and what about this man?" Jesus said to him, "If I want him to remain until I come, what is that to you? You follow Me!" (John 21:21-22)

We need to keep our focus on the only prize that ultimately matters, and the prize-Giver, and not on other people. Your destiny is dependent on understanding your starting point, learning how to identify and engage what God has given you, so you can have a desirable end. Each person's experience is unique and cannot be replicated. We need to resist trying to become like another person, unless that person is Jesus.

God is jealous for you to be you! He is not looking for copies, clones, or counterfeits, but longs to see the emergence and development of His original. We are a reflection of His glory and He takes great pride in us as His sons and daughters. When we seek to become someone else, we basically are saying that what God created in us is not good. What He created is good.

That goodness is authenticated by transforming a world characterized by Volatility, Uncertainty, Complexity, and Ambiguity through Vision, Understanding, Clarity, and Authenticity. This is our birthright. We create, build and multiply, so that we can rule and release the government of Jesus. His government's operating system is love, joy, peace, righteousness and justice. It is administered by people partnering with the Person (God) in the NOW - the "new operating wisdom". The Ancient of Days is the source of the administration of that wisdom.

The Father has given us a DNA code not only to achieve success, but significance. That significance is found in the Convergence of relationship through sonship – that is being God's sons and daughters. It is not just who we are, but what we will become. It is not just about surviving, but is also about being successful. We are called to steward the resources God has given us to become fruitful in every venue of life. But, there is something beyond success that everyone longs for, and that is significance.

All that we are and all that we do, must converge in something greater than ourselves. Destiny without understanding your design and purpose will be a disappointment. Our Connection must be maintained through the development process of fulfilling our Calling. The Connection – our bond with God – must be inseparable.

Living in the place of significance is the seed bed for us to achieve greatness – the place of Convergence. Greatness is about relationally impacting our Culture, growing in Capacity, and is expressed through our Communication, Collaboration, Creativity, and Compassion. It is a partnership designed in heaven to be realized in the earth so we reflect our heavenly Father as Champions.

How do you measure greatness?

Somehow I believe that our Father measures greatness in ways that we might not consider, such as how we:

- Love deeply

- Utilize our gifts and talents to build

- Overcome adversity and obstacles

- Persevere in weakness

- Sacrifice when no one else sees

- Make the right choices regardless of the cost

- Take the path of humility over preeminence and exaltation

- Lay down our lives and serve others

- Choose to forgive rather than be bitter

- Embrace mercy when it is in our power to punish

- Walk in faith against the tide and opposition

- Give freely, with joy, even when it hurts

- Rejoice in another's success even when we are overlooked

- Learn to receive gifts that we do not deserve

- Embrace suffering so we can comfort others and partake of His glory

The list above expresses choices that will release God's greatness in us. Our choices and responses will either cause the acceleration of growth or cause people to stumble. We want to be those who remove the obstacles and stumbling blocks. Jesus, when speaking about heaven and hell in

Mark 9:42-48, exhorted us to cut off that which causes us to stumble and live with the loss rather than going to hell. These are strong words and contrasts.

The choices we make will determine the destination we arrive at. Jesus clearly defines the risks and rewards. God does not leave us without His resources from heaven to enable us to walk with Him. He gives us His Holy Spirit! He also provides us with another divine accelerator which is mentioned at the end of this text in Mark.

> *For everyone will be salted with fire. Salt is good and useful; but if salt has lost its saltiness (purpose), how will you make it salty? Have salt within yourselves continually, and be at peace with one another.* (Mark 9:49-50, AMP)

Our lives will be salted with fire to purify, preserve, prove, and perfect us that we would bring forth value worthy of the Lamb and be at peace with one another. We choose to embrace with gratitude the seasons when our lives are salted with fire. It is the signet of your sonship – being branded as His sons and daughters. I believe Peter's life was salted with fire and he wrote about it.

> *In this you greatly rejoice, even though now for a little while, if necessary, you have been distressed by various trials, so that the proof of your faith, being more precious than gold which is perishable, even though tested by fire, may be found to result in praise and glory and honor at the revelation of Jesus Christ; and though you have not seen Him, you love Him, and though you do not see Him now, but believe in Him, you greatly rejoice with joy inexpressible and full of glory.* (1 Pet. 1:6-8)

The Father's heart is deeply invested in your development. He has given us His greatest resource to make a way for your success so we can live in significance with Him. There is great increase that will come through experiencing God's glory. In those seasons of great increase and blessing, we do not forget that God is the glory and the lifter of our heads. He sustains us.

But You, O Lord, are a shield about me, My glory, and the One who lifts my head. I was crying to the Lord with my voice, And He answered me from His holy mountain. (Psa. 3:3-4)

You hear our voice and you will answer us from your holy mountain!

Jesus is our Dread Champion.

He is our Calling, the resource of our Competencies, the bond of our Connection, our Capacity in the crucible, the divine space of Convergence, our Catalyst and the best Communicator that transforms Cultures through Creativity, Compassion and Collaboration.

It is my hope that this perspective expressed through NOW Leadership has encouraged, strengthened, and called you to a deeper place to run your race – that is to run your race with all your strength, passion and wisdom, and all that is within you.

It is the passion God put in me that I have shared with you.

Run your Race!

"Peace be with you; as the Father has sent Me, I also send you."

—*Jesus*

ABOUT THE AUTHOR

Will Meier has an assignment to release the Father's dreams and raise up a company of Champions that will awaken, revive and reform the global landscape. He is an authentic communicator, leadership architect, and C-level coach who releases the Father's heart to empower kingdom destiny in individuals, organizations, and nations. He is a frequent speaker at conferences and churches. He is a commissioned apostle and prophet in the body of Christ, and is the founder of Awakening Destiny Global and Leaders for Life Global. He and his wife live in the New England area near Hartford, Connecticut. and are the parents of two grown sons. He became a Christian in 1980, was commissioned in 2015 and 2017, and ordained in Christian ministry in 2018.

Will is a mechanical engineer and leads and manages technical, multidisciplinary teams for a Fortune 50 company. He has a successful 35 year career in business and industry. Will has a bachelors of science in mechanical engineering from the University of Connecticut and a masters degree in Leadership Coaching from Regent University.

CONTACT WILL MEIER:

Website:
www.leadersforlife.global

Email:
info@leadersforlife.global

GLOSSARY

Common words can sometimes convey diverse meanings to different groups of people. The best way to ensure we are all on the same page is to make sure we are all speaking the same language. Following are some definitions that are important to the message contained within this book.

- **ANOINTING:** This refers to the supernatural ability or grace God gives people to perform specific assignments or tasks. (Isa. 10:27; Mark 6:13; Acts 10:38; 1 John 2:27)

- **ASSIGNMENT:** This is a specific task or project that only you can accomplish based on your unique abilities, talents, personal experience, training, and gifts. Typically, God's favor is upon your assignment because it is related to accomplishing kingdom work.

- **FLOW:** The state of being completely present and fully immersed in a task where you have connection with your Creator and creative outcomes result.

- **KINGDOM:** This is referring to the Kingdom of Heaven. Most easily explained, it is the rule and reign of Jesus. The Bible says the kingdom of heaven is righteousness, peace and joy in the Holy Spirit (Rom. 14:7). More generally, this refers to God's sons and daughters who live in abundance and not scarcity, and are fulfilling their assignments and are not caught up in the religious system and order. It includes making disciples of nations, that is, leaders who will change the world.

They are motivated with servant hearts and do not care about affiliations, associations, titles, and religious power structures.

- **LEADER:** Is anyone who is influencing someone or thing or has someone following them. This is very inclusive, including parents, teachers, businesspeople, CEO's, teenagers, marketplace experts. This also includes leaders who have been given as gifts from Jesus in Eph. 4:11 – the apostle, prophet, teacher, pastor, and evangelist – as well as the Rom. 12:8 gift of leadership and governance.

- **MOUNTAIN:** Mountains in the Scriptures are symbolic of kingdoms. There is a movement that identifies the Seven Mountains of Culture including religion, education, business, family, media, government, arts and entertainment. The 8th Mountain has been used to describe the Lord's mountain (heaven, or Mount Zion).

- **SPHERE OF INFLUENCE:** This is the area or domain that God has given you authority to influence. It can be a region, territory, location, nation, industry, sector, sphere, mountain or people group (see 2 Cor. 10:15). Also read Acts 16:6-10 and the story of the apostle Paul and the Macedonian call.

- **SWEET SPOT:** This was originally a term that came from the sport of tennis. The sweet spot on your tennis racket is the center where the player gets the most energy out of their swing. This term is used to mean that there is a place and state where you are really effective in the things that you do, with a sense of effortlessness. We use this term in relationship to Convergence.